CHICAGO ORGANIZED WORKERS LEAGUE

C O W L

1949

EQUITAS VENERATIO POTENTIA

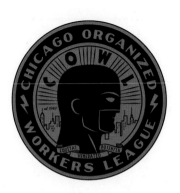

**IMAGE COMICS, INC.**
**Robert Kirkman** – Chief Operating Officer
**Erik Larsen** – Chief Financial Officer
**Todd McFarlane** – President
**Marc Silvestri** – Chief Executive Officer
**Jim Valentino** – Vice-President

**Eric Stephenson** – Publisher
**Corey Murphy** – Director of Sales
**Jeremy Sullivan** – Director of Digital Sales
**Kat Salazar** – Director of PR & Marketing
**Emily Miller** – Director of Operations
**Branwyn Bigglestone** – Senior Accounts Manager
**Sarah Mello** – Accounts Manager
**Drew Gill** – Art Director
**Jonathan Chan** – Production Manager
**Meredith Wallace** – Print Manager
**Randy Okamura** – Marketing Production Designer
**David Brothers** – Branding Manager
**Ally Power** – Content Manager
**Addison Duke** – Production Artist
**Vincent Kukua** – Production Artist
**Sasha Head** – Production Artist
**Tricia Ramos** – Production Artist
**Emilio Bautista** – Sales Assistant
**Chloe Ramos-Peterson** – Administrative Assistant
**IMAGECOMICS.COM**

C.O.W.L. VOL. 2: THE GREATER GOOD. First Printing. August 2015. Copyrig
© 2015 Kyle Higgins & Alec Siegel. All rights reserved. Published by Image
Comics, Inc. Office of publication: 2001 Center Street, Sixth Floor, Berkeley,
CA 94704. Originally published in single magazine form as C.O.W.L. #7-11,
Image Comics. "C.O.W.L.," its logos, and the likenesses of all characters here
are trademarks of Kyle Higgins & Alec Siegel, unless otherwise noted. "Image
and the Image Comics logos are registered trademarks of Image Comics, Inc.
No part of this publication may be reproduced or transmitted, in any form or
by any means (except for short excerpts for journalistic or review purposes),
without the express written permission of Kyle Higgins & Alec Siegel or Image
Comics, Inc. All names, characters, events, and locales in this publication are
entirely fictional. Any resemblance to actual persons (living or dead), events,
places, without satiric intent, is coincidental. Printed in the USA. For informati
regarding the CPSIA on this printed material call: 203-595-3636 and provide
reference #RICH-632036. For international rights, contact: foreignlicensing@
imagecomics.com. ISBN: 978-1-63215-326-5

*image*

# C.O.W.L.
### CHICAGO ORGANIZED WORKERS LEAGUE

# The Greater Good

## KYLE HIGGINS     ALEC SIEGEL
### STORY

## ROD REIS
### ART

## TROY PETERI
#### LETTERS

## TREVOR MCCARTHY & ROD REIS
#### COVERS

## RICH BLOOM
#### DESIGN

#### LOGO BY ERIC WIGHT

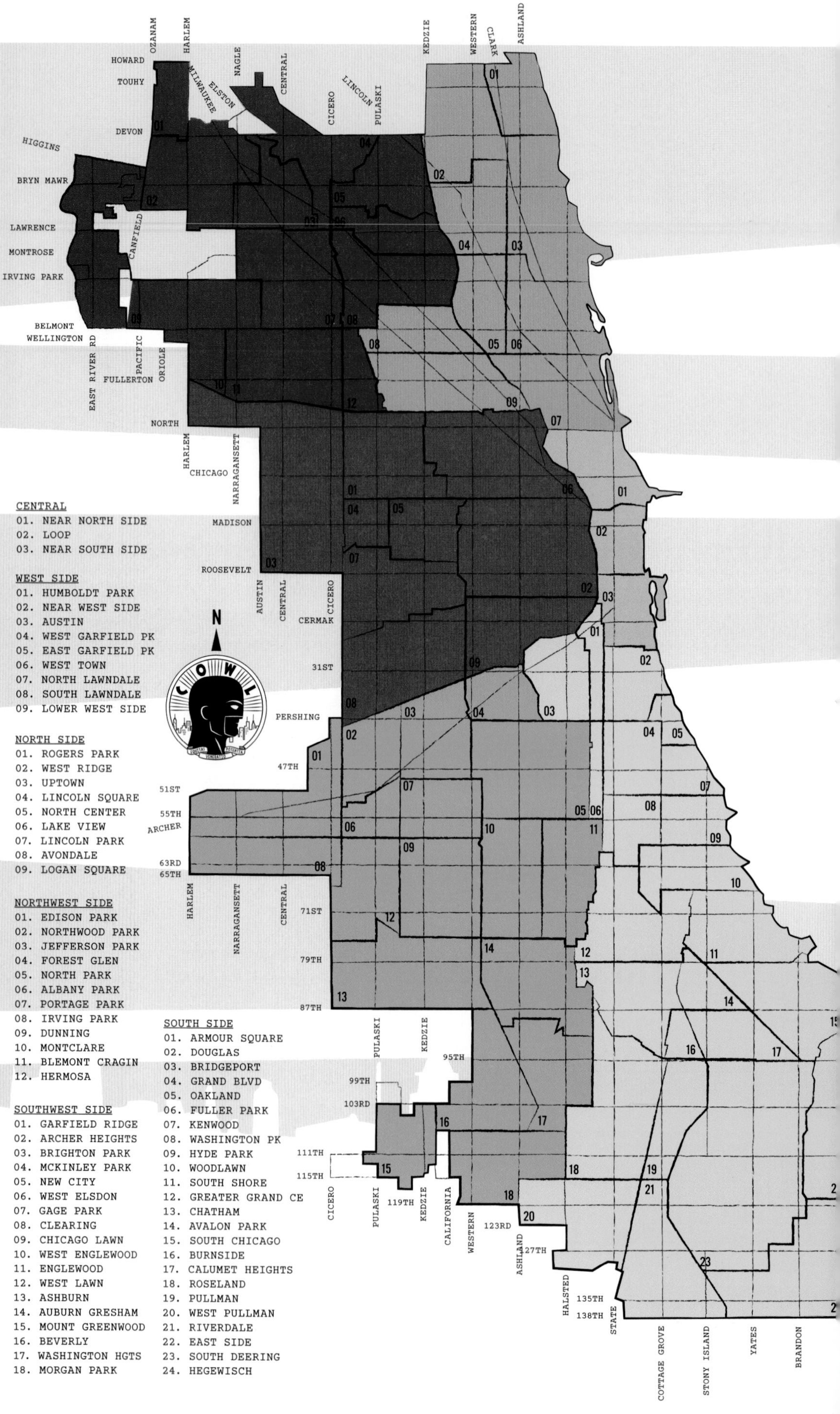
CENTRAL
01. NEAR NORTH SIDE
02. LOOP
03. NEAR SOUTH SIDE
WEST SIDE
01. HUMBOLDT PARK
02. NEAR WEST SIDE
03. AUSTIN
04. WEST GARFIELD PK
05. EAST GARFIELD PK
06. WEST TOWN
07. NORTH LAWNDALE
08. SOUTH LAWNDALE
09. LOWER WEST SIDE
NORTH SIDE
01. ROGERS PARK
02. WEST RIDGE
03. UPTOWN
04. LINCOLN SQUARE
05. NORTH CENTER
06. LAKE VIEW
07. LINCOLN PARK
08. AVONDALE
09. LOGAN SQUARE
NORTHWEST SIDE
01. EDISON PARK
02. NORTHWOOD PARK
03. JEFFERSON PARK
04. FOREST GLEN
05. NORTH PARK
06. ALBANY PARK
07. PORTAGE PARK
08. IRVING PARK
09. DUNNING
10. MONTCLARE
11. BLEMONT CRAGIN
12. HERMOSA
SOUTHWEST SIDE
01. GARFIELD RIDGE
02. ARCHER HEIGHTS
03. BRIGHTON PARK
04. MCKINLEY PARK
05. NEW CITY
06. WEST ELSDON
07. GAGE PARK
08. CLEARING
09. CHICAGO LAWN
10. WEST ENGLEWOOD
11. ENGLEWOOD
12. WEST LAWN
13. ASHBURN
14. AUBURN GRESHAM
15. MOUNT GREENWOOD
16. BEVERLY
17. WASHINGTON HGTS
18. MORGAN PARK
SOUTH SIDE
01. ARMOUR SQUARE
02. DOUGLAS
03. BRIDGEPORT
04. GRAND BLVD
05. OAKLAND
06. FULLER PARK
07. KENWOOD
08. WASHINGTON PK
09. HYDE PARK
10. WOODLAWN
11. SOUTH SHORE
12. GREATER GRAND CE
13. CHATHAM
14. AVALON PARK
15. SOUTH CHICAGO
16. BURNSIDE
17. CALUMET HEIGHTS
18. ROSELAND
19. PULLMAN
20. WEST PULLMAN
21. RIVERDALE
22. EAST SIDE
23. SOUTH DEERING
24. HEGEWISCH
N
COWL
OZANAM
HARLEM
KEDZIE
WESTERN
CLARK
ASHLAND
HOWARD
TOUHY
MILWAUKEE
ELSTON
NAGLE
CENTRAL
LINCOLN
CICERO
PULASKI
DEVON
HIGGINS
BRYN MAWR
LAWRENCE
MONTROSE
IRVING PARK
CANFIELD
BELMONT
WELLINGTON
EAST RIVER RD
PACIFIC
ORIOLE
FULLERTON
NORTH
HARLEM
CHICAGO
NARRAGANSETT
MADISON
ROOSEVELT
AUSTIN
CENTRAL
CICERO
CERMAK
31ST
PERSHING
47TH
51ST
55TH
ARCHER
63RD
65TH
HARLEM
NARRAGANSETT
CENTRAL
71ST
79TH
87TH
PULASKI
KEDZIE
95TH
99TH
103RD
111TH
115TH
CICERO
PULASKI
119TH
KEDZIE
CALIFORNIA
WESTERN
123RD
ASHLAND
127TH
HALSTED
135TH
138TH
STATE
COTTAGE GROVE
STONY ISLAND
YATES
BRANDON

## Geoffrey Warner (The Grey Raven)
**C.O.W.L. Chief**
Sharpshooter, Master Strategist, Unpowered

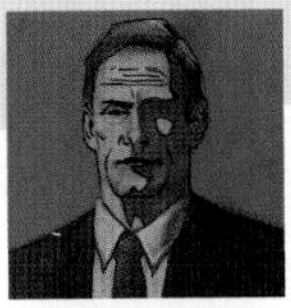

## Reginald Davis (Blaze)
**Deputy C.O.W.L. Chief/Head of Tactical**
Zero–Point Energy Gauntlet

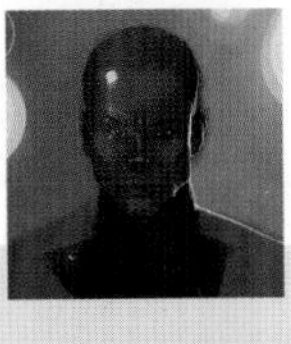

## Kathryn Mitchell (Radia)
**Tactical Division**
Telekinesis

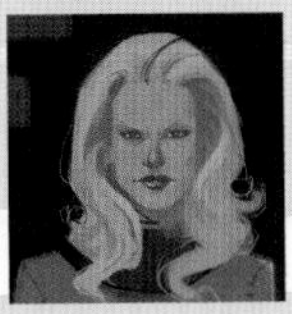

## Tom Hayden (Arclight)
**Tactical Division**
Flight, Focused Energy Bursts

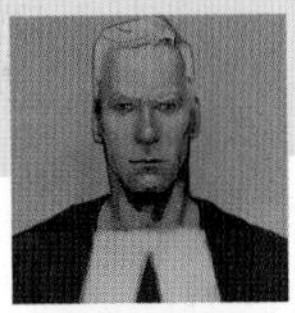

## John Pierce
**Investigations**
Detective, Unpowered

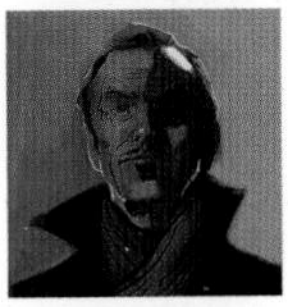

## Grant Marlow
**Patrol Division – West Side**
Sharpshooter, Unpowered

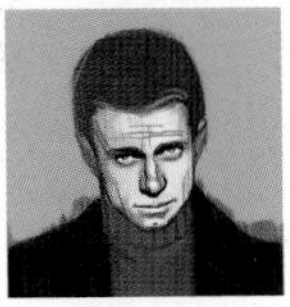

## Karl Samoski (Eclipse)
**Patrol Division – West Side**
Anti–Kinetics, Power Disruption

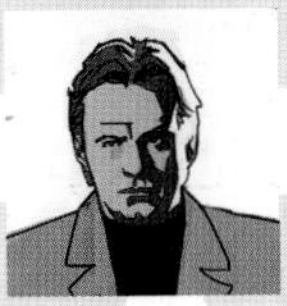

PATROL DISTRICTS

CENTRAL
NORTH
NORTHWEST
SOUTH
SOUTHWEST
WEST SIDE

# CHICAGO, 1962

# Introduction

You hold in your hands the final collection (for now, I hope) of *C.O.W.L.* and, damn, if it isn't extremely unsatisfying and 100% what it needs to be. That unsatisfied feeling is all about the complex, sleazy, backstabbing, hypocritical world of behind-the-scenes politics. You see, just like in real life, the games never end, the machinations get more labyrinthine and no one—even when they get what they think they want—has a truly happy ending. No riding off into the sunset. No reuniting atop the Empire State Building. No passionate kisses and declarations of love in the rain. Life just goes on and we have to deal with it.

And that is why I fucking LOVE *C.O.W.L.*

The team behind the book has been firing on all cylinders since the first panel of the first page of the first issue and never once let up. They tell their story with truth and reality and no fear of expectation. And they are to be commended.

The pull-no-punches look behind the curtain of Chicago politics crosses genre lines effortlessly. In Hollywood, I'd say it's *The Wire* meets *Hoffa* meets *The Avengers* meets *Mad Men*. (That's my superpower: I'm *Reductive Man*.) But those comparisons seem weak when one actually dives into the vivid, rotting-from-the-inside world Kyle, Alec, and Rod have created. This is a wholly original series evocative of many things, but with its own distinct flavor (and deliciously nasty aftertaste).

There are lots of comics out there that try the "what if super heroes existed in the real world?" concept, but none have felt quite so real since *Watchmen*. Maybe even more so. You see—SPOILER ALERT—in Moore and Gibbons' masterwork, the "costumes" are behind it all, but in *C.O.W.L.*'s '60s era Chicago, true power doesn't come from flying or eye beams or super strength. It's the players behind-the-scenes—amoral, wealth-obsessed, but decidedly flesh-and-blood men—who move demigods like so many chess pieces. And, as the Presidential election season begins again, we see the only thing different from the world of *C.O.W.L.* and our very own is a few capes. (And *C.O.W.L.* has much better art direction than we do).

So, roll up your sleeves and dig into the world of *C.O.W.L.* It's a dirty place, but, goddamn, if i don't love to wallow in it.

**Marc Andreyko**
Los Angeles, 2015

*Marc Andreyko is the* New York Times *bestselling, Harvey and Eisner nominated writer behind such books as* Torso *(w/ Brian Bendis),* Manhunter, The Illegitimates *(w/ Taran Killam), and the smash hit* Wonder Woman '77, *among his many credits. He lives in Los Angeles with his books, Blu-Rays, and his awesome dog, Frederick.*

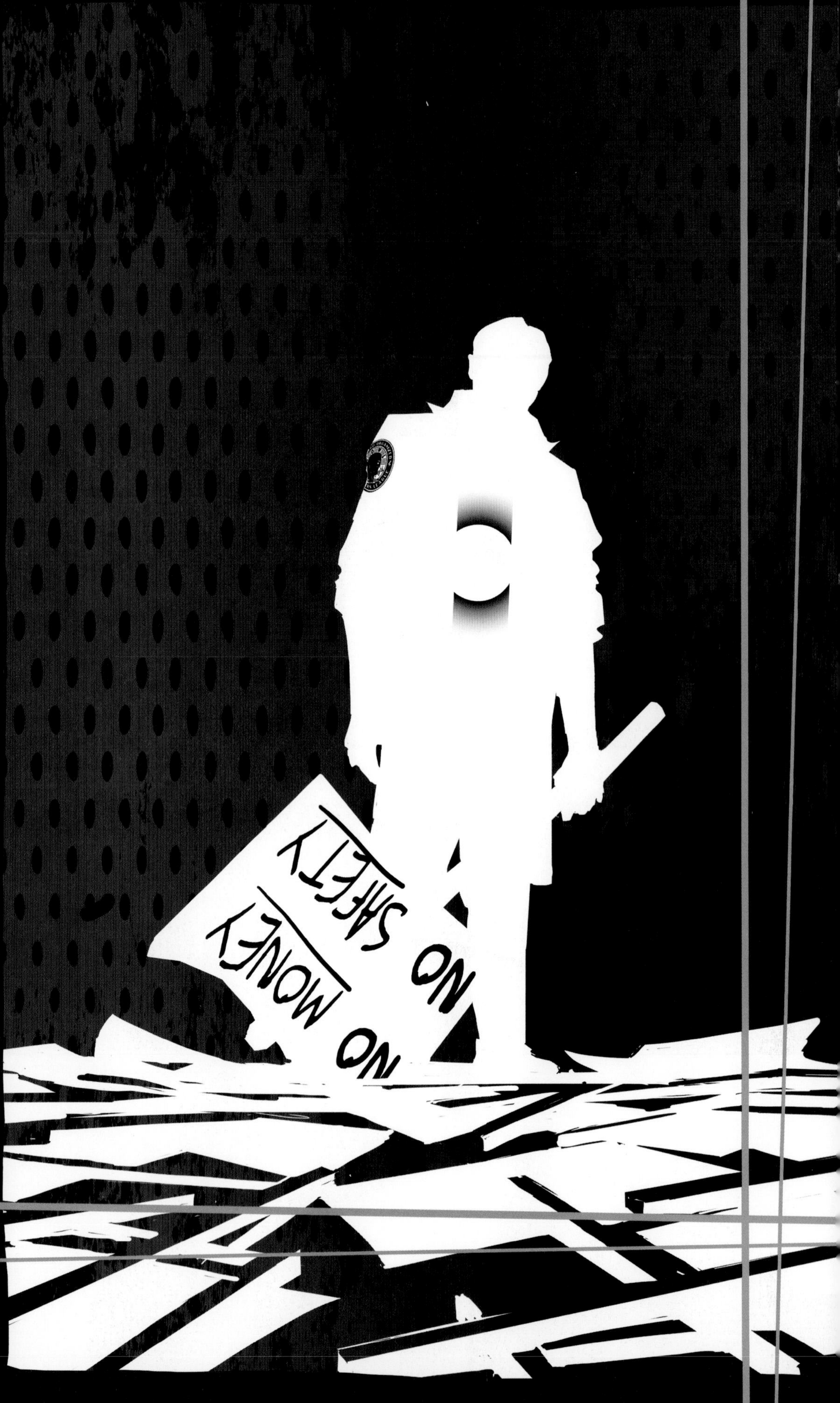
NO MONEY
NO SAFETY

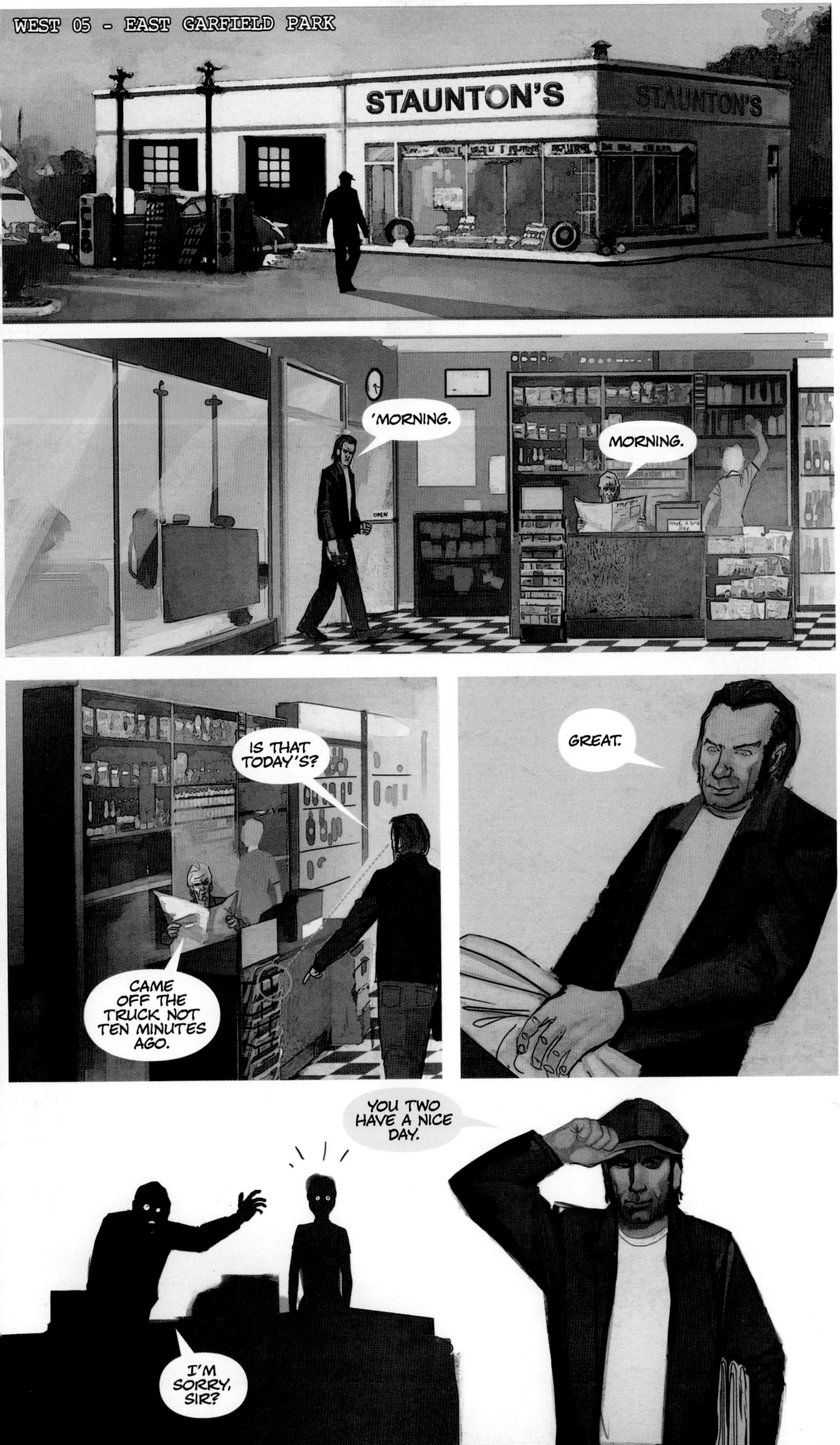
WEST 05 - EAST GARFIELD PARK
STAUNTON'S
STAUNTON'S
'MORNING.
MORNING.
IS THAT TODAY'S?
CAME OFF THE TRUCK NOT TEN MINUTES AGO.
GREAT.
YOU TWO HAVE A NICE DAY.
I'M SORRY, SIR?

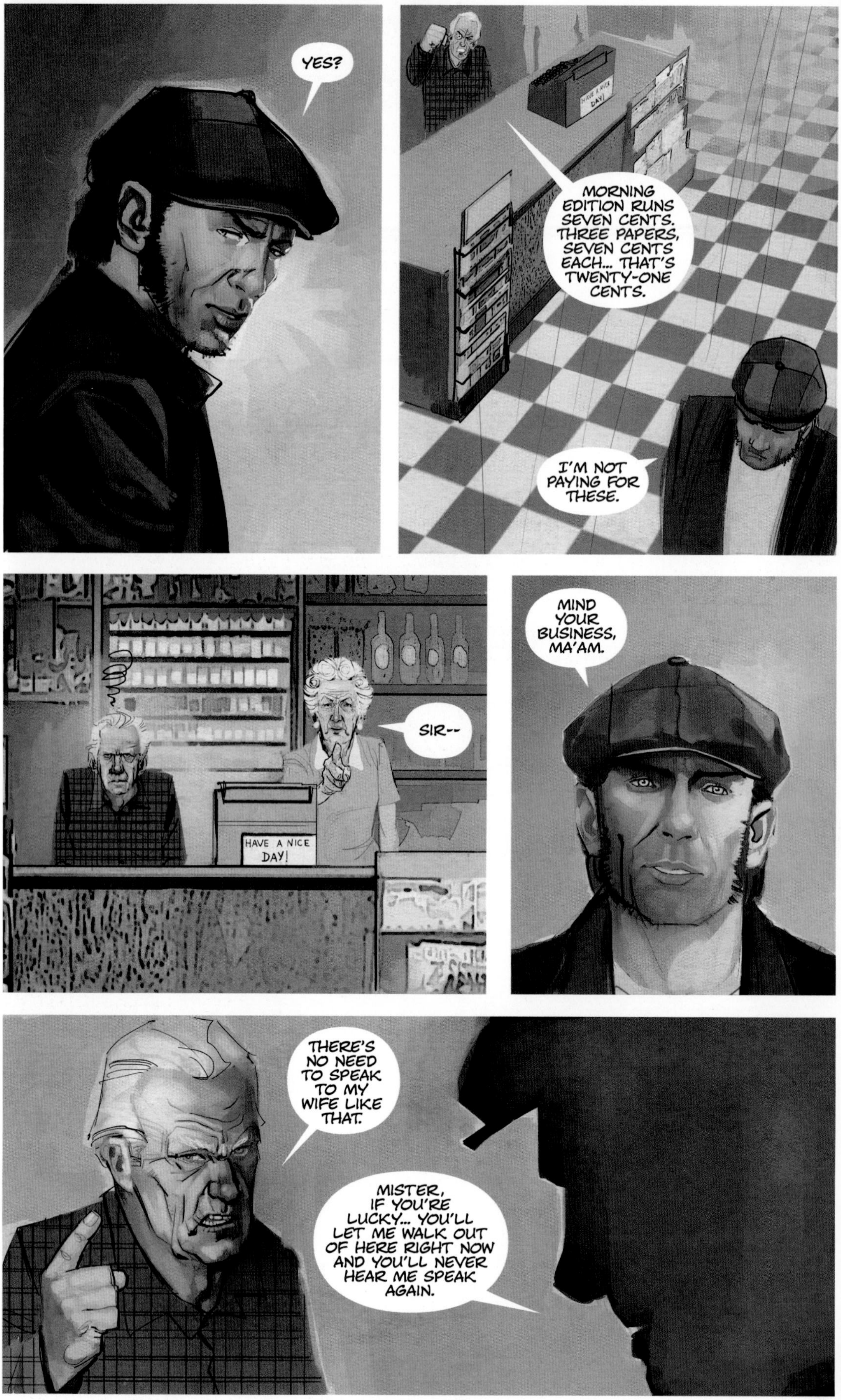
YES?
HAVE A NICE DAY!
MORNING EDITION RUNS SEVEN CENTS. THREE PAPERS, SEVEN CENTS EACH... THAT'S TWENTY-ONE CENTS.
I'M NOT PAYING FOR THESE.
SIR--
HAVE A NICE DAY!
MIND YOUR BUSINESS, MA'AM.
THERE'S NO NEED TO SPEAK TO MY WIFE LIKE THAT.
MISTER, IF YOU'RE LUCKY... YOU'LL LET ME WALK OUT OF HERE RIGHT NOW AND YOU'LL NEVER HEAR ME SPEAK AGAIN.

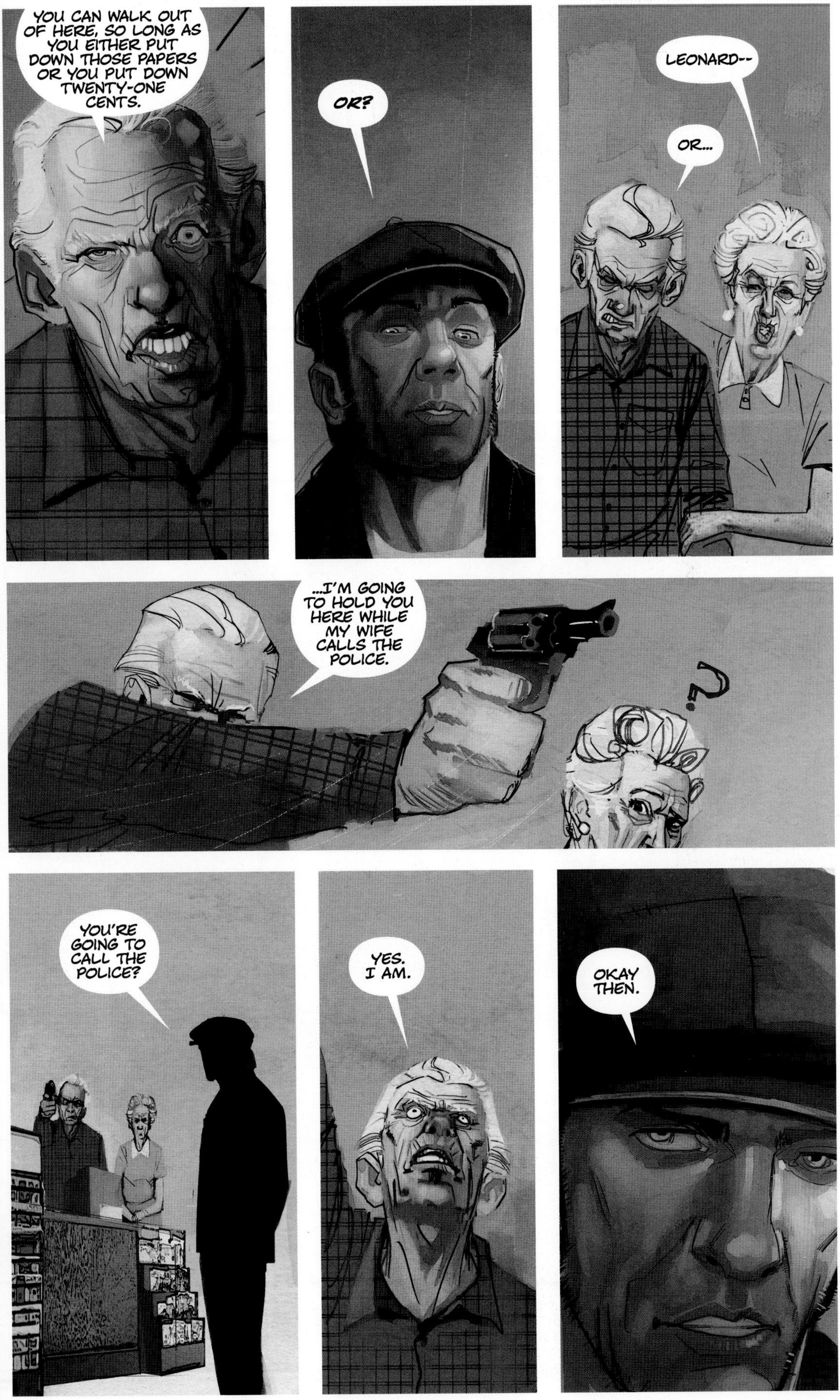
YOU CAN WALK OUT OF HERE, SO LONG AS YOU EITHER PUT DOWN THOSE PAPERS OR YOU PUT DOWN TWENTY-ONE CENTS.
OR?
LEONARD--
OR...
...I'M GOING TO HOLD YOU HERE WHILE MY WIFE CALLS THE POLICE.
?
YOU'RE GOING TO CALL THE POLICE?
YES. I AM.
OKAY THEN.

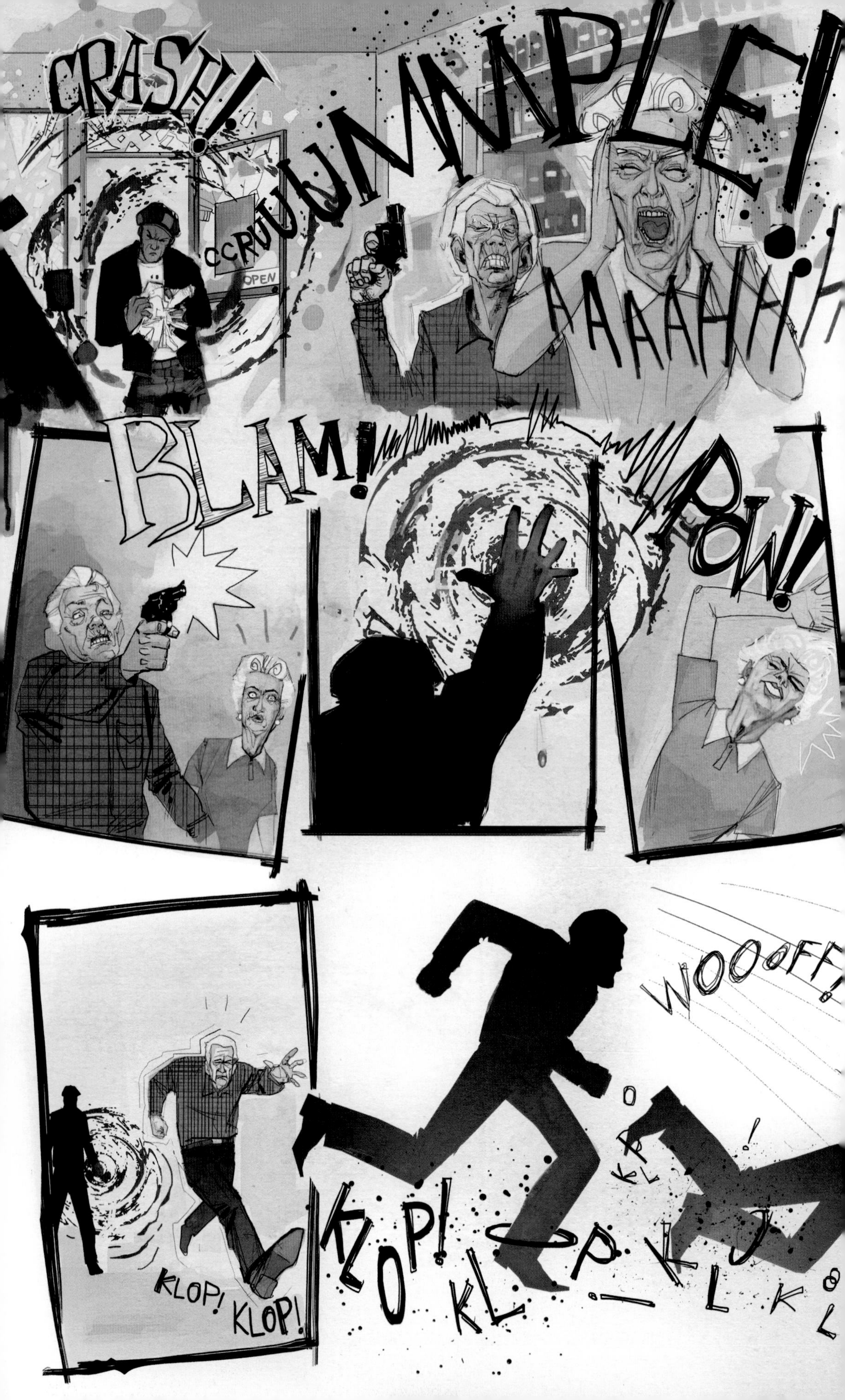
CRASH!
OPEN
AAAAHHH
BLAM!
POW!
WOOOFF!
KLOP! KLOP!
KLOP!

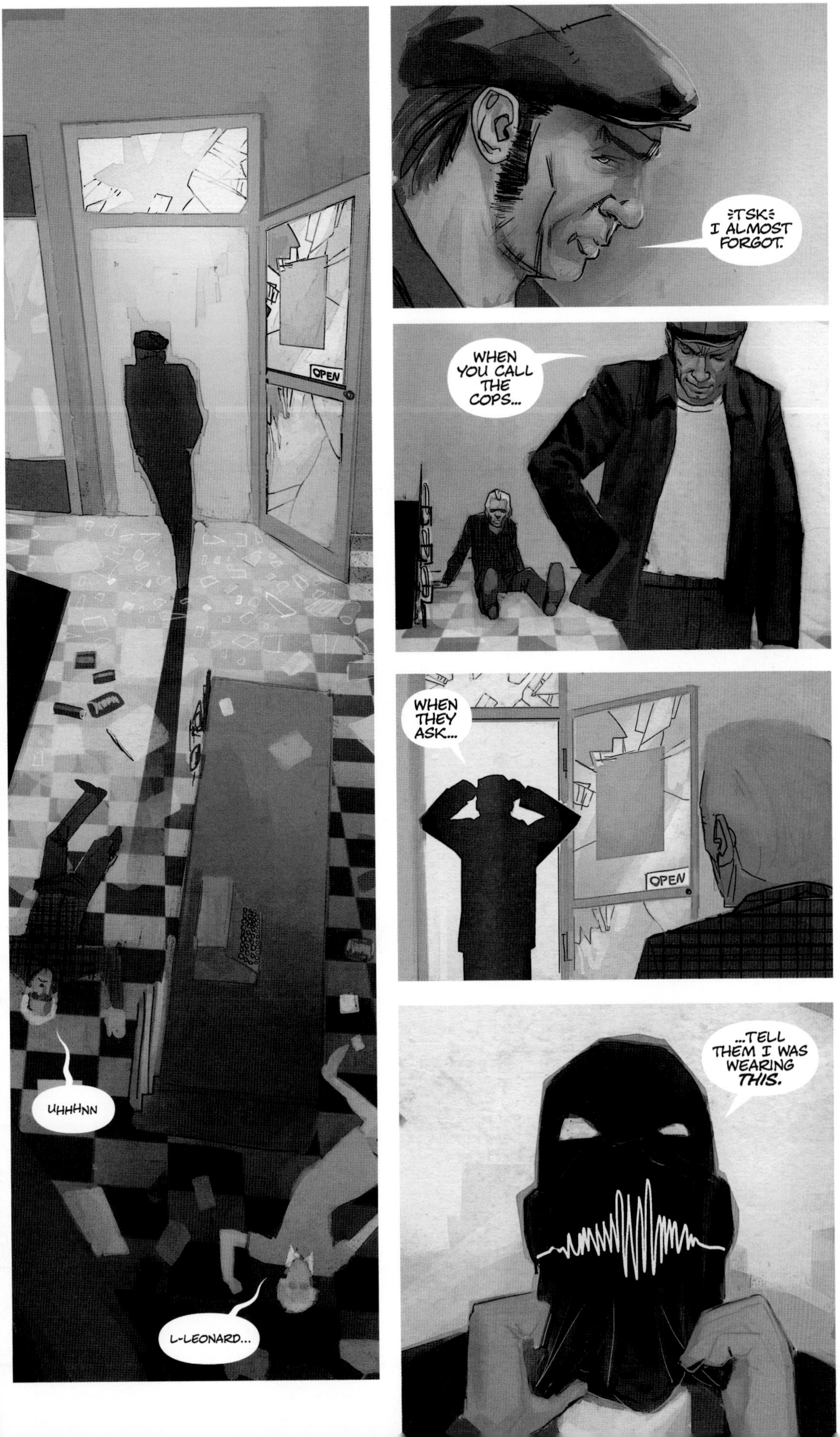
OPEN
UHHHNN
L-LEONARD...
TSK
I ALMOST FORGOT.
WHEN YOU CALL THE COPS...
WHEN THEY ASK...
OPEN
...TELL THEM I WAS WEARING *THIS.*

# CHAPTER 1
## At the Brink

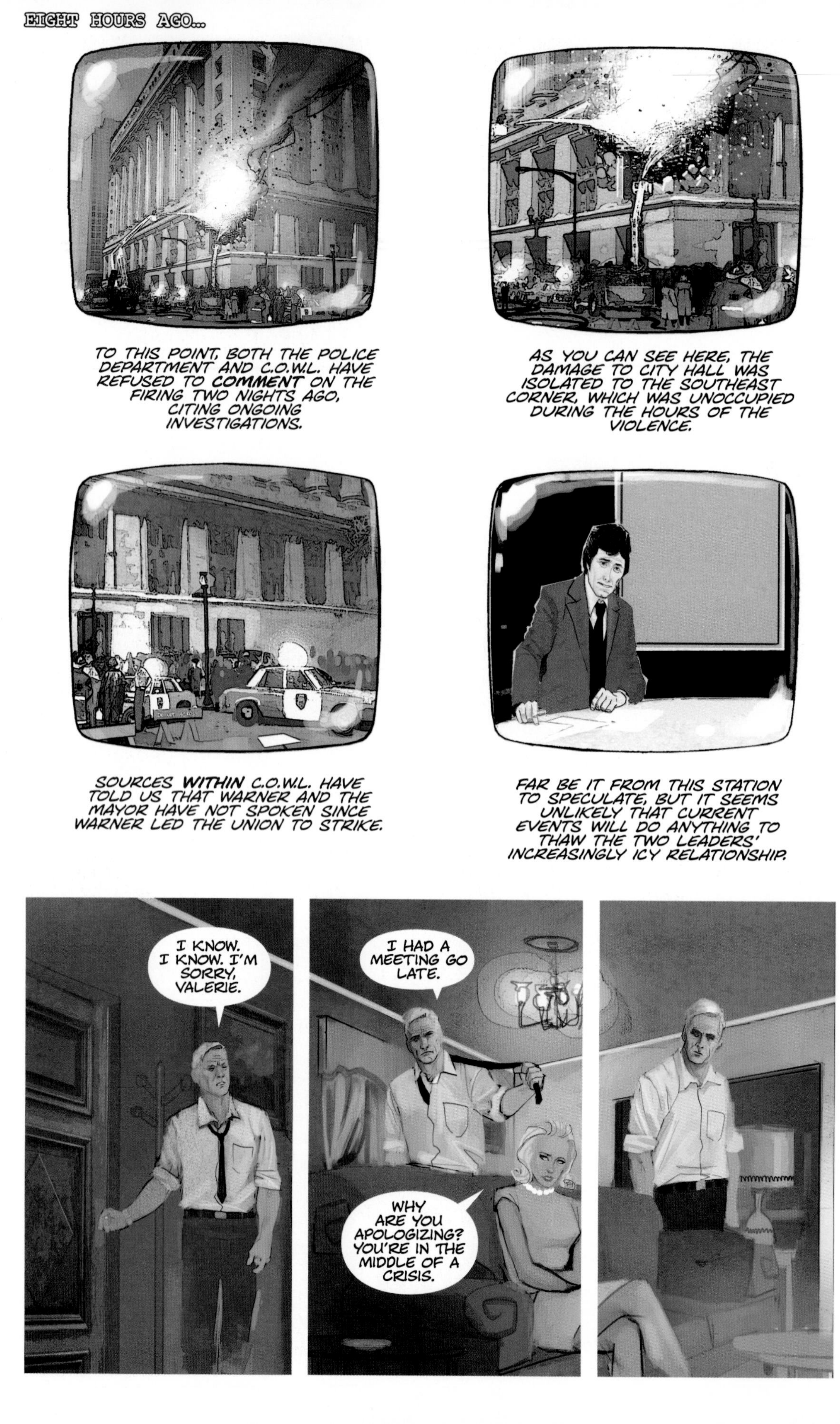
EIGHT HOURS AGO...
TO THIS POINT, BOTH THE POLICE DEPARTMENT AND C.O.W.L. HAVE REFUSED TO COMMENT ON THE FIRING TWO NIGHTS AGO, CITING ONGOING INVESTIGATIONS.
AS YOU CAN SEE HERE, THE DAMAGE TO CITY HALL WAS ISOLATED TO THE SOUTHEAST CORNER, WHICH WAS UNOCCUPIED DURING THE HOURS OF THE VIOLENCE.
SOURCES WITHIN C.O.W.L. HAVE TOLD US THAT WARNER AND THE MAYOR HAVE NOT SPOKEN SINCE WARNER LED THE UNION TO STRIKE.
FAR BE IT FROM THIS STATION TO SPECULATE, BUT IT SEEMS UNLIKELY THAT CURRENT EVENTS WILL DO ANYTHING TO THAW THE TWO LEADERS' INCREASINGLY ICY RELATIONSHIP.
I KNOW. I KNOW. I'M SORRY, VALERIE.
I HAD A MEETING GO LATE.
WHY ARE YOU APOLOGIZING? YOU'RE IN THE MIDDLE OF A CRISIS.

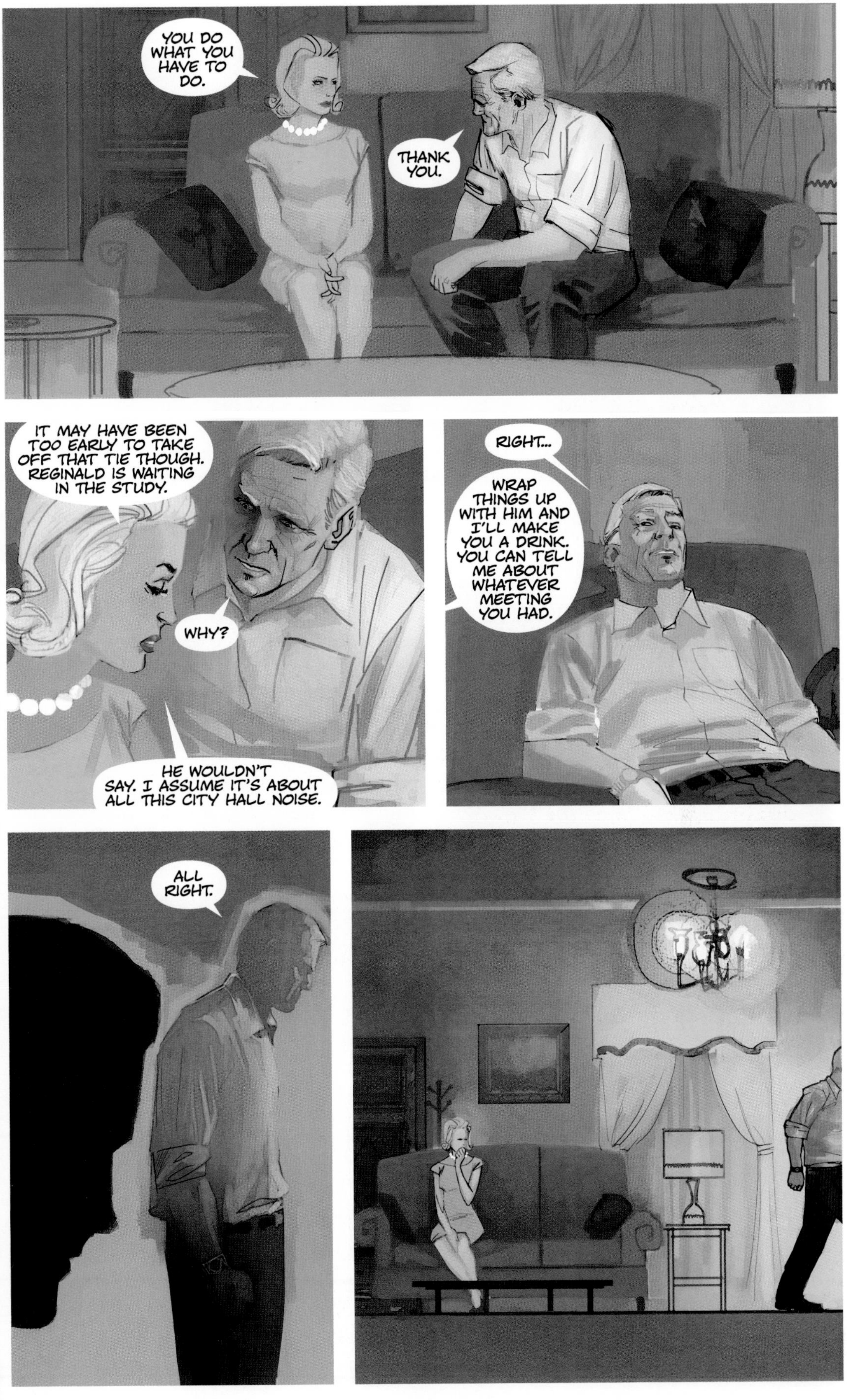
YOU DO WHAT YOU HAVE TO DO.
THANK YOU.
IT MAY HAVE BEEN TOO EARLY TO TAKE OFF THAT TIE THOUGH. REGINALD IS WAITING IN THE STUDY.
WHY?
HE WOULDN'T SAY. I ASSUME IT'S ABOUT ALL THIS CITY HALL NOISE.
RIGHT...
WRAP THINGS UP WITH HIM AND I'LL MAKE YOU A DRINK. YOU CAN TELL ME ABOUT WHATEVER MEETING YOU HAD.
ALL RIGHT.

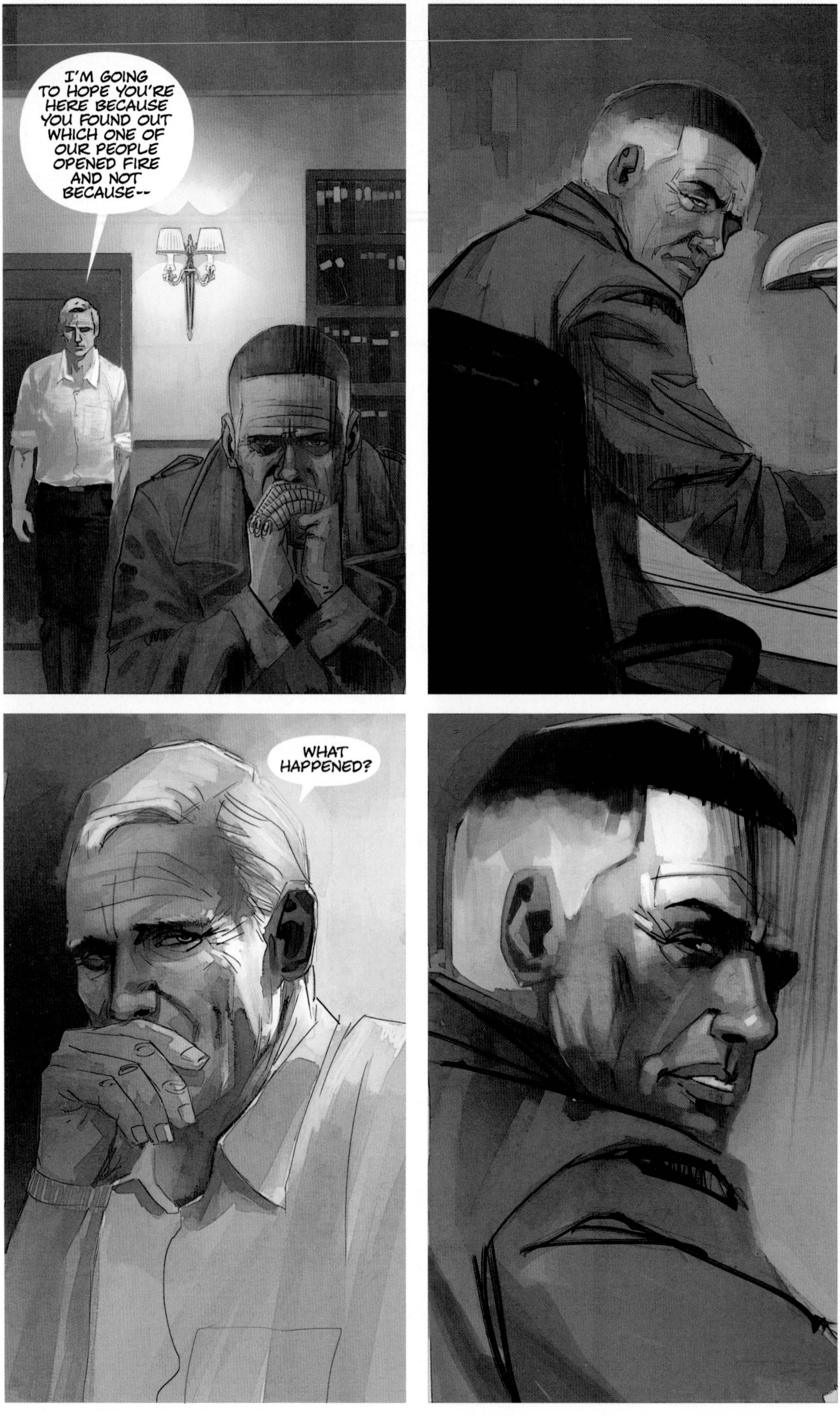
I'M GOING TO HOPE YOU'RE HERE BECAUSE YOU FOUND OUT WHICH ONE OF OUR PEOPLE OPENED FIRE AND NOT BECAUSE--
WHAT HAPPENED?

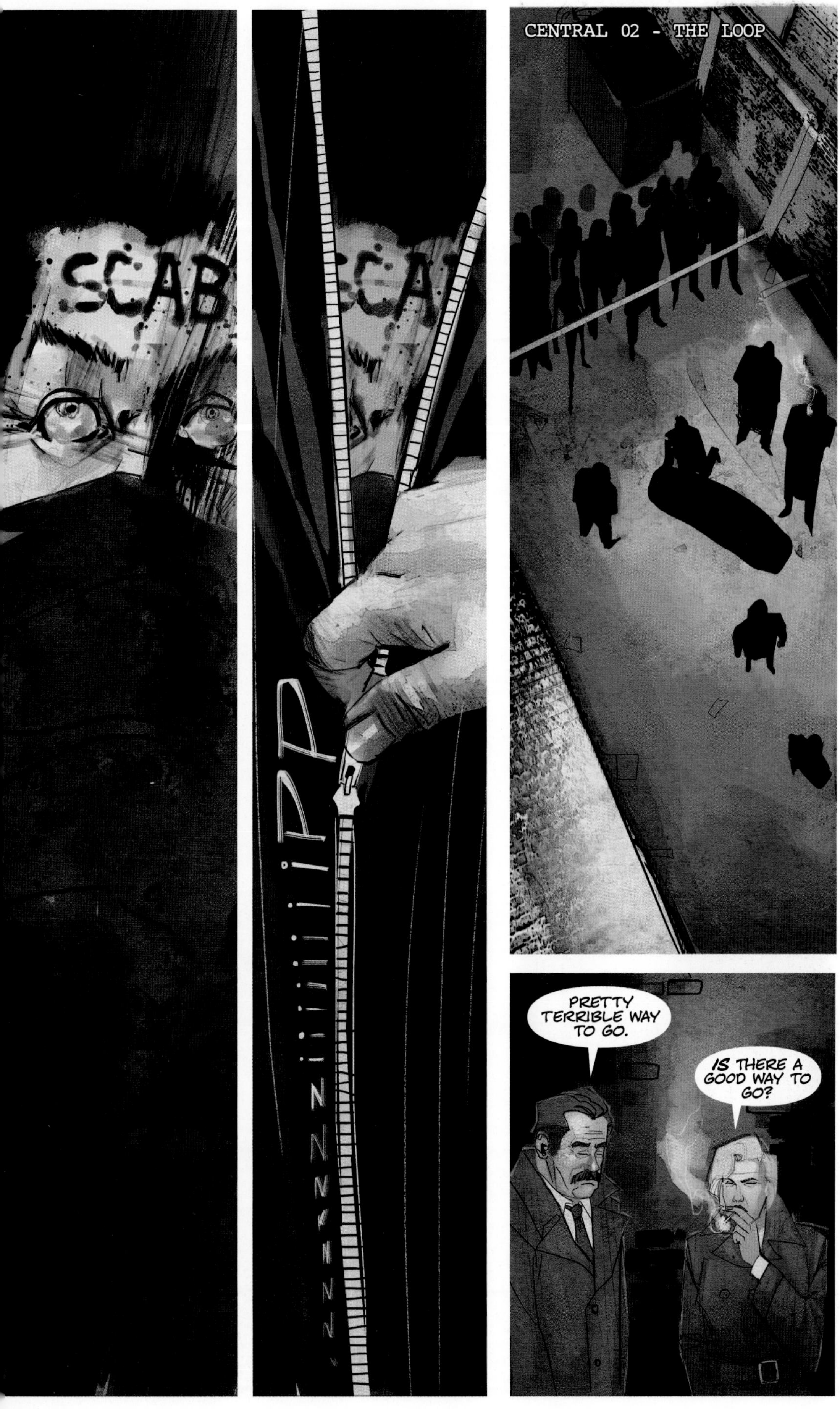
SCAB
SCA
ZIPPP...
ZZZZNNNN
CENTRAL 02 - THE LOOP
PRETTY TERRIBLE WAY TO GO.
IS THERE A GOOD WAY TO GO?

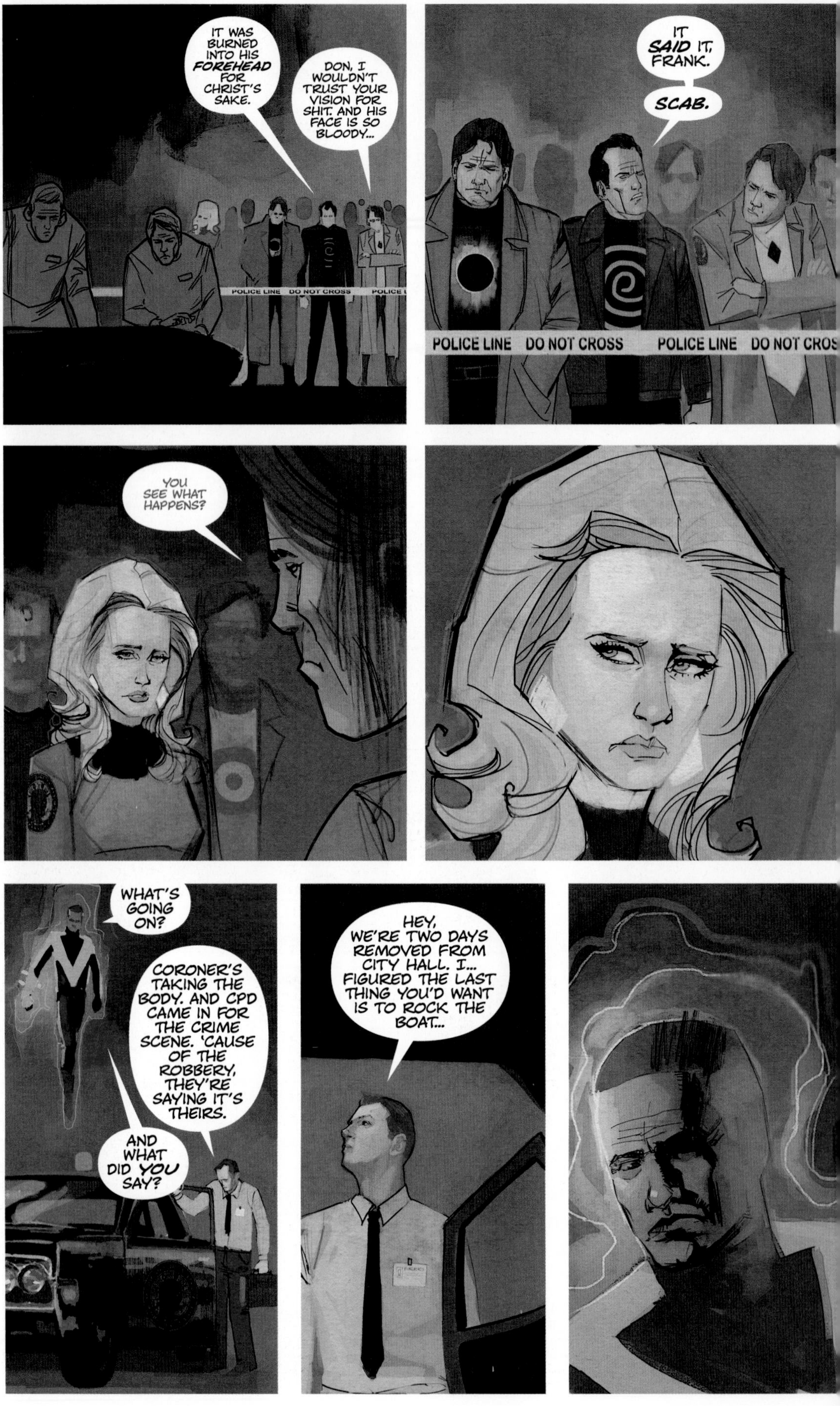
IT WAS BURNED INTO HIS FOREHEAD FOR CHRIST'S SAKE.
DON, I WOULDN'T TRUST YOUR VISION FOR SHIT. AND HIS FACE IS SO BLOODY...
POLICE LINE DO NOT CROSS POLICE L
IT SAID IT, FRANK.
SCAB.
POLICE LINE DO NOT CROSS POLICE LINE DO NOT CROS
YOU SEE WHAT HAPPENS?
WHAT'S GOING ON?
CORONER'S TAKING THE BODY. AND CPD CAME IN FOR THE CRIME SCENE. 'CAUSE OF THE ROBBERY, THEY'RE SAYING IT'S THEIRS.
AND WHAT DID YOU SAY?
HEY, WE'RE TWO DAYS REMOVED FROM CITY HALL. I... FIGURED THE LAST THING YOU'D WANT IS TO ROCK THE BOAT...

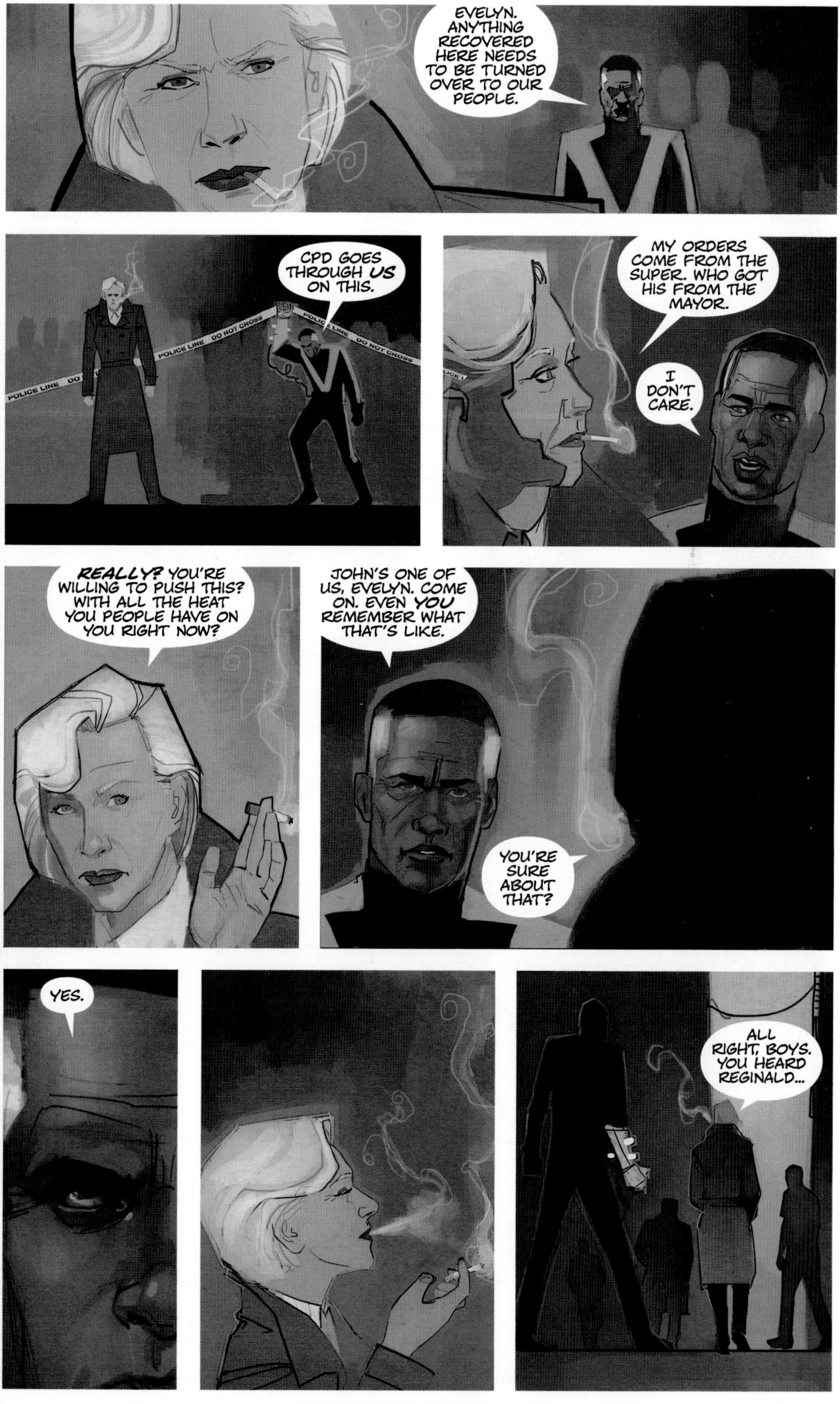
EVELYN. ANYTHING RECOVERED HERE NEEDS TO BE TURNED OVER TO OUR PEOPLE.
CPD GOES THROUGH *US* ON THIS.
POLICE LINE DO NOT CROSS
MY ORDERS COME FROM THE SUPER. WHO GOT HIS FROM THE MAYOR.
I DON'T CARE.
*REALLY?* YOU'RE WILLING TO PUSH THIS? WITH ALL THE HEAT YOU PEOPLE HAVE ON YOU RIGHT NOW?
JOHN'S ONE OF US, EVELYN. COME ON. EVEN *YOU* REMEMBER WHAT THAT'S LIKE.
YOU'RE SURE ABOUT THAT?
YES.
ALL RIGHT, BOYS. YOU HEARD REGINALD...

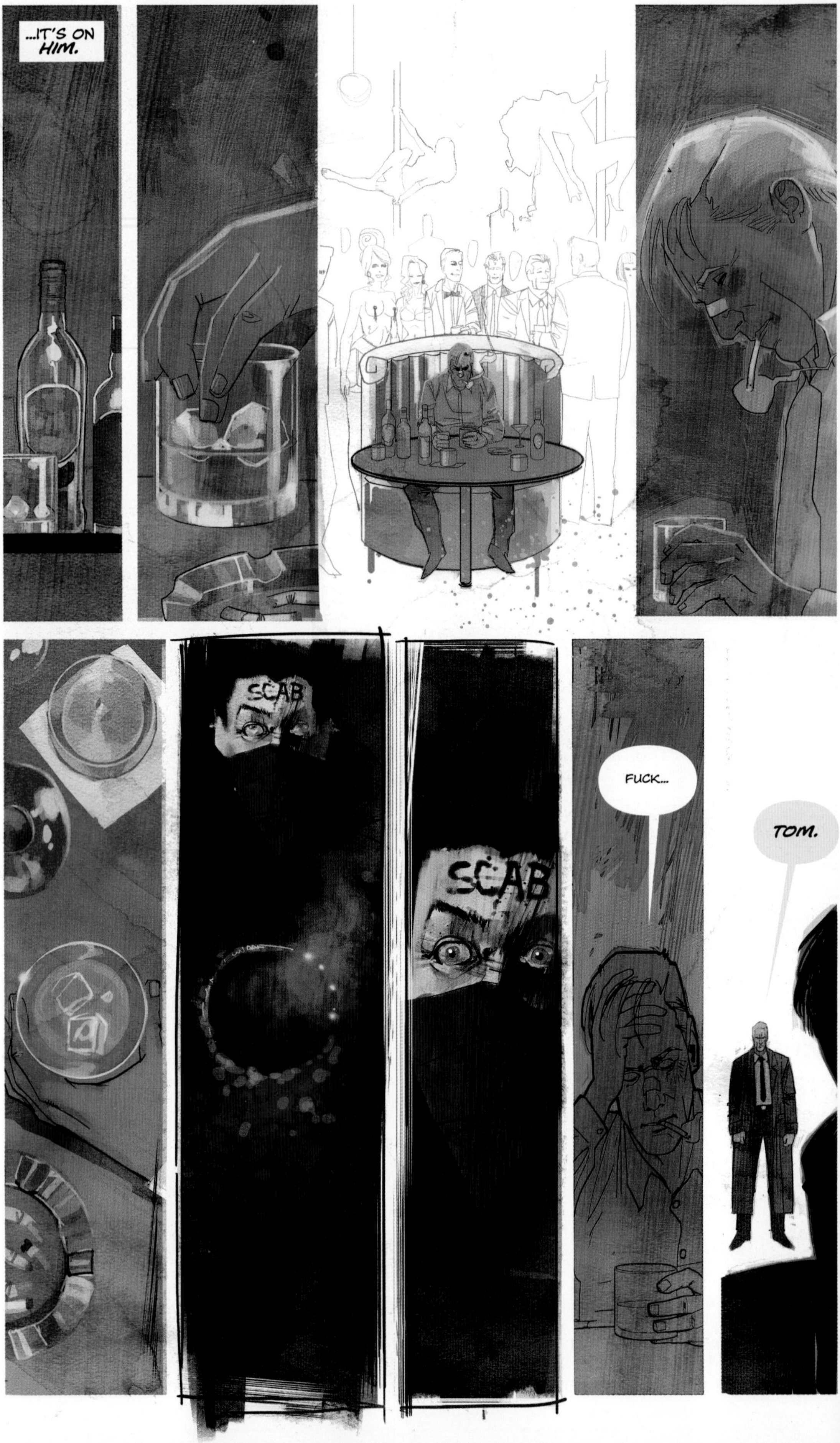
...IT'S ON HIM.
SCAB
SCAB
FUCK...
TOM.

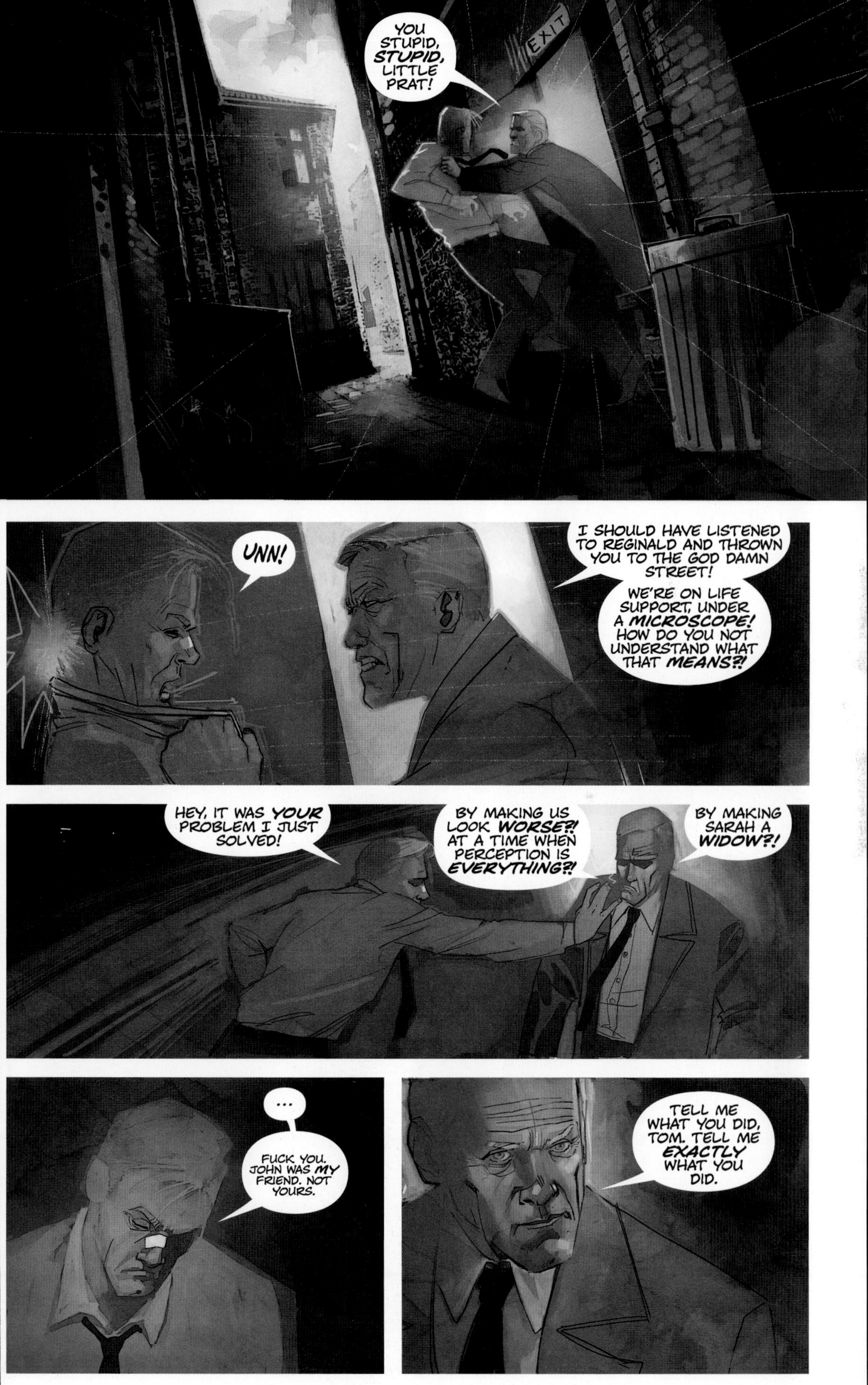

YOU STUPID, STUPID, LITTLE PRAT!
EXIT
UNN!
I SHOULD HAVE LISTENED TO REGINALD AND THROWN YOU TO THE GOD DAMN STREET!
WE'RE ON LIFE SUPPORT, UNDER A MICROSCOPE! HOW DO YOU NOT UNDERSTAND WHAT THAT MEANS?!
HEY, IT WAS YOUR PROBLEM I JUST SOLVED!
BY MAKING US LOOK WORSE?! AT A TIME WHEN PERCEPTION IS EVERYTHING?!
BY MAKING SARAH A WIDOW?!
...
FUCK YOU. JOHN WAS MY FRIEND. NOT YOURS.
TELL ME WHAT YOU DID, TOM. TELL ME EXACTLY WHAT YOU DID.

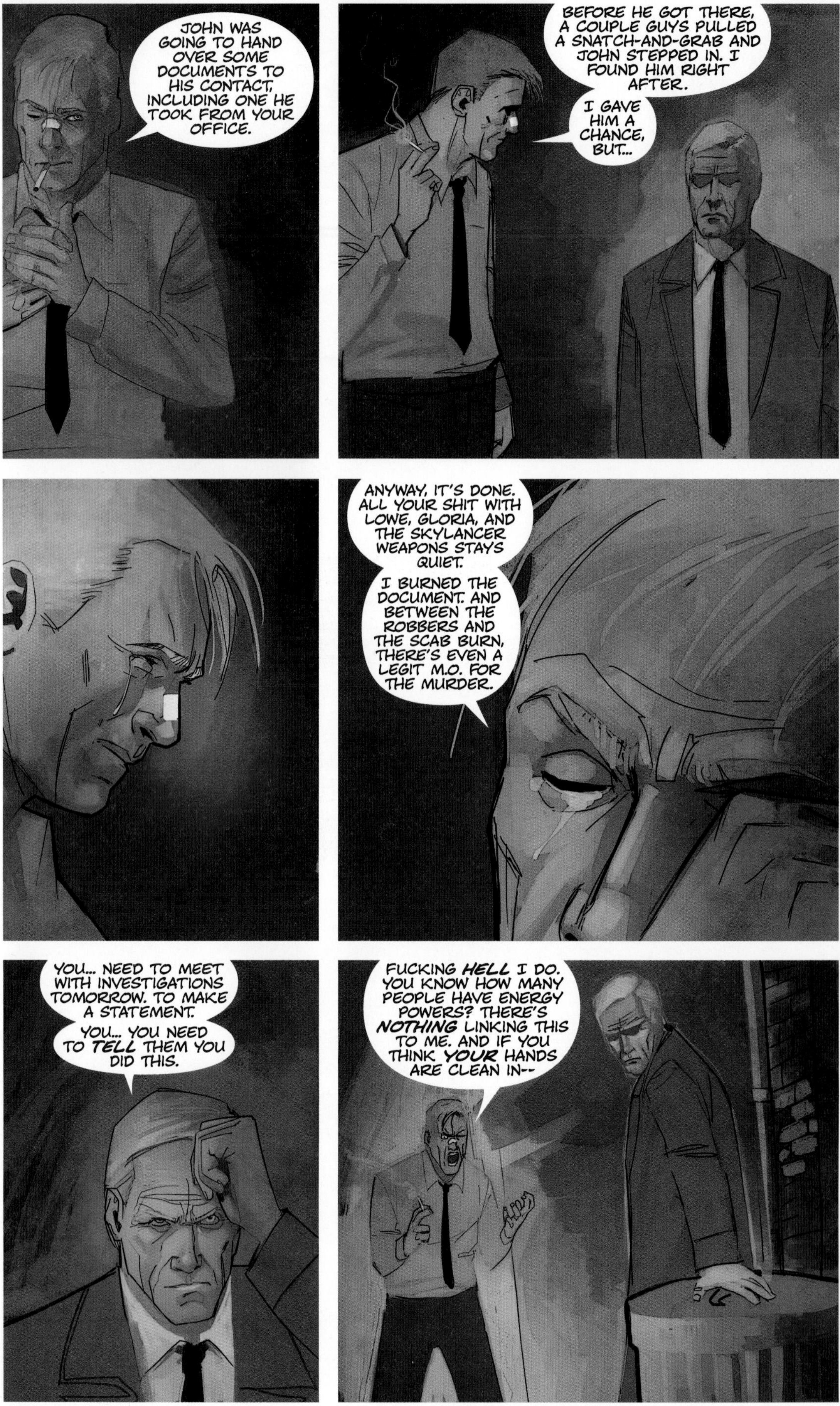
JOHN WAS GOING TO HAND OVER SOME DOCUMENTS TO HIS CONTACT, INCLUDING ONE HE TOOK FROM YOUR OFFICE.
BEFORE HE GOT THERE, A COUPLE GUYS PULLED A SNATCH-AND-GRAB AND JOHN STEPPED IN. I FOUND HIM RIGHT AFTER.
I GAVE HIM A CHANCE, BUT...
ANYWAY, IT'S DONE. ALL YOUR SHIT WITH LOWE, GLORIA, AND THE SKYLANCER WEAPONS STAYS QUIET.
I BURNED THE DOCUMENT. AND BETWEEN THE ROBBERS AND THE SCAB BURN, THERE'S EVEN A LEGIT M.O. FOR THE MURDER.
YOU... NEED TO MEET WITH INVESTIGATIONS TOMORROW. TO MAKE A STATEMENT.
YOU... YOU NEED TO ***TELL*** THEM YOU DID THIS.
FUCKING ***HELL*** I DO. YOU KNOW HOW MANY PEOPLE HAVE ENERGY POWERS? THERE'S ***NOTHING*** LINKING THIS TO ME. AND IF YOU THINK ***YOUR*** HANDS ARE CLEAN IN--

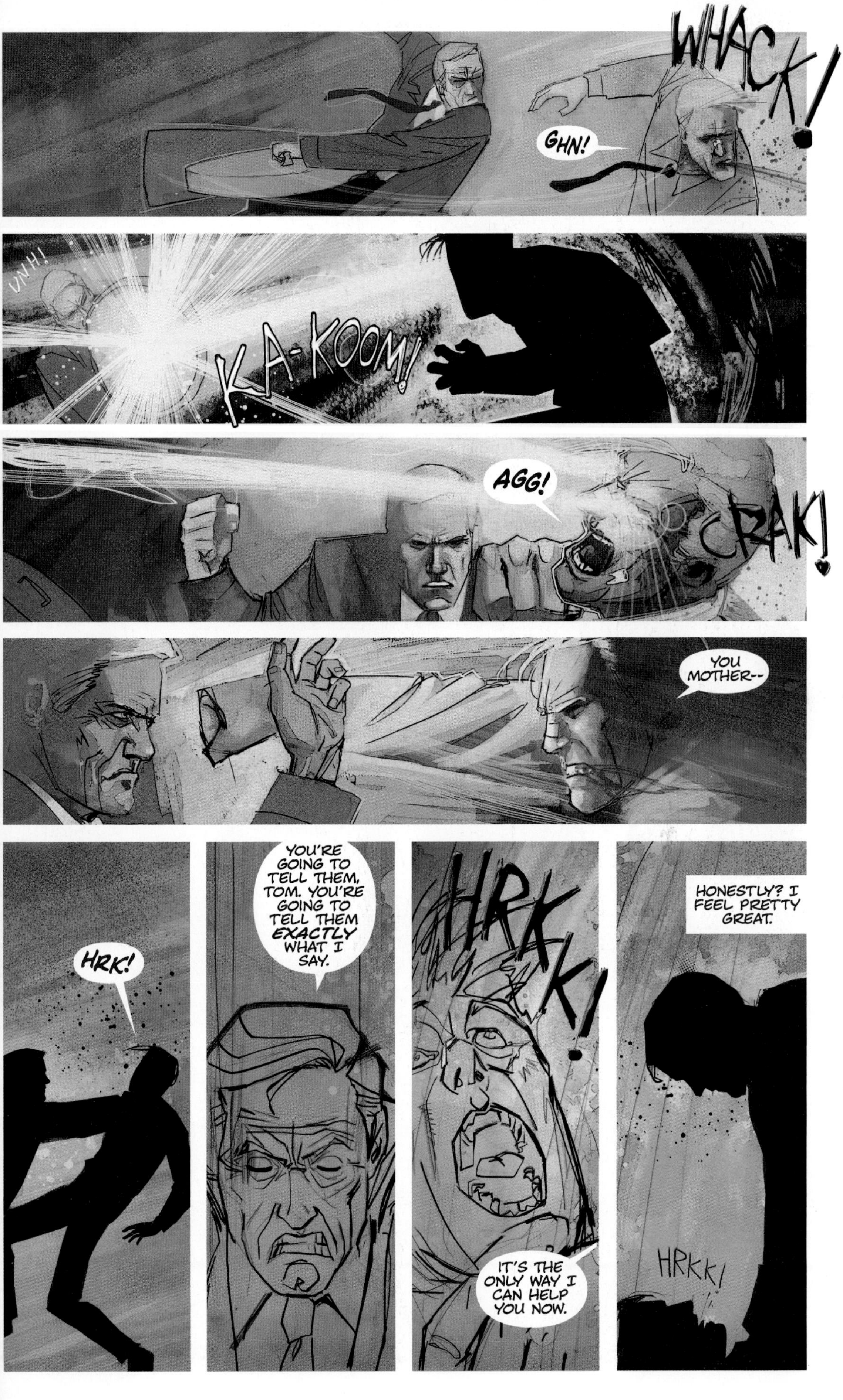
WHACK!
GHN!
UNH!
KA-KOOM!
AGG!
CRAK!
YOU MOTHER--
HRK!
YOU'RE GOING TO TELL THEM, TOM. YOU'RE GOING TO TELL THEM EXACTLY WHAT I SAY.
HRKK!
IT'S THE ONLY WAY I CAN HELP YOU NOW.
HONESTLY? I FEEL PRETTY GREAT.
HRKK!

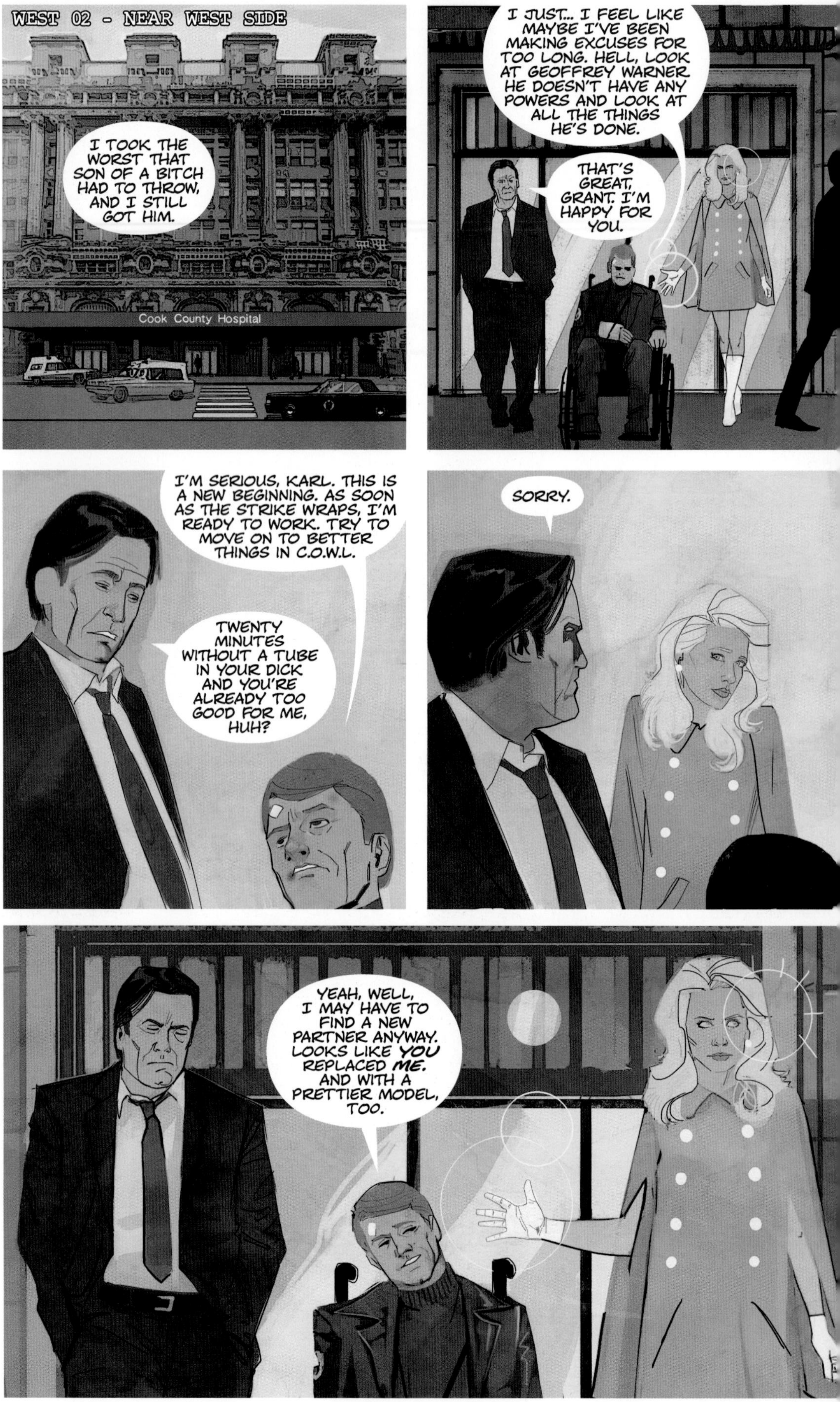
WEST 02 - NEAR WEST SIDE
Cook County Hospital
I TOOK THE WORST THAT SON OF A BITCH HAD TO THROW, AND I STILL GOT HIM.
I JUST... I FEEL LIKE MAYBE I'VE BEEN MAKING EXCUSES FOR TOO LONG. HELL, LOOK AT GEOFFREY WARNER HE DOESN'T HAVE ANY POWERS AND LOOK AT ALL THE THINGS HE'S DONE.
THAT'S GREAT, GRANT. I'M HAPPY FOR YOU.
I'M SERIOUS, KARL. THIS IS A NEW BEGINNING. AS SOON AS THE STRIKE WRAPS, I'M READY TO WORK. TRY TO MOVE ON TO BETTER THINGS IN C.O.W.L.
TWENTY MINUTES WITHOUT A TUBE IN YOUR DICK AND YOU'RE ALREADY TOO GOOD FOR ME, HUH?
SORRY.
YEAH, WELL, I MAY HAVE TO FIND A NEW PARTNER ANYWAY. LOOKS LIKE *YOU* REPLACED *ME.* AND WITH A PRETTIER MODEL, TOO.

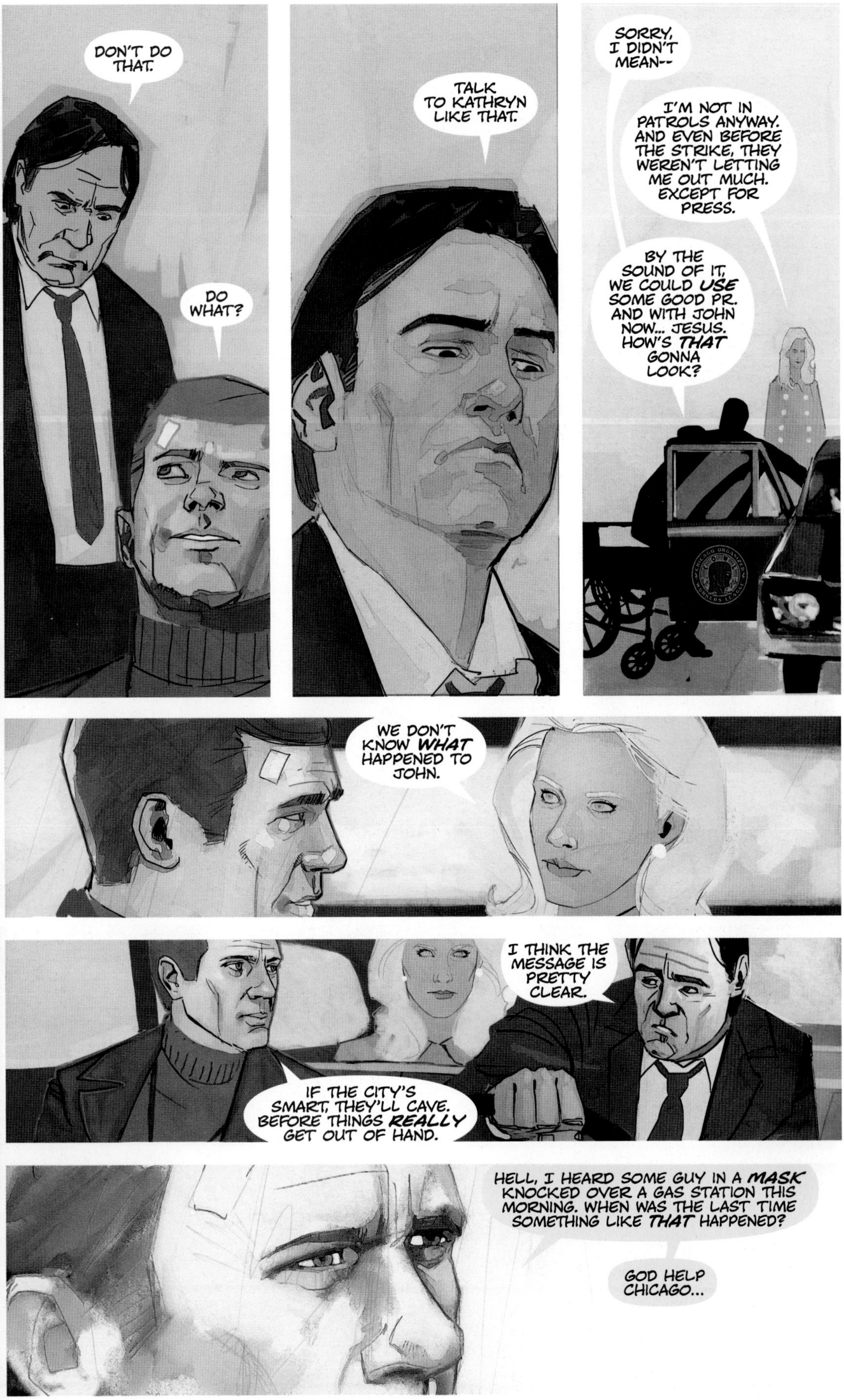

DON'T DO THAT.
DO WHAT?
TALK TO KATHRYN LIKE THAT.
SORRY, I DIDN'T MEAN--
I'M NOT IN PATROLS ANYWAY. AND EVEN BEFORE THE STRIKE, THEY WEREN'T LETTING ME OUT MUCH. EXCEPT FOR PRESS.
BY THE SOUND OF IT, WE COULD *USE* SOME GOOD PR. AND WITH JOHN NOW... JESUS. HOW'S *THAT* GONNA LOOK?
WE DON'T KNOW *WHAT* HAPPENED TO JOHN.
I THINK THE MESSAGE IS PRETTY CLEAR.
IF THE CITY'S SMART, THEY'LL CAVE. BEFORE THINGS *REALLY* GET OUT OF HAND.
HELL, I HEARD SOME GUY IN A *MASK* KNOCKED OVER A GAS STATION THIS MORNING. WHEN WAS THE LAST TIME SOMETHING LIKE *THAT* HAPPENED?
GOD HELP CHICAGO...

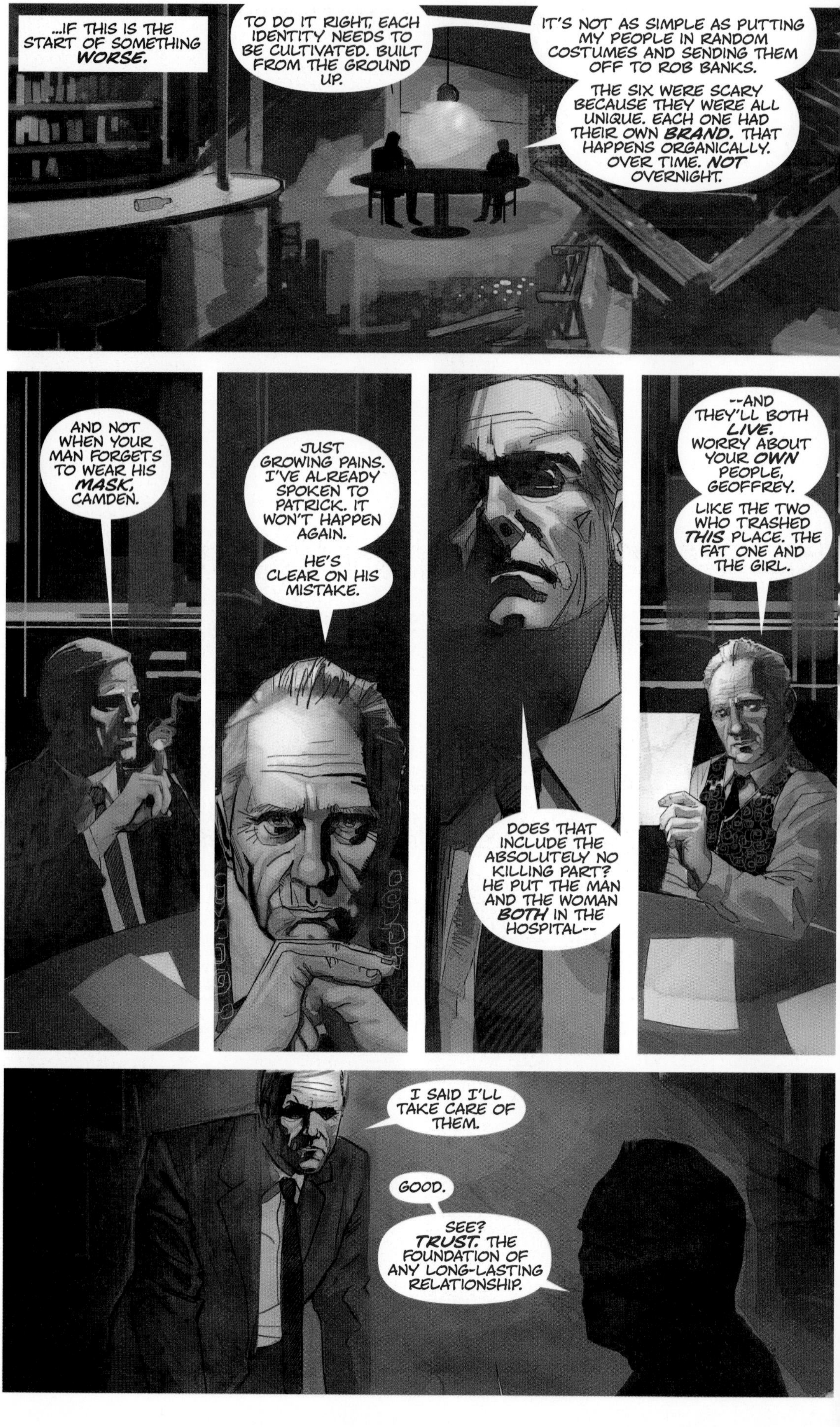
...IF THIS IS THE START OF SOMETHING WORSE.
TO DO IT RIGHT, EACH IDENTITY NEEDS TO BE CULTIVATED. BUILT FROM THE GROUND UP.
IT'S NOT AS SIMPLE AS PUTTING MY PEOPLE IN RANDOM COSTUMES AND SENDING THEM OFF TO ROB BANKS.
THE SIX WERE SCARY BECAUSE THEY WERE ALL UNIQUE. EACH ONE HAD THEIR OWN BRAND. THAT HAPPENS ORGANICALLY. OVER TIME. NOT OVERNIGHT.
AND NOT WHEN YOUR MAN FORGETS TO WEAR HIS MASK, CAMDEN.
JUST GROWING PAINS. I'VE ALREADY SPOKEN TO PATRICK. IT WON'T HAPPEN AGAIN.
HE'S CLEAR ON HIS MISTAKE.
DOES THAT INCLUDE THE ABSOLUTELY NO KILLING PART? HE PUT THE MAN AND THE WOMAN BOTH IN THE HOSPITAL--
--AND THEY'LL BOTH LIVE. WORRY ABOUT YOUR OWN PEOPLE, GEOFFREY.
LIKE THE TWO WHO TRASHED THIS PLACE. THE FAT ONE AND THE GIRL.
I SAID I'LL TAKE CARE OF THEM.
GOOD.
SEE? TRUST. THE FOUNDATION OF ANY LONG-LASTING RELATIONSHIP.

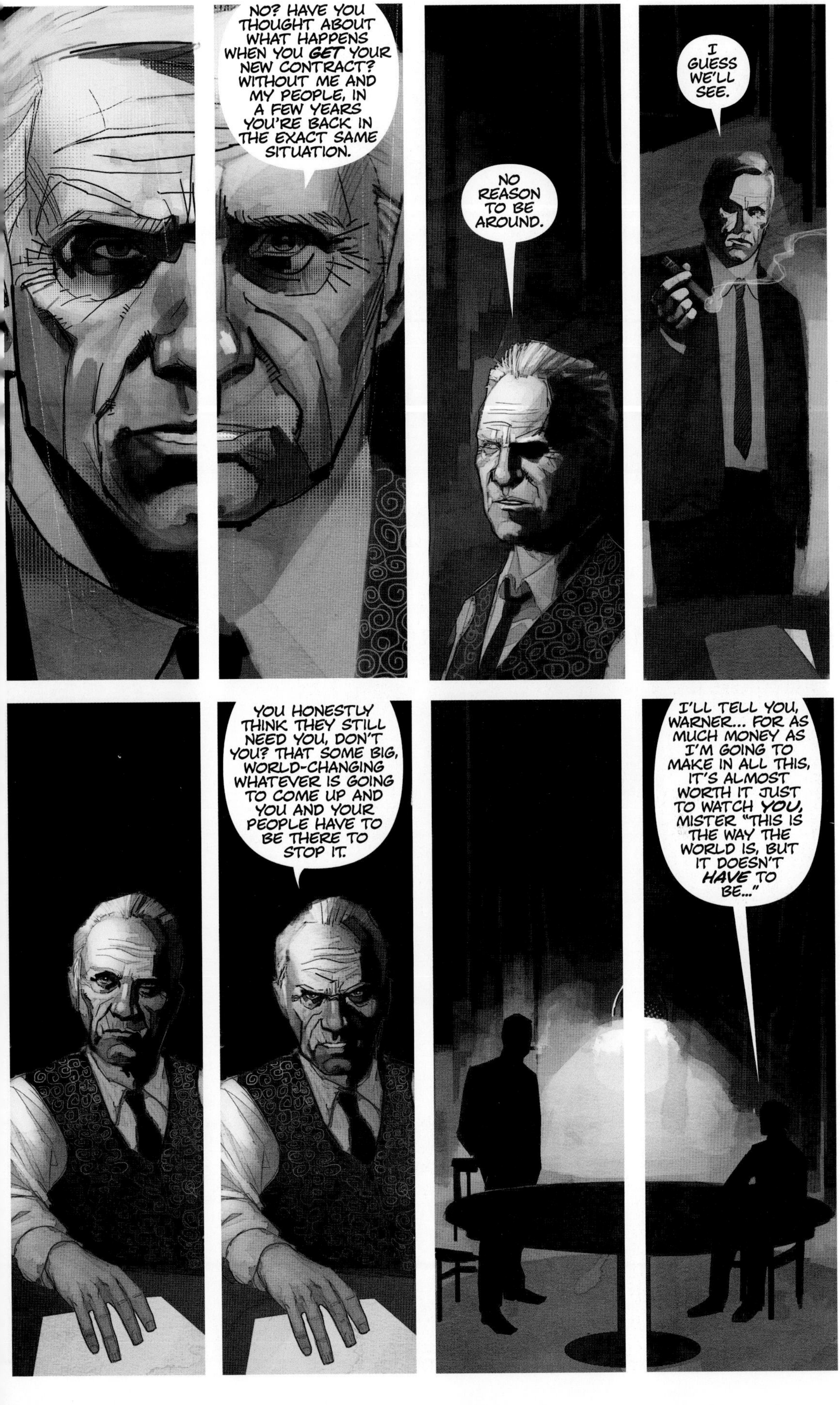
NO? HAVE YOU THOUGHT ABOUT WHAT HAPPENS WHEN YOU GET YOUR NEW CONTRACT? WITHOUT ME AND MY PEOPLE, IN A FEW YEARS YOU'RE BACK IN THE EXACT SAME SITUATION.
NO REASON TO BE AROUND.
I GUESS WE'LL SEE.
YOU HONESTLY THINK THEY STILL NEED YOU, DON'T YOU? THAT SOME BIG, WORLD-CHANGING WHATEVER IS GOING TO COME UP AND YOU AND YOUR PEOPLE HAVE TO BE THERE TO STOP IT.
I'LL TELL YOU, WARNER... FOR AS MUCH MONEY AS I'M GOING TO MAKE IN ALL THIS, IT'S ALMOST WORTH IT JUST TO WATCH YOU, MISTER "THIS IS THE WAY THE WORLD IS, BUT IT DOESN'T HAVE TO BE..."

...COME CRASHING BACK TO *EARTH*.

KNOK
KNOK
KNOK

YES?

GOOD EVENING, MRS. PIERCE. MY NAME IS EVELYN THOMPSON. I'M A DETECTIVE WITH THE CHICAGO POLICE.

I'M SURE THIS IS A TERRIBLE TIME, AND I'M SO SORRY FOR YOUR LOSS... BUT I WAS WONDERING IF WE COULD SPEAK FOR A FEW MINUTES? ABOUT WHY YOUR HUSBAND WAS MURDERED.

JOHN WAS KILLED FOR CROSSING THE PICKET LINE, MS. THOMPSON. I... DON'T THINK THERE'S ANYTHING ELSE TO SAY...

I WAS HIS CONTACT, SARAH.

...OH.

HE WOULDN'T TELL ME WHAT HE HAD. BUT IF YOU HAVE ANY IDEA...

NO. WHATEVER IT WAS... IT DOESN'T MATTER ANYMORE.

I KNOW YOU DON'T HAVE A LOT OF REASON TO TRUST ME, SARAH... BUT JOHN *DID*.

OUTSIDE OF THIS HOUSE, I WAS PROBABLY THE ONLY PERSON WHO KNEW WHO HE REALLY WAS, AND WHY HE BELIEVED IN C.O.W.L. SO MUCH.

I'M THE ONLY OTHER PERSON WHO KNEW HE WAS ONE OF THE CHICAGO SIX.

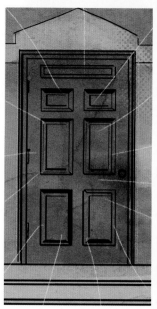

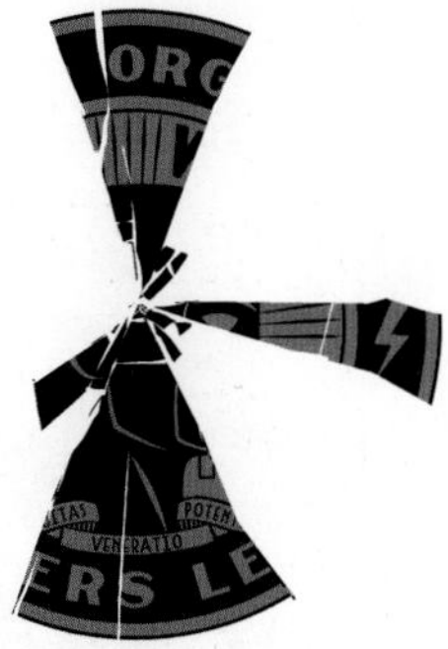
ORG
VENERATIO
POTEN
ERS LE

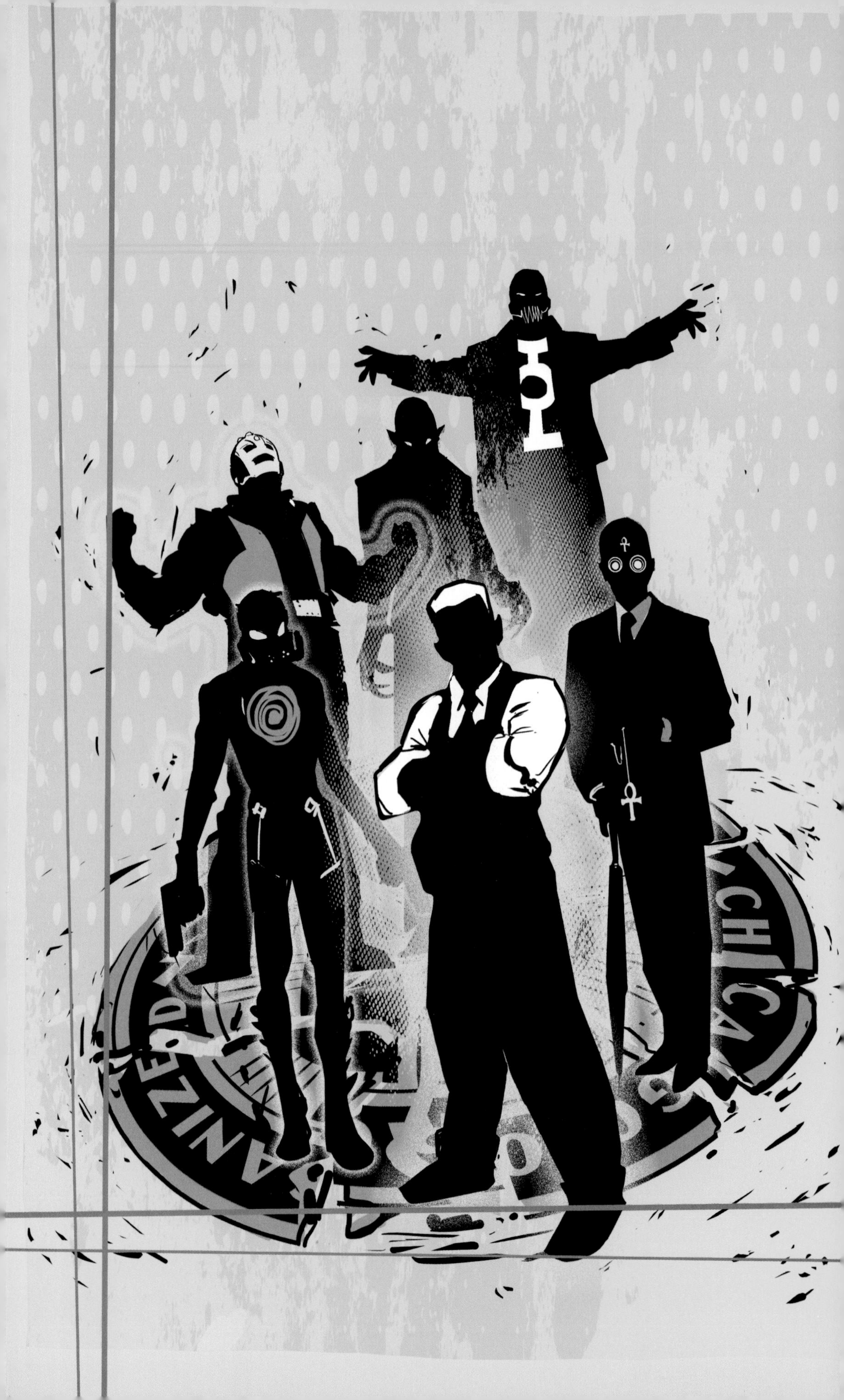

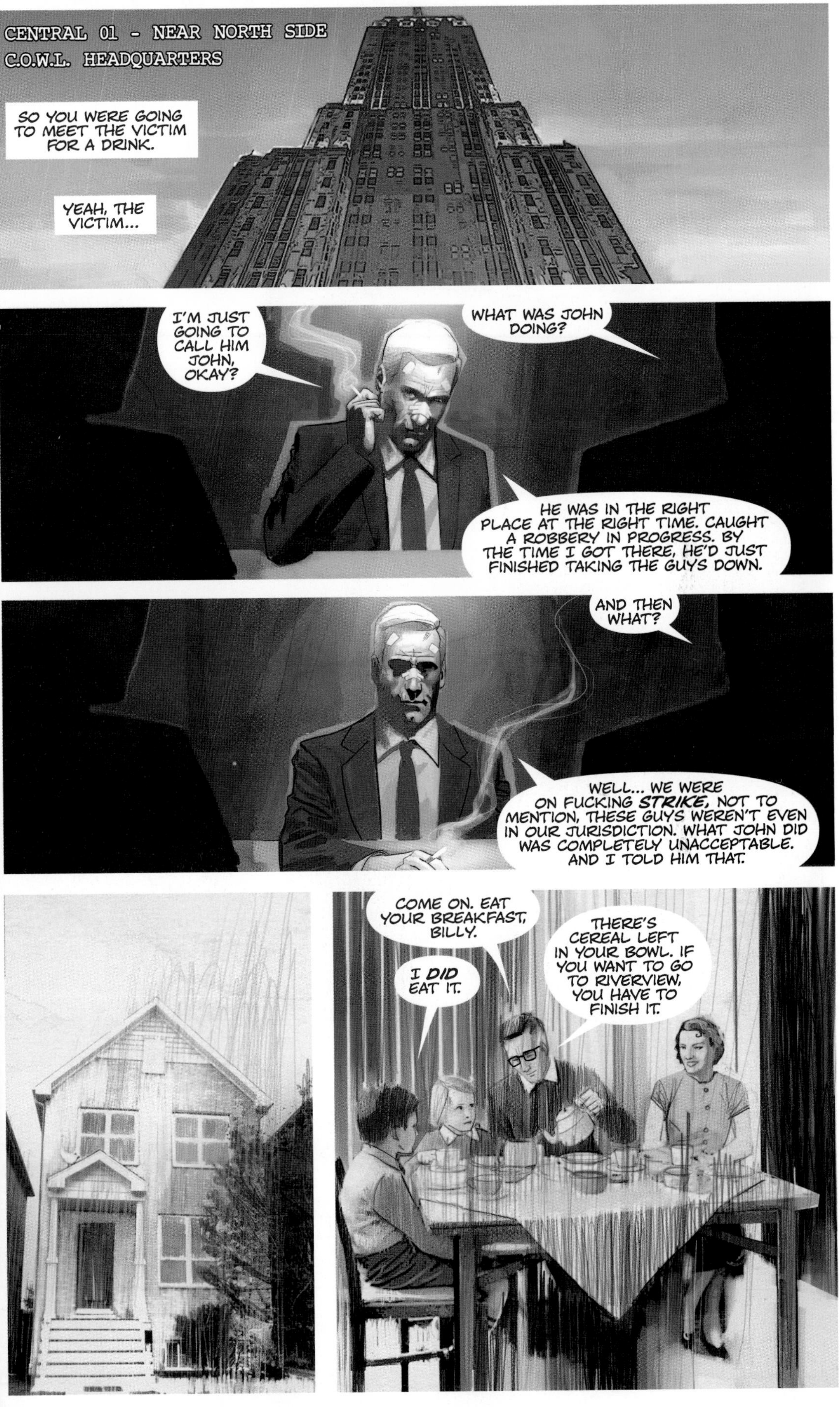
CENTRAL 01 - NEAR NORTH SIDE
C.O.W.L. HEADQUARTERS
SO YOU WERE GOING TO MEET THE VICTIM FOR A DRINK.
YEAH, THE VICTIM...
I'M JUST GOING TO CALL HIM JOHN, OKAY?
WHAT WAS JOHN DOING?
HE WAS IN THE RIGHT PLACE AT THE RIGHT TIME. CAUGHT A ROBBERY IN PROGRESS. BY THE TIME I GOT THERE, HE'D JUST FINISHED TAKING THE GUYS DOWN.
AND THEN WHAT?
WELL... WE WERE ON FUCKING STRIKE, NOT TO MENTION, THESE GUYS WEREN'T EVEN IN OUR JURISDICTION. WHAT JOHN DID WAS COMPLETELY UNACCEPTABLE. AND I TOLD HIM THAT.
COME ON. EAT YOUR BREAKFAST, BILLY.
I DID EAT IT.
THERE'S CEREAL LEFT IN YOUR BOWL. IF YOU WANT TO GO TO RIVERVIEW, YOU HAVE TO FINISH IT.

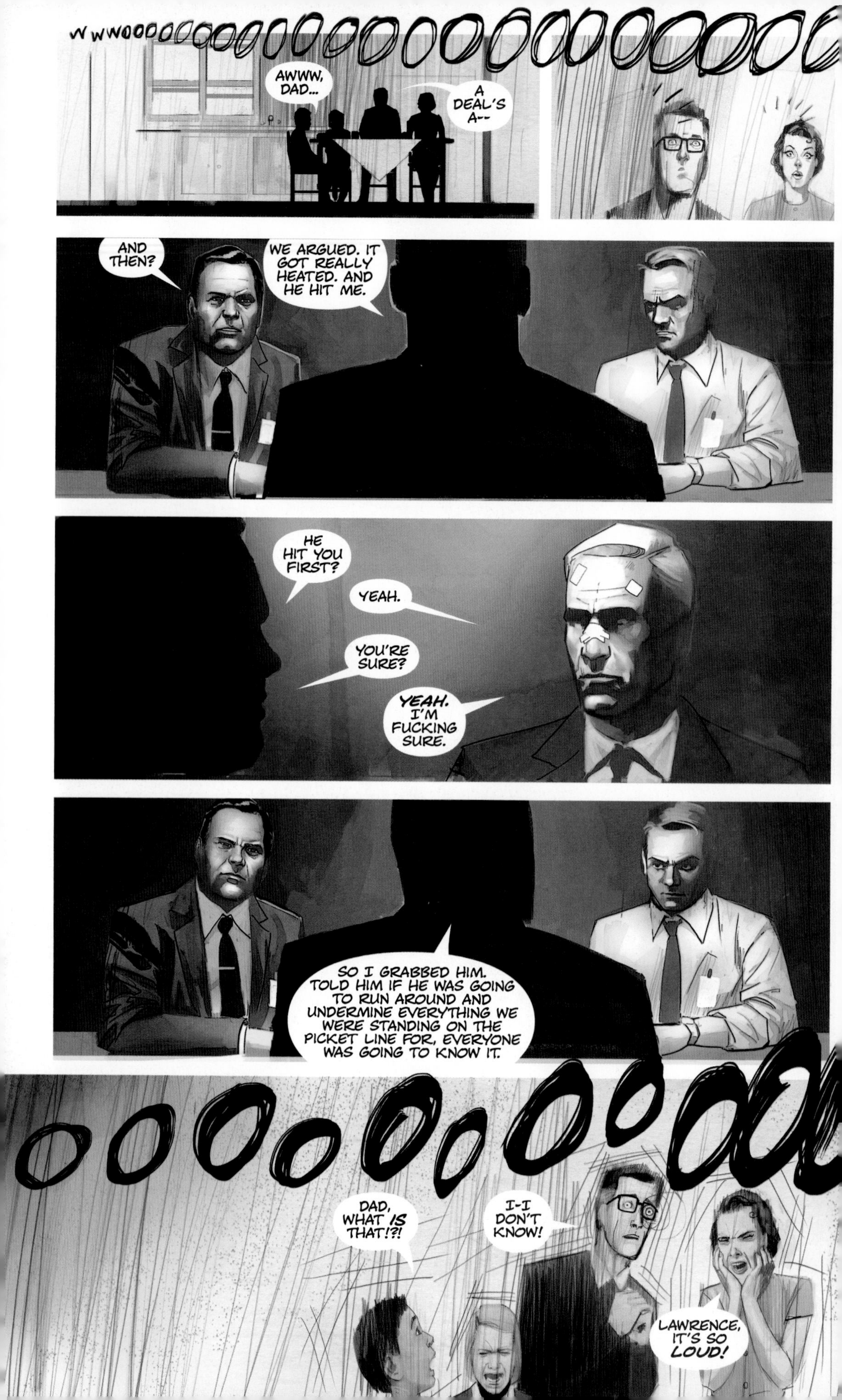
WWWOOOOOOOOOOOOOOOOOOOOOOO
AWWW, DAD...
A DEAL'S A--
AND THEN?
WE ARGUED. IT GOT REALLY HEATED. AND HE HIT ME.
HE HIT YOU FIRST?
YEAH.
YOU'RE SURE?
YEAH. I'M FUCKING SURE.
SO I GRABBED HIM. TOLD HIM IF HE WAS GOING TO RUN AROUND AND UNDERMINE EVERYTHING WE WERE STANDING ON THE PICKET LINE FOR, EVERYONE WAS GOING TO KNOW IT.
OOOOOOOOOOOOOOO
DAD, WHAT IS THAT!?!
I-I DON'T KNOW!
LAWRENCE, IT'S SO LOUD!

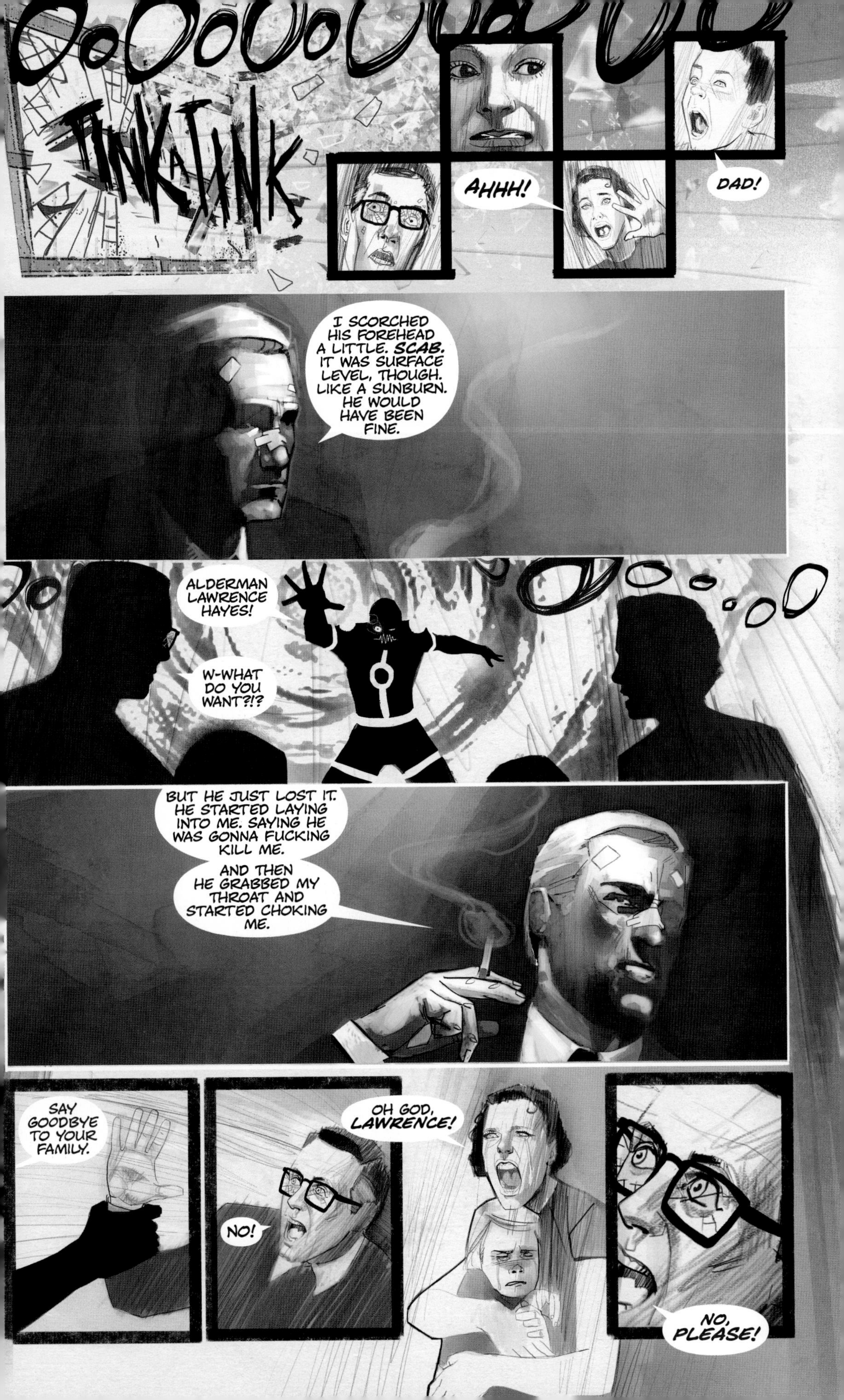

TINKATINK
AHHH!
DAD!
I SCORCHED HIS FOREHEAD A LITTLE. SCAB. IT WAS SURFACE LEVEL, THOUGH. LIKE A SUNBURN. HE WOULD HAVE BEEN FINE.
ALDERMAN LAWRENCE HAYES!
W-WHAT DO YOU WANT?!?
BUT HE JUST LOST IT. HE STARTED LAYING INTO ME. SAYING HE WAS GONNA FUCKING KILL ME.
AND THEN HE GRABBED MY THROAT AND STARTED CHOKING ME.
SAY GOODBYE TO YOUR FAMILY.
NO!
OH GOD, LAWRENCE!
NO, PLEASE!

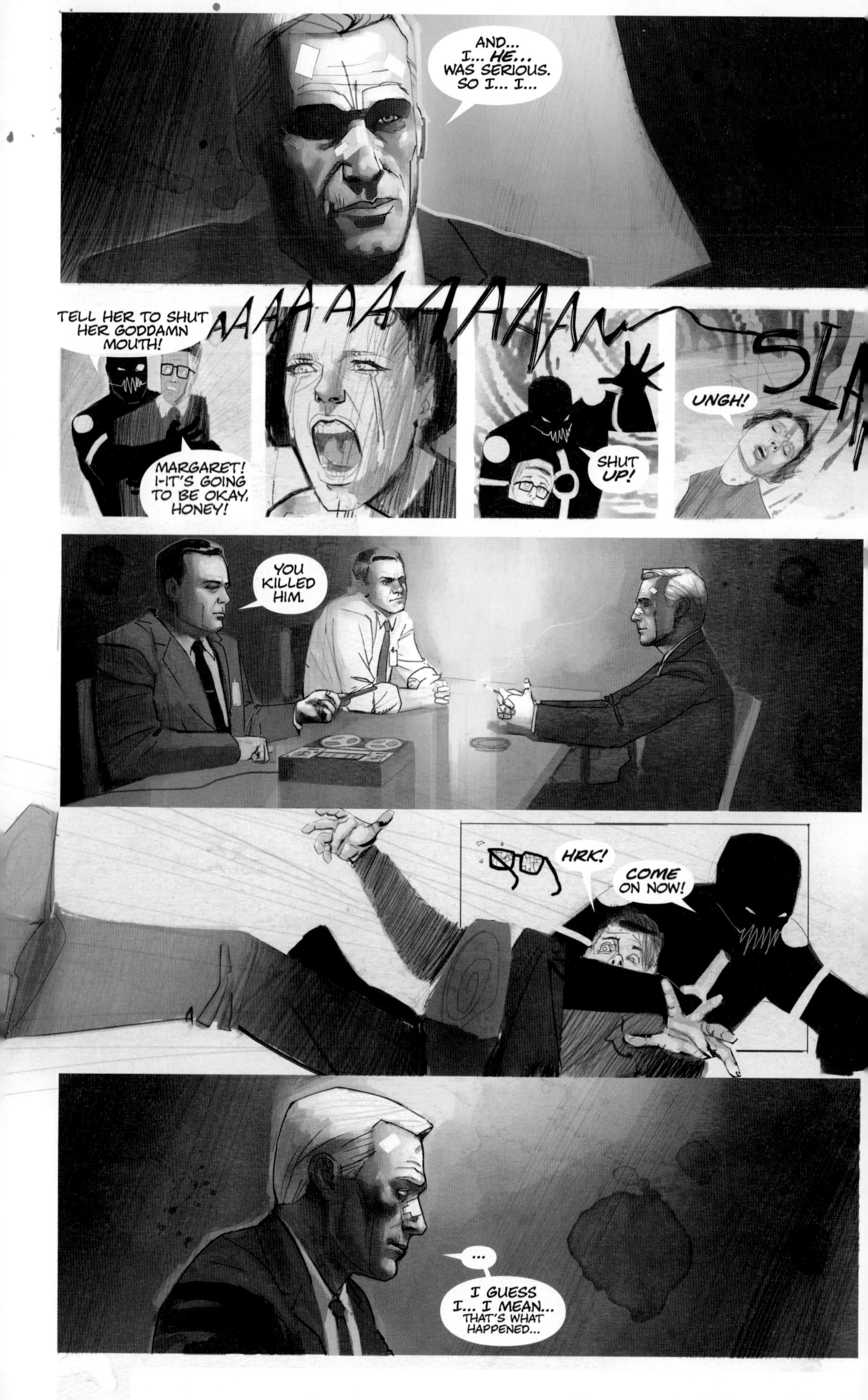
AND... I... HE... WAS SERIOUS. SO I... I...
TELL HER TO SHUT HER GODDAMN MOUTH!
MARGARET! I-IT'S GOING TO BE OKAY, HONEY!
AAAAAAAAAAA
SHUT UP!
UNGH!
SLA
YOU KILLED HIM.
HRK!
COME ON NOW!
...
I GUESS I... I MEAN... THAT'S WHAT HAPPENED...

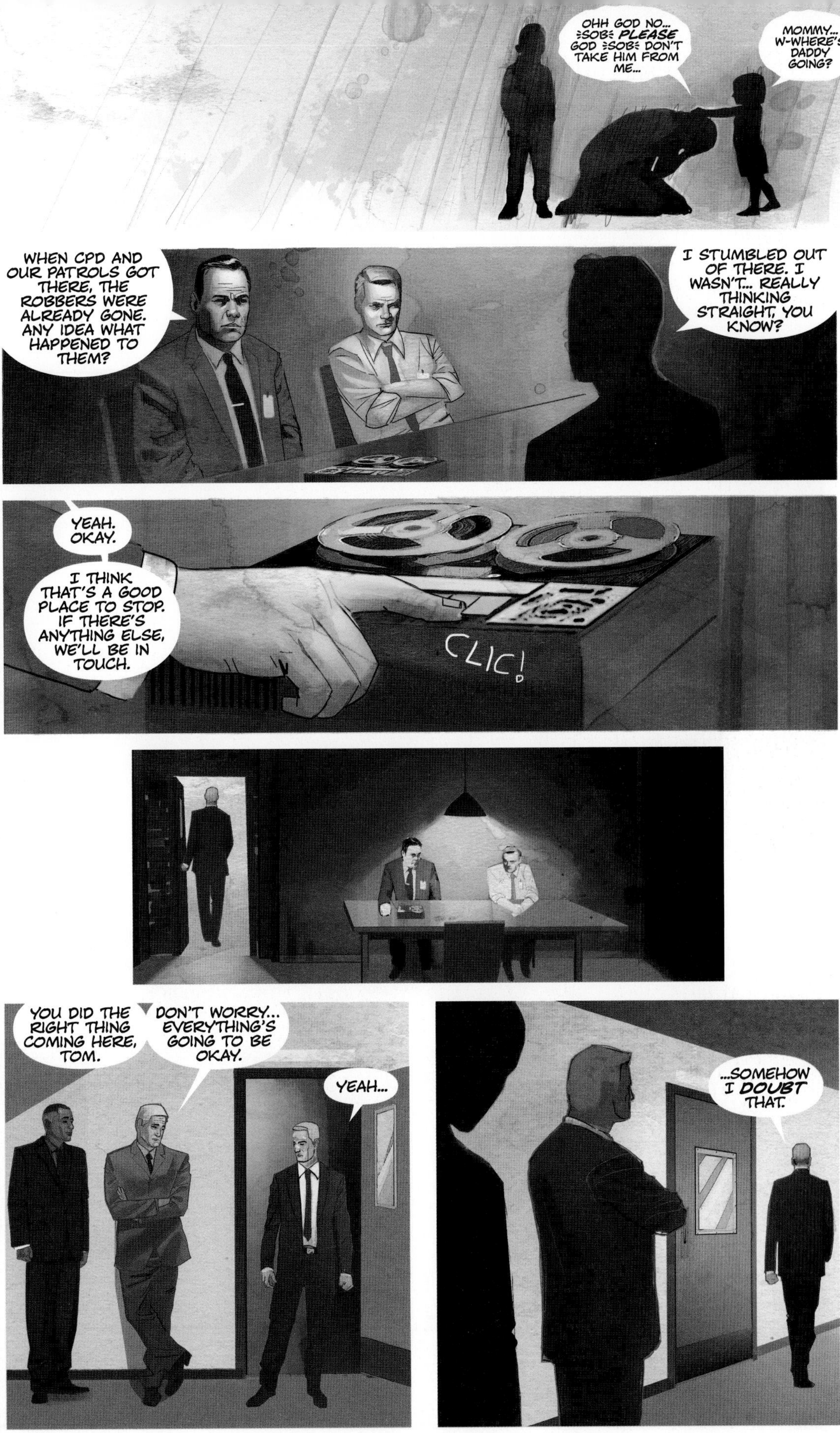
OHH GOD NO... ⋚SOB⋛ PLEASE GOD ⋚SOB⋛ DON'T TAKE HIM FROM ME...
MOMMY... W-WHERE'S DADDY GOING?
WHEN CPD AND OUR PATROLS GOT THERE, THE ROBBERS WERE ALREADY GONE. ANY IDEA WHAT HAPPENED TO THEM?
I STUMBLED OUT OF THERE. I WASN'T... REALLY THINKING STRAIGHT, YOU KNOW?
YEAH. OKAY.
I THINK THAT'S A GOOD PLACE TO STOP. IF THERE'S ANYTHING ELSE, WE'LL BE IN TOUCH.
CLIC!
YOU DID THE RIGHT THING COMING HERE, TOM.
DON'T WORRY... EVERYTHING'S GOING TO BE OKAY.
YEAH...
...SOMEHOW I DOUBT THAT.

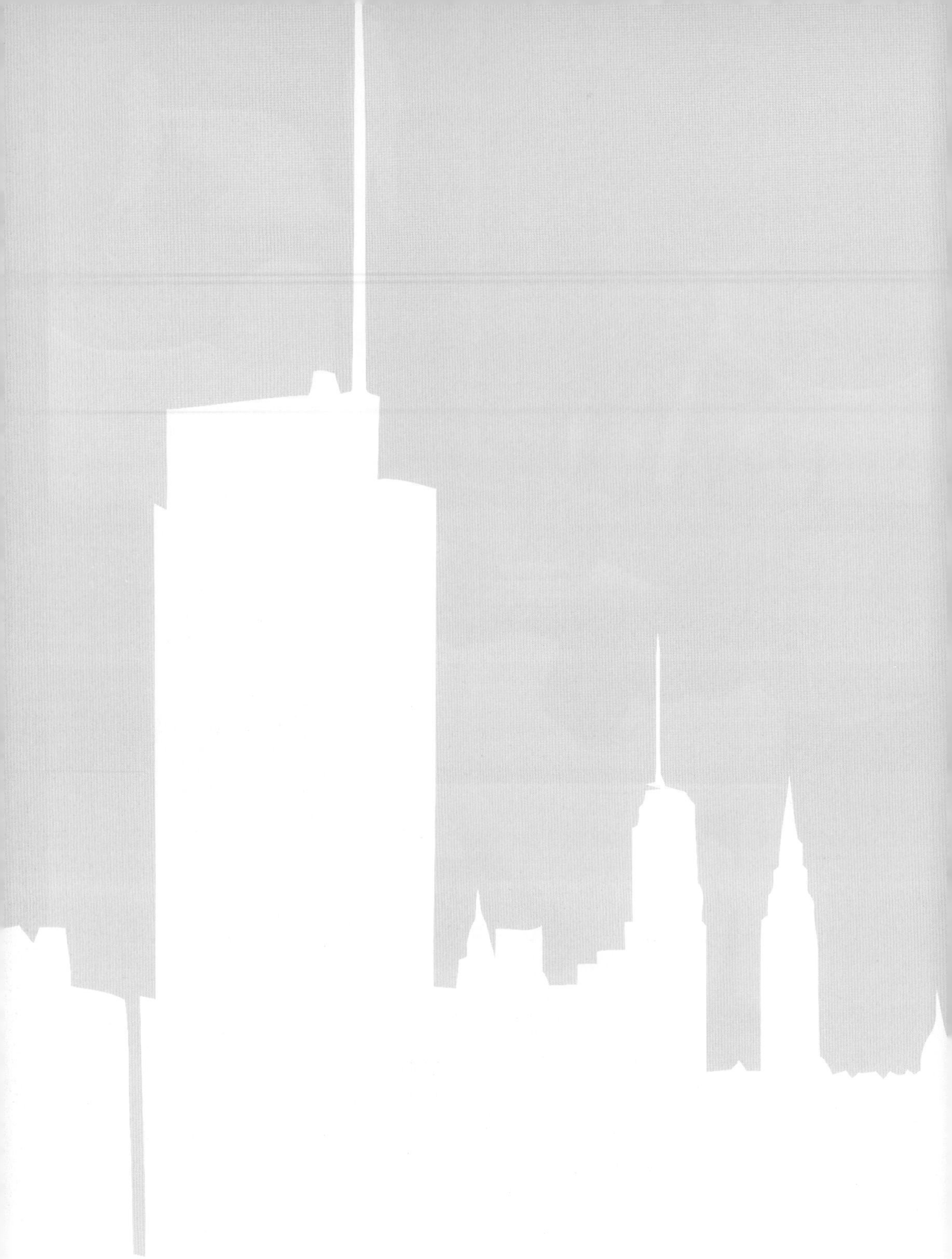

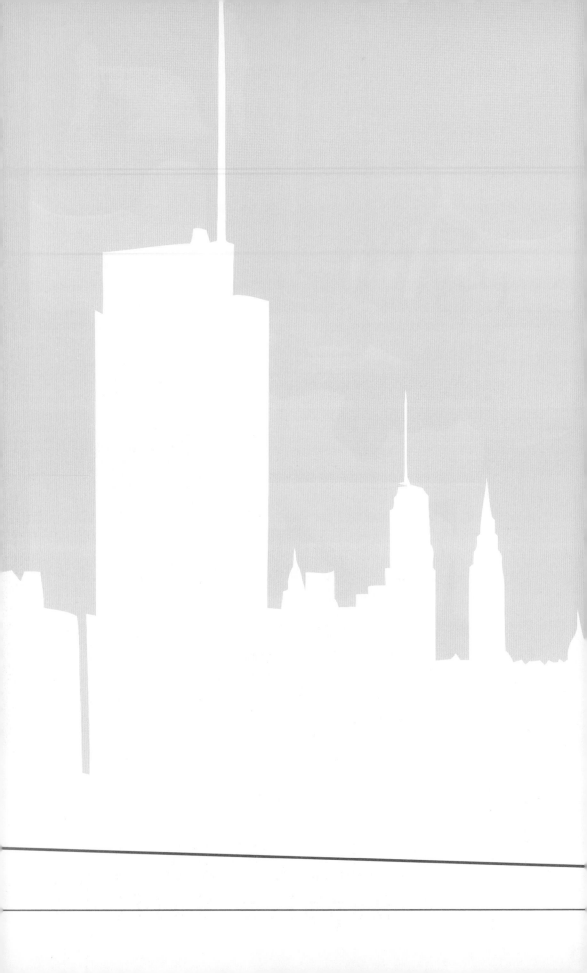

# CHAPTER 2
## Doppler Shift

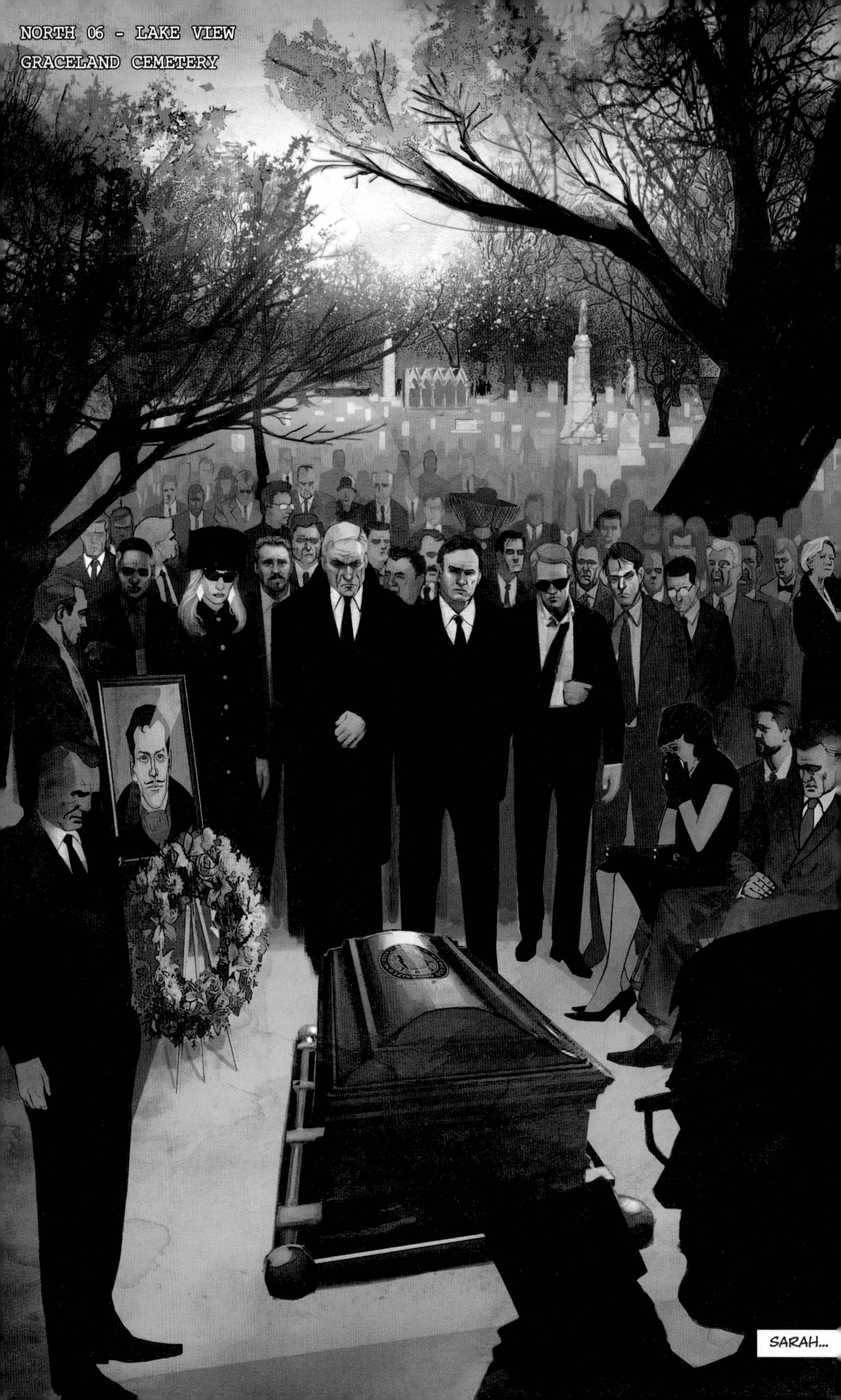
NORTH 06 - LAKE VIEW
GRACELAND CEMETERY
SARAH...

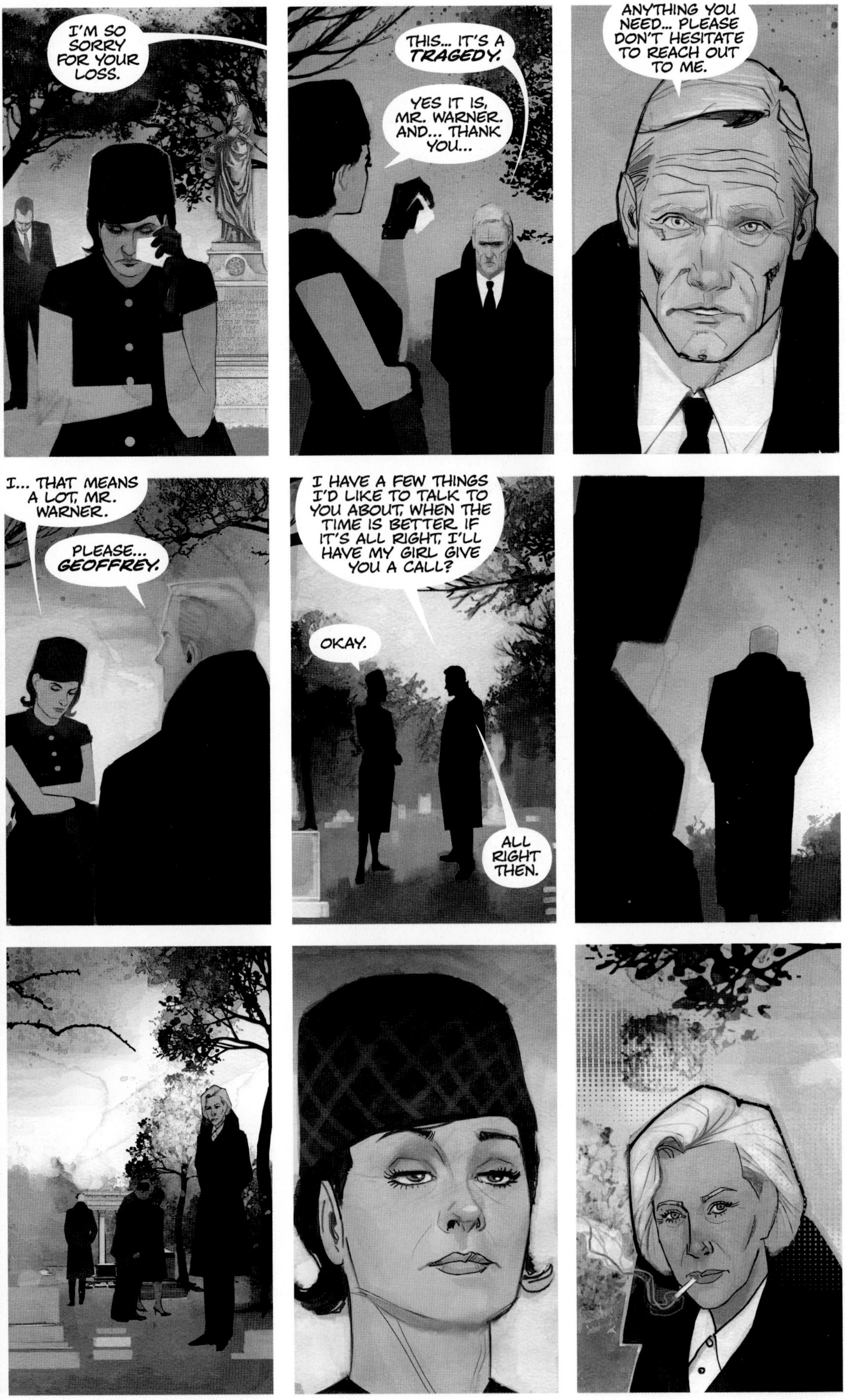

I'M SO SORRY FOR YOUR LOSS.
THIS... IT'S A TRAGEDY.
YES IT IS, MR. WARNER. AND... THANK YOU...
ANYTHING YOU NEED... PLEASE DON'T HESITATE TO REACH OUT TO ME.
I... THAT MEANS A LOT, MR. WARNER.
PLEASE... GEOFFREY.
I HAVE A FEW THINGS I'D LIKE TO TALK TO YOU ABOUT, WHEN THE TIME IS BETTER. IF IT'S ALL RIGHT, I'LL HAVE MY GIRL GIVE YOU A CALL?
OKAY.
ALL RIGHT THEN.

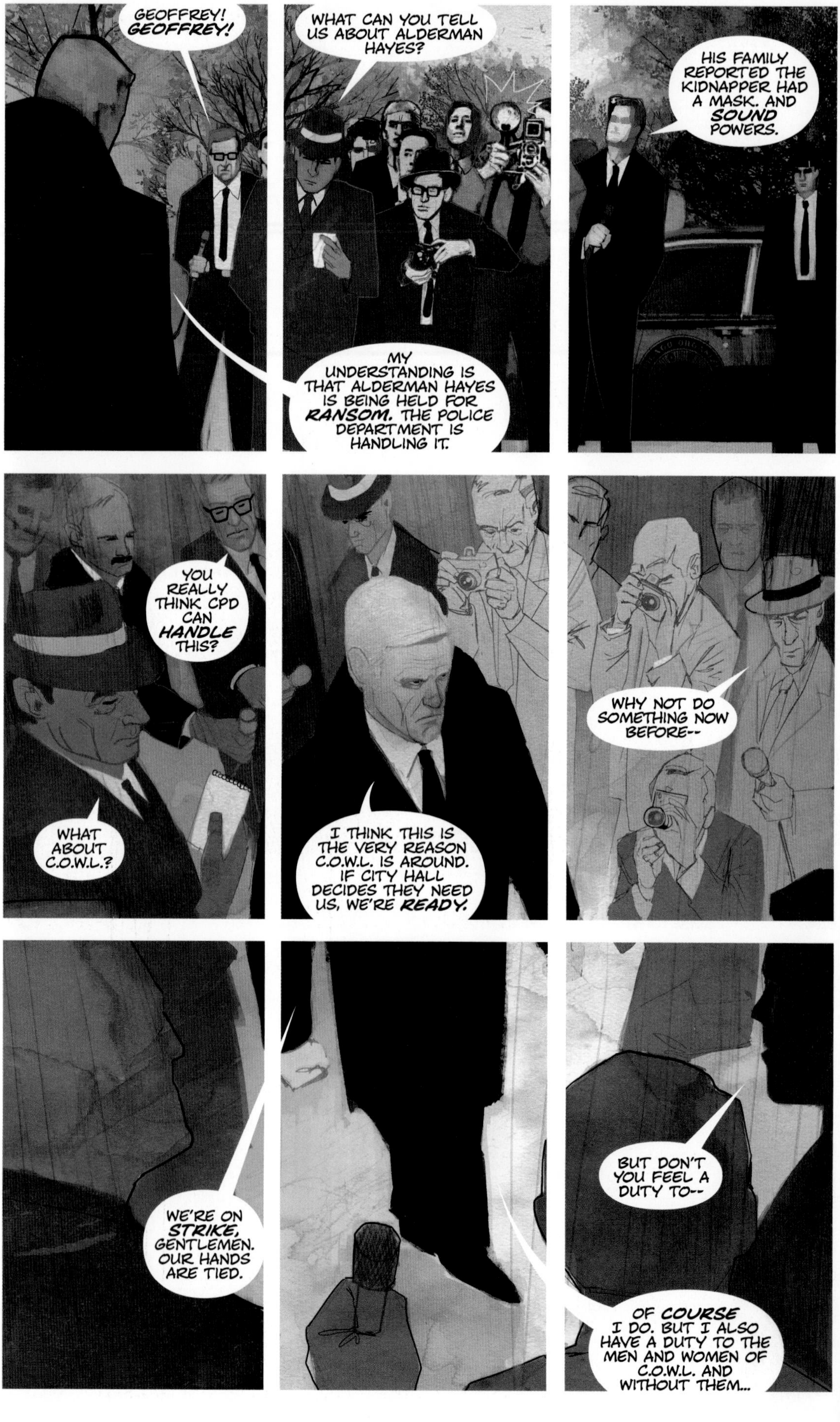
GEOFFREY! GEOFFREY!
WHAT CAN YOU TELL US ABOUT ALDERMAN HAYES?
MY UNDERSTANDING IS THAT ALDERMAN HAYES IS BEING HELD FOR RANSOM. THE POLICE DEPARTMENT IS HANDLING IT.
HIS FAMILY REPORTED THE KIDNAPPER HAD A MASK. AND SOUND POWERS.
YOU REALLY THINK CPD CAN HANDLE THIS?
WHAT ABOUT C.O.W.L.?
I THINK THIS IS THE VERY REASON C.O.W.L. IS AROUND. IF CITY HALL DECIDES THEY NEED US, WE'RE READY.
WHY NOT DO SOMETHING NOW BEFORE--
WE'RE ON STRIKE, GENTLEMEN. OUR HANDS ARE TIED.
BUT DON'T YOU FEEL A DUTY TO--
OF COURSE I DO. BUT I ALSO HAVE A DUTY TO THE MEN AND WOMEN OF C.O.W.L. AND WITHOUT THEM...

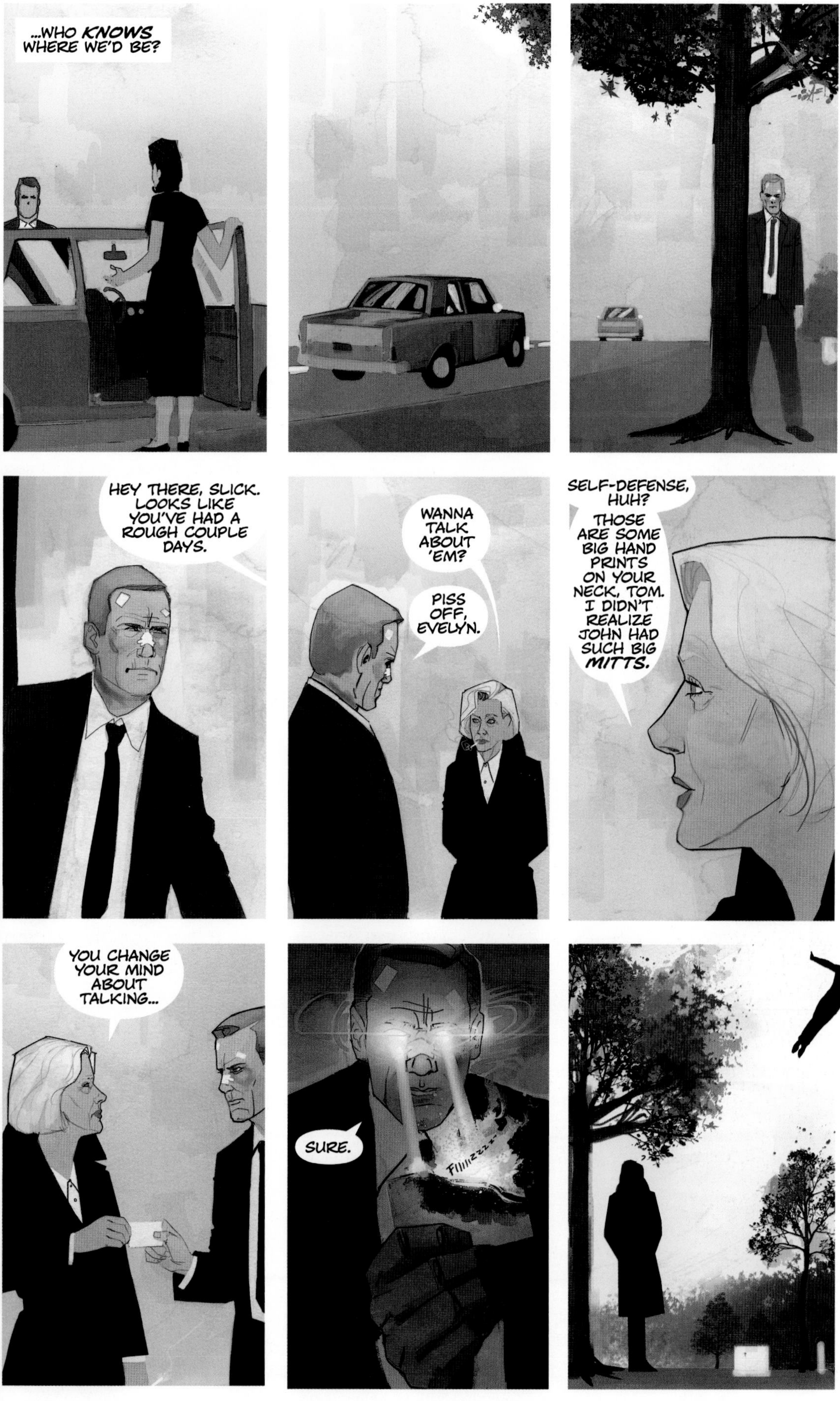
...WHO KNOWS WHERE WE'D BE?
HEY THERE, SLICK. LOOKS LIKE YOU'VE HAD A ROUGH COUPLE DAYS.
WANNA TALK ABOUT 'EM?
PISS OFF, EVELYN.
SELF-DEFENSE, HUH? THOSE ARE SOME BIG HAND PRINTS ON YOUR NECK, TOM. I DIDN'T REALIZE JOHN HAD SUCH BIG MITTS.
YOU CHANGE YOUR MIND ABOUT TALKING...
SURE.
FIIIIIzzzz

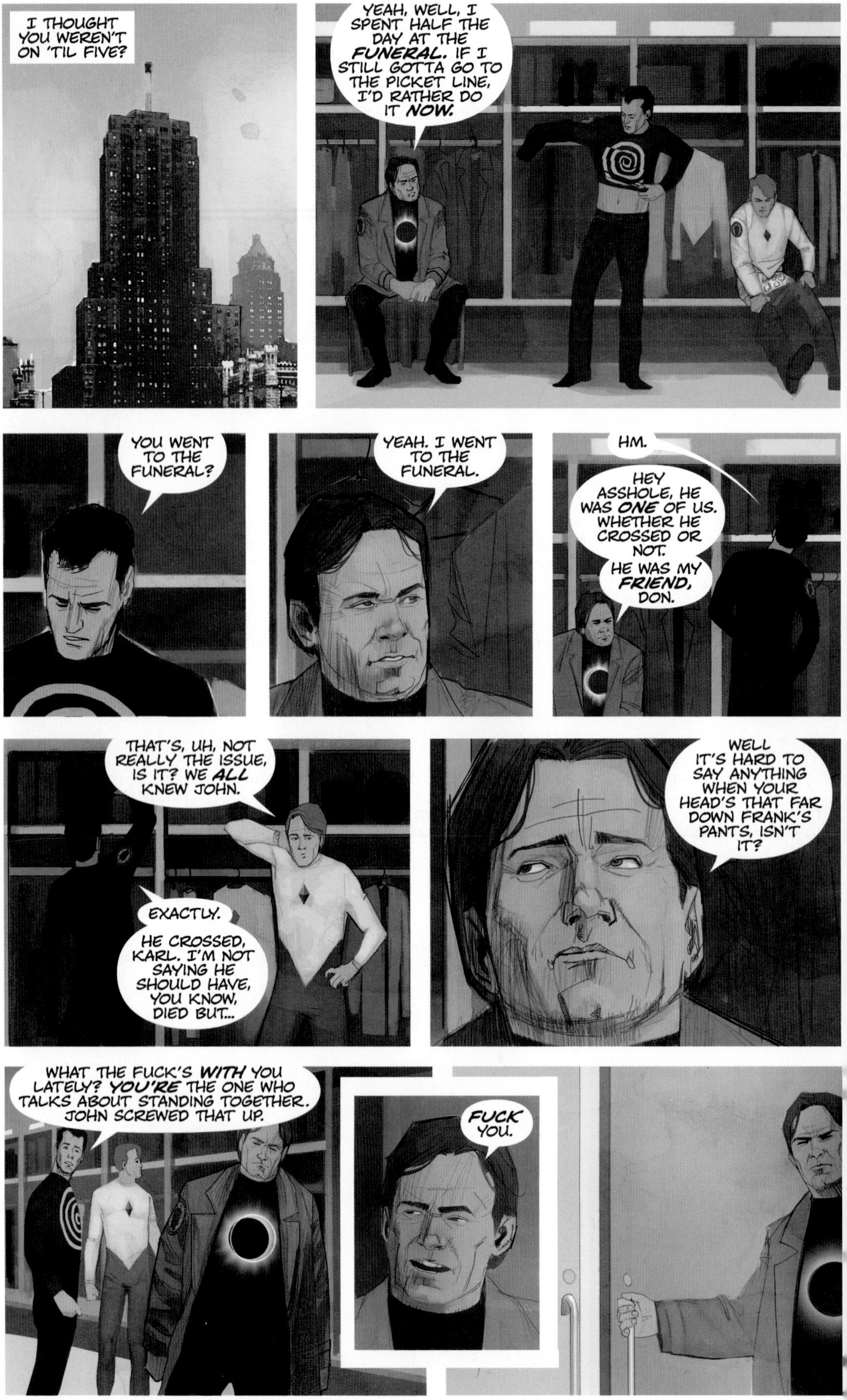
I THOUGHT YOU WEREN'T ON 'TIL FIVE?
YEAH, WELL, I SPENT HALF THE DAY AT THE FUNERAL. IF I STILL GOTTA GO TO THE PICKET LINE, I'D RATHER DO IT NOW.
YOU WENT TO THE FUNERAL?
YEAH. I WENT TO THE FUNERAL.
HM.
HEY ASSHOLE, HE WAS ONE OF US. WHETHER HE CROSSED OR NOT.
HE WAS MY FRIEND, DON.
THAT'S, UH, NOT REALLY THE ISSUE, IS IT? WE ALL KNEW JOHN.
EXACTLY.
HE CROSSED, KARL. I'M NOT SAYING HE SHOULD HAVE, YOU KNOW, DIED BUT...
WELL IT'S HARD TO SAY ANYTHING WHEN YOUR HEAD'S THAT FAR DOWN FRANK'S PANTS, ISN'T IT?
WHAT THE FUCK'S WITH YOU LATELY? YOU'RE THE ONE WHO TALKS ABOUT STANDING TOGETHER. JOHN SCREWED THAT UP.
FUCK YOU.

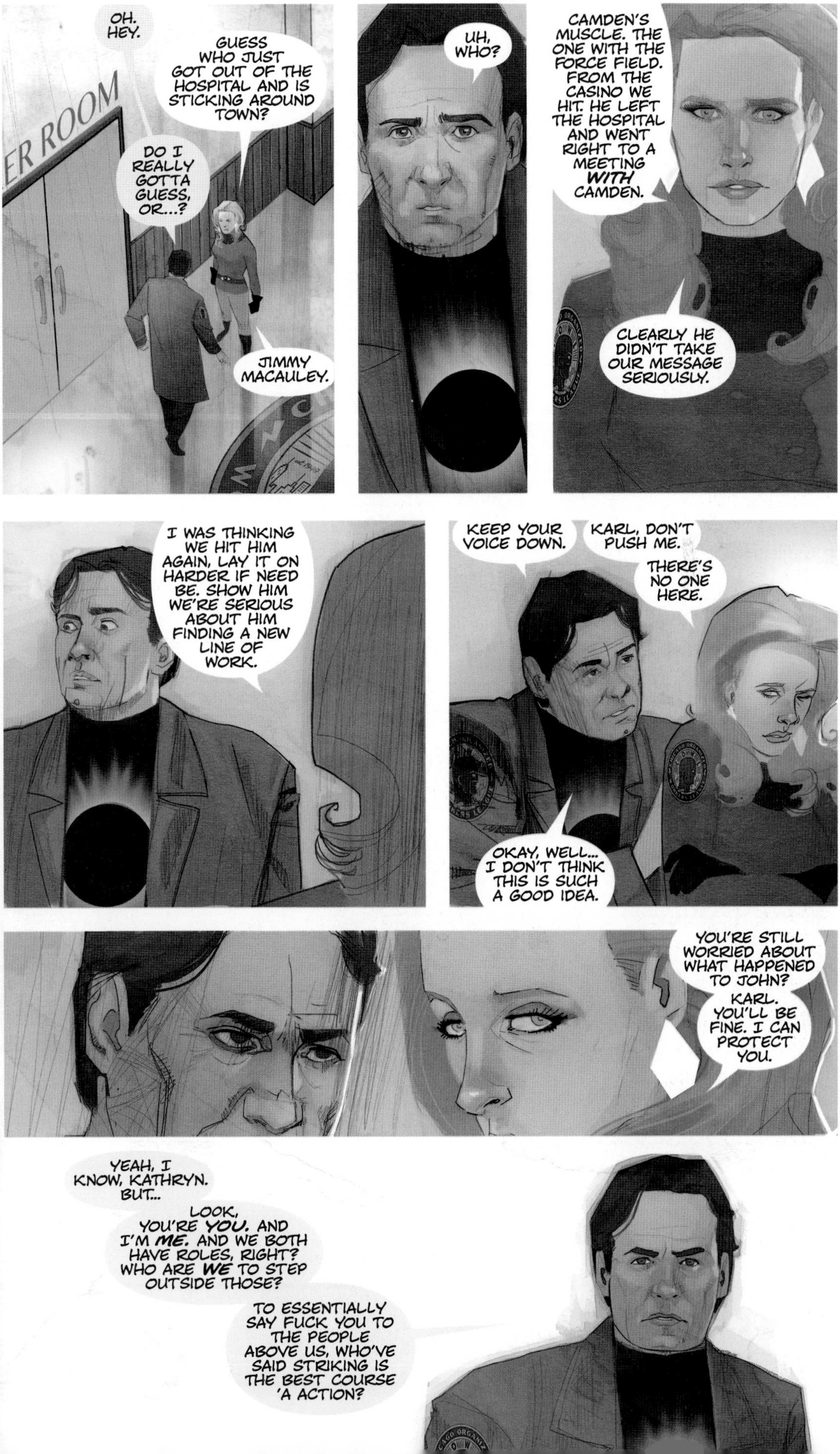
ER ROOM
OH. HEY.
GUESS WHO JUST GOT OUT OF THE HOSPITAL AND IS STICKING AROUND TOWN?
DO I REALLY GOTTA GUESS, OR...?
JIMMY MACAULEY.
UH, WHO?
CAMDEN'S MUSCLE. THE ONE WITH THE FORCE FIELD. FROM THE CASINO WE HIT. HE LEFT THE HOSPITAL AND WENT RIGHT TO A MEETING *WITH* CAMDEN.
CLEARLY HE DIDN'T TAKE OUR MESSAGE SERIOUSLY.
I WAS THINKING WE HIT HIM AGAIN, LAY IT ON HARDER IF NEED BE. SHOW HIM WE'RE SERIOUS ABOUT HIM FINDING A NEW LINE OF WORK.
KEEP YOUR VOICE DOWN.
KARL, DON'T PUSH ME.
THERE'S NO ONE HERE.
OKAY, WELL... I DON'T THINK THIS IS SUCH A GOOD IDEA.
YOU'RE STILL WORRIED ABOUT WHAT HAPPENED TO JOHN?
KARL. YOU'LL BE FINE. I CAN PROTECT YOU.
YEAH, I KNOW, KATHRYN. BUT...
LOOK, YOU'RE *YOU.* AND I'M *ME.* AND WE BOTH HAVE ROLES, RIGHT? WHO ARE *WE* TO STEP OUTSIDE THOSE?
TO ESSENTIALLY SAY FUCK YOU TO THE PEOPLE ABOVE US, WHO'VE SAID STRIKING IS THE BEST COURSE 'A ACTION?

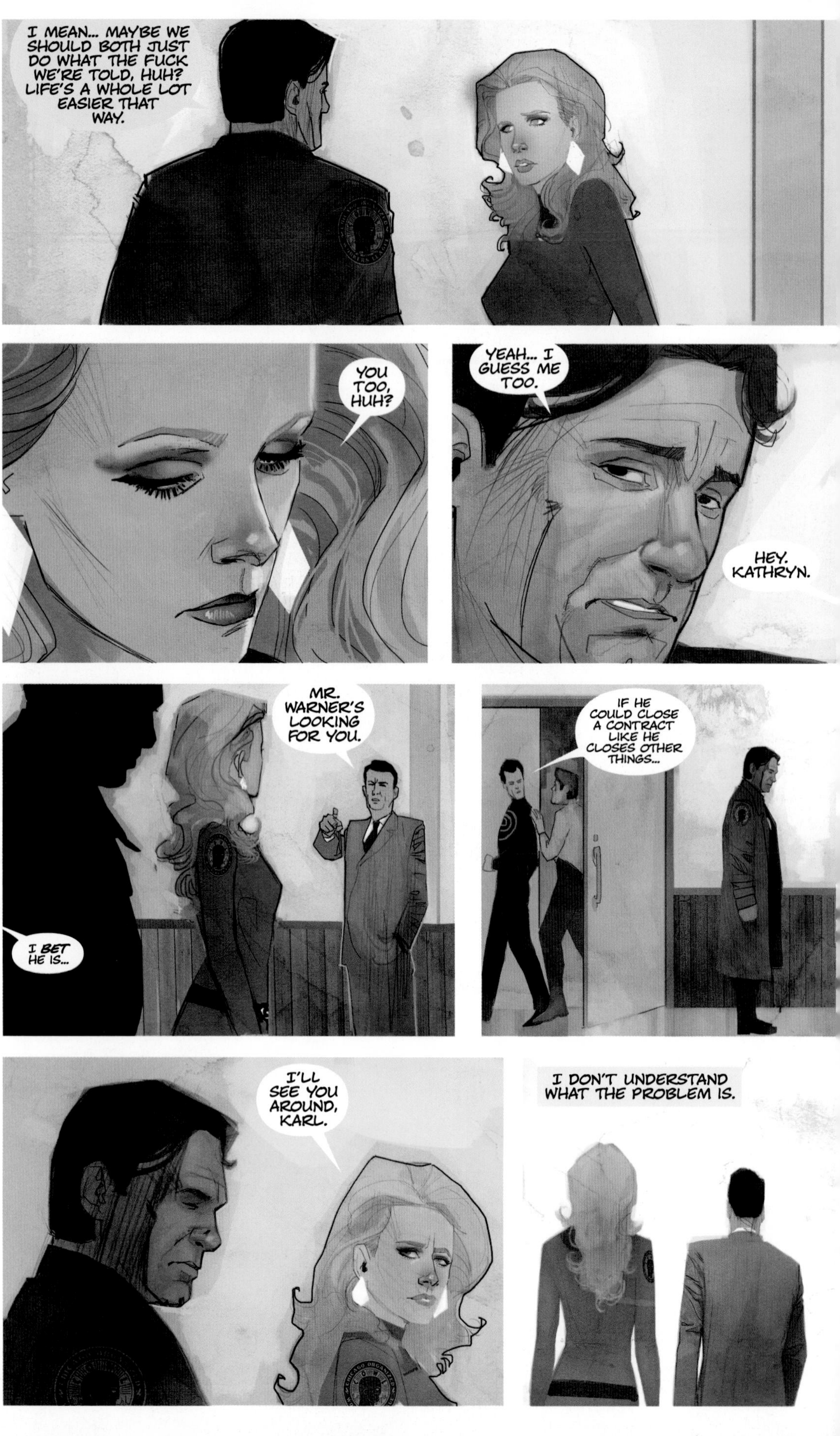
I MEAN... MAYBE WE SHOULD BOTH JUST DO WHAT THE FUCK WE'RE TOLD, HUH? LIFE'S A WHOLE LOT EASIER THAT WAY.
YOU TOO, HUH?
YEAH... I GUESS ME TOO.
HEY. KATHRYN.
MR. WARNER'S LOOKING FOR YOU.
I BET HE IS...
IF HE COULD CLOSE A CONTRACT LIKE HE CLOSES OTHER THINGS...
I'LL SEE YOU AROUND, KARL.
I DON'T UNDERSTAND WHAT THE PROBLEM IS.

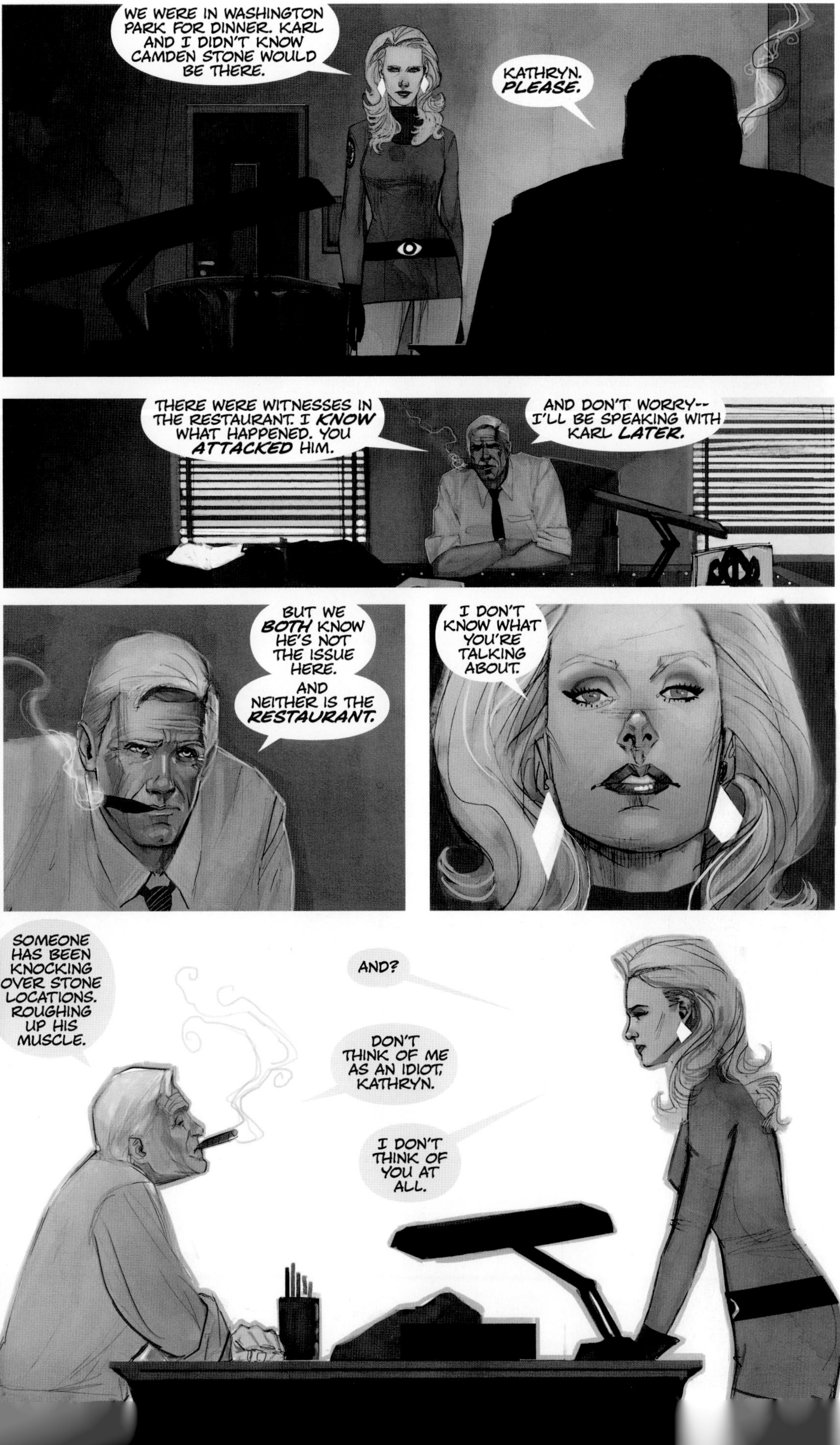
WE WERE IN WASHINGTON PARK FOR DINNER. KARL AND I DIDN'T KNOW CAMDEN STONE WOULD BE THERE.
KATHRYN. PLEASE.
THERE WERE WITNESSES IN THE RESTAURANT. I KNOW WHAT HAPPENED. YOU ATTACKED HIM.
AND DON'T WORRY-- I'LL BE SPEAKING WITH KARL LATER.
BUT WE BOTH KNOW HE'S NOT THE ISSUE HERE.
AND NEITHER IS THE RESTAURANT.
I DON'T KNOW WHAT YOU'RE TALKING ABOUT.
SOMEONE HAS BEEN KNOCKING OVER STONE LOCATIONS. ROUGHING UP HIS MUSCLE.
AND?
DON'T THINK OF ME AS AN IDIOT, KATHRYN.
I DON'T THINK OF YOU AT ALL.

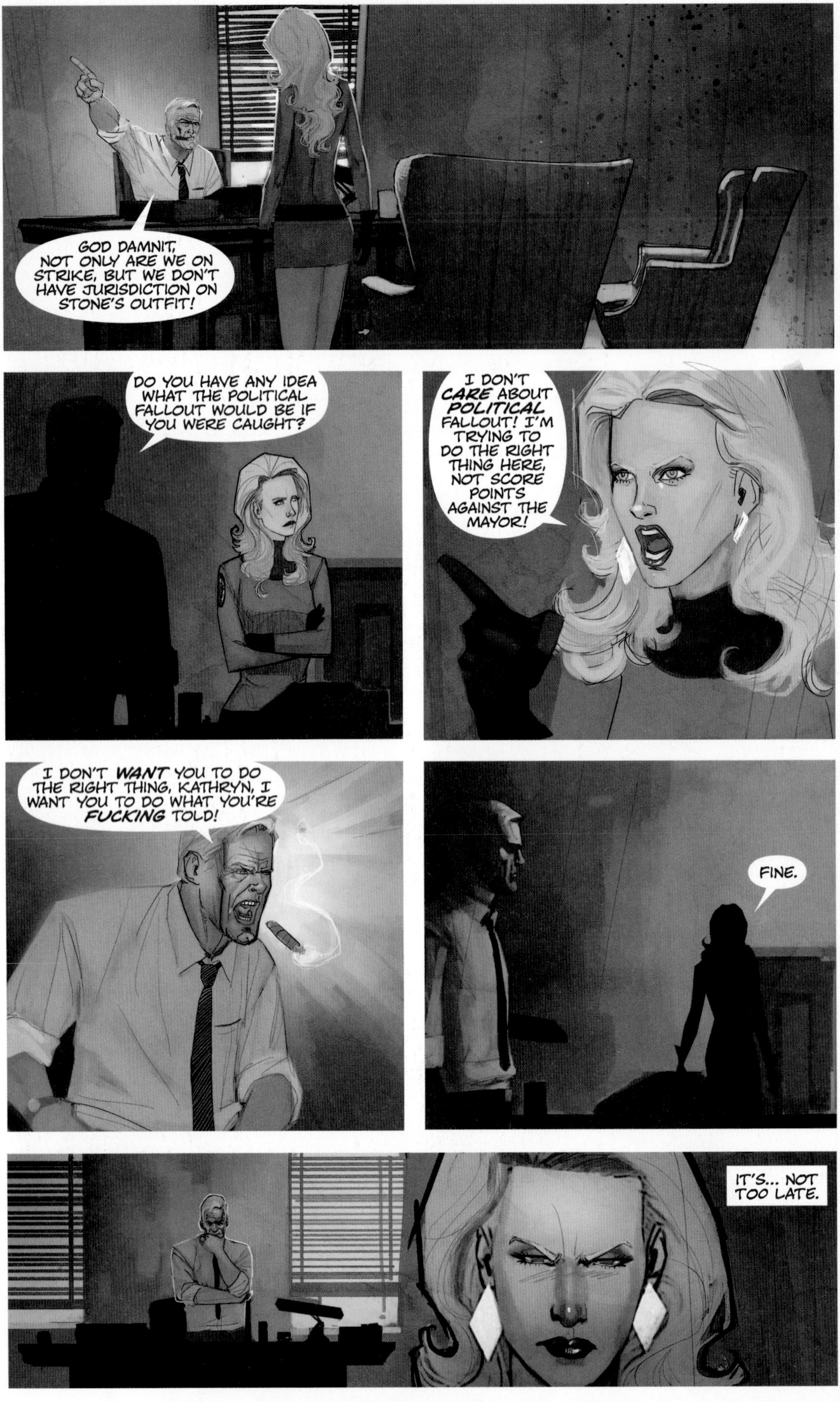
GOD DAMNIT, NOT ONLY ARE WE ON STRIKE, BUT WE DON'T HAVE JURISDICTION ON STONE'S OUTFIT!
DO YOU HAVE ANY IDEA WHAT THE POLITICAL FALLOUT WOULD BE IF YOU WERE CAUGHT?
I DON'T CARE ABOUT POLITICAL FALLOUT! I'M TRYING TO DO THE RIGHT THING HERE, NOT SCORE POINTS AGAINST THE MAYOR!
I DON'T WANT YOU TO DO THE RIGHT THING, KATHRYN, I WANT YOU TO DO WHAT YOU'RE FUCKING TOLD!
FINE.
IT'S... NOT TOO LATE.

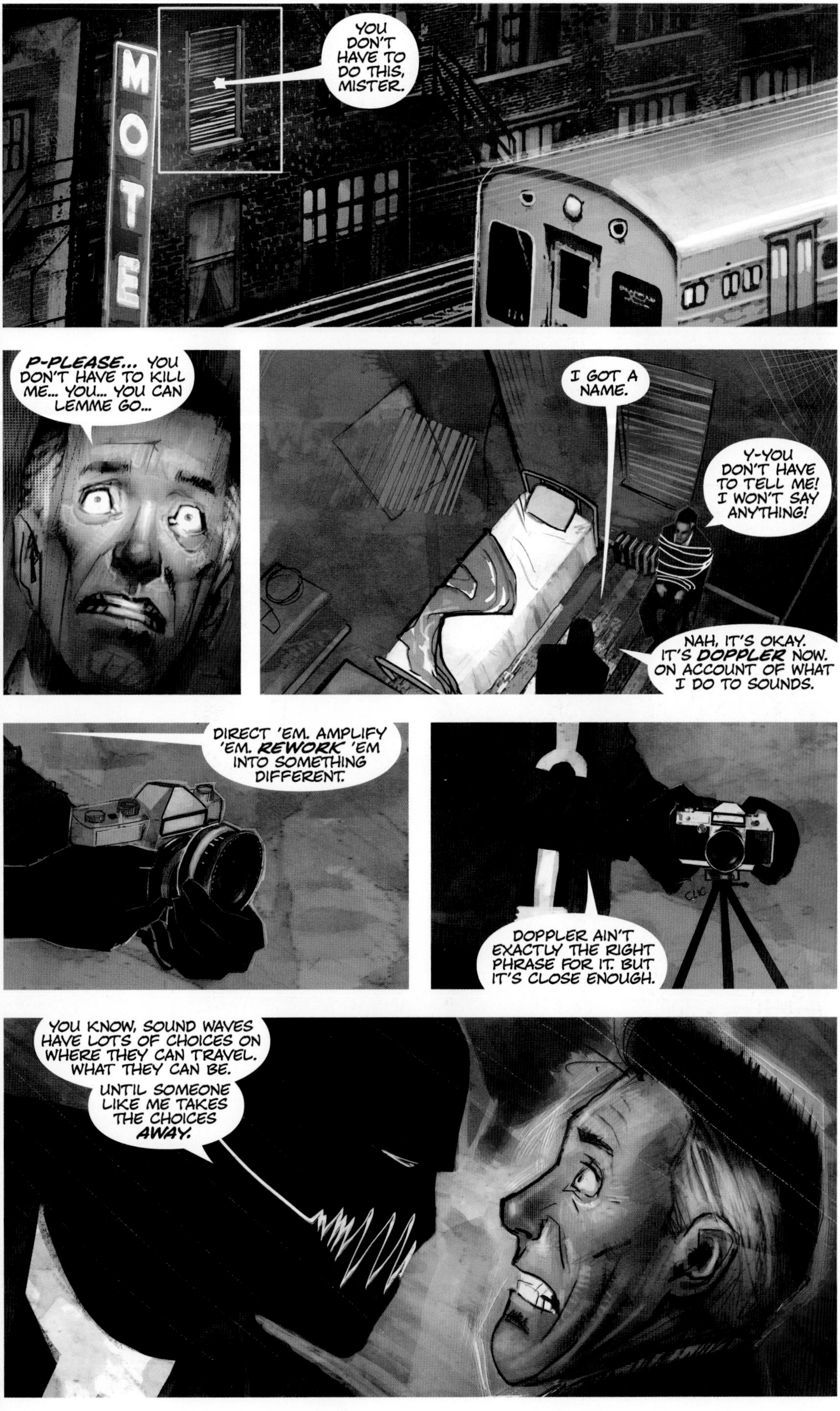
MOTE
YOU DON'T HAVE TO DO THIS, MISTER.
P-PLEASE... YOU DON'T HAVE TO KILL ME... YOU... YOU CAN LEMME GO...
I GOT A NAME.
Y-YOU DON'T HAVE TO TELL ME! I WON'T SAY ANYTHING!
NAH, IT'S OKAY. IT'S DOPPLER NOW. ON ACCOUNT OF WHAT I DO TO SOUNDS.
DIRECT 'EM. AMPLIFY 'EM. REWORK 'EM INTO SOMETHING DIFFERENT.
DOPPLER AIN'T EXACTLY THE RIGHT PHRASE FOR IT. BUT IT'S CLOSE ENOUGH.
YOU KNOW, SOUND WAVES HAVE LOTS OF CHOICES ON WHERE THEY CAN TRAVEL. WHAT THEY CAN BE.
UNTIL SOMEONE LIKE ME TAKES THE CHOICES AWAY.

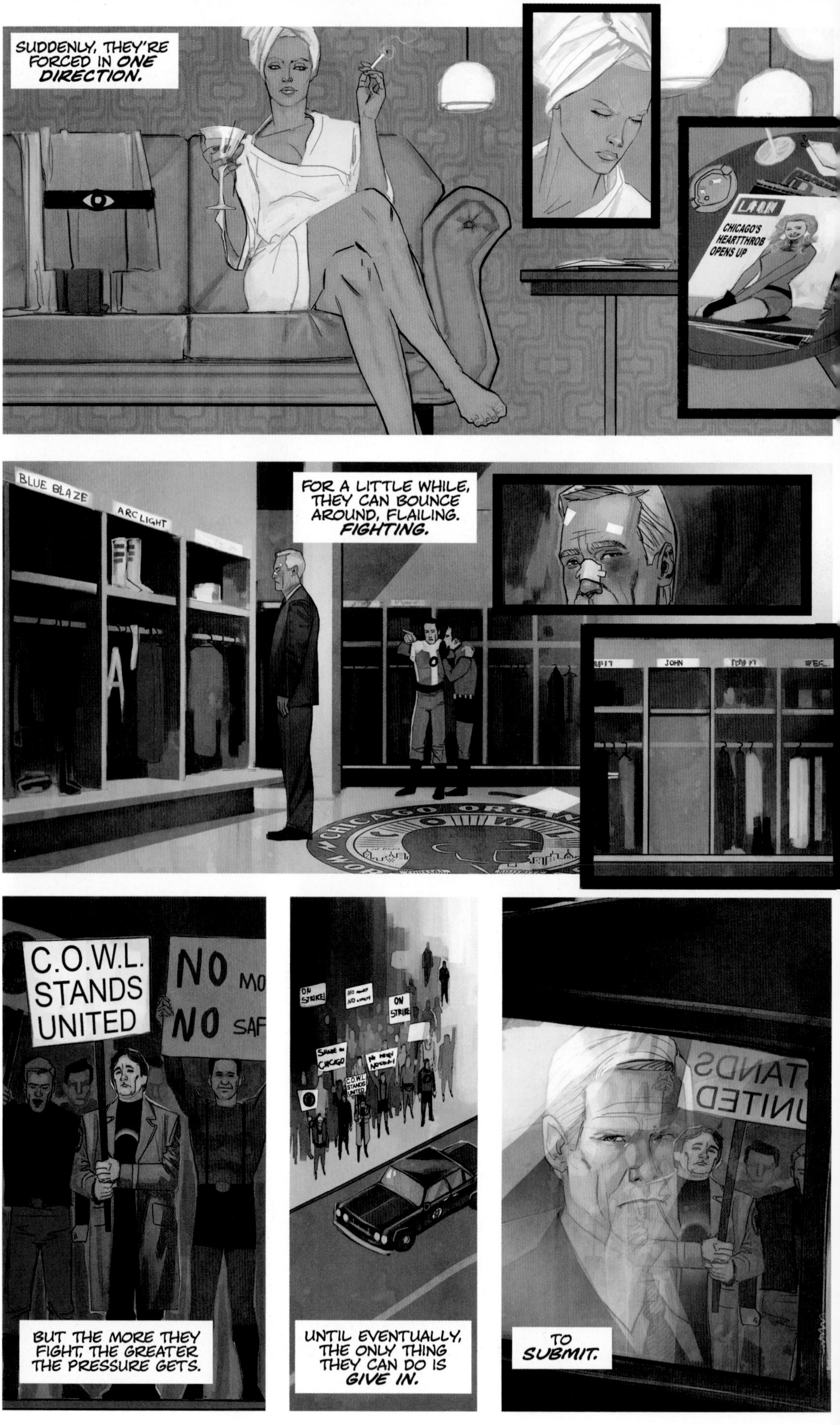
SUDDENLY, THEY'RE FORCED IN ONE DIRECTION.
CHICAGO'S HEARTTHROB OPENS UP
FOR A LITTLE WHILE, THEY CAN BOUNCE AROUND, FLAILING. FIGHTING.
BLUE BLAZE
ARC LIGHT
JOHN
C.O.W.L. STANDS UNITED
NO
NO
BUT THE MORE THEY FIGHT, THE GREATER THE PRESSURE GETS.
ON STRIKE!
ON STRIKE
C.O.W.L. STANDS UNITED
UNTIL EVENTUALLY, THE ONLY THING THEY CAN DO IS GIVE IN.
TO SUBMIT.

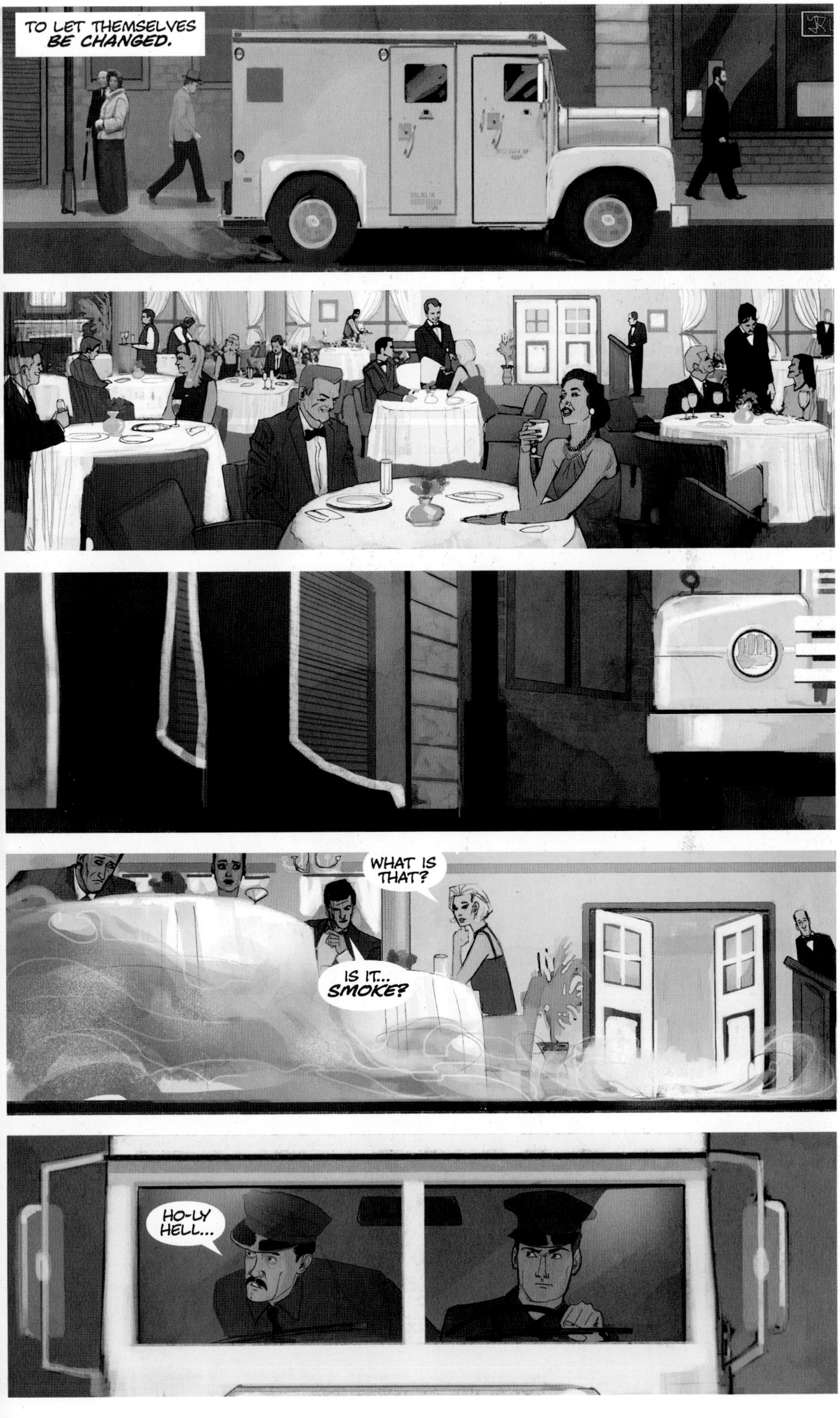
TO LET THEMSELVES
BE CHANGED.
WHAT IS THAT?
IS IT... SMOKE?
HO-LY HELL...

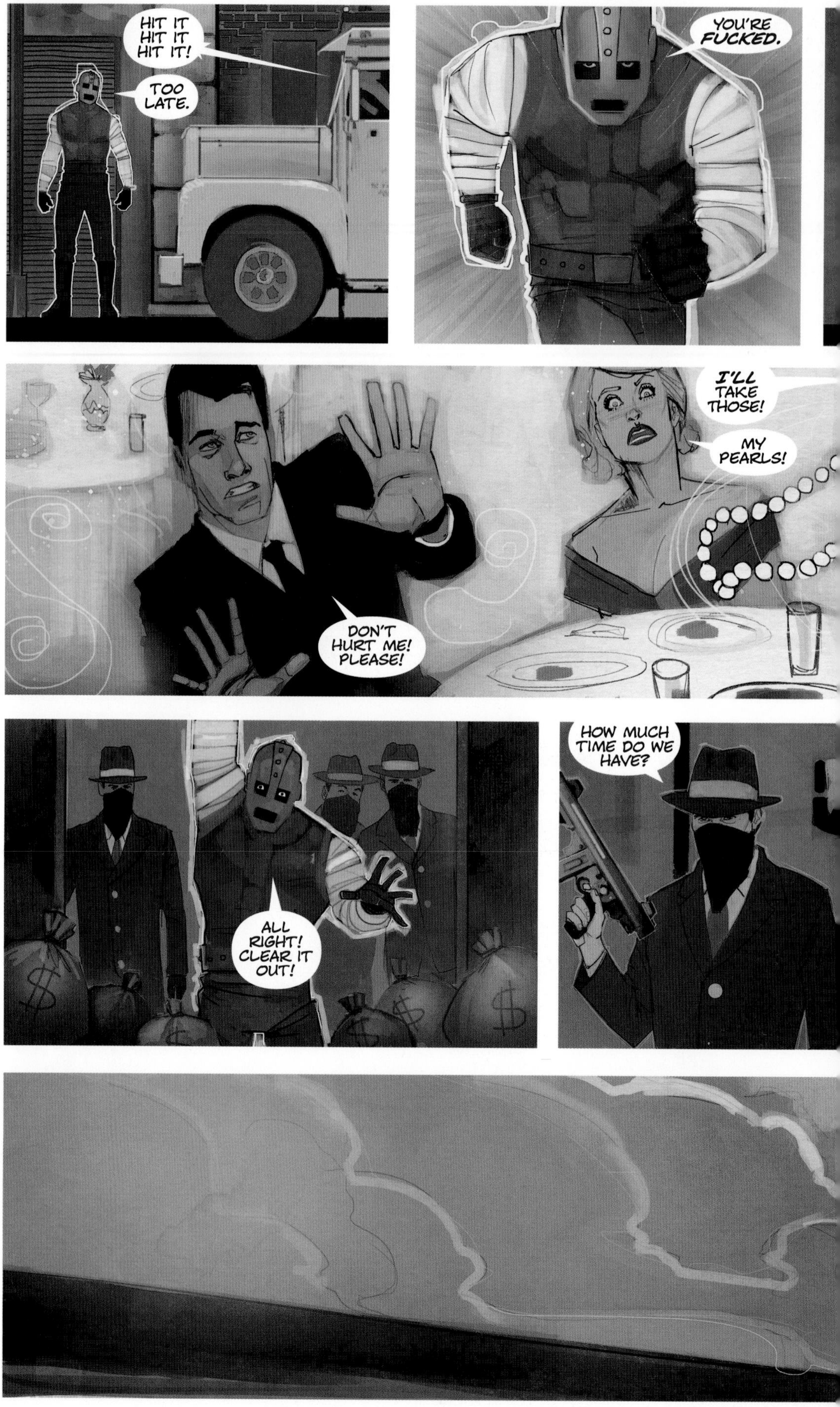
HIT IT
HIT IT
HIT IT!
TOO LATE.
YOU'RE *FUCKED.*
*I'LL* TAKE THOSE!
MY PEARLS!
DON'T HURT ME! PLEASE!
ALL RIGHT! CLEAR IT OUT!
HOW MUCH TIME DO WE HAVE?

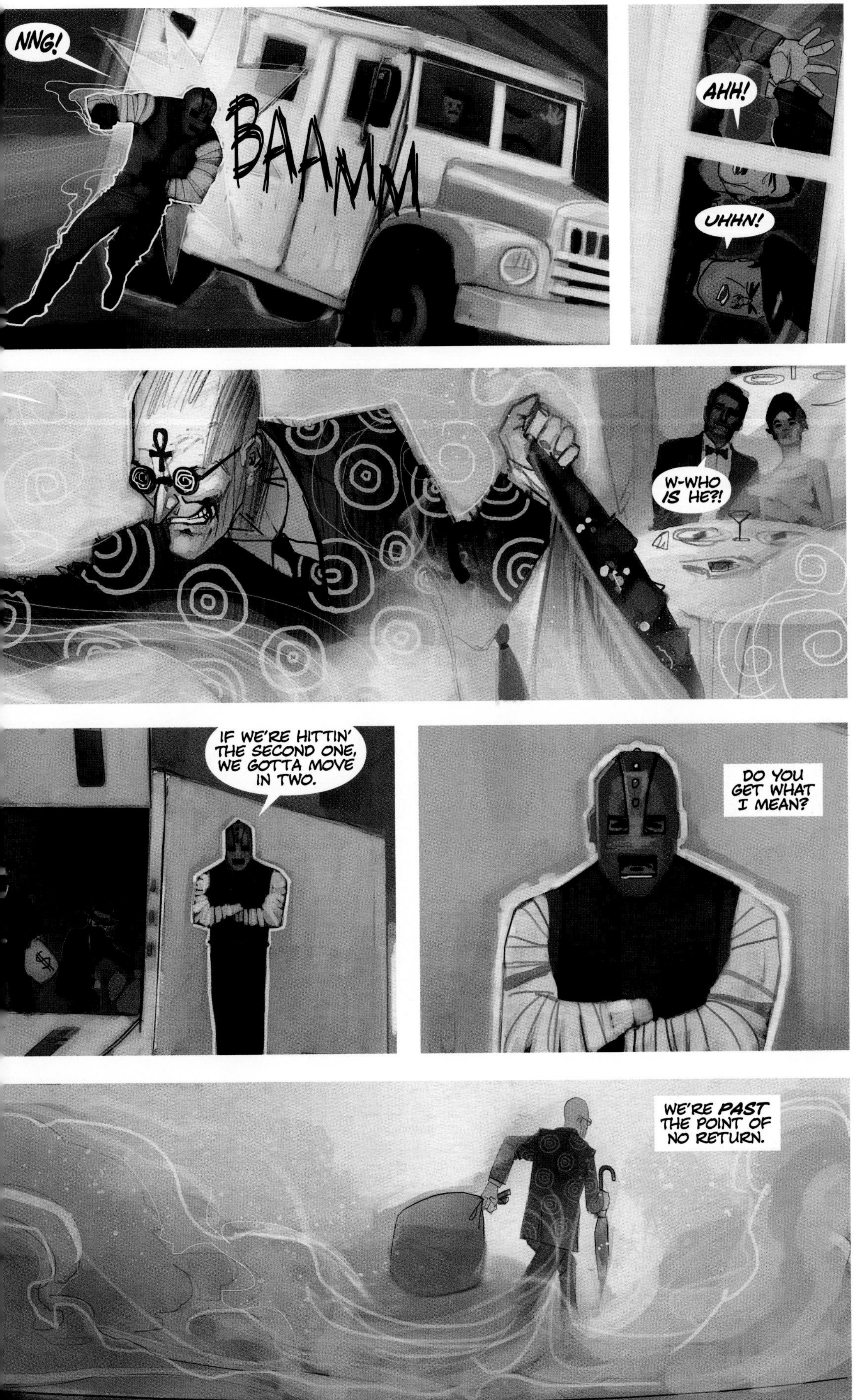
NNG!
BAAMM
AHH!
UHHN!
W-WHO IS HE?!
IF WE'RE HITTIN' THE SECOND ONE, WE GOTTA MOVE IN TWO.
DO YOU GET WHAT I MEAN?
WE'RE PAST THE POINT OF NO RETURN.

KLIK

BBRRRRIIIIIIIIINNNGGGGGG

BBBBRRRIIIIIIIINNNGGGGG

BBRRRRIIIIIIIINNNGGGGG

BBRRRRIIIIIIIINNNGGGGG

STRIKE!

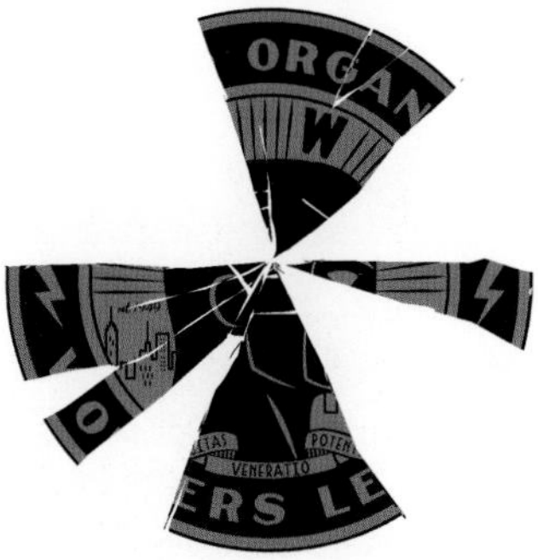
ORGAN
W
VENERATIO
ERS LE

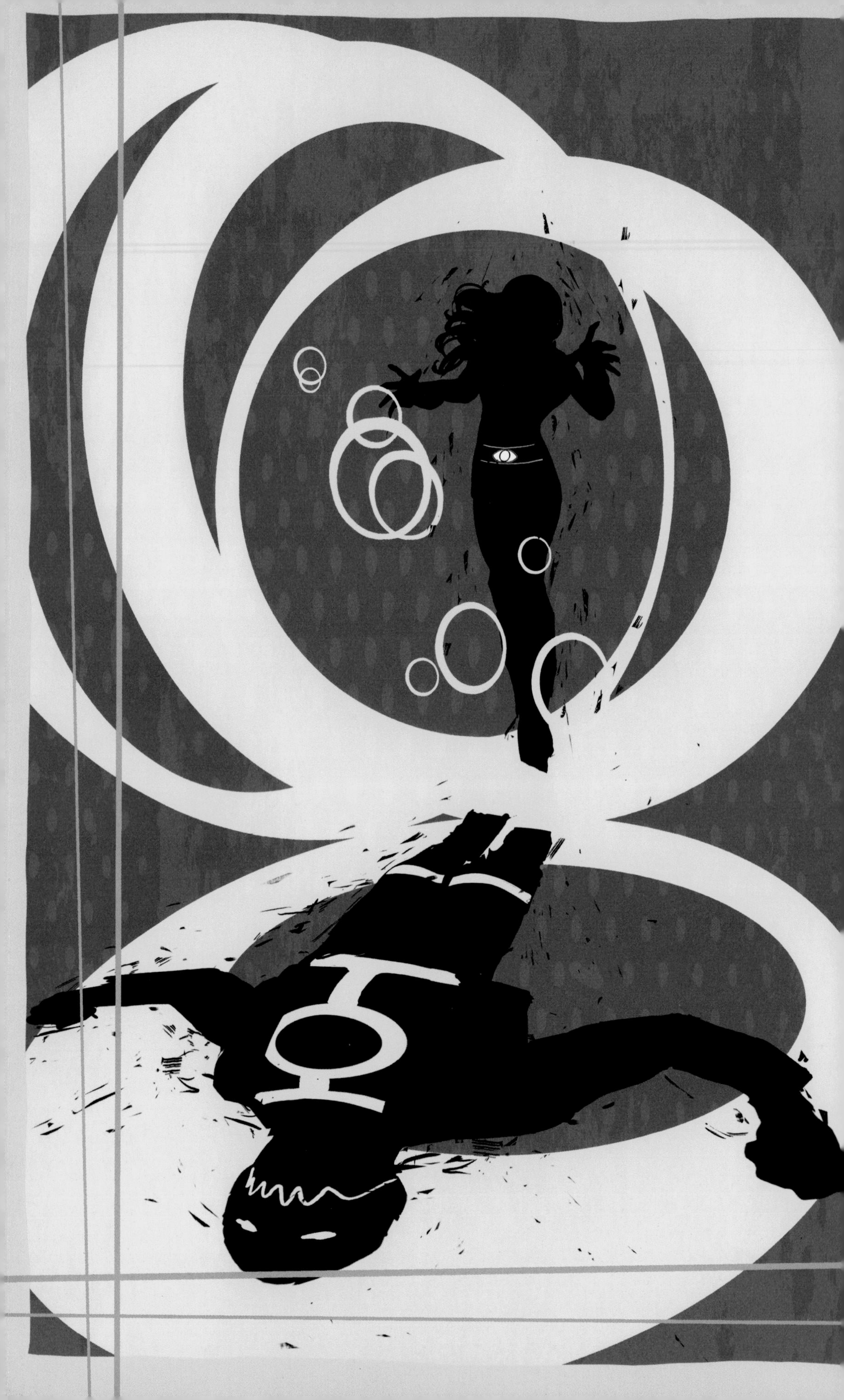

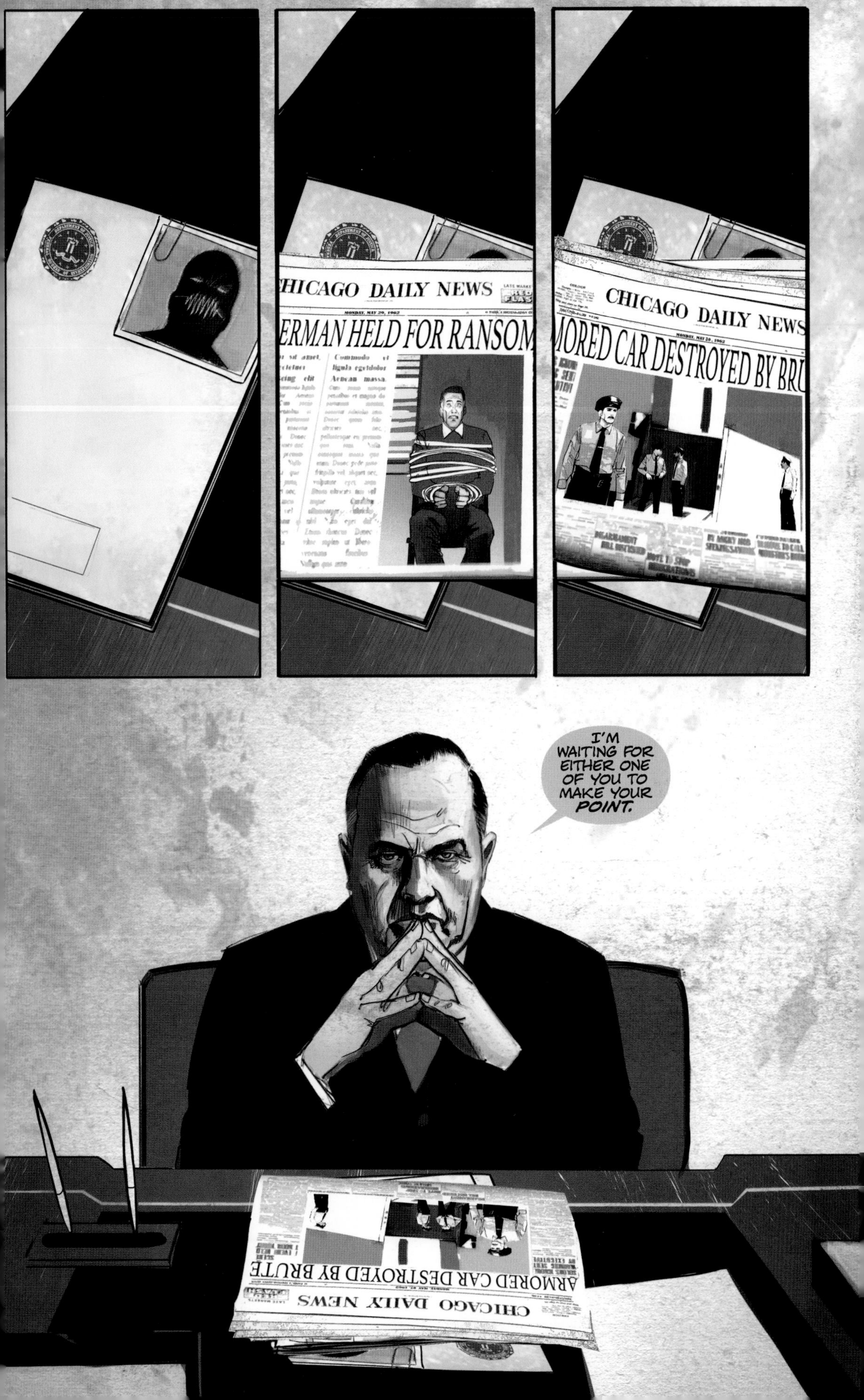
CHICAGO DAILY NEWS
MONDAY, MAY 29, 1962
ERMAN HELD FOR RANSOM
CHICAGO DAILY NEWS
MONDAY, MAY 30, 1962
ORED CAR DESTROYED BY BRU
I'M WAITING FOR EITHER ONE OF YOU TO MAKE YOUR *POINT.*
CHICAGO DAILY NEWS
ARMORED CAR DESTROYED BY BRUTE

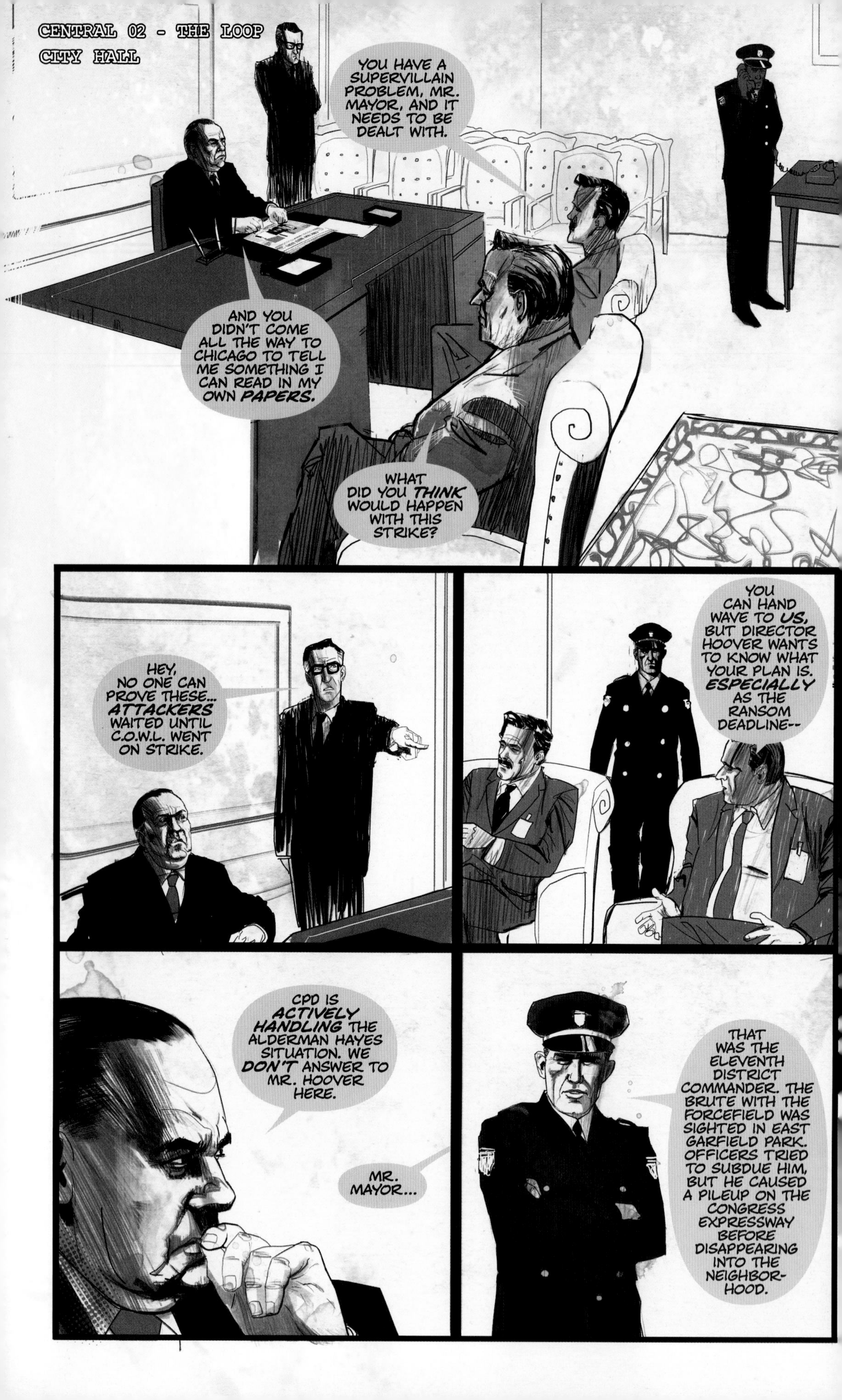
CENTRAL 02 - THE LOOP
CITY HALL
YOU HAVE A SUPERVILLAIN PROBLEM, MR. MAYOR, AND IT NEEDS TO BE DEALT WITH.
AND YOU DIDN'T COME ALL THE WAY TO CHICAGO TO TELL ME SOMETHING I CAN READ IN MY OWN PAPERS.
WHAT DID YOU THINK WOULD HAPPEN WITH THIS STRIKE?
HEY, NO ONE CAN PROVE THESE... ATTACKERS WAITED UNTIL C.O.W.L. WENT ON STRIKE.
YOU CAN HAND WAVE TO US, BUT DIRECTOR HOOVER WANTS TO KNOW WHAT YOUR PLAN IS. ESPECIALLY AS THE RANSOM DEADLINE--
CPD IS ACTIVELY HANDLING THE ALDERMAN HAYES SITUATION. WE DON'T ANSWER TO MR. HOOVER HERE.
MR. MAYOR...
THAT WAS THE ELEVENTH DISTRICT COMMANDER. THE BRUTE WITH THE FORCEFIELD WAS SIGHTED IN EAST GARFIELD PARK. OFFICERS TRIED TO SUBDUE HIM, BUT HE CAUSED A PILEUP ON THE CONGRESS EXPRESSWAY BEFORE DISAPPEARING INTO THE NEIGHBOR-HOOD.

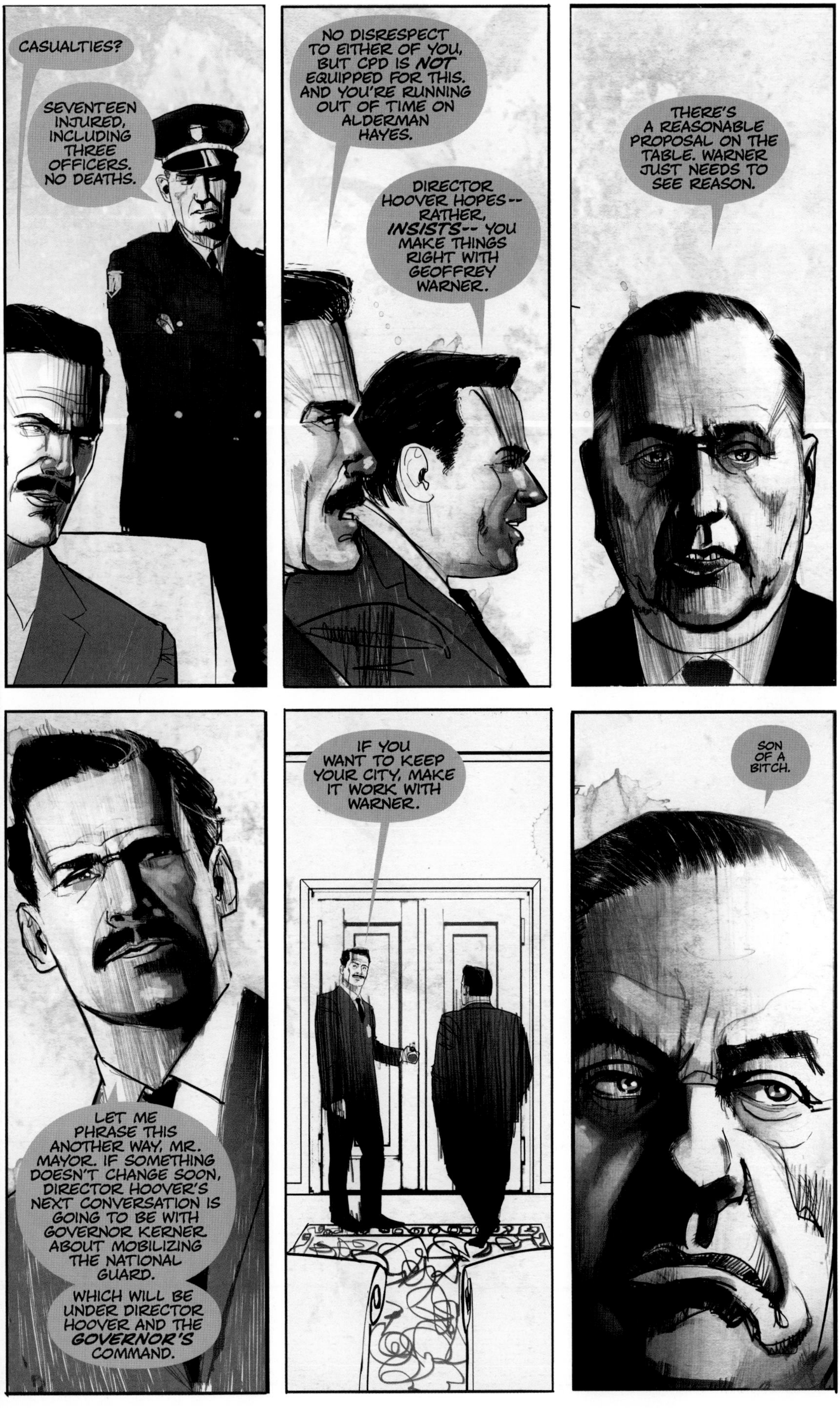
CASUALTIES?
SEVENTEEN INJURED, INCLUDING THREE OFFICERS. NO DEATHS.
NO DISRESPECT TO EITHER OF YOU, BUT CPD IS NOT EQUIPPED FOR THIS. AND YOU'RE RUNNING OUT OF TIME ON ALDERMAN HAYES.
DIRECTOR HOOVER HOPES-- RATHER, INSISTS-- YOU MAKE THINGS RIGHT WITH GEOFFREY WARNER.
THERE'S A REASONABLE PROPOSAL ON THE TABLE. WARNER JUST NEEDS TO SEE REASON.
LET ME PHRASE THIS ANOTHER WAY, MR. MAYOR. IF SOMETHING DOESN'T CHANGE SOON, DIRECTOR HOOVER'S NEXT CONVERSATION IS GOING TO BE WITH GOVERNOR KERNER ABOUT MOBILIZING THE NATIONAL GUARD.
WHICH WILL BE UNDER DIRECTOR HOOVER AND THE GOVERNOR'S COMMAND.
IF YOU WANT TO KEEP YOUR CITY, MAKE IT WORK WITH WARNER.
SON OF A BITCH.

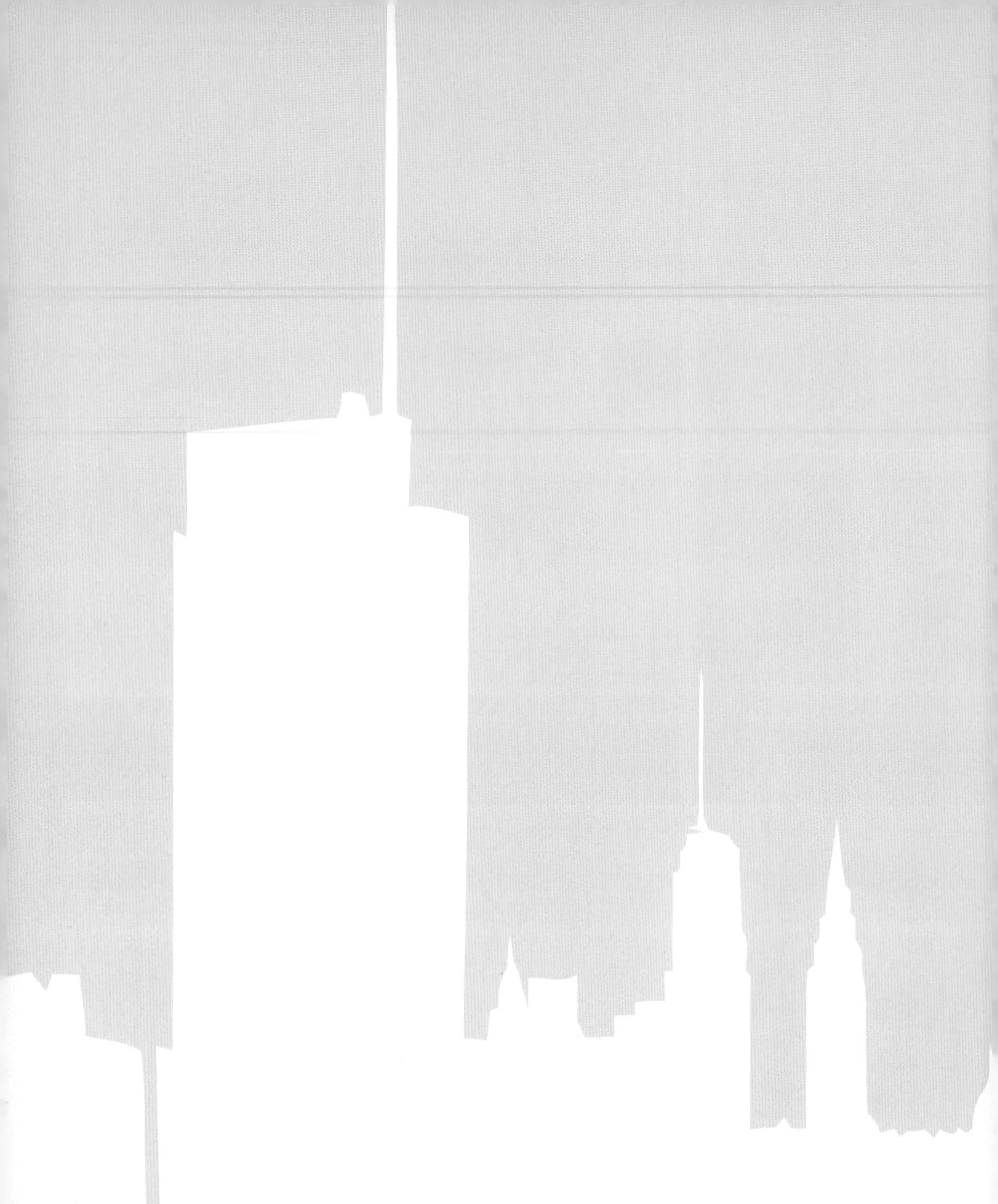

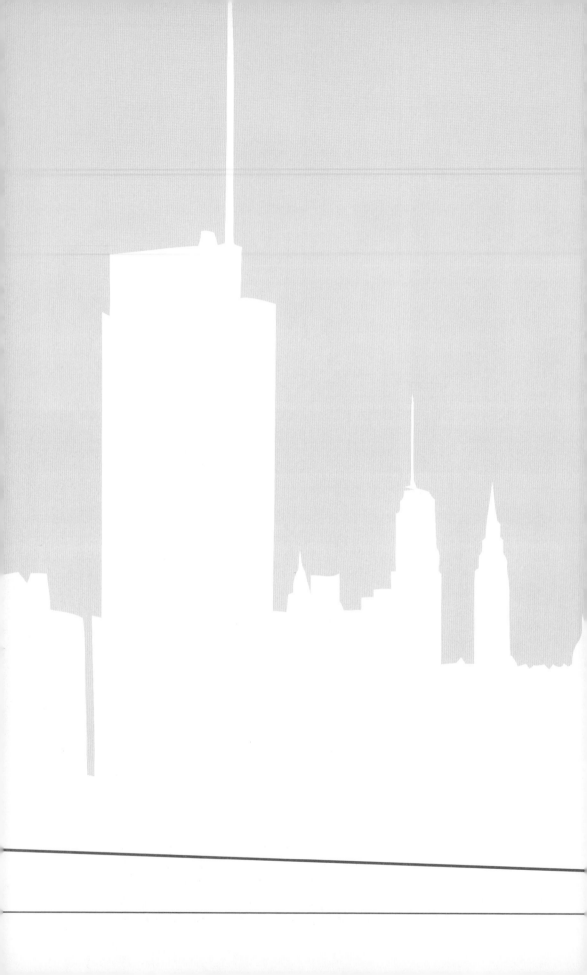

# CHAPTER 3
## The High Ground

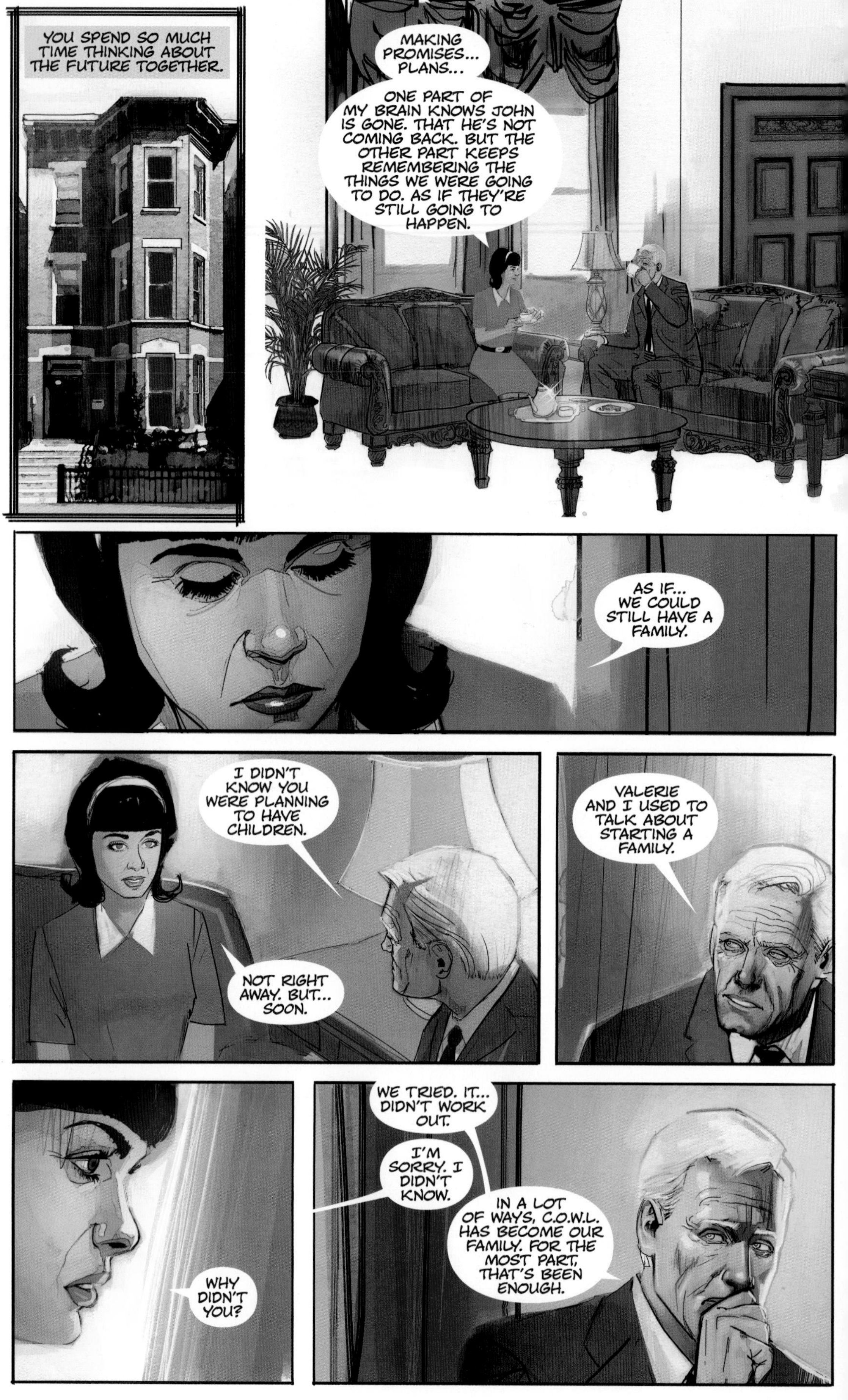
YOU SPEND SO MUCH TIME THINKING ABOUT THE FUTURE TOGETHER.
MAKING PROMISES... PLANS...
ONE PART OF MY BRAIN KNOWS JOHN IS GONE. THAT HE'S NOT COMING BACK. BUT THE OTHER PART KEEPS REMEMBERING THE THINGS WE WERE GOING TO DO. AS IF THEY'RE STILL GOING TO HAPPEN.
AS IF... WE COULD STILL HAVE A FAMILY.
I DIDN'T KNOW YOU WERE PLANNING TO HAVE CHILDREN.
NOT RIGHT AWAY. BUT... SOON.
VALERIE AND I USED TO TALK ABOUT STARTING A FAMILY.
WHY DIDN'T YOU?
WE TRIED. IT... DIDN'T WORK OUT.
I'M SORRY. I DIDN'T KNOW.
IN A LOT OF WAYS, C.O.W.L. HAS BECOME OUR FAMILY. FOR THE MOST PART, THAT'S BEEN ENOUGH.

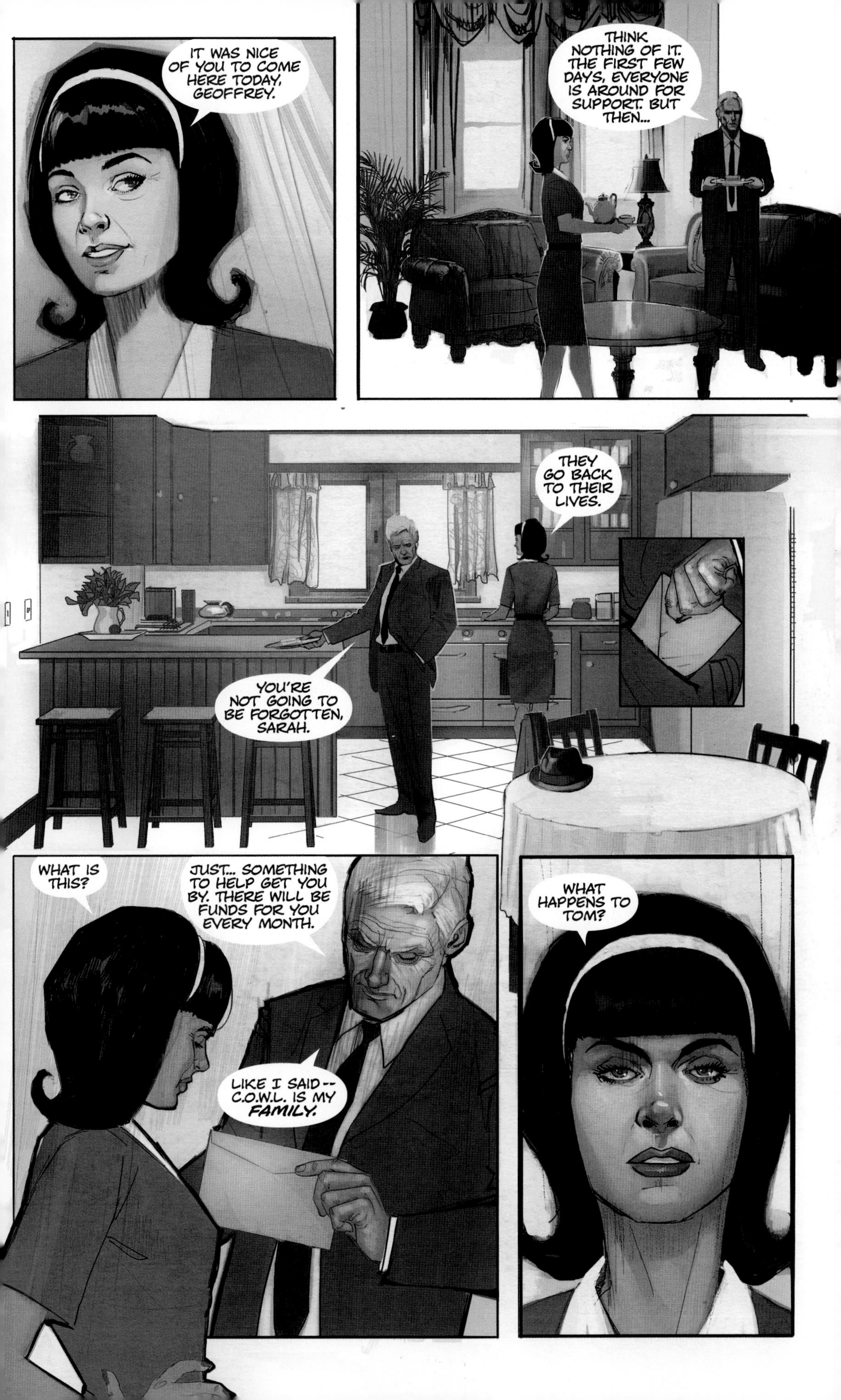
IT WAS NICE OF YOU TO COME HERE TODAY, GEOFFREY.
THINK NOTHING OF IT. THE FIRST FEW DAYS, EVERYONE IS AROUND FOR SUPPORT. BUT THEN...
THEY GO BACK TO THEIR LIVES.
YOU'RE NOT GOING TO BE FORGOTTEN, SARAH.
WHAT IS THIS?
JUST... SOMETHING TO HELP GET YOU BY. THERE WILL BE FUNDS FOR YOU EVERY MONTH.
LIKE I SAID-- C.O.W.L. IS MY *FAMILY.*
WHAT HAPPENS TO TOM?

THAT'S UP TO THE INTERNAL AFFAIRS BOARD.

DO YOU REALLY THINK IT WAS SELF DEFENSE?

TOM'S INJURIES SEEM TO SUPPORT IT. I'M GETTING THE SENSE YOU DON'T BELIEVE HIM?

I DIDN'T SAY THAT.

THE ONLY PART THAT SEEMS OUT OF PLACE IS WHY JOHN WAS IN THAT PART OF TOWN TO BEGIN WITH.

MAYBE IT WAS SOMETHING HE WAS WORKING ON?

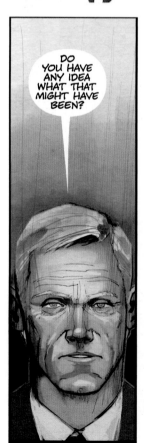

DO YOU HAVE ANY IDEA WHAT THAT MIGHT HAVE BEEN?

NO. JOHN NEVER TALKED ABOUT THE CASES HE WAS WORKING.

HE ALWAYS HAD HIS SECRETS.

WELL, I'D BETTER GET BACK.

IF YOU THINK OF ANYTHING ELSE...

YOU'LL BE THE FIRST TO HEAR ABOUT IT.

BLAM!

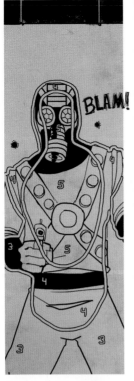

BLAM!

BLAM!

HEY, TWO OUTTA THREE ONLY GETS YOU KILLED TWICE. NOT BAD, MARLOW.

DON'T YOU HAVE ANYTHING BETTER TO DO?

AND MISS *THIS* SHOWCASE?

LIGHTEN THE FUCK UP, DON. IT'S BEEN A WHILE SINCE HE'S BEEN ON THE FIRING LINE.

AH, COME ON. I'M JUST GIVING HIM SHIT.

DON'T WORRY, GRANT. TAKE YOUR TIME. GET BACK RIGHT.

SCREW TAKING MY TIME. WE GET CALLED TO MOVE ON THAT SOUND FREAK, I'M GONNA BE THERE.

I HEARD INVESTIGATIONS ALREADY HAS HIM STAKED OUT.

PHIL, YOU WERE AT CITY HALL THE NIGHT OF THE 10TH, RIGHT?

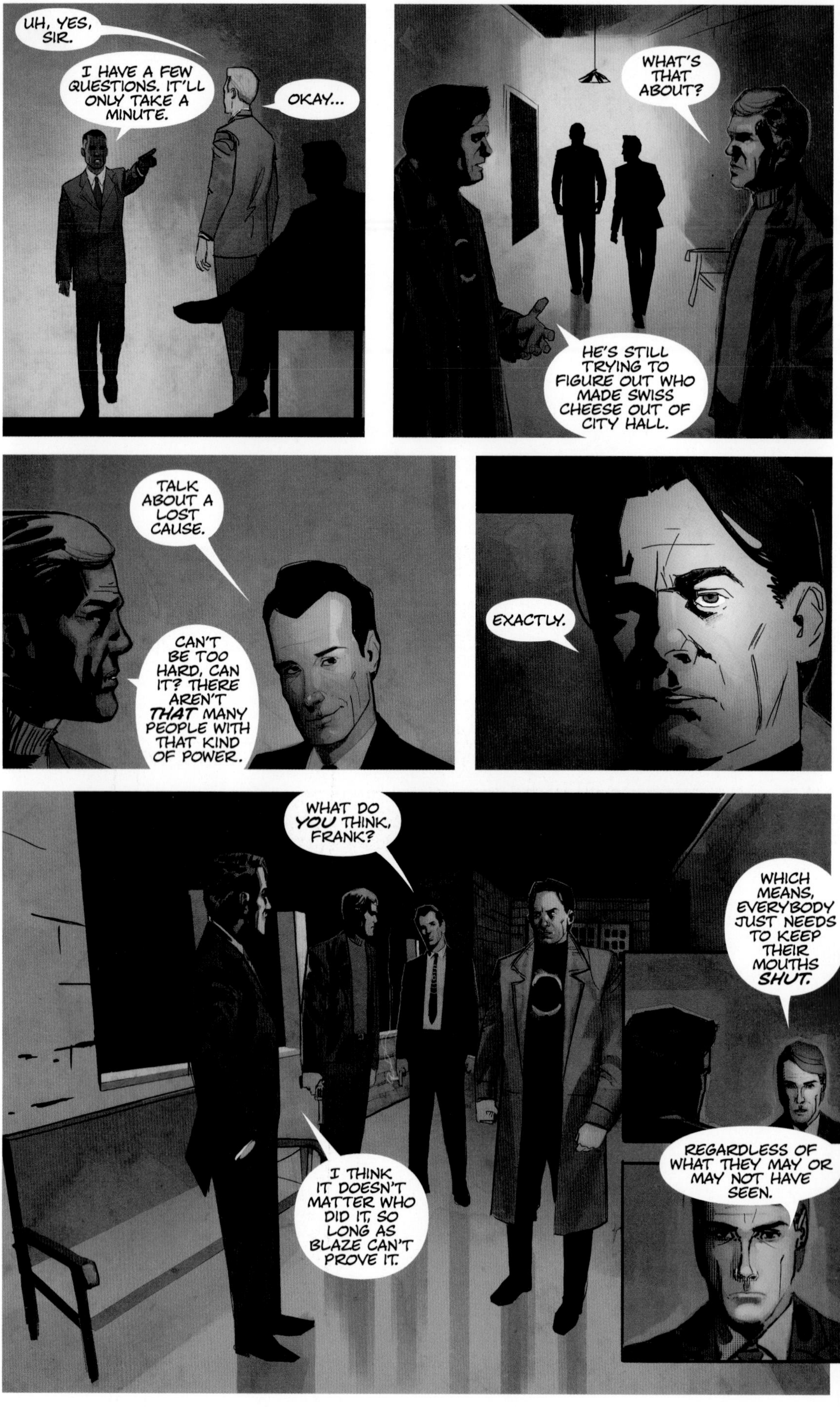
UH, YES, SIR.
I HAVE A FEW QUESTIONS. IT'LL ONLY TAKE A MINUTE.
OKAY...
WHAT'S THAT ABOUT?
HE'S STILL TRYING TO FIGURE OUT WHO MADE SWISS CHEESE OUT OF CITY HALL.
TALK ABOUT A LOST CAUSE.
CAN'T BE TOO HARD, CAN IT? THERE AREN'T THAT MANY PEOPLE WITH THAT KIND OF POWER.
EXACTLY.
WHAT DO YOU THINK, FRANK?
I THINK IT DOESN'T MATTER WHO DID IT, SO LONG AS BLAZE CAN'T PROVE IT.
WHICH MEANS, EVERYBODY JUST NEEDS TO KEEP THEIR MOUTHS SHUT.
REGARDLESS OF WHAT THEY MAY OR MAY NOT HAVE SEEN.

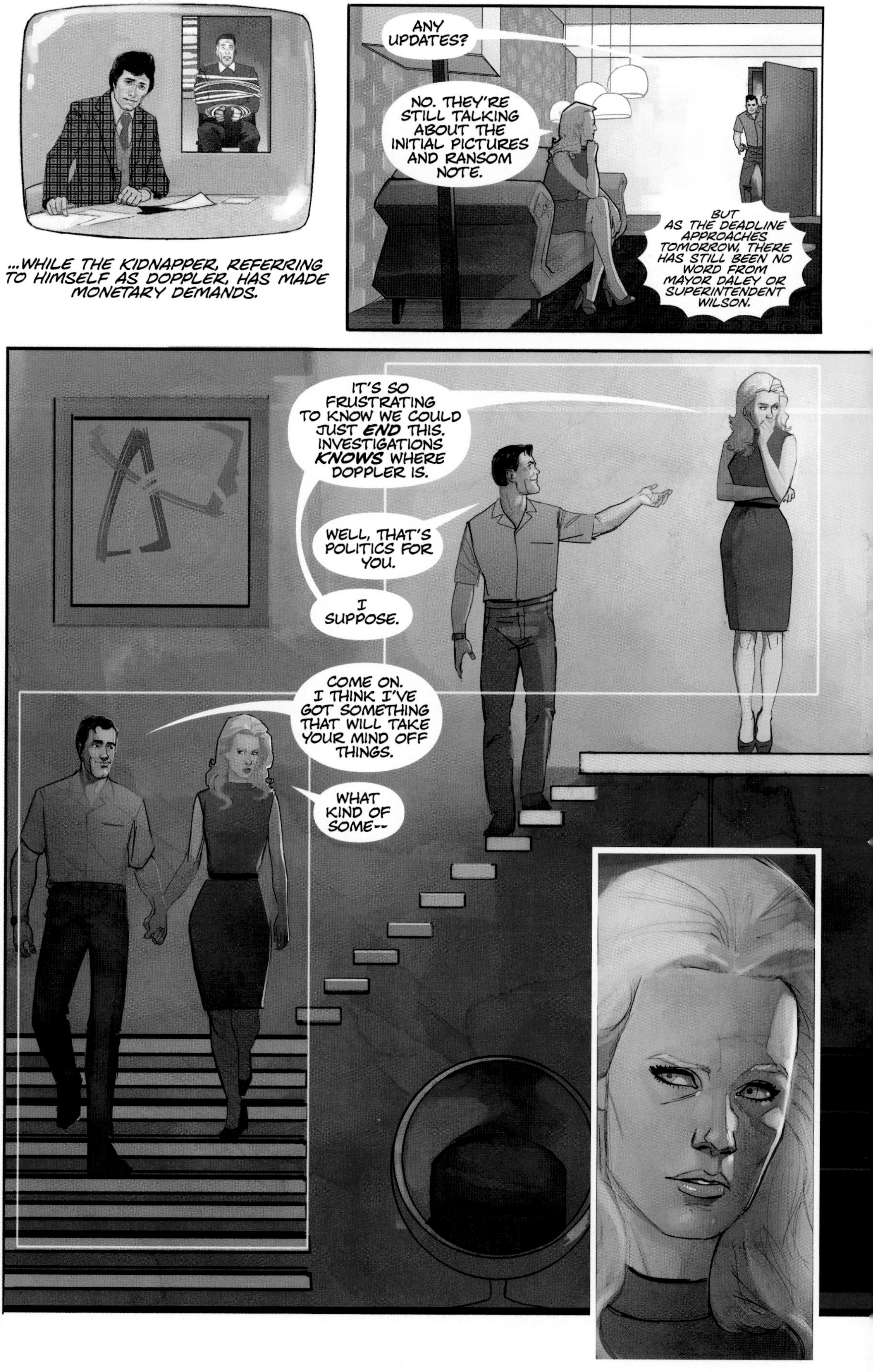
...WHILE THE KIDNAPPER, REFERRING TO HIMSELF AS DOPPLER, HAS MADE MONETARY DEMANDS.
ANY UPDATES?
NO. THEY'RE STILL TALKING ABOUT THE INITIAL PICTURES AND RANSOM NOTE.
BUT AS THE DEADLINE APPROACHES TOMORROW, THERE HAS STILL BEEN NO WORD FROM MAYOR DALEY OR SUPERINTENDENT WILSON.
IT'S SO FRUSTRATING TO KNOW WE COULD JUST END THIS. INVESTIGATIONS KNOWS WHERE DOPPLER IS.
WELL, THAT'S POLITICS FOR YOU.
I SUPPOSE.
COME ON. I THINK I'VE GOT SOMETHING THAT WILL TAKE YOUR MIND OFF THINGS.
WHAT KIND OF SOME--

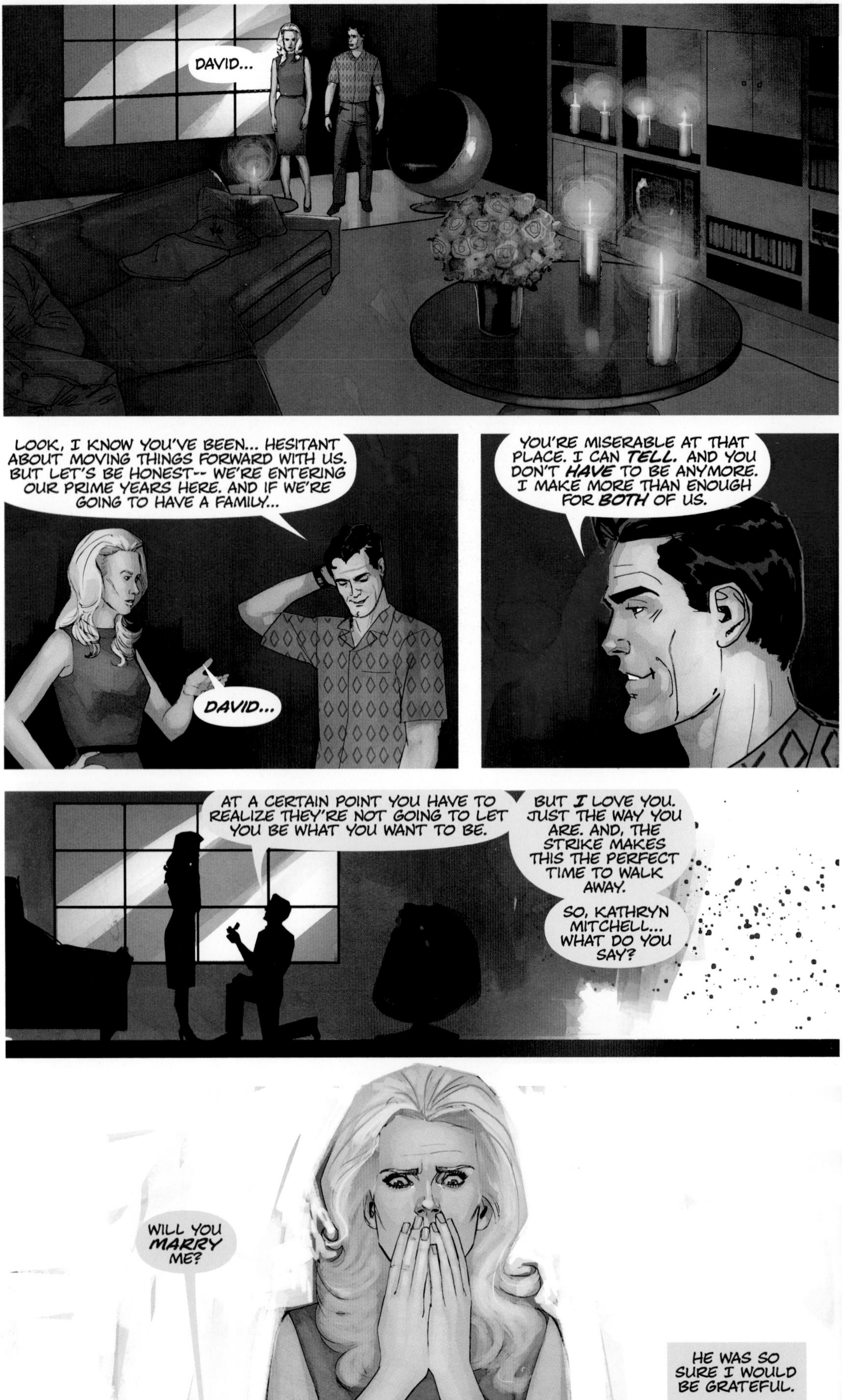
DAVID...
LOOK, I KNOW YOU'VE BEEN... HESITANT ABOUT MOVING THINGS FORWARD WITH US. BUT LET'S BE HONEST-- WE'RE ENTERING OUR PRIME YEARS HERE. AND IF WE'RE GOING TO HAVE A FAMILY...
DAVID...
YOU'RE MISERABLE AT THAT PLACE. I CAN TELL. AND YOU DON'T HAVE TO BE ANYMORE. I MAKE MORE THAN ENOUGH FOR BOTH OF US.
AT A CERTAIN POINT YOU HAVE TO REALIZE THEY'RE NOT GOING TO LET YOU BE WHAT YOU WANT TO BE.
BUT I LOVE YOU. JUST THE WAY YOU ARE. AND, THE STRIKE MAKES THIS THE PERFECT TIME TO WALK AWAY.
SO, KATHRYN MITCHELL... WHAT DO YOU SAY?
WILL YOU MARRY ME?
HE WAS SO SURE I WOULD BE GRATEFUL.

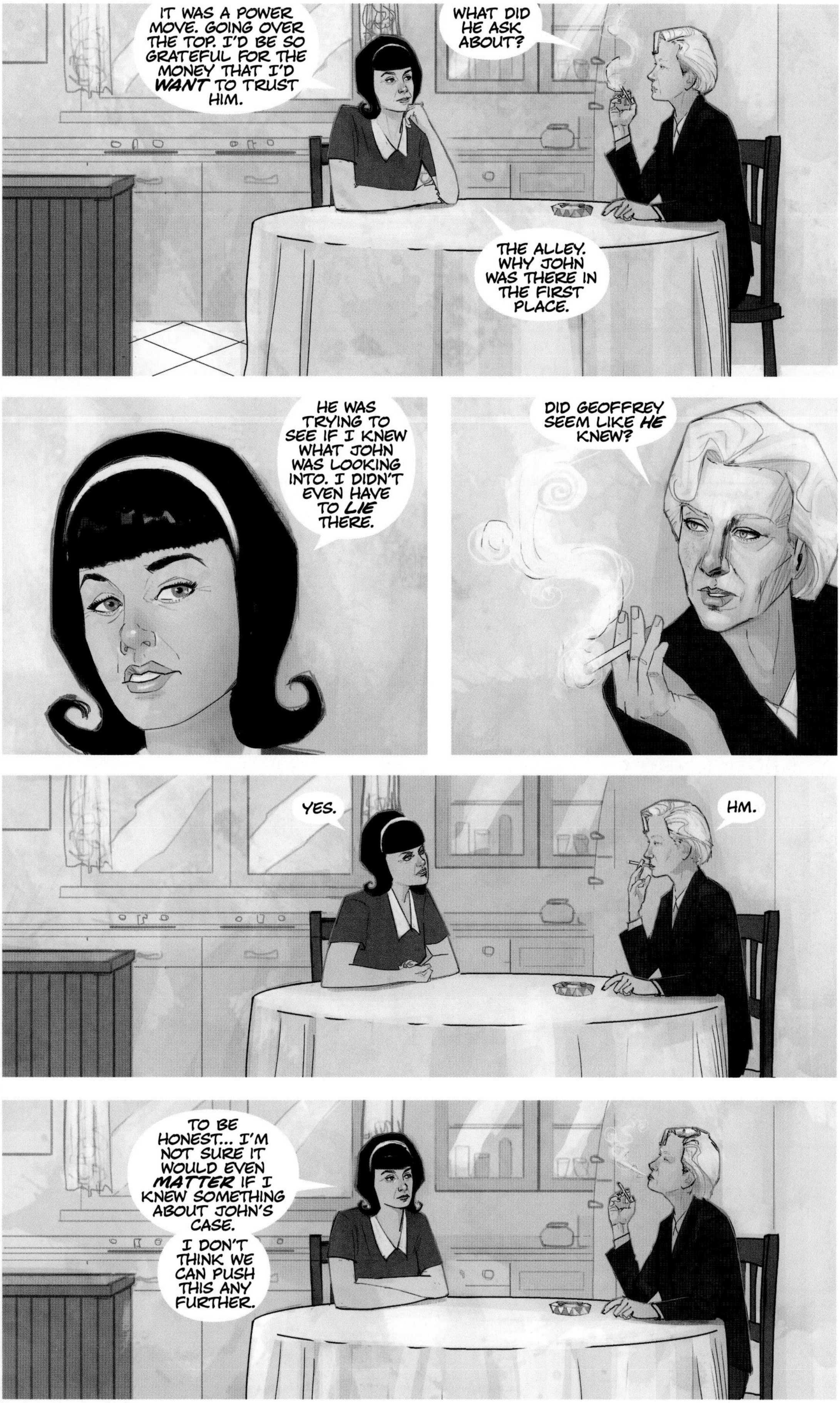
IT WAS A POWER MOVE. GOING OVER THE TOP. I'D BE SO GRATEFUL FOR THE MONEY THAT I'D *WANT* TO TRUST HIM.
WHAT DID HE ASK ABOUT?
THE ALLEY. WHY JOHN WAS THERE IN THE FIRST PLACE.
HE WAS TRYING TO SEE IF I KNEW WHAT JOHN WAS LOOKING INTO. I DIDN'T EVEN HAVE TO *LIE* THERE.
DID GEOFFREY SEEM LIKE *HE* KNEW?
YES.
HM.
TO BE HONEST... I'M NOT SURE IT WOULD EVEN *MATTER* IF I KNEW SOMETHING ABOUT JOHN'S CASE.
I DON'T THINK WE CAN PUSH THIS ANY FURTHER.

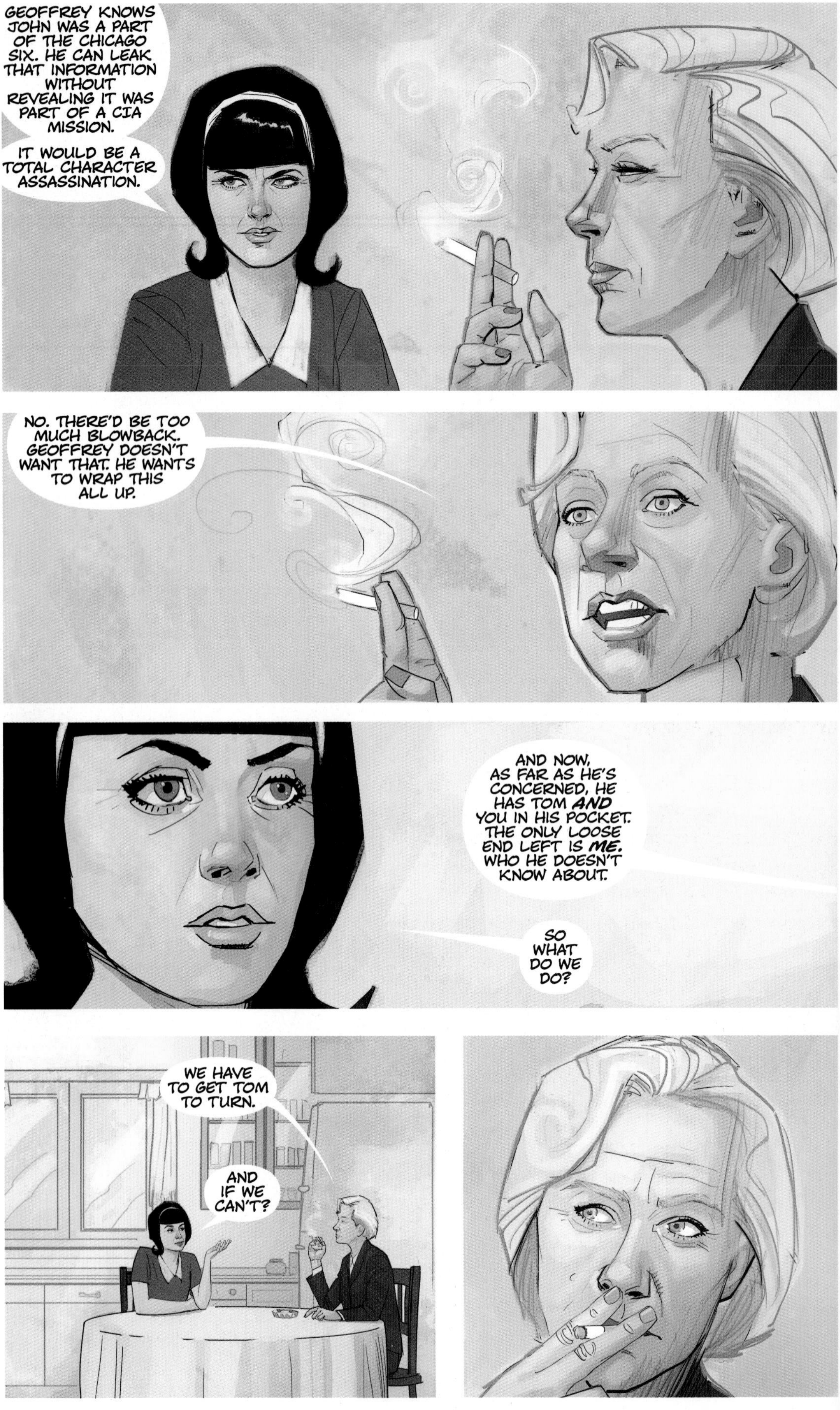
GEOFFREY KNOWS JOHN WAS A PART OF THE CHICAGO SIX. HE CAN LEAK THAT INFORMATION WITHOUT REVEALING IT WAS PART OF A CIA MISSION.
IT WOULD BE A TOTAL CHARACTER ASSASSINATION.
NO. THERE'D BE TOO MUCH BLOWBACK. GEOFFREY DOESN'T WANT THAT. HE WANTS TO WRAP THIS ALL UP.
AND NOW, AS FAR AS HE'S CONCERNED, HE HAS TOM *AND* YOU IN HIS POCKET. THE ONLY LOOSE END LEFT IS *ME*. WHO HE DOESN'T KNOW ABOUT.
SO WHAT DO WE DO?
WE HAVE TO GET TOM TO TURN.
AND IF WE CAN'T?

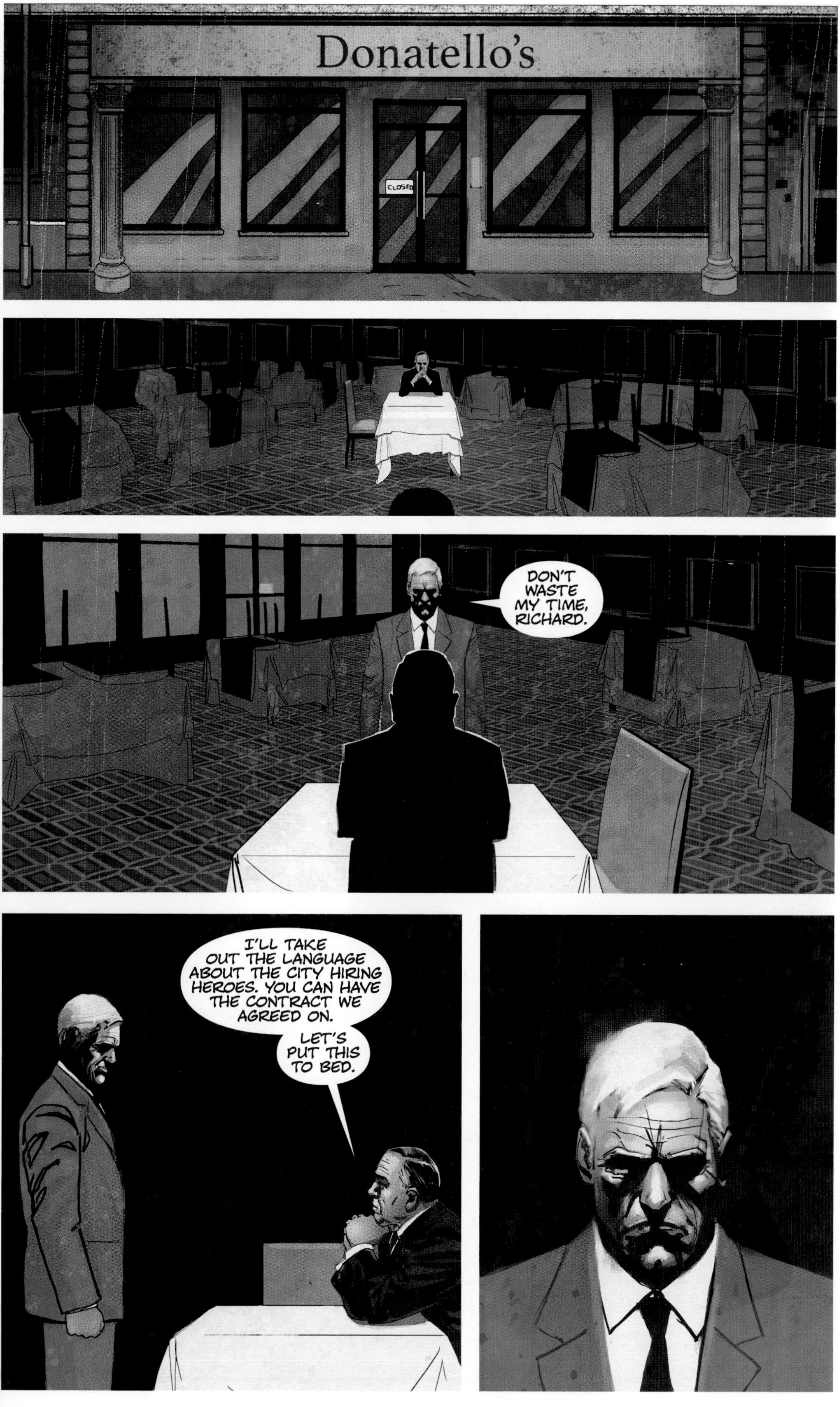
Donatello's
CLOSED
DON'T WASTE MY TIME, RICHARD.
I'LL TAKE OUT THE LANGUAGE ABOUT THE CITY HIRING HEROES. YOU CAN HAVE THE CONTRACT WE AGREED ON.
LET'S PUT THIS TO BED.

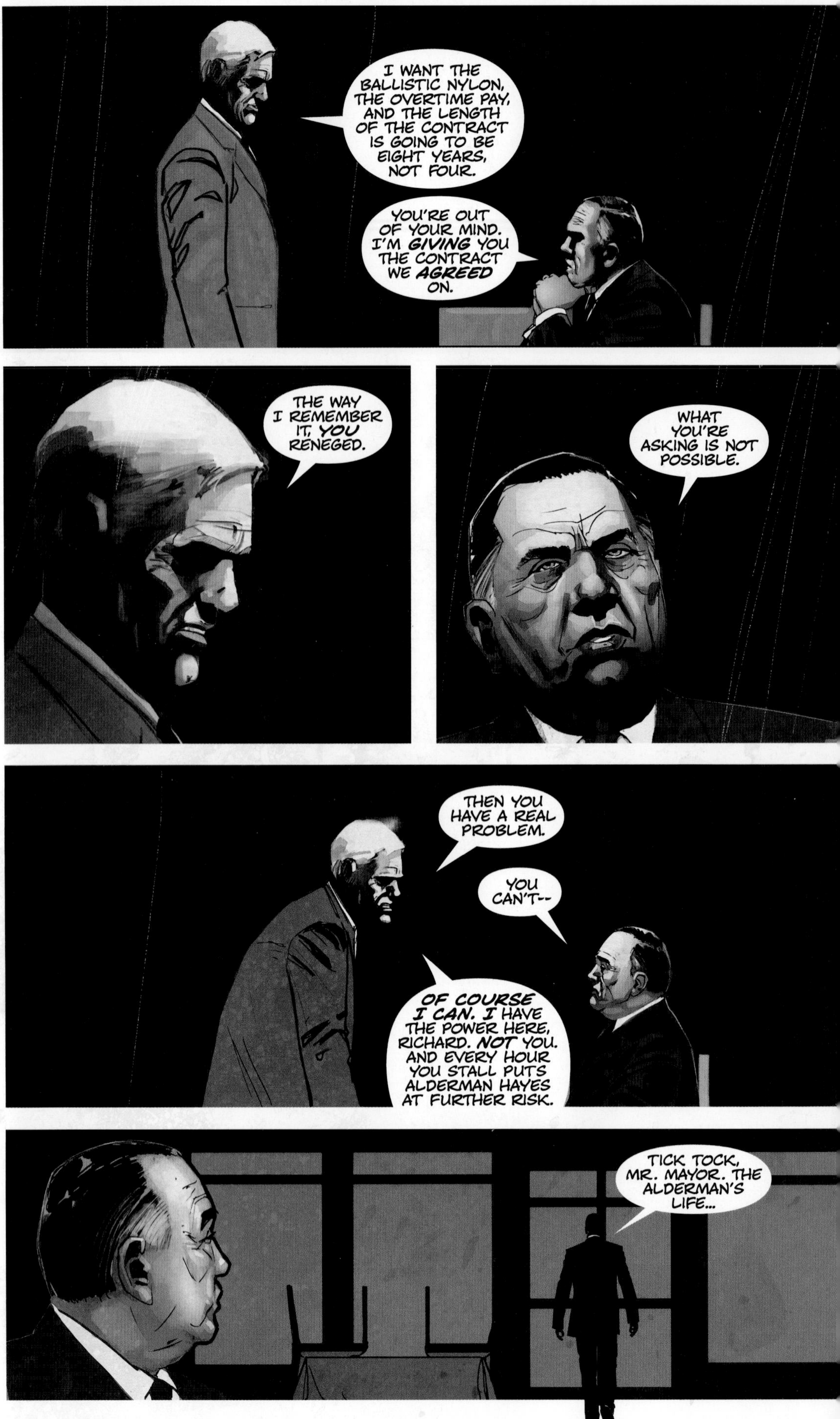

I WANT THE BALLISTIC NYLON, THE OVERTIME PAY, AND THE LENGTH OF THE CONTRACT IS GOING TO BE EIGHT YEARS, NOT FOUR.
YOU'RE OUT OF YOUR MIND. I'M GIVING YOU THE CONTRACT WE AGREED ON.
THE WAY I REMEMBER IT, YOU RENEGED.
WHAT YOU'RE ASKING IS NOT POSSIBLE.
THEN YOU HAVE A REAL PROBLEM.
YOU CAN'T--
OF COURSE I CAN. I HAVE THE POWER HERE, RICHARD. NOT YOU. AND EVERY HOUR YOU STALL PUTS ALDERMAN HAYES AT FURTHER RISK.
TICK TOCK, MR. MAYOR. THE ALDERMAN'S LIFE...

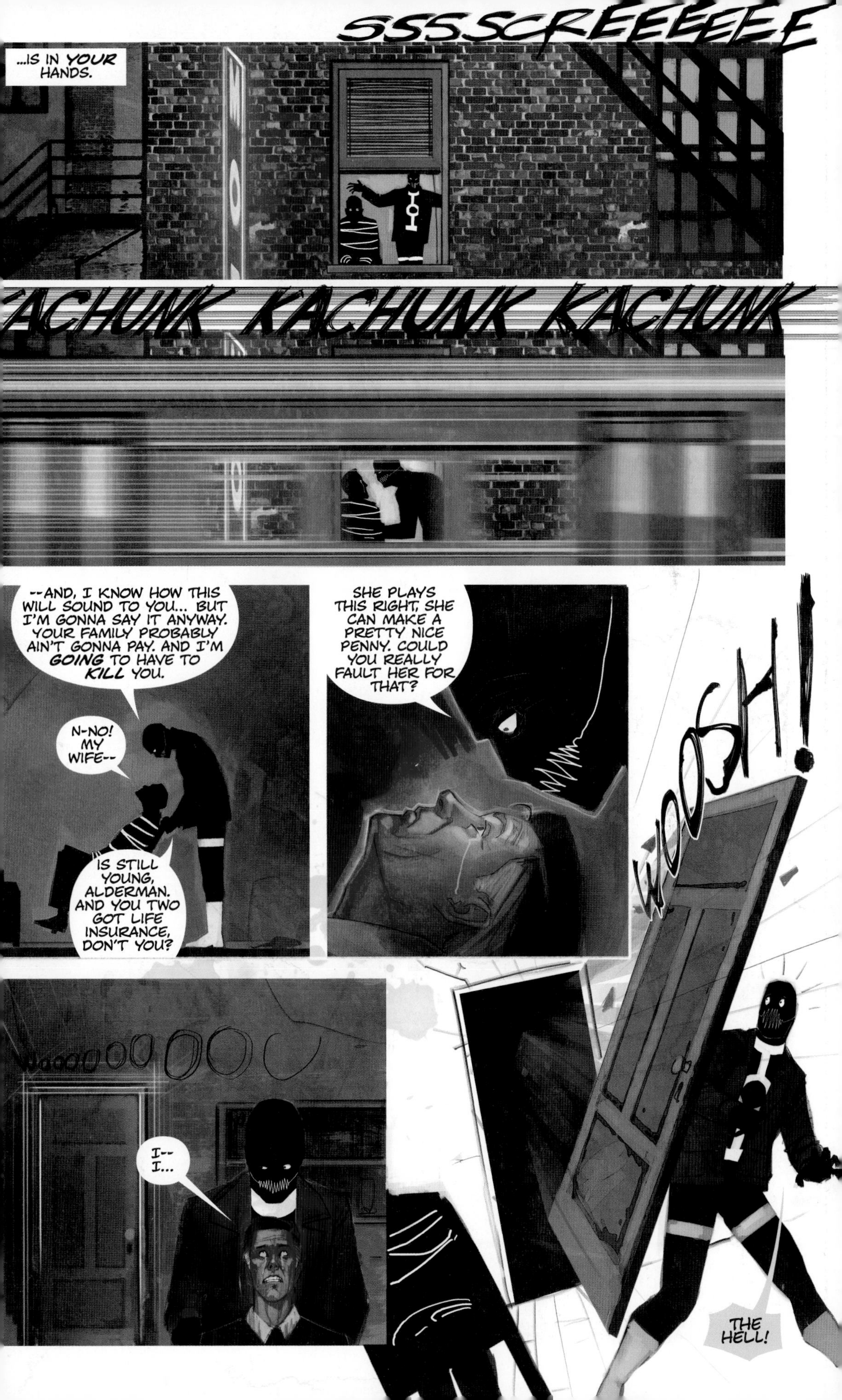
SSSSCREEEEEEE
...IS IN YOUR HANDS.
KACHUNK KACHUNK KACHUNK
--AND, I KNOW HOW THIS WILL SOUND TO YOU... BUT I'M GONNA SAY IT ANYWAY. YOUR FAMILY PROBABLY AIN'T GONNA PAY. AND I'M GOING TO HAVE TO KILL YOU.
N-NO! MY WIFE--
IS STILL YOUNG, ALDERMAN. AND YOU TWO GOT LIFE INSURANCE, DON'T YOU?
SHE PLAYS THIS RIGHT, SHE CAN MAKE A PRETTY NICE PENNY. COULD YOU REALLY FAULT HER FOR THAT?
WOOSH!
WoooOOOOO
I-- I...
THE HELL!

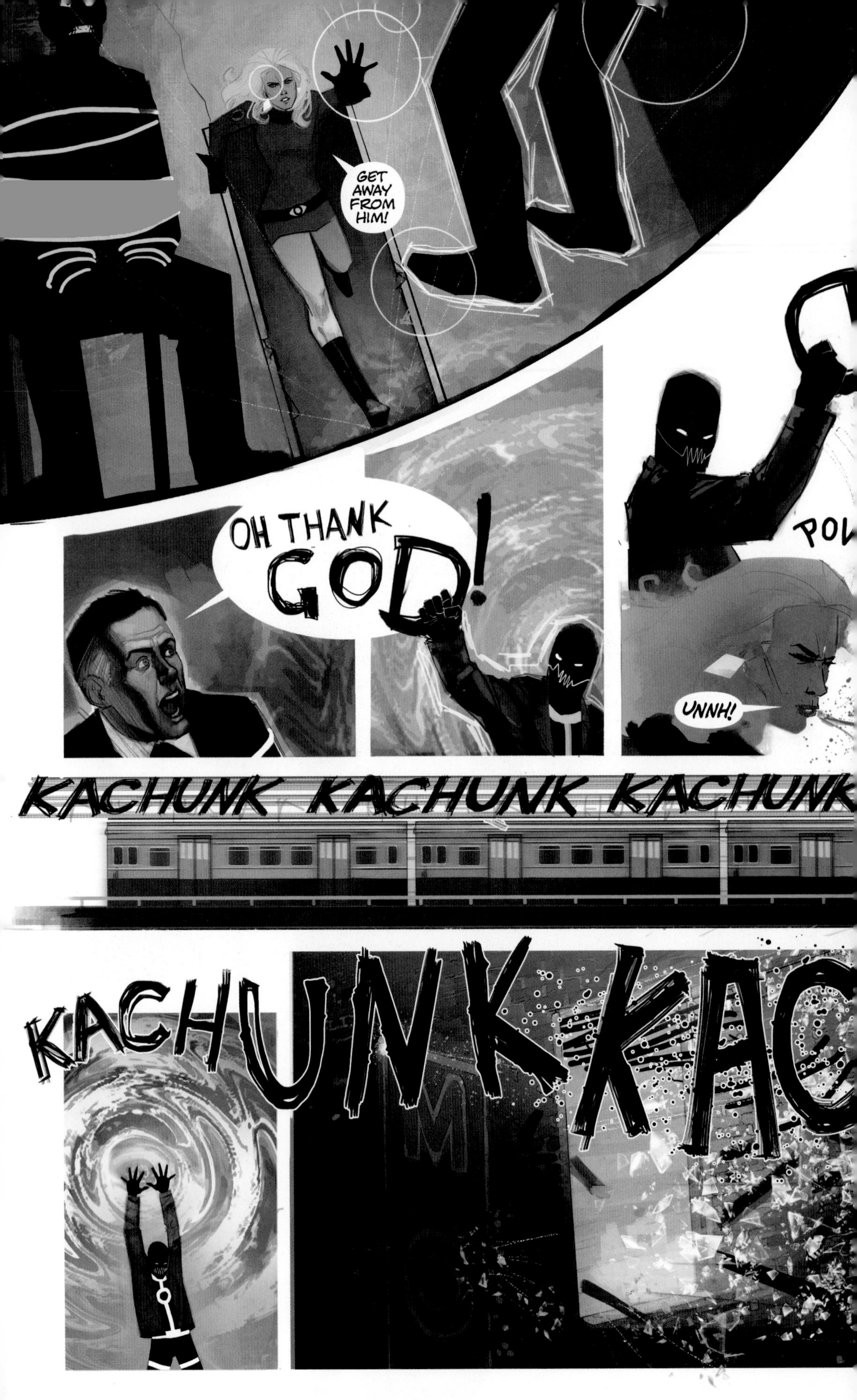
GET AWAY FROM HIM!
OH THANK GOD!
UNNH!
KACHUNK KACHUNK KACHUNK
KACHUNK

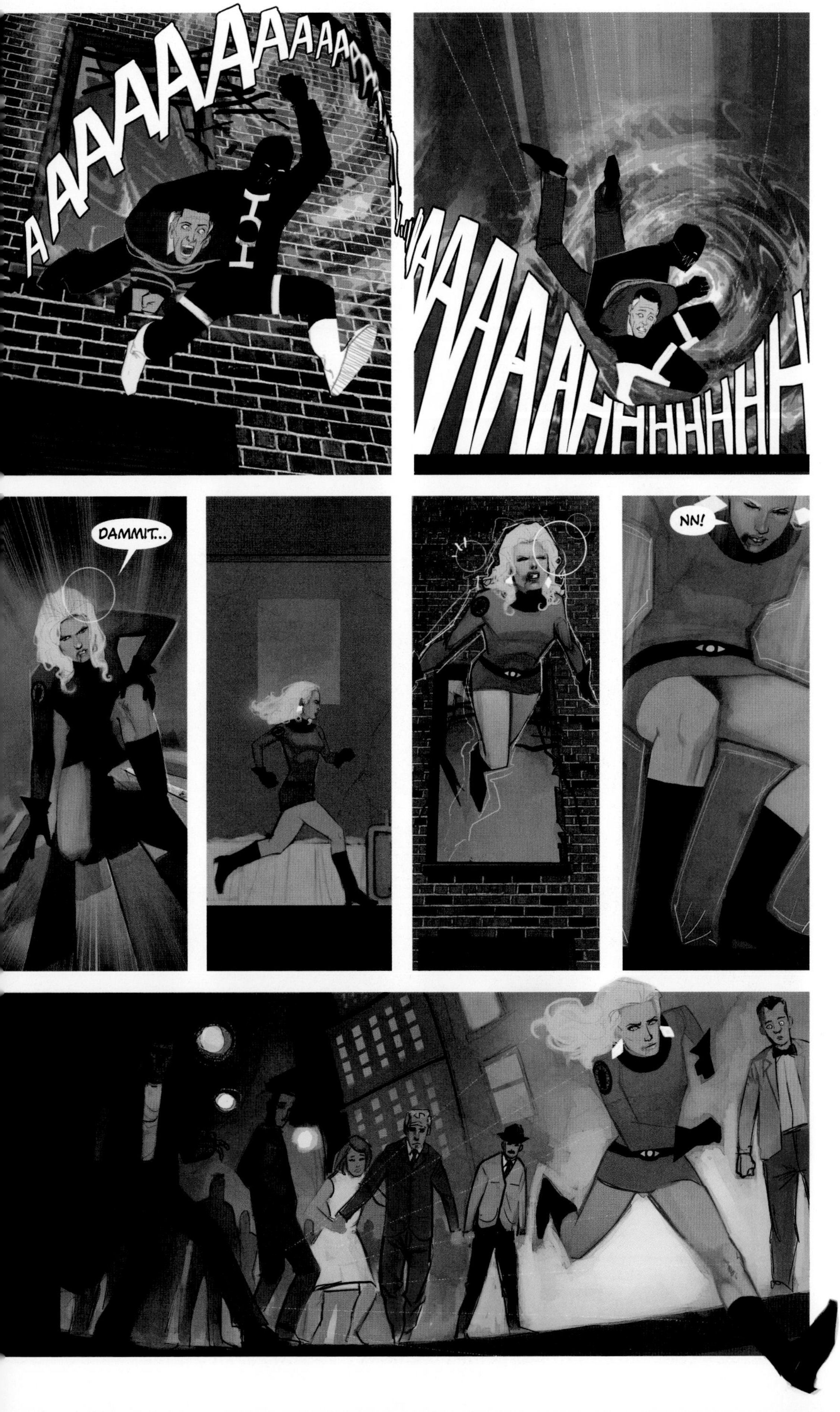
AAAAAAAAAAAAAAAAAAAAAAAAAAAHHHHHHHH
DAMMIT...
NN!

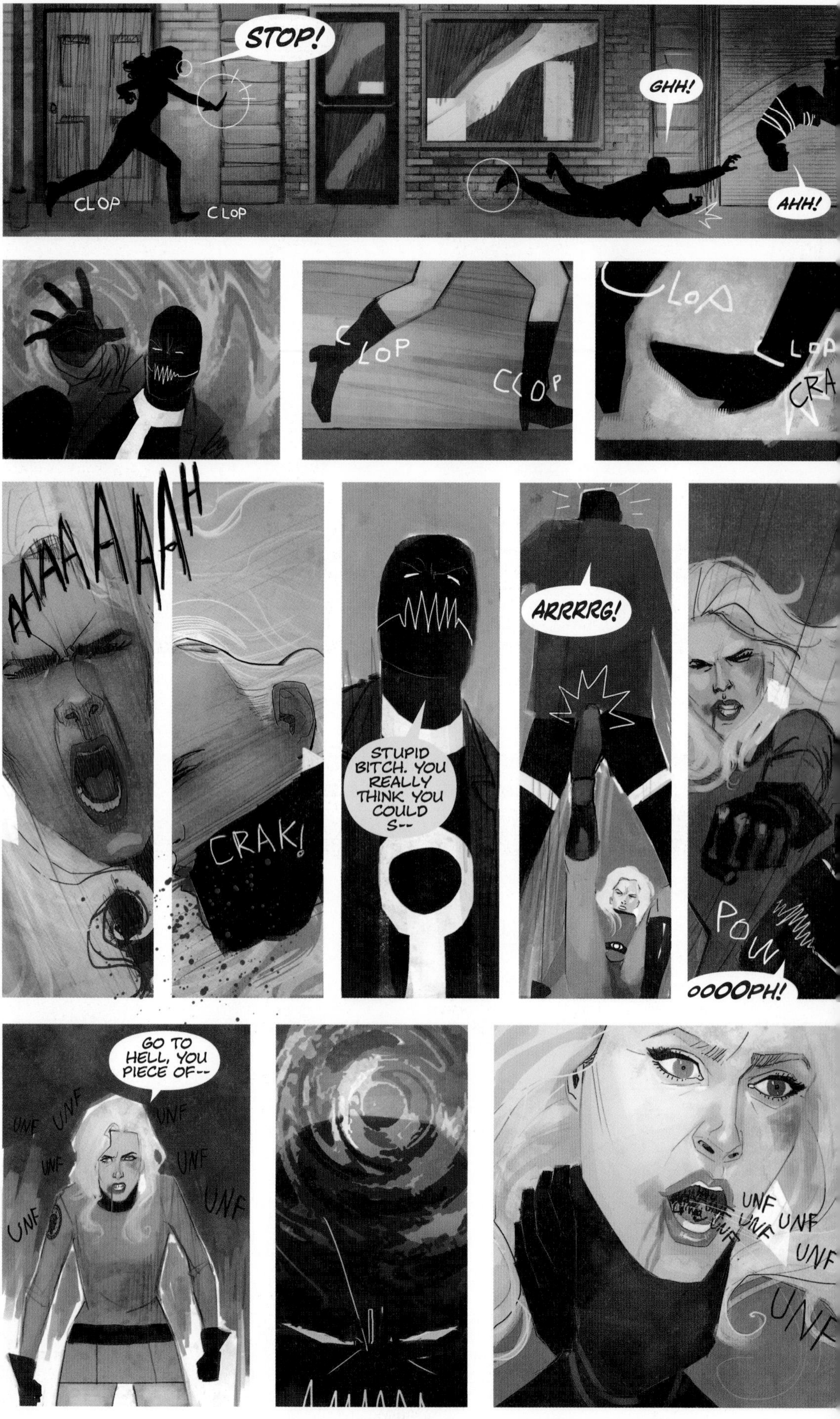
STOP!
CLOP
CLOP
GHH!
AHH!
CLOP
CLOP
CLOP
CLOP
CRA
AAAAAAAAH
CRAK!
STUPID BITCH. YOU REALLY THINK YOU COULD S--
ARRRRG!
POW
OOOOPH!
GO TO HELL, YOU PIECE OF--
UNF
UNF
UNF
UNF
UNF
UNF
UNF
UNF
UNF
UNF
UNF
UNF
UNF

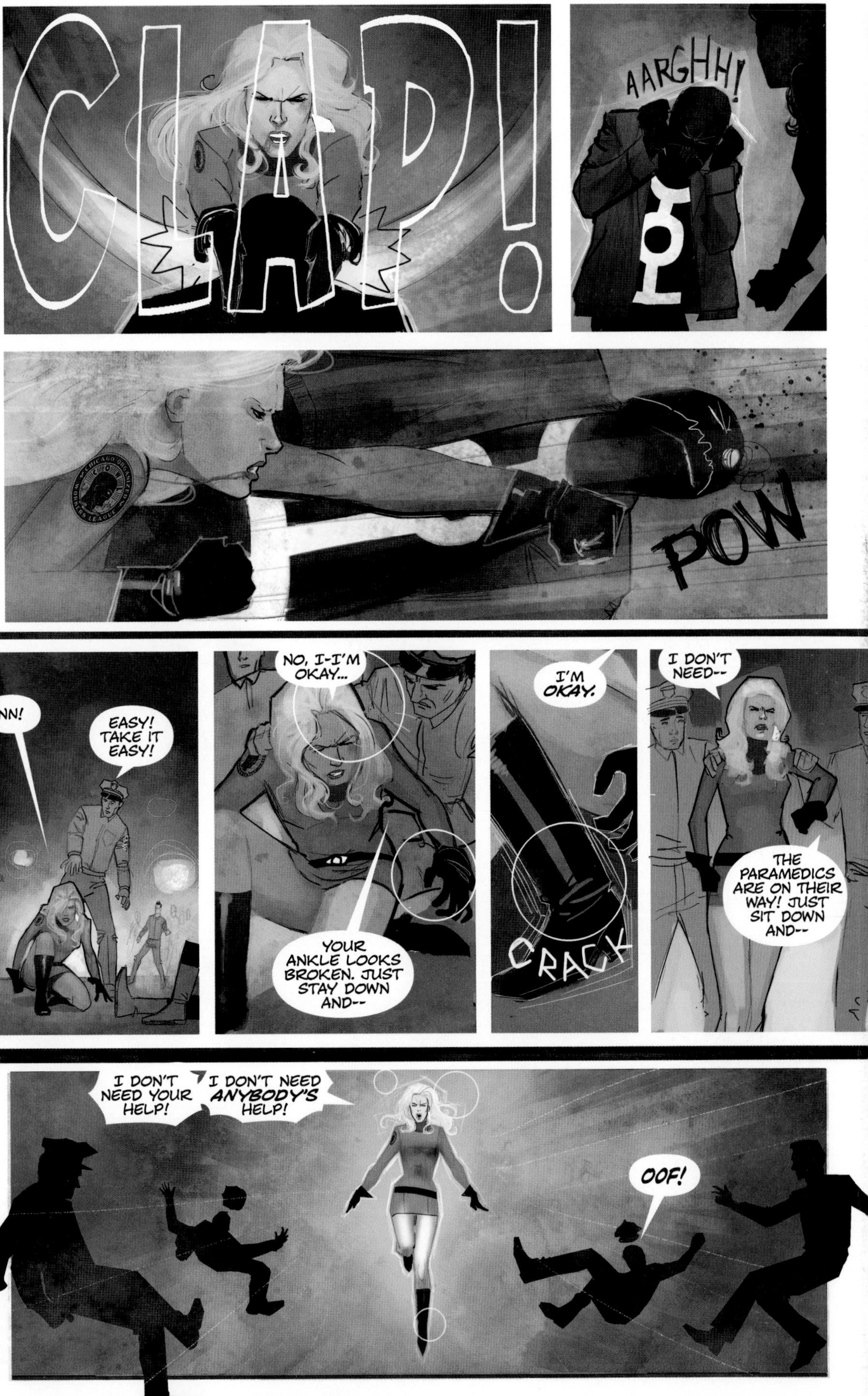
CLAP!
AARGHH!
POW
NN!
EASY! TAKE IT EASY!
NO, I-I'M OKAY...
YOUR ANKLE LOOKS BROKEN. JUST STAY DOWN AND--
I'M OKAY.
CRACK
I DON'T NEED--
THE PARAMEDICS ARE ON THEIR WAY! JUST SIT DOWN AND--
I DON'T NEED YOUR HELP!
I DON'T NEED ANYBODY'S HELP!
OOF!

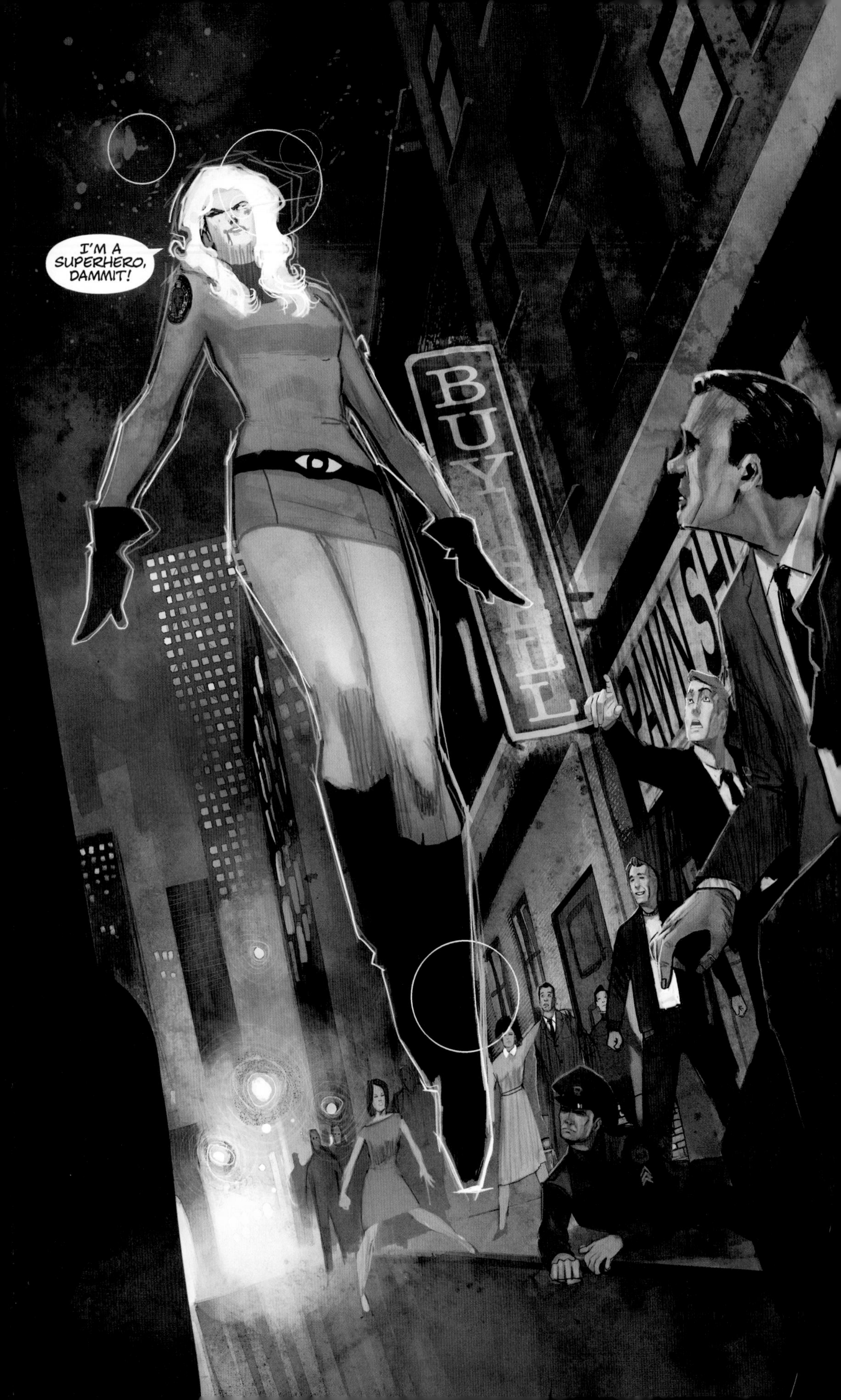
I'M A SUPERHERO, DAMMIT!
BUY

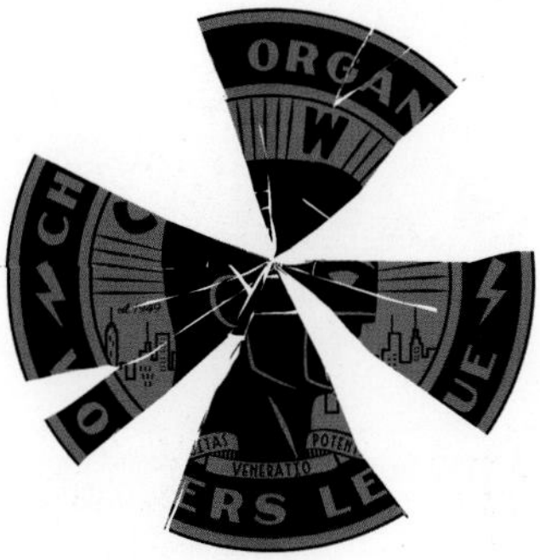
ORGAN
W
CH
UE
ERS LE
VENERATIO

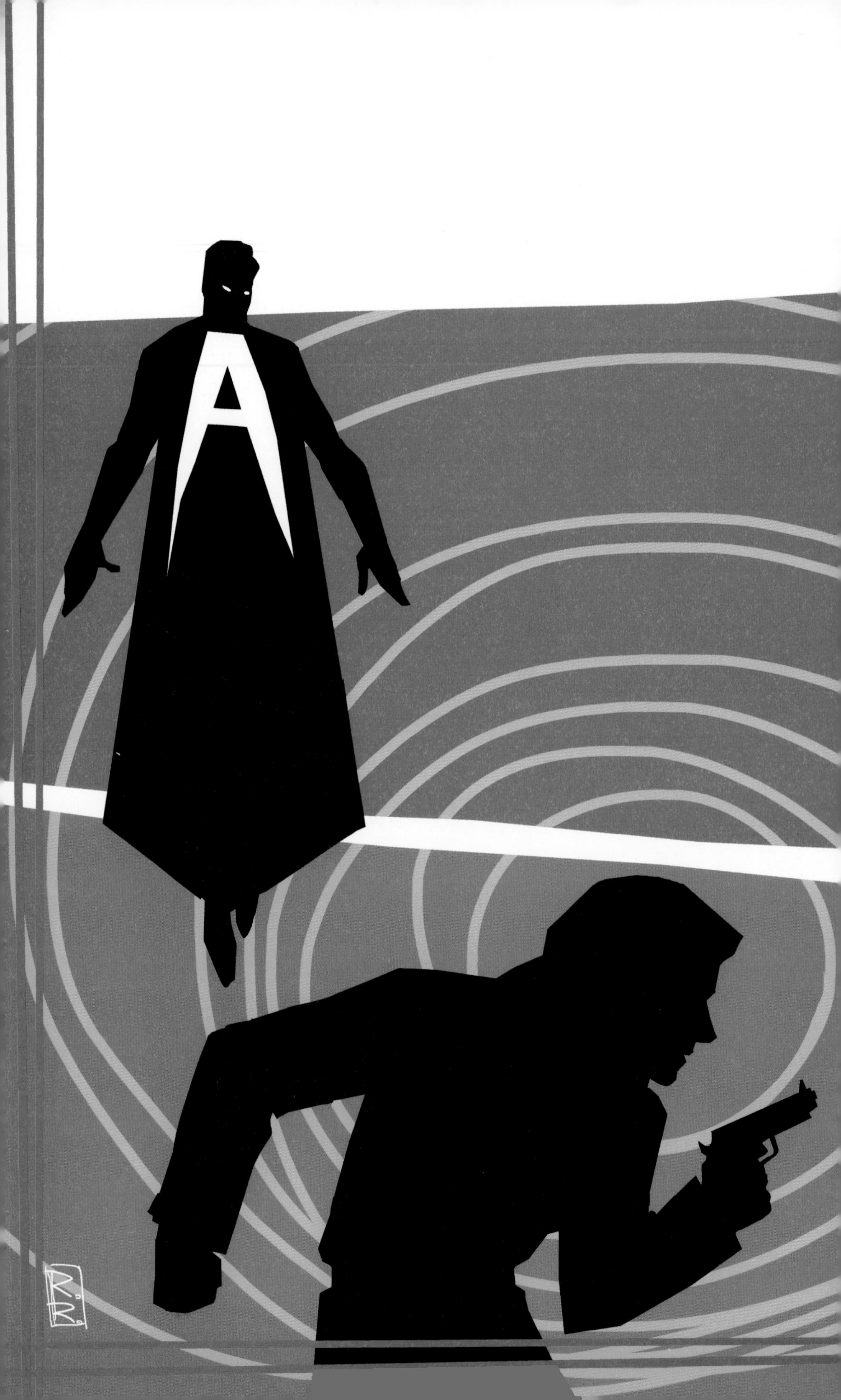

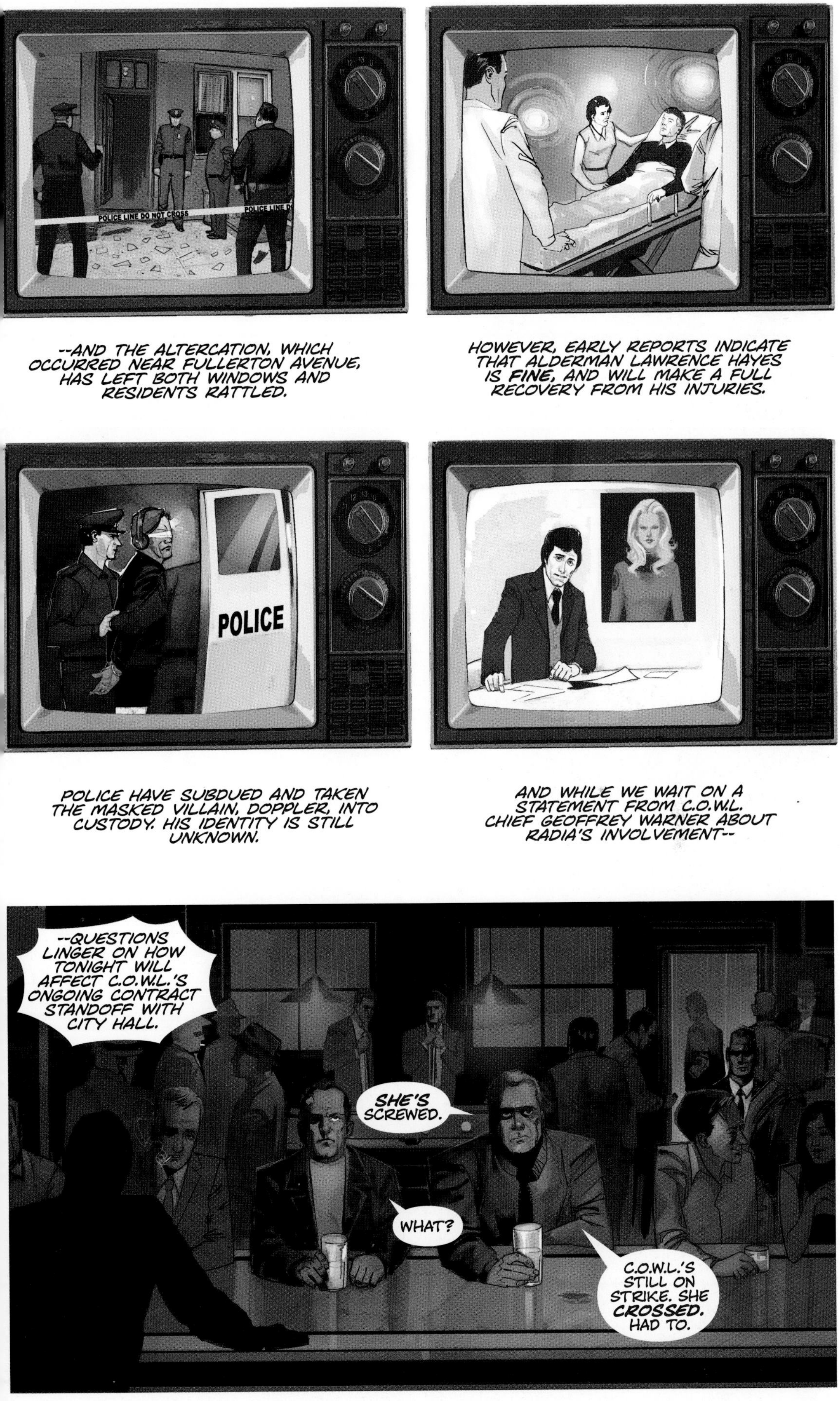
POLICE LINE DO NOT CROSS
--AND THE ALTERCATION, WHICH OCCURRED NEAR FULLERTON AVENUE, HAS LEFT BOTH WINDOWS AND RESIDENTS RATTLED.
HOWEVER, EARLY REPORTS INDICATE THAT ALDERMAN LAWRENCE HAYES IS FINE, AND WILL MAKE A FULL RECOVERY FROM HIS INJURIES.
POLICE
POLICE HAVE SUBDUED AND TAKEN THE MASKED VILLAIN, DOPPLER, INTO CUSTODY. HIS IDENTITY IS STILL UNKNOWN.
AND WHILE WE WAIT ON A STATEMENT FROM C.O.W.L. CHIEF GEOFFREY WARNER ABOUT RADIA'S INVOLVEMENT--
--QUESTIONS LINGER ON HOW TONIGHT WILL AFFECT C.O.W.L.'S ONGOING CONTRACT STANDOFF WITH CITY HALL.
SHE'S SCREWED.
WHAT?
C.O.W.L.'S STILL ON STRIKE. SHE CROSSED. HAD TO.

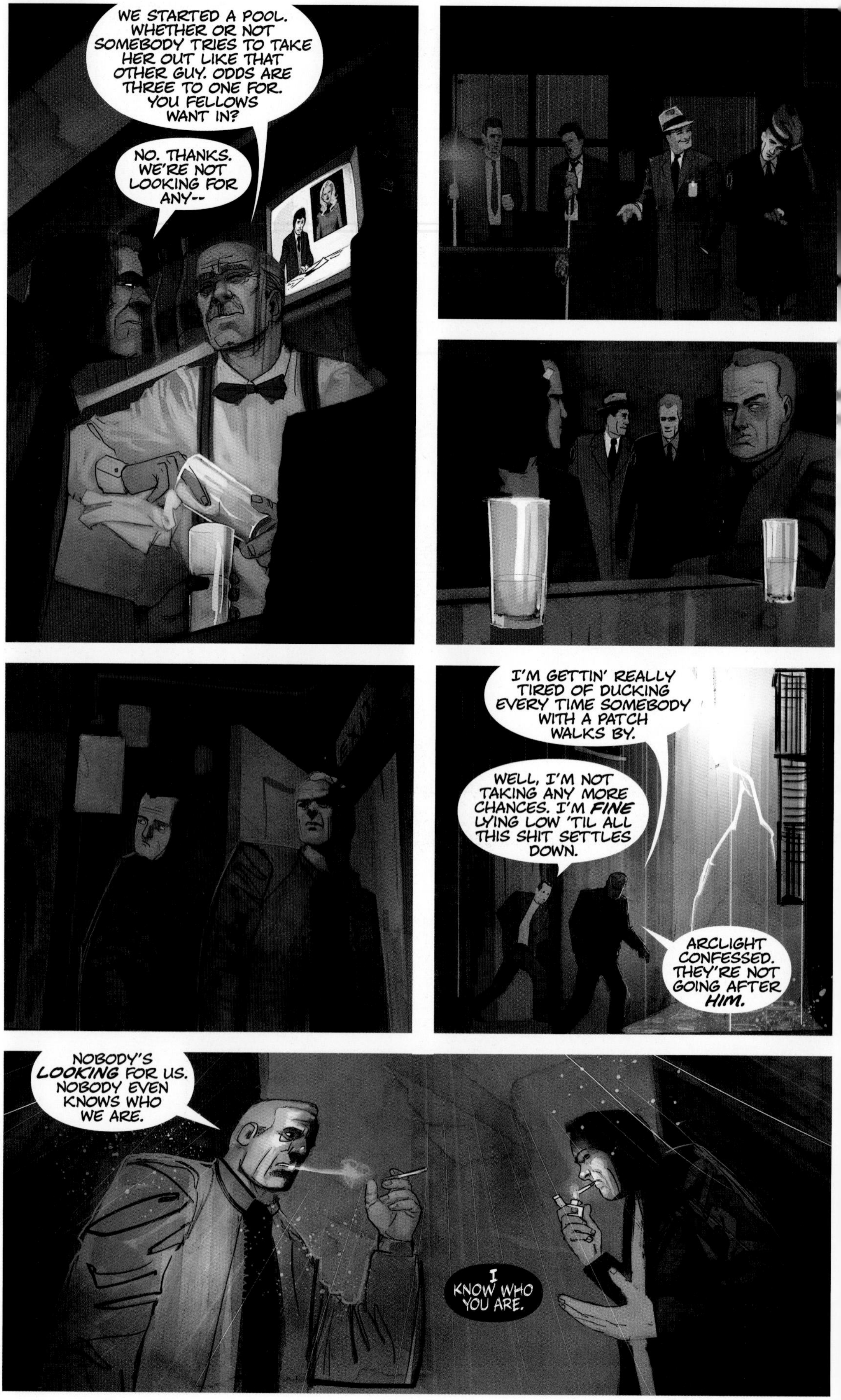
WE STARTED A POOL. WHETHER OR NOT SOMEBODY TRIES TO TAKE HER OUT LIKE THAT OTHER GUY. ODDS ARE THREE TO ONE FOR. YOU FELLOWS WANT IN?
NO. THANKS. WE'RE NOT LOOKING FOR ANY--
I'M GETTIN' REALLY TIRED OF DUCKING EVERY TIME SOMEBODY WITH A PATCH WALKS BY.
WELL, I'M NOT TAKING ANY MORE CHANCES. I'M *FINE* LYING LOW 'TIL ALL THIS SHIT SETTLES DOWN.
ARCLIGHT CONFESSED. THEY'RE NOT GOING AFTER *HIM.*
NOBODY'S *LOOKING* FOR US. NOBODY EVEN KNOWS WHO WE ARE.
I KNOW WHO YOU ARE.

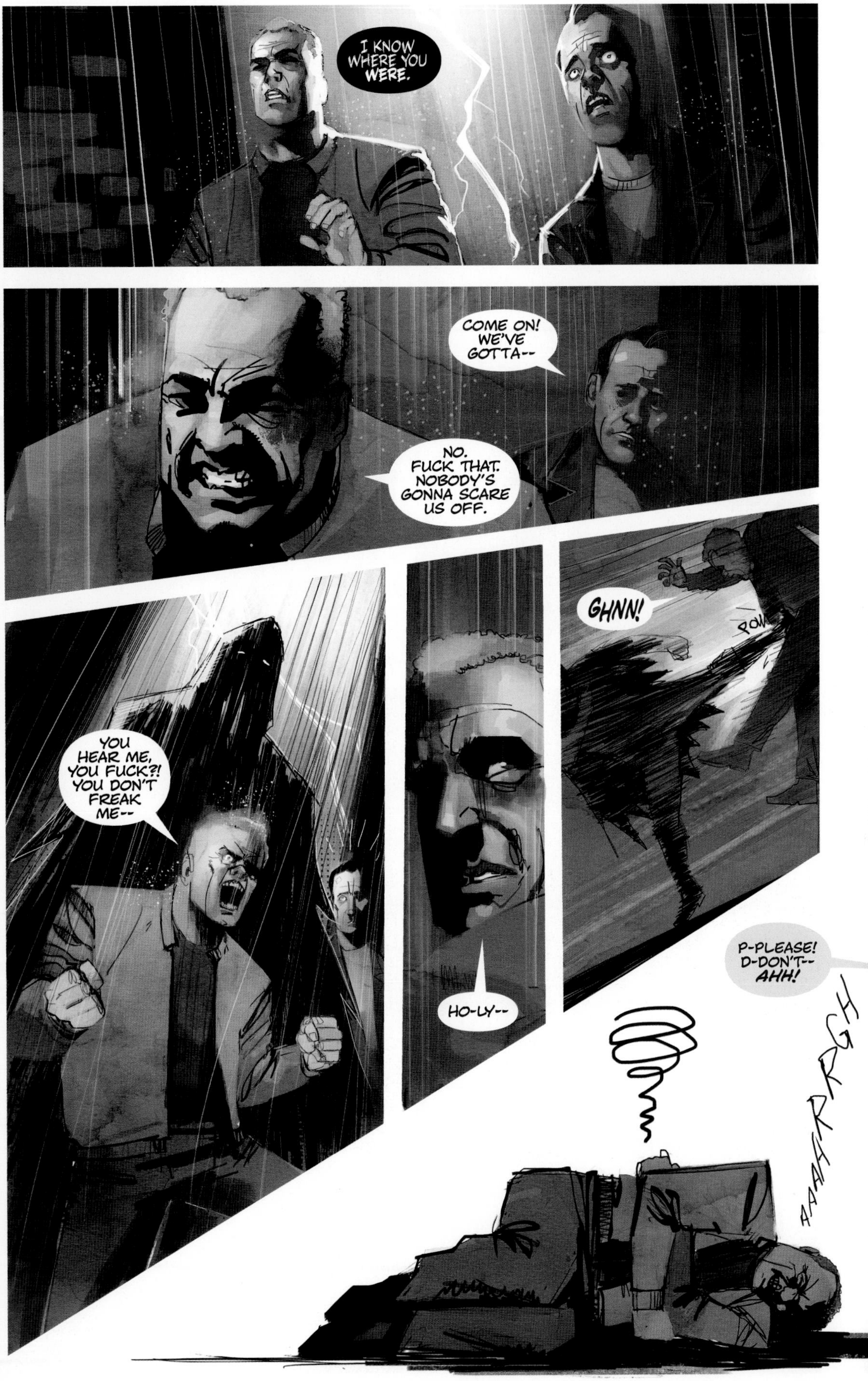
I KNOW WHERE YOU WERE.
COME ON! WE'VE GOTTA--
NO. FUCK THAT. NOBODY'S GONNA SCARE US OFF.
YOU HEAR ME, YOU FUCK?! YOU DON'T FREAK ME--
HO-LY--
GHNN!
POW
P-PLEASE! D-DON'T-- AHH!
AAAHRRGH

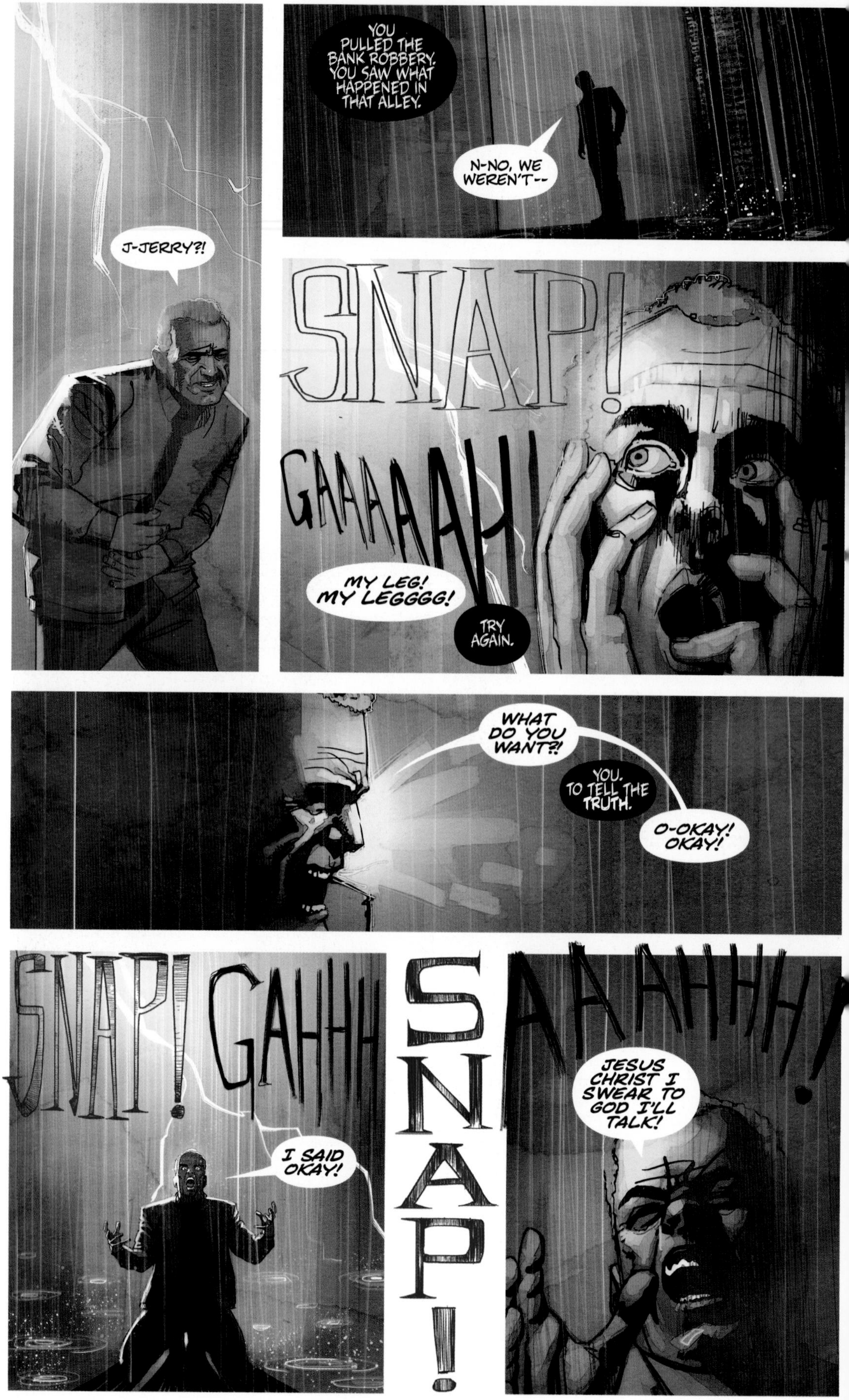
J-JERRY?!
YOU PULLED THE BANK ROBBERY. YOU SAW WHAT HAPPENED IN THAT ALLEY.
N-NO, WE WEREN'T--
SNAP!
GAAAAAH!
MY LEG! MY LEGGGG!
TRY AGAIN.
WHAT DO YOU WANT?!
YOU. TO TELL THE TRUTH.
O-OKAY! OKAY!
SNAP!
GAHHH
I SAID OKAY!
SNAP!
AAAHHH!
JESUS CHRIST I SWEAR TO GOD I'LL TALK!

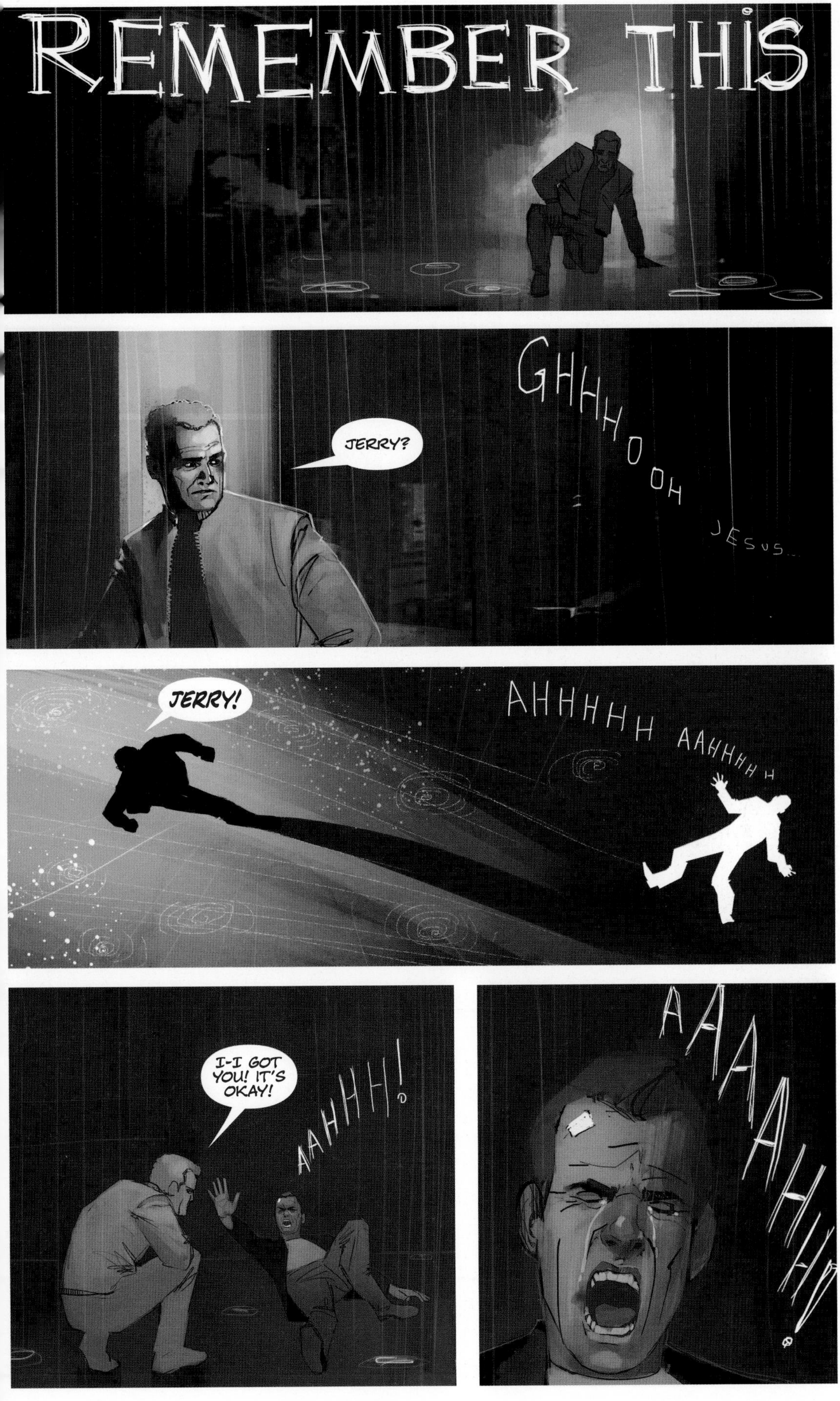
REMEMBER THIS
JERRY?
GHHHOOH
JESUS...
JERRY!
AHHHHH AAHHHHH
I-I GOT YOU! IT'S OKAY!
AAHHH!
AAAAAHHH!

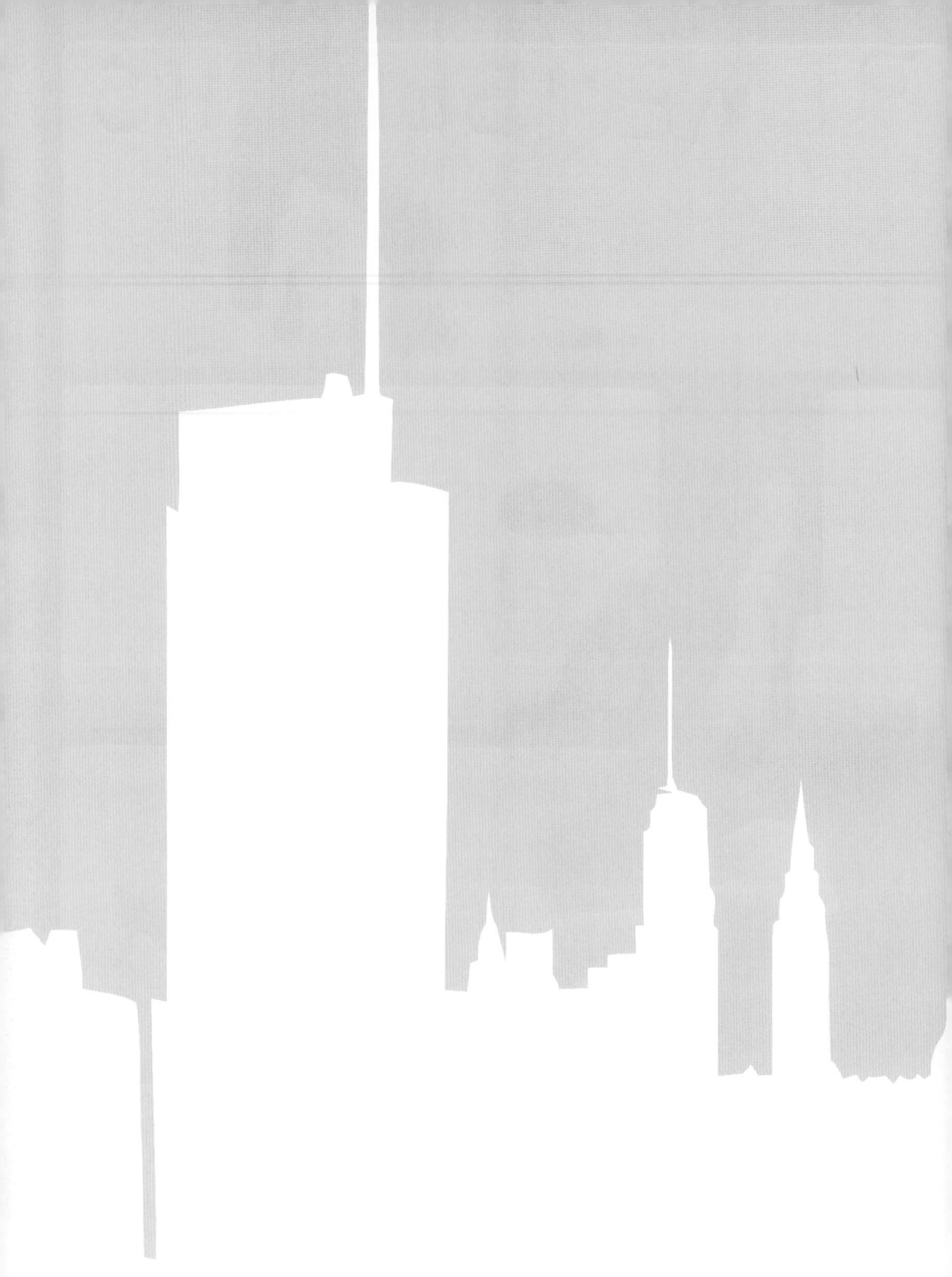

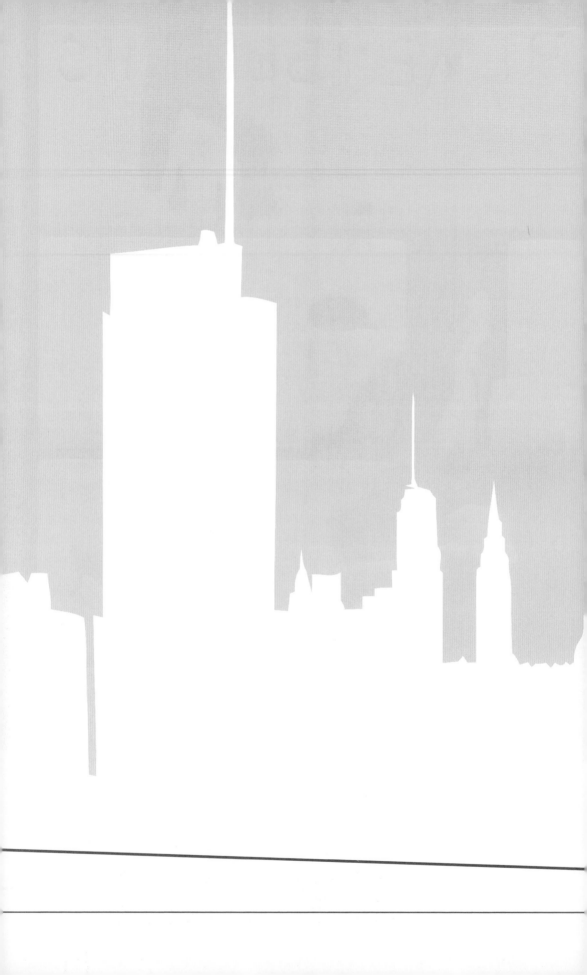

# CHAPTER 4
## Full Disclosure

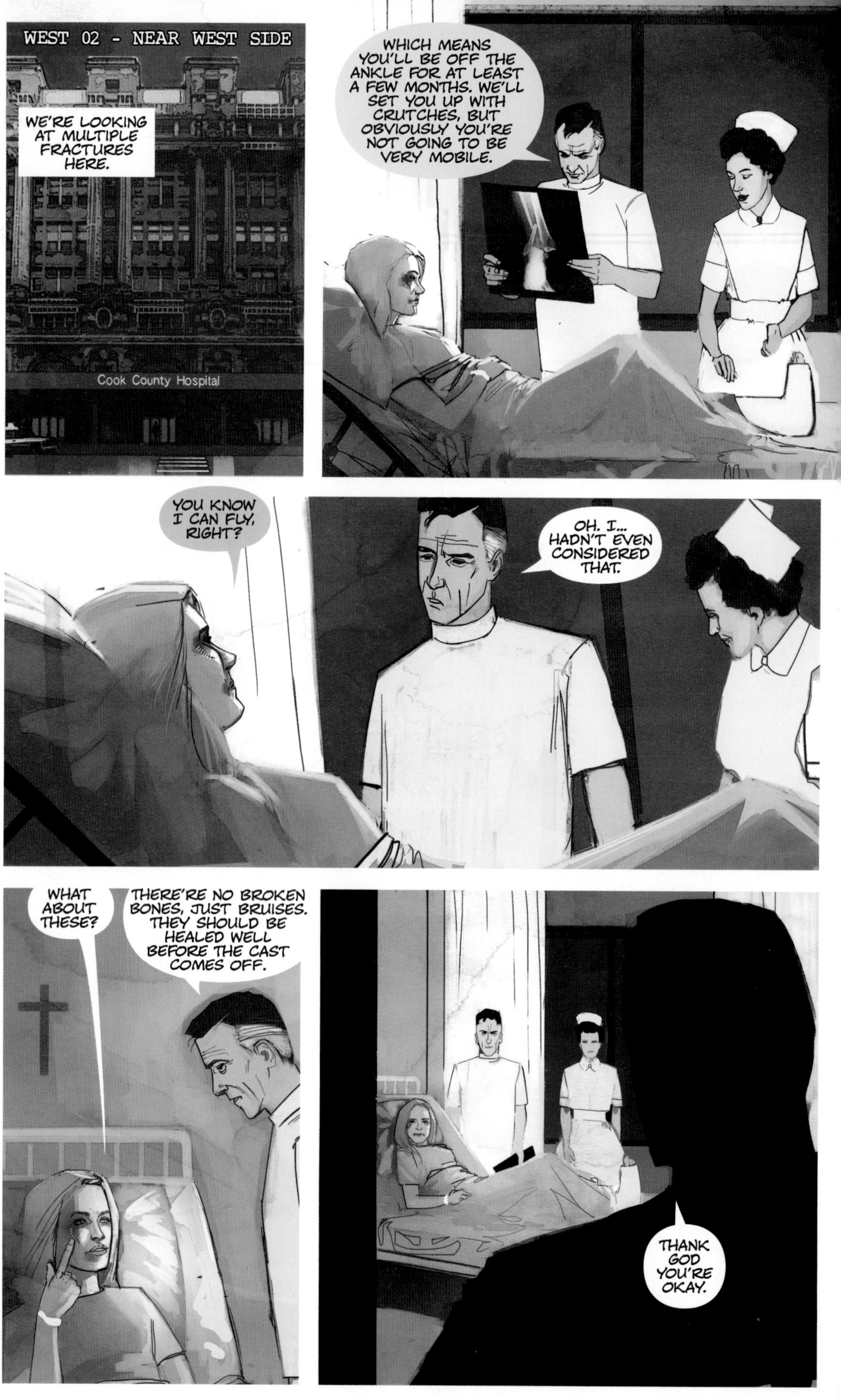
WEST 02 - NEAR WEST SIDE
WE'RE LOOKING AT MULTIPLE FRACTURES HERE.
Cook County Hospital
WHICH MEANS YOU'LL BE OFF THE ANKLE FOR AT LEAST A FEW MONTHS. WE'LL SET YOU UP WITH CRUTCHES, BUT OBVIOUSLY YOU'RE NOT GOING TO BE VERY MOBILE.
YOU KNOW I CAN FLY, RIGHT?
OH. I... HADN'T EVEN CONSIDERED THAT.
WHAT ABOUT THESE?
THERE'RE NO BROKEN BONES, JUST BRUISES. THEY SHOULD BE HEALED WELL BEFORE THE CAST COMES OFF.
THANK GOD YOU'RE OKAY.

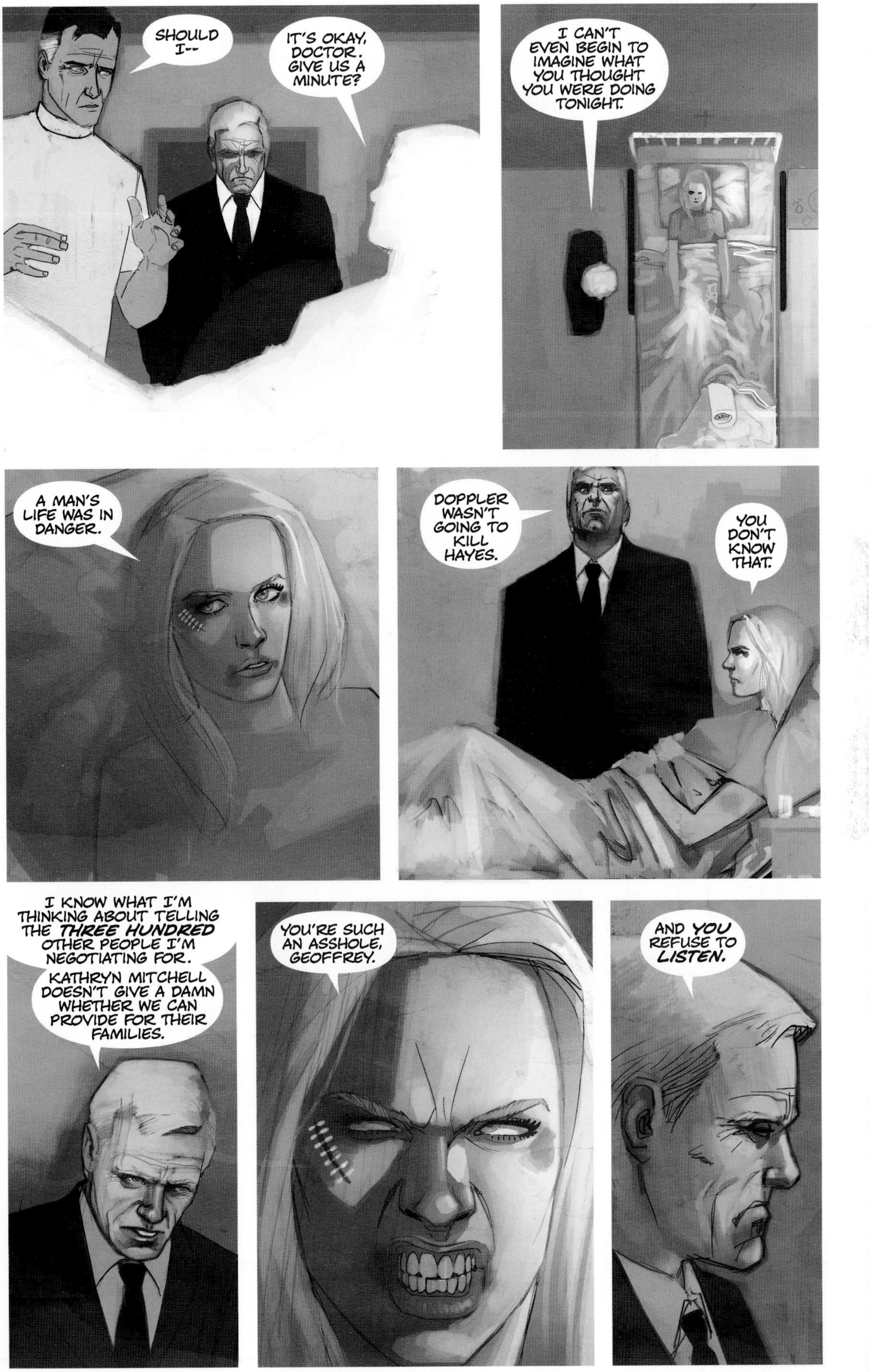
SHOULD I--
IT'S OKAY, DOCTOR. GIVE US A MINUTE?
I CAN'T EVEN BEGIN TO IMAGINE WHAT YOU THOUGHT YOU WERE DOING TONIGHT.
A MAN'S LIFE WAS IN DANGER.
DOPPLER WASN'T GOING TO KILL HAYES.
YOU DON'T KNOW THAT.
I KNOW WHAT I'M THINKING ABOUT TELLING THE THREE HUNDRED OTHER PEOPLE I'M NEGOTIATING FOR.
KATHRYN MITCHELL DOESN'T GIVE A DAMN WHETHER WE CAN PROVIDE FOR THEIR FAMILIES.
YOU'RE SUCH AN ASSHOLE, GEOFFREY.
AND YOU REFUSE TO LISTEN.

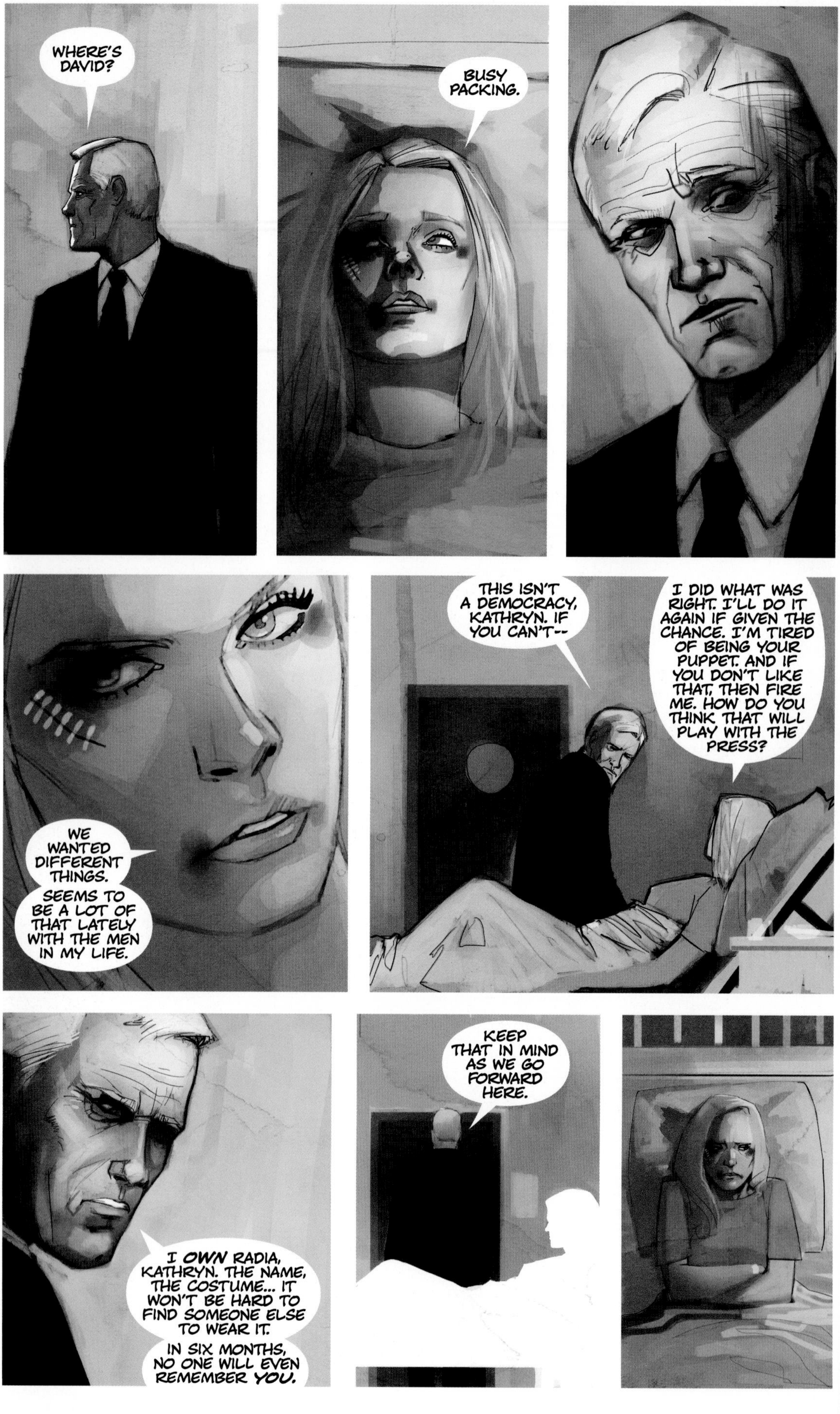
WHERE'S DAVID?
BUSY PACKING.
WE WANTED DIFFERENT THINGS.
SEEMS TO BE A LOT OF THAT LATELY WITH THE MEN IN MY LIFE.
THIS ISN'T A DEMOCRACY, KATHRYN. IF YOU CAN'T--
I DID WHAT WAS RIGHT. I'LL DO IT AGAIN IF GIVEN THE CHANCE. I'M TIRED OF BEING YOUR PUPPET. AND IF YOU DON'T LIKE THAT, THEN FIRE ME. HOW DO YOU THINK THAT WILL PLAY WITH THE PRESS?
I OWN RADIA, KATHRYN. THE NAME, THE COSTUME... IT WON'T BE HARD TO FIND SOMEONE ELSE TO WEAR IT.
IN SIX MONTHS, NO ONE WILL EVEN REMEMBER YOU.
KEEP THAT IN MIND AS WE GO FORWARD HERE.

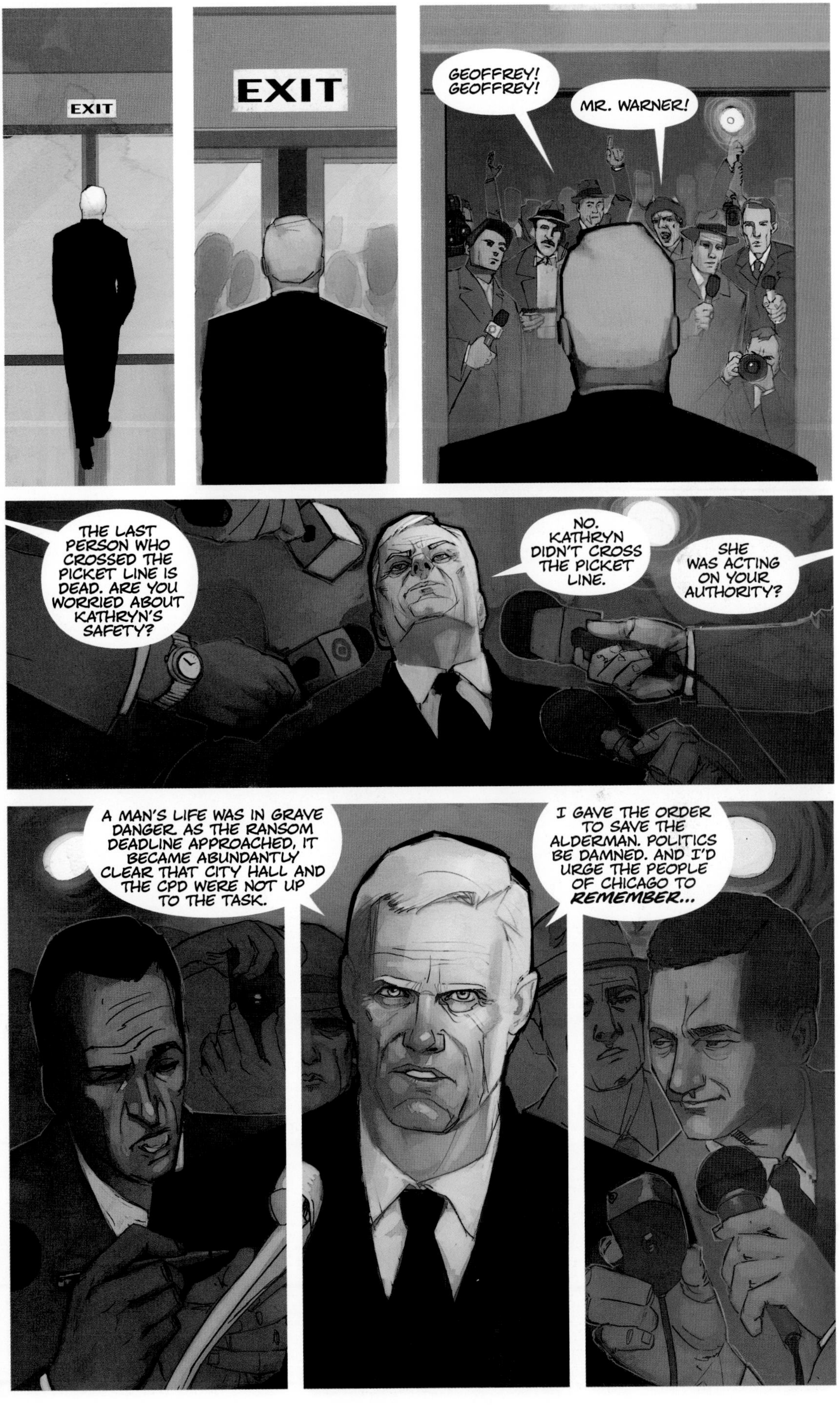
EXIT
EXIT
GEOFFREY! GEOFFREY!
MR. WARNER!
THE LAST PERSON WHO CROSSED THE PICKET LINE IS DEAD. ARE YOU WORRIED ABOUT KATHRYN'S SAFETY?
NO. KATHRYN DIDN'T CROSS THE PICKET LINE.
SHE WAS ACTING ON YOUR AUTHORITY?
A MAN'S LIFE WAS IN GRAVE DANGER AS THE RANSOM DEADLINE APPROACHED, IT BECAME ABUNDANTLY CLEAR THAT CITY HALL AND THE CPD WERE NOT UP TO THE TASK.
I GAVE THE ORDER TO SAVE THE ALDERMAN. POLITICS BE DAMNED. AND I'D URGE THE PEOPLE OF CHICAGO TO *REMEMBER...*

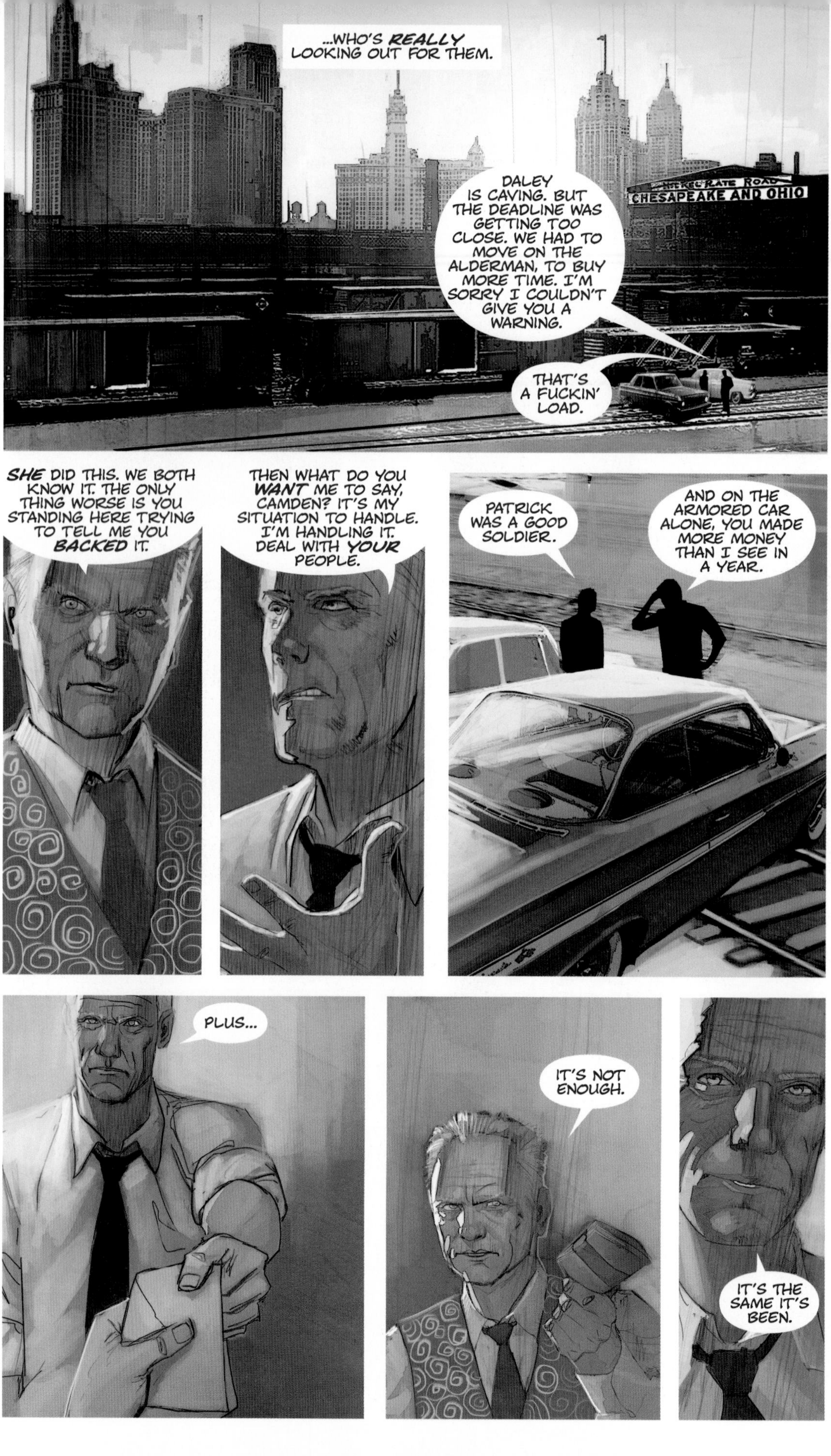
...WHO'S REALLY LOOKING OUT FOR THEM.
NICKEL PLATE ROAD
CHESAPEAKE AND OHIO
DALEY IS CAVING. BUT THE DEADLINE WAS GETTING TOO CLOSE. WE HAD TO MOVE ON THE ALDERMAN, TO BUY MORE TIME. I'M SORRY I COULDN'T GIVE YOU A WARNING.
THAT'S A FUCKIN' LOAD.
SHE DID THIS. WE BOTH KNOW IT. THE ONLY THING WORSE IS YOU STANDING HERE TRYING TO TELL ME YOU BACKED IT.
THEN WHAT DO YOU WANT ME TO SAY, CAMDEN? IT'S MY SITUATION TO HANDLE. I'M HANDLING IT. DEAL WITH YOUR PEOPLE.
PATRICK WAS A GOOD SOLDIER.
AND ON THE ARMORED CAR ALONE, YOU MADE MORE MONEY THAN I SEE IN A YEAR.
PLUS...
IT'S NOT ENOUGH.
IT'S THE SAME IT'S BEEN.

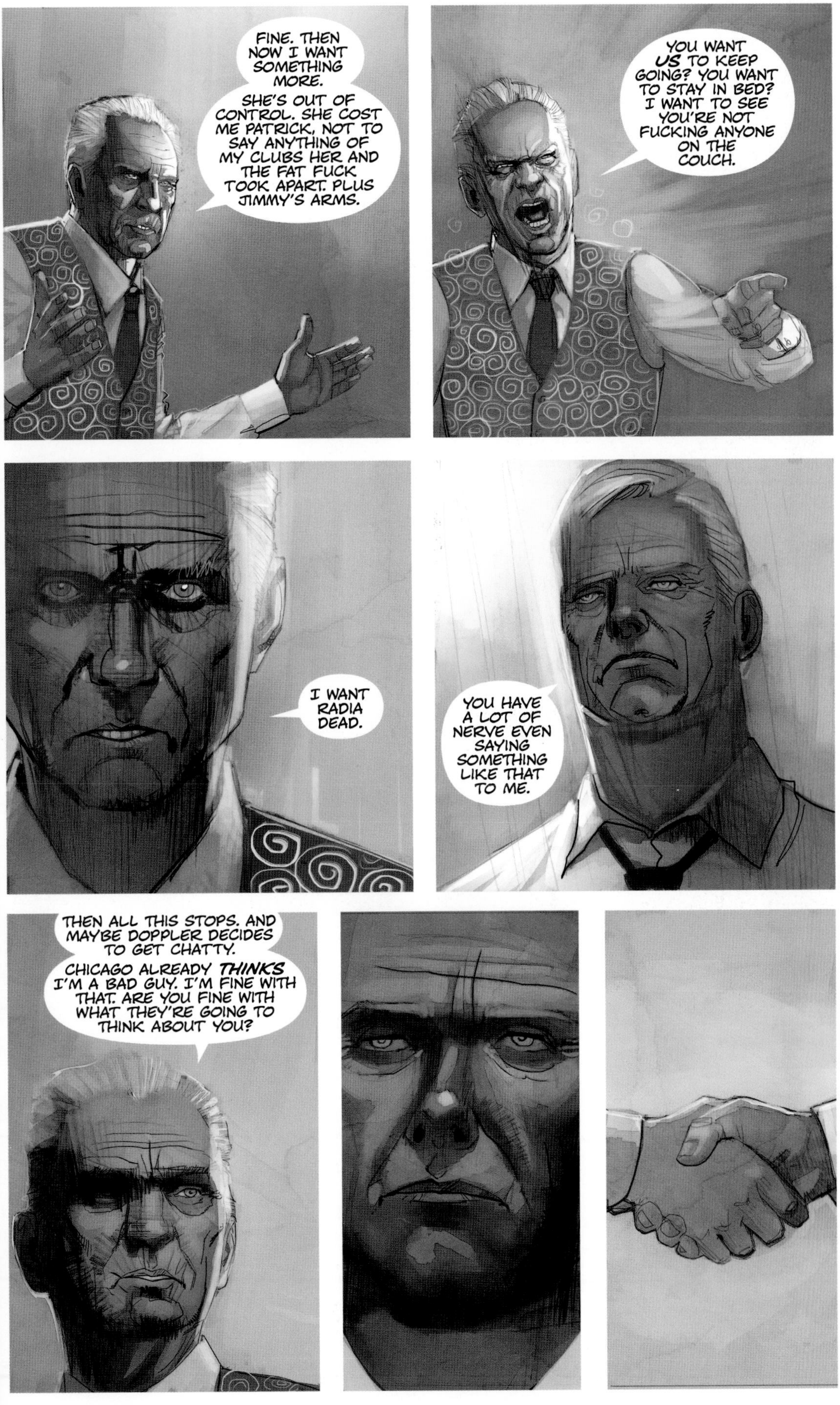
FINE. THEN NOW I WANT SOMETHING MORE.
SHE'S OUT OF CONTROL. SHE COST ME PATRICK, NOT TO SAY ANYTHING OF MY CLUBS HER AND THE FAT FUCK TOOK APART. PLUS JIMMY'S ARMS.
YOU WANT US TO KEEP GOING? YOU WANT TO STAY IN BED? I WANT TO SEE YOU'RE NOT FUCKING ANYONE ON THE COUCH.
I WANT RADIA DEAD.
YOU HAVE A LOT OF NERVE EVEN SAYING SOMETHING LIKE THAT TO ME.
THEN ALL THIS STOPS. AND MAYBE DOPPLER DECIDES TO GET CHATTY.
CHICAGO ALREADY THINKS I'M A BAD GUY. I'M FINE WITH THAT. ARE YOU FINE WITH WHAT THEY'RE GOING TO THINK ABOUT YOU?

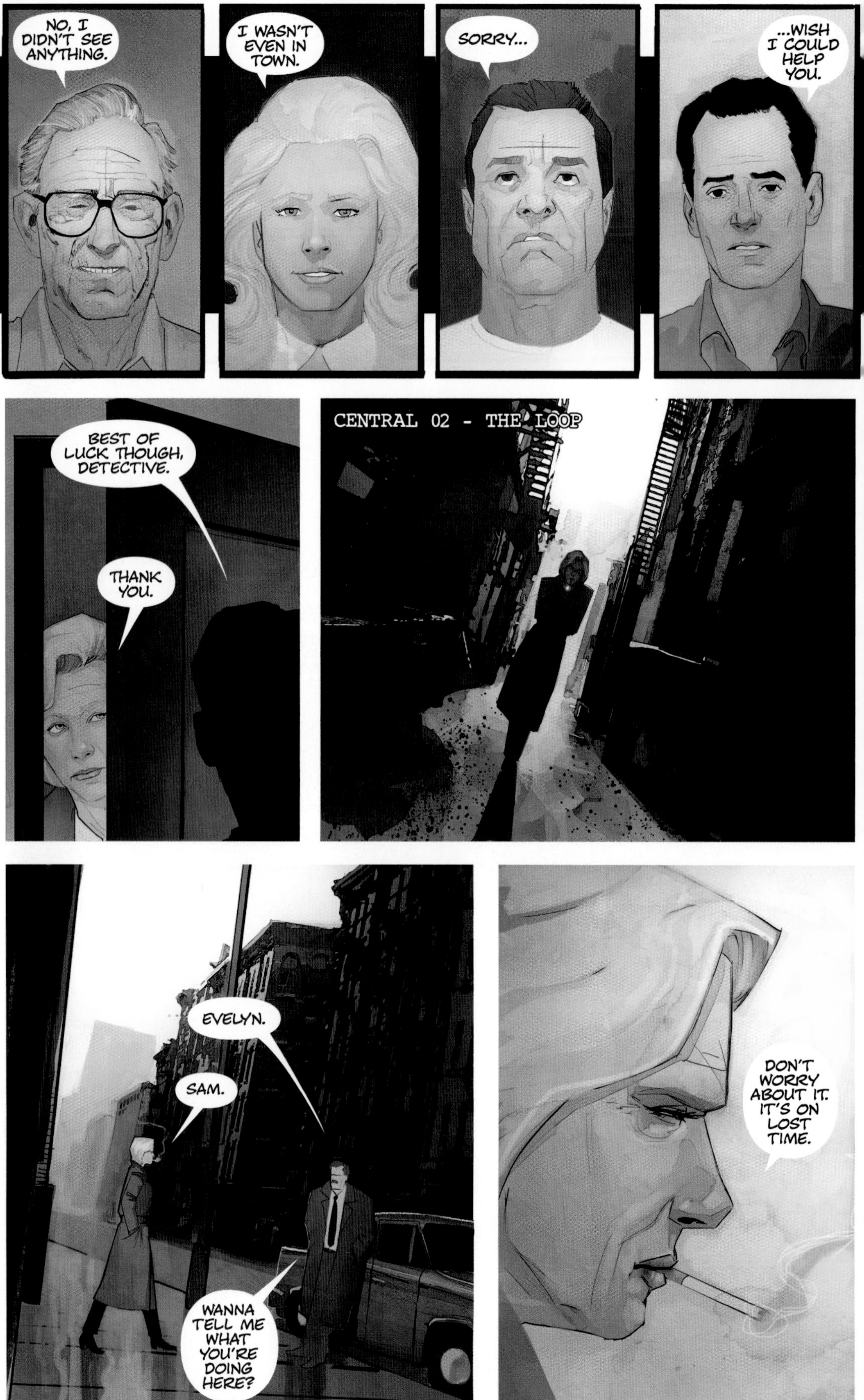
NO, I DIDN'T SEE ANYTHING.
I WASN'T EVEN IN TOWN.
SORRY...
...WISH I COULD HELP YOU.
BEST OF LUCK THOUGH, DETECTIVE.
THANK YOU.
CENTRAL 02 - THE LOOP
EVELYN.
SAM.
WANNA TELL ME WHAT YOU'RE DOING HERE?
DON'T WORRY ABOUT IT. IT'S ON LOST TIME.

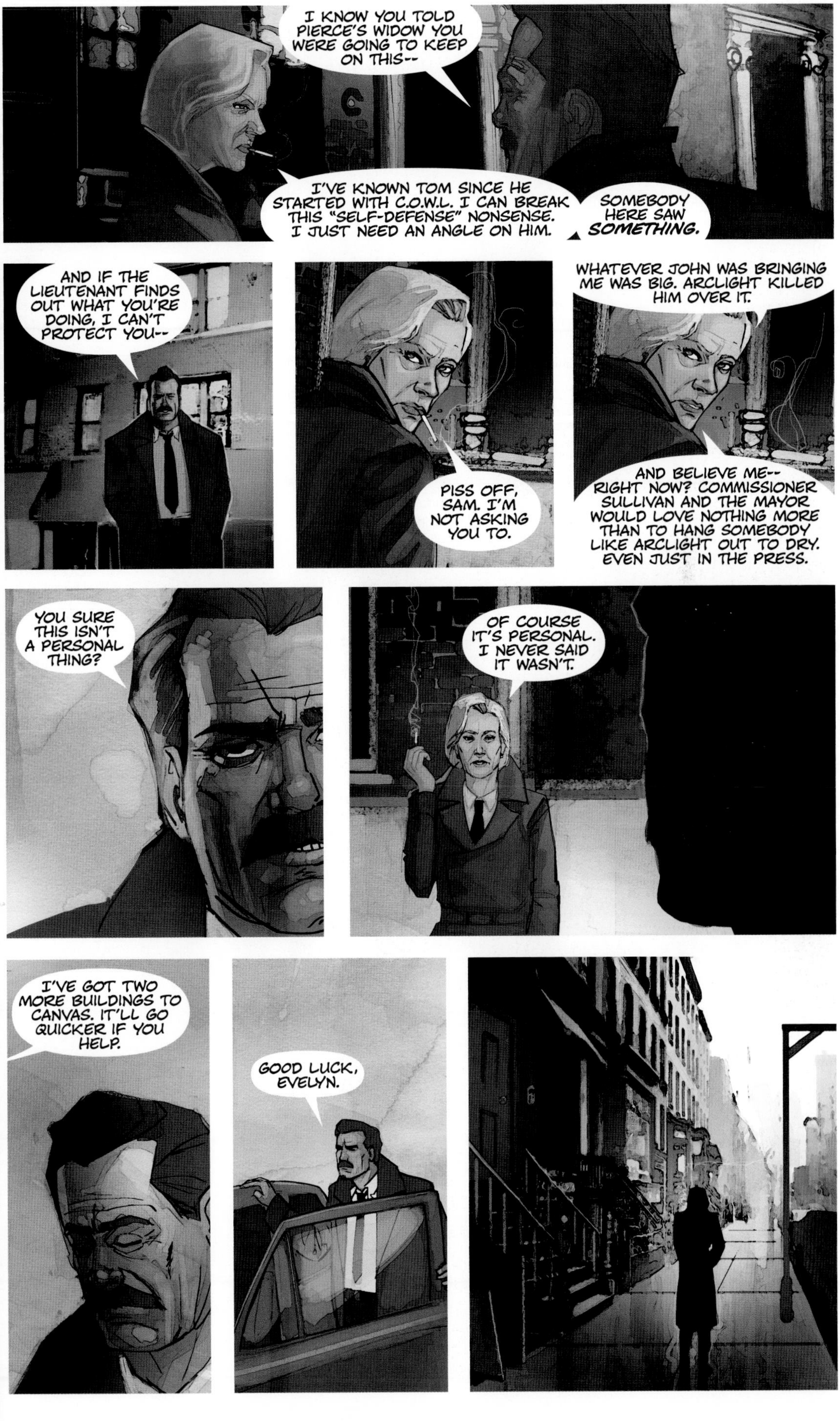
I KNOW YOU TOLD PIERCE'S WIDOW YOU WERE GOING TO KEEP ON THIS--
I'VE KNOWN TOM SINCE HE STARTED WITH C.O.W.L. I CAN BREAK THIS "SELF-DEFENSE" NONSENSE. I JUST NEED AN ANGLE ON HIM.
SOMEBODY HERE SAW *SOMETHING.*
AND IF THE LIEUTENANT FINDS OUT WHAT YOU'RE DOING, I CAN'T PROTECT YOU--
PISS OFF, SAM. I'M NOT ASKING YOU TO.
WHATEVER JOHN WAS BRINGING ME WAS BIG. ARCLIGHT KILLED HIM OVER IT.
AND BELIEVE ME--RIGHT NOW? COMMISSIONER SULLIVAN AND THE MAYOR WOULD LOVE NOTHING MORE THAN TO HANG SOMEBODY LIKE ARCLIGHT OUT TO DRY. EVEN JUST IN THE PRESS.
YOU SURE THIS ISN'T A PERSONAL THING?
OF COURSE IT'S PERSONAL. I NEVER SAID IT WASN'T.
I'VE GOT TWO MORE BUILDINGS TO CANVAS. IT'LL GO QUICKER IF YOU HELP.
GOOD LUCK, EVELYN.

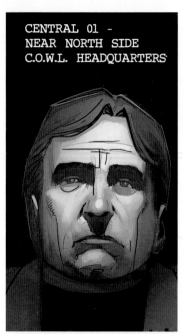

CENTRAL 01 -
NEAR NORTH SIDE
C.O.W.L. HEADQUARTERS

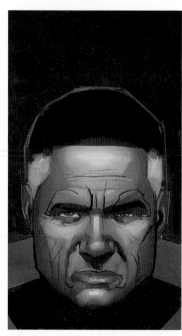

I DON'T KNOW ANYTHING.

SURE YOU DO, KARL. YOU KNOW WHAT I KNOW. YOU WERE AT THE PICKET LINE. YOU WERE WITH THE GROUP WHEN THE RIOT STARTED. YOU SAW FRANK FIRE OFF A BLAST THAT TORE APART CITY HALL.

WOW. THAT... SOUNDS REALLY SPECIFIC. LIKE SOMETHING I'D *REMEMBER* SEEING.

HM. I GUESS YOU'RE RIGHT. BUT, YOU KNOW HOW MEMORY IS. PLUS, YOU WERE PROBABLY PRETTY TIRED AFTER THE DAY YOU HAD WITH KATHRYN.

TEARING THROUGH CAMDEN STONE'S CASINO.

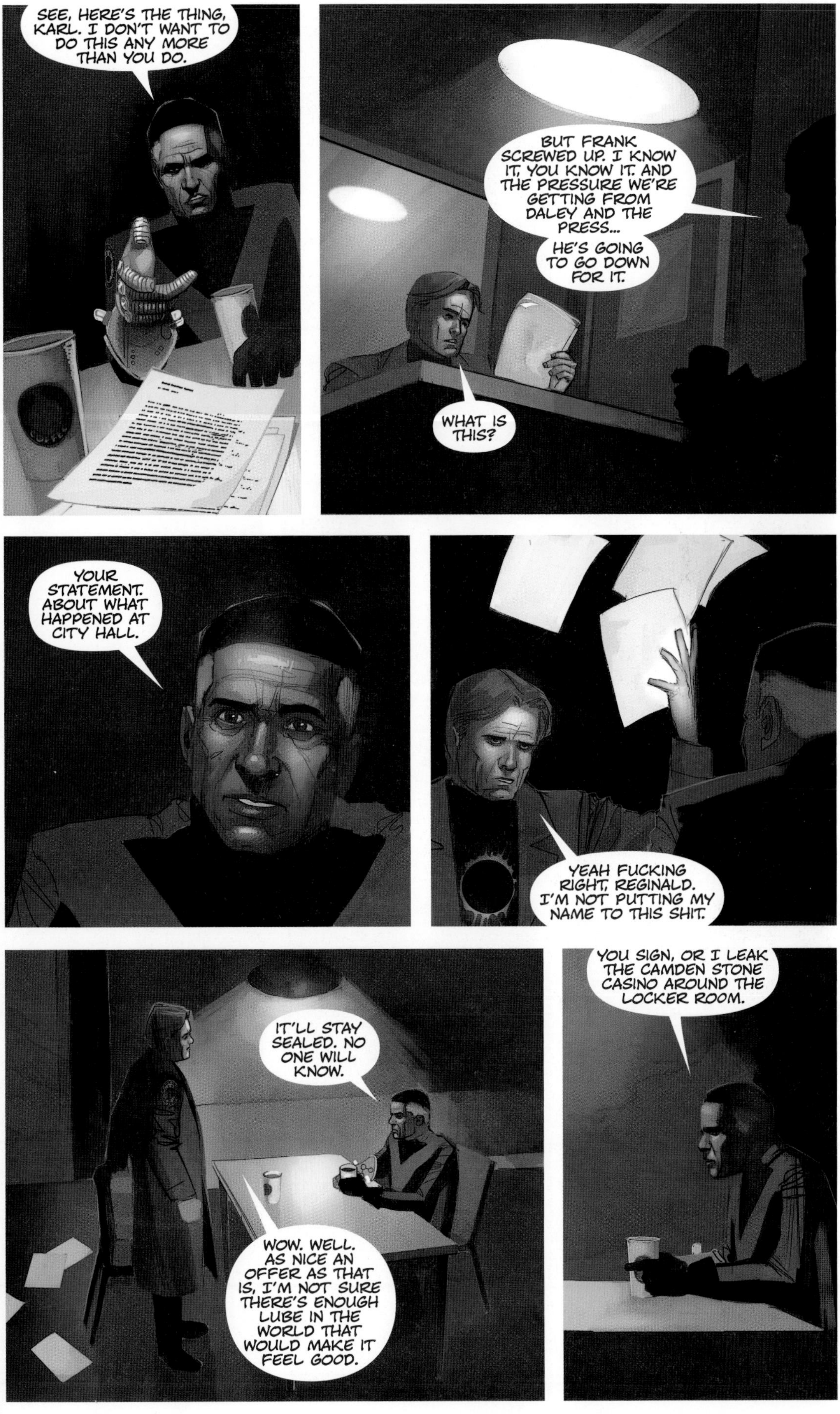

SEE, HERE'S THE THING, KARL. I DON'T WANT TO DO THIS ANY MORE THAN YOU DO.
BUT FRANK SCREWED UP. I KNOW IT, YOU KNOW IT. AND THE PRESSURE WE'RE GETTING FROM DALEY AND THE PRESS...
HE'S GOING TO GO DOWN FOR IT.
WHAT IS THIS?
YOUR STATEMENT. ABOUT WHAT HAPPENED AT CITY HALL.
YEAH FUCKING RIGHT, REGINALD. I'M NOT PUTTING MY NAME TO THIS SHIT.
IT'LL STAY SEALED. NO ONE WILL KNOW.
WOW. WELL. AS NICE AN OFFER AS THAT IS, I'M NOT SURE THERE'S ENOUGH LUBE IN THE WORLD THAT WOULD MAKE IT FEEL GOOD.
YOU SIGN, OR I LEAK THE CAMDEN STONE CASINO AROUND THE LOCKER ROOM.

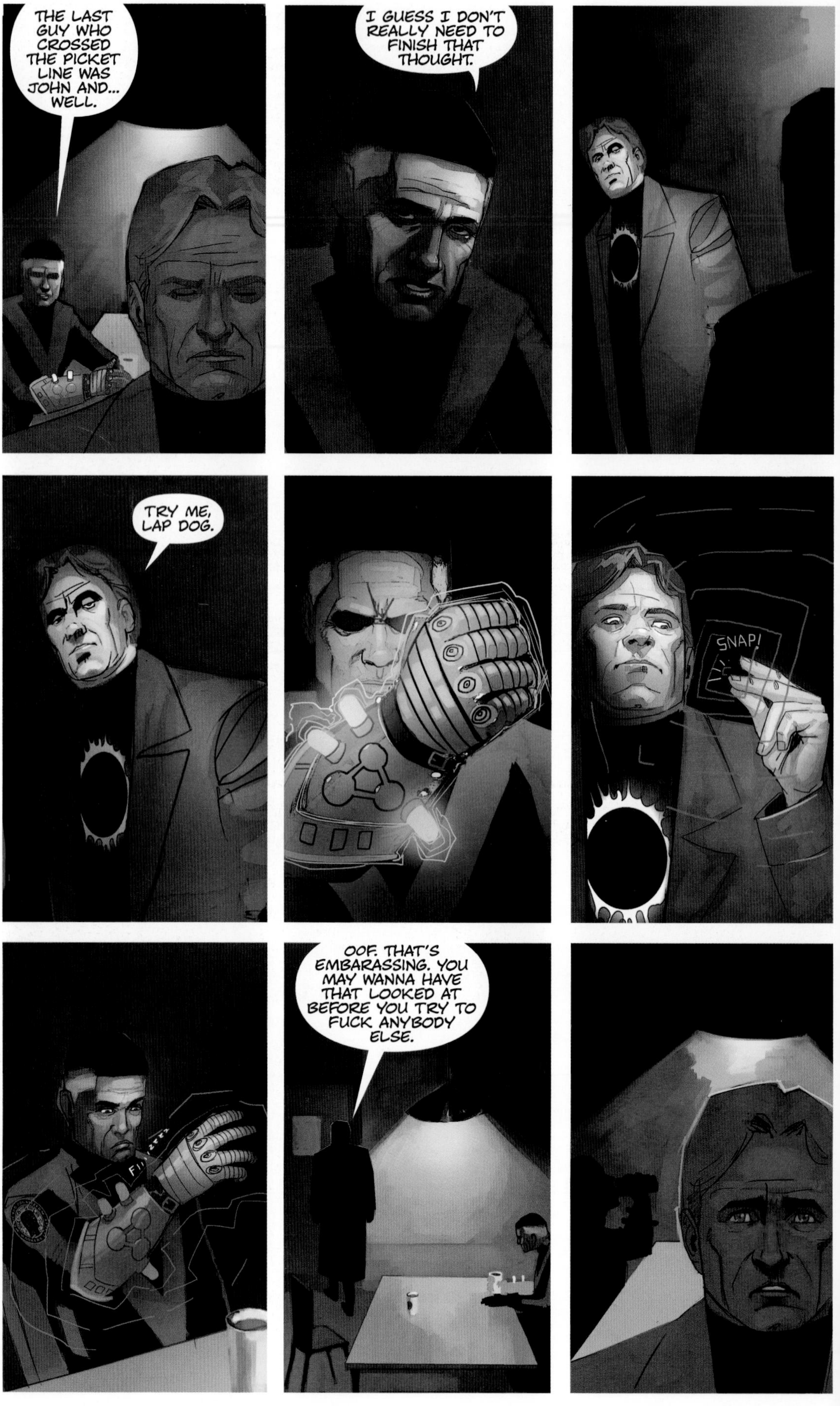
THE LAST GUY WHO CROSSED THE PICKET LINE WAS JOHN AND... WELL.
I GUESS I DON'T REALLY NEED TO FINISH THAT THOUGHT.
TRY ME, LAP DOG.
SNAP!
OOF. THAT'S EMBARASSING. YOU MAY WANNA HAVE THAT LOOKED AT BEFORE YOU TRY TO FUCK ANYBODY ELSE.

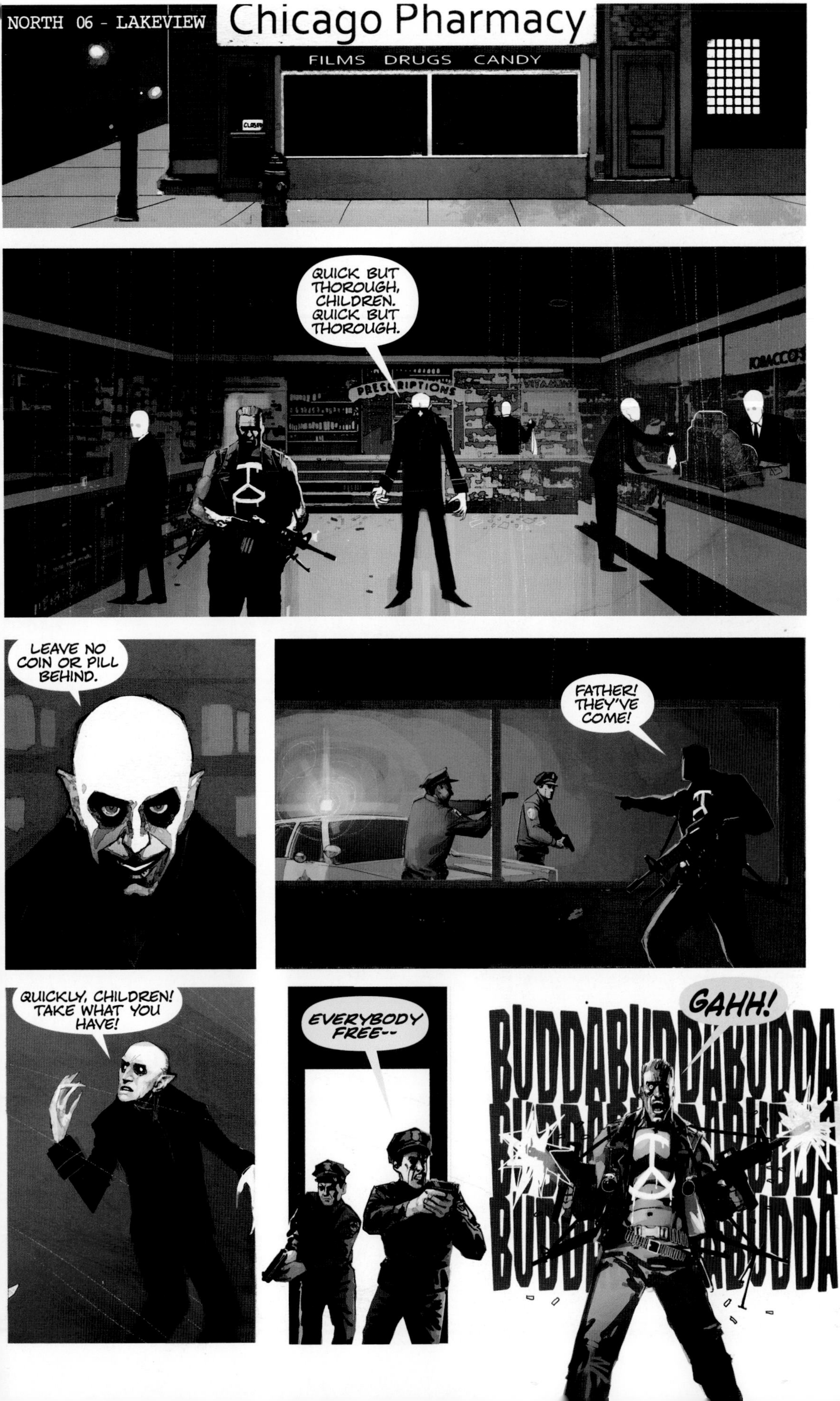
NORTH 06 - LAKEVIEW
Chicago Pharmacy
FILMS DRUGS CANDY
QUICK BUT THOROUGH, CHILDREN. QUICK BUT THOROUGH.
PRESCRIPTIONS
LEAVE NO COIN OR PILL BEHIND.
FATHER! THEY'VE COME!
QUICKLY, CHILDREN! TAKE WHAT YOU HAVE!
EVERYBODY FREE--
GAHH!
BUDDABUDDABUDDA

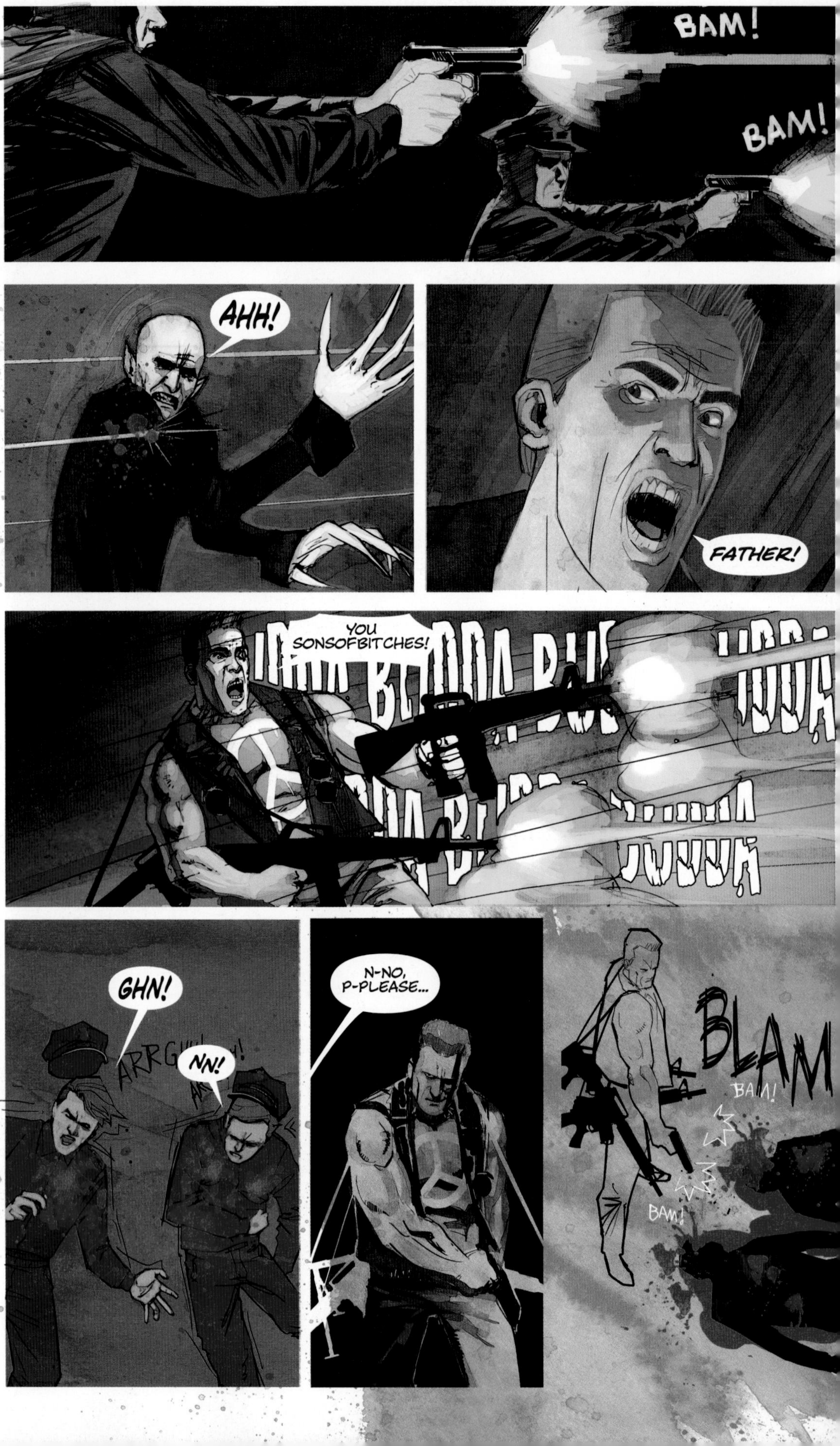
BAM!
BAM!
AHH!
FATHER!
YOU SONSOFBITCHES!
GHN!
NN!
N-NO, P-PLEASE...
BLAM
BAM!
BAM!

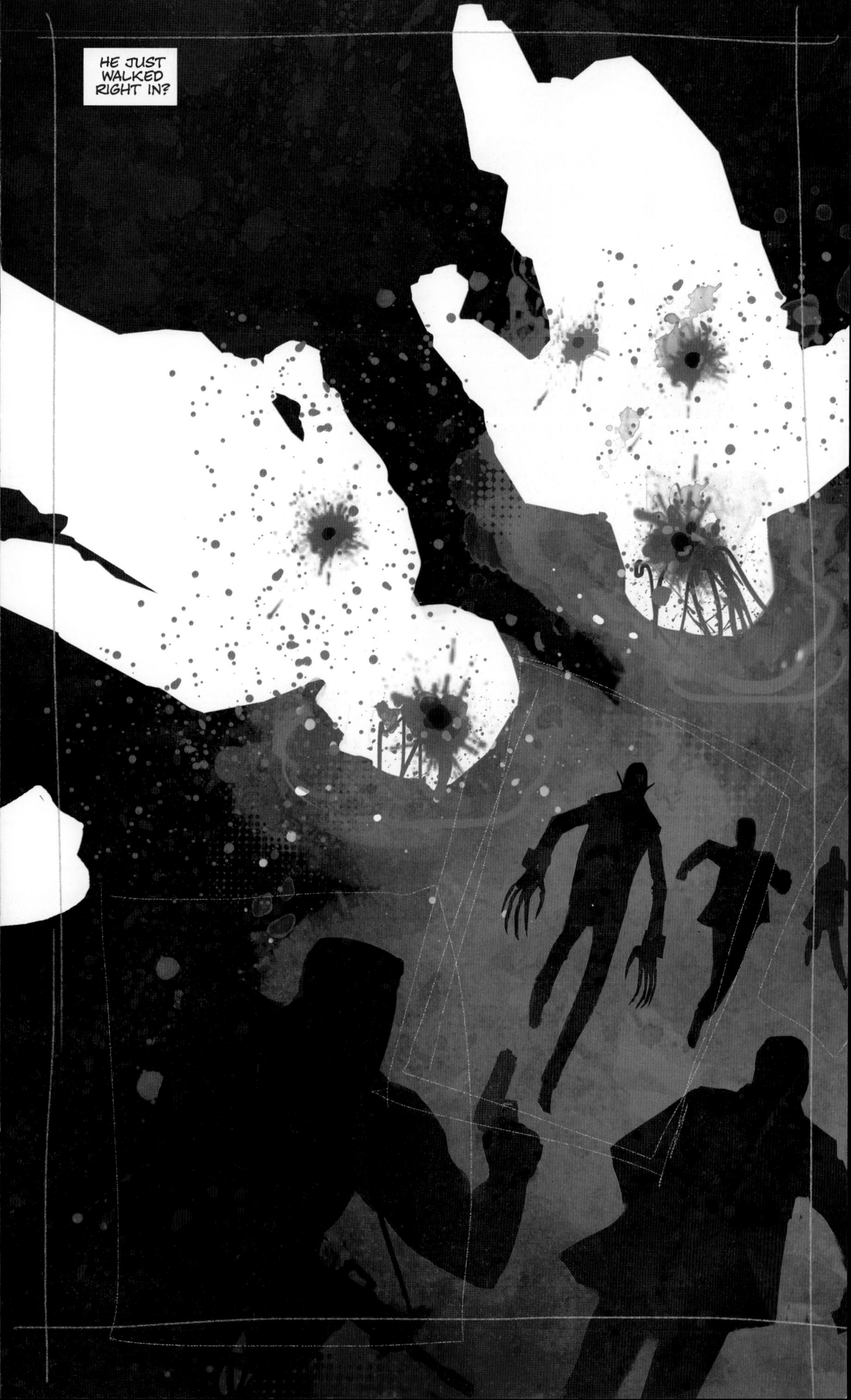
HE JUST WALKED RIGHT IN?

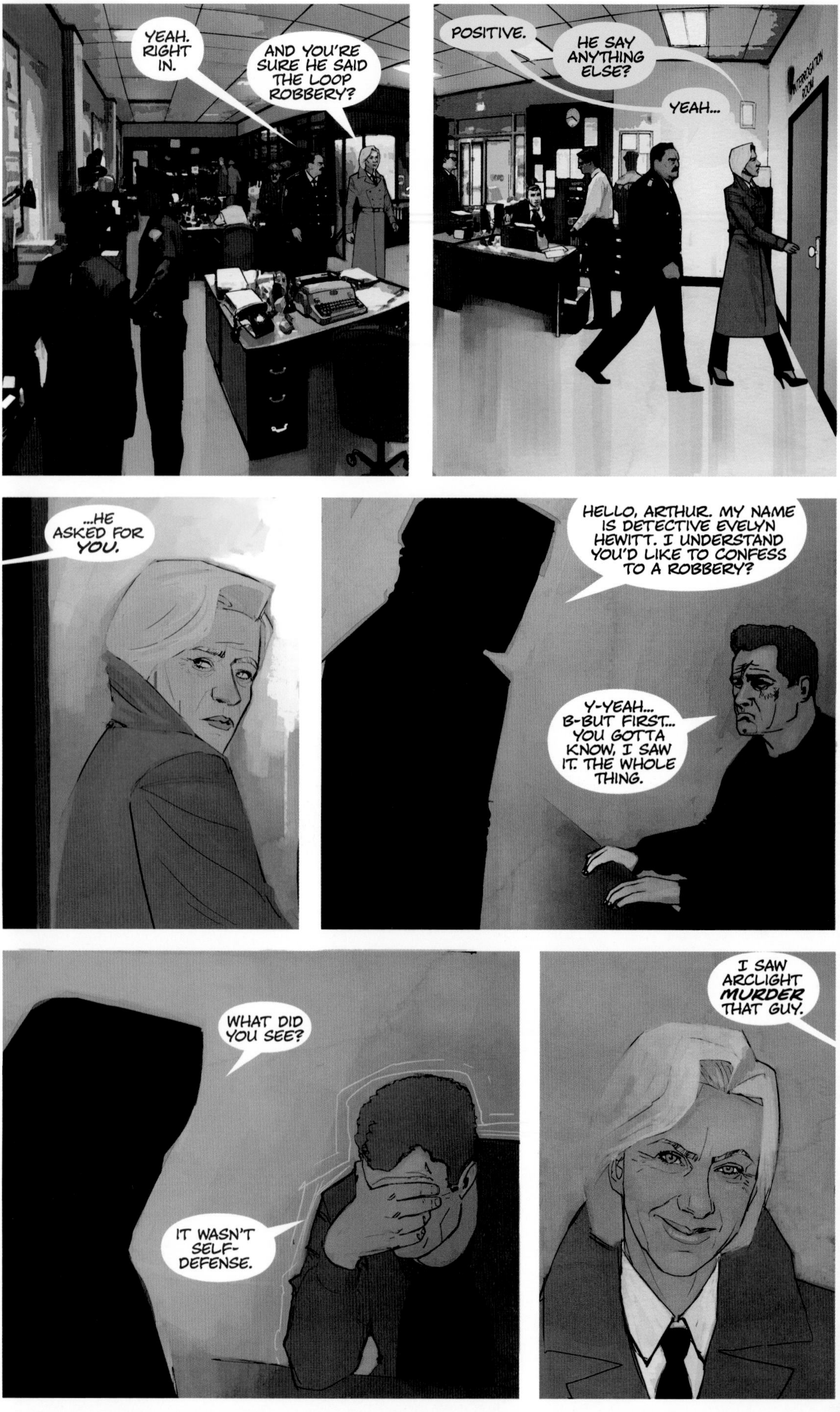
YEAH. RIGHT IN.
AND YOU'RE SURE HE SAID THE LOOP ROBBERY?
POSITIVE.
HE SAY ANYTHING ELSE?
YEAH...
INTERROGATION ROOM
...HE ASKED FOR *YOU.*
HELLO, ARTHUR. MY NAME IS DETECTIVE EVELYN HEWITT. I UNDERSTAND YOU'D LIKE TO CONFESS TO A ROBBERY?
Y-YEAH... B-BUT FIRST... YOU GOTTA KNOW, I SAW IT. THE WHOLE THING.
WHAT DID YOU SEE?
IT WASN'T SELF-DEFENSE.
I SAW ARCLIGHT *MURDER* THAT GUY.

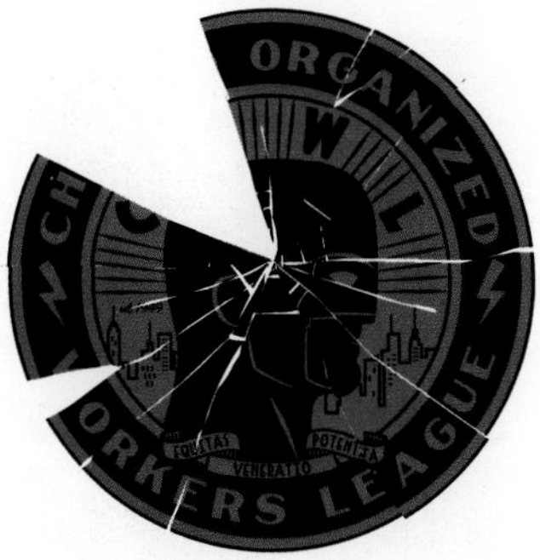
ORGANIZED
WORKERS LEAGUE

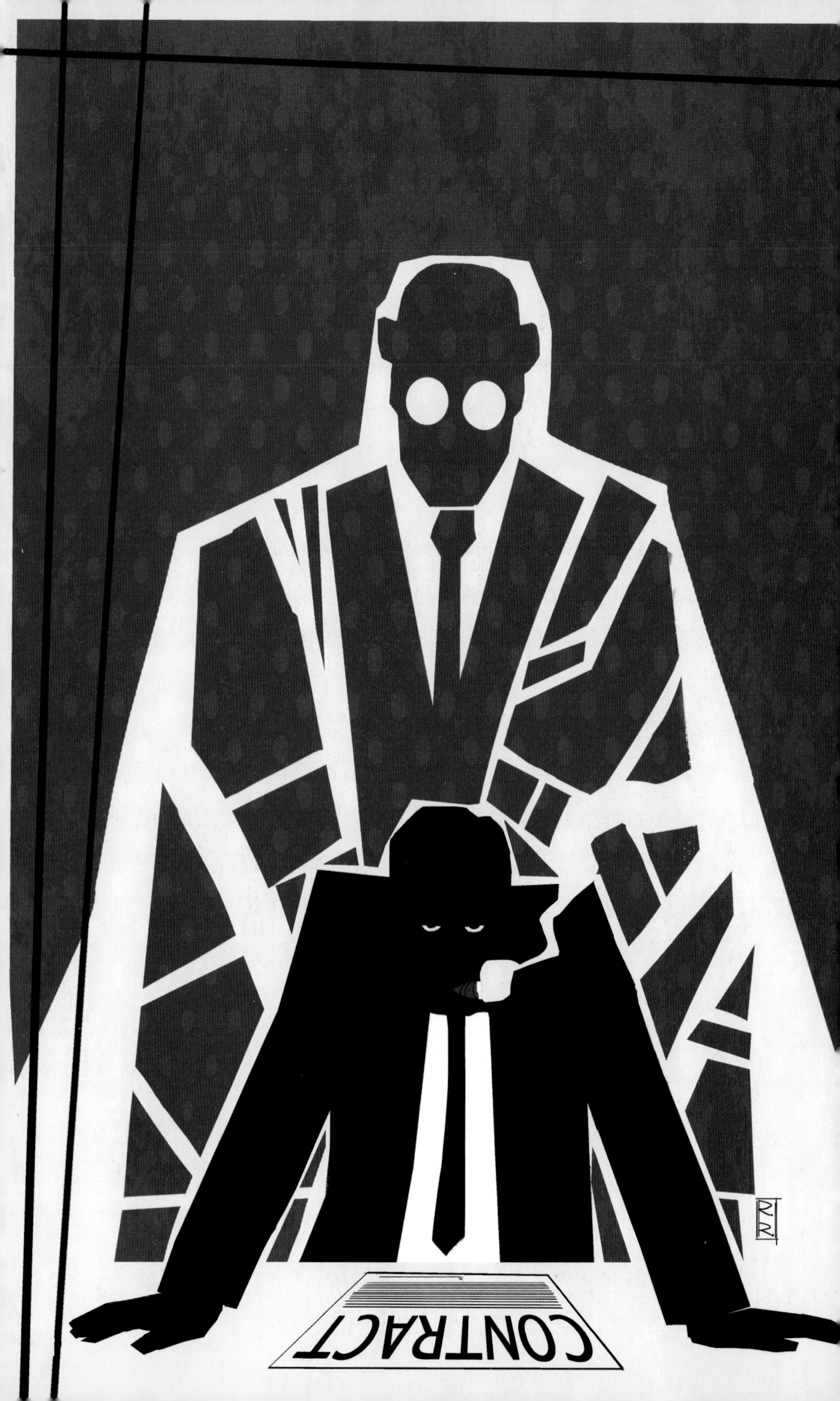
CONTRACT

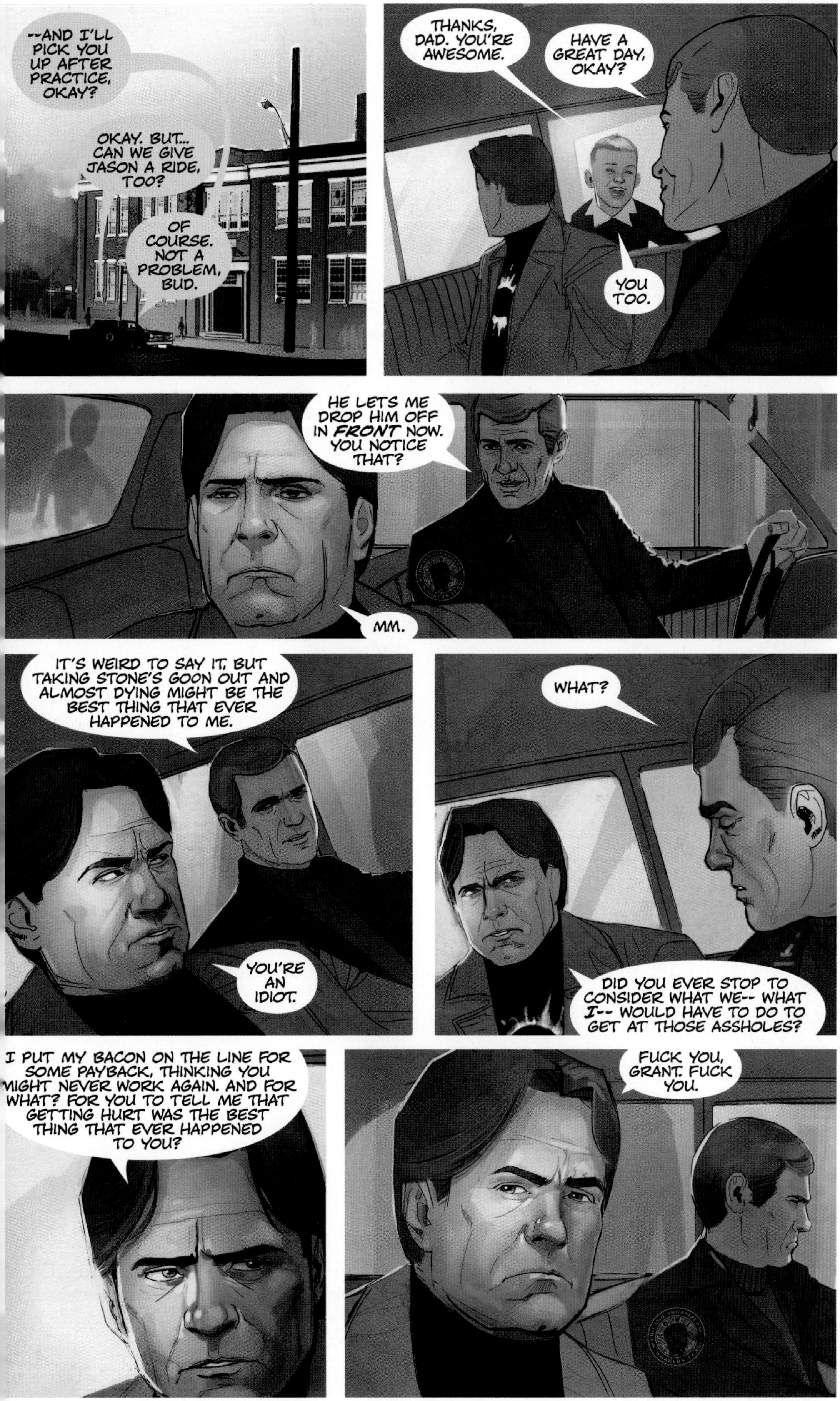
--AND I'LL PICK YOU UP AFTER PRACTICE, OKAY?
OKAY. BUT... CAN WE GIVE JASON A RIDE, TOO?
OF COURSE. NOT A PROBLEM, BUD.
THANKS, DAD. YOU'RE AWESOME.
HAVE A GREAT DAY, OKAY?
YOU TOO.
HE LETS ME DROP HIM OFF IN FRONT NOW. YOU NOTICE THAT?
MM.
IT'S WEIRD TO SAY IT, BUT TAKING STONE'S GOON OUT AND ALMOST DYING MIGHT BE THE BEST THING THAT EVER HAPPENED TO ME.
YOU'RE AN IDIOT.
WHAT?
DID YOU EVER STOP TO CONSIDER WHAT WE-- WHAT I-- WOULD HAVE TO DO TO GET AT THOSE ASSHOLES?
I PUT MY BACON ON THE LINE FOR SOME PAYBACK, THINKING YOU MIGHT NEVER WORK AGAIN. AND FOR WHAT? FOR YOU TO TELL ME THAT GETTING HURT WAS THE BEST THING THAT EVER HAPPENED TO YOU?
FUCK YOU, GRANT. FUCK YOU.

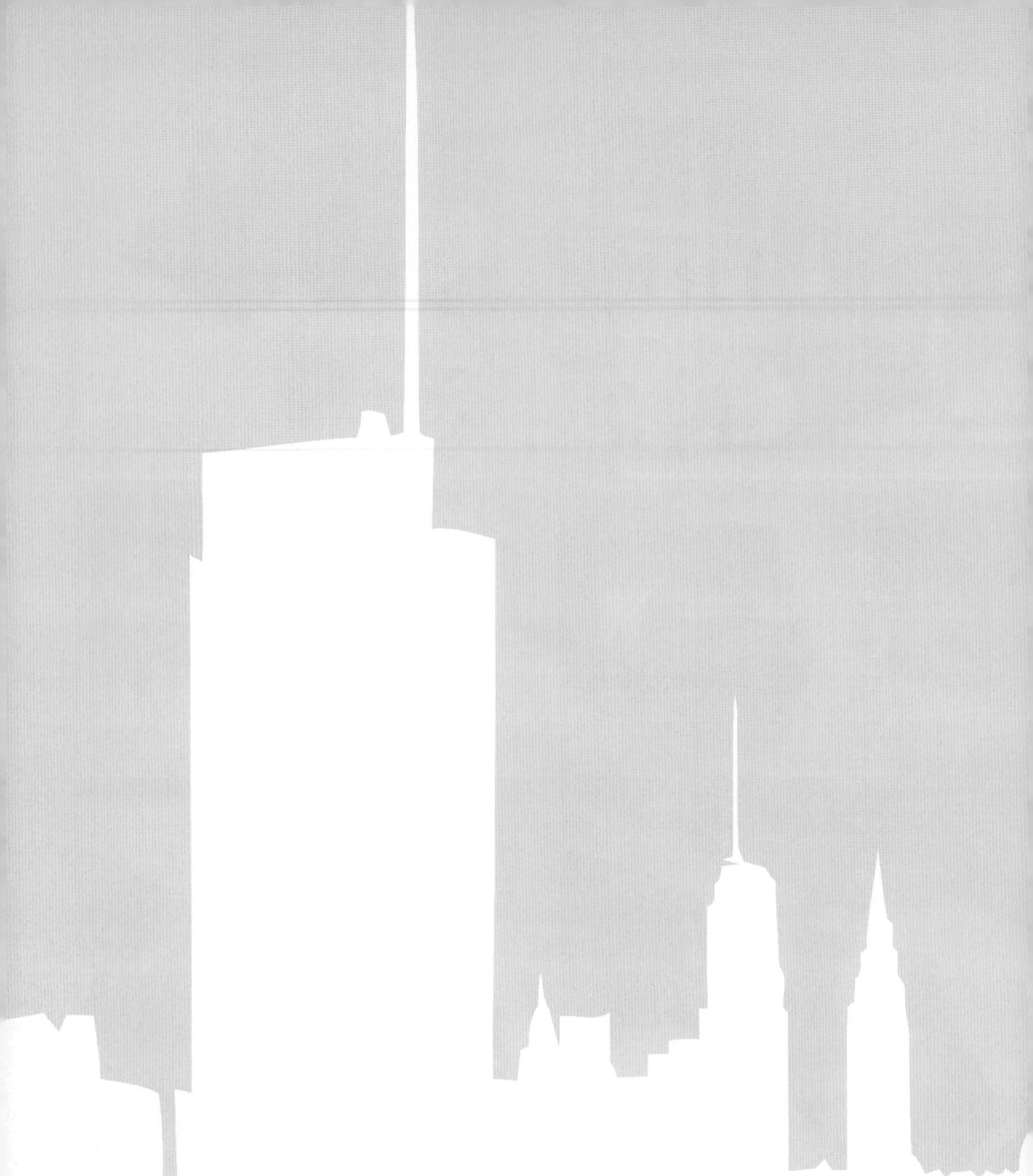

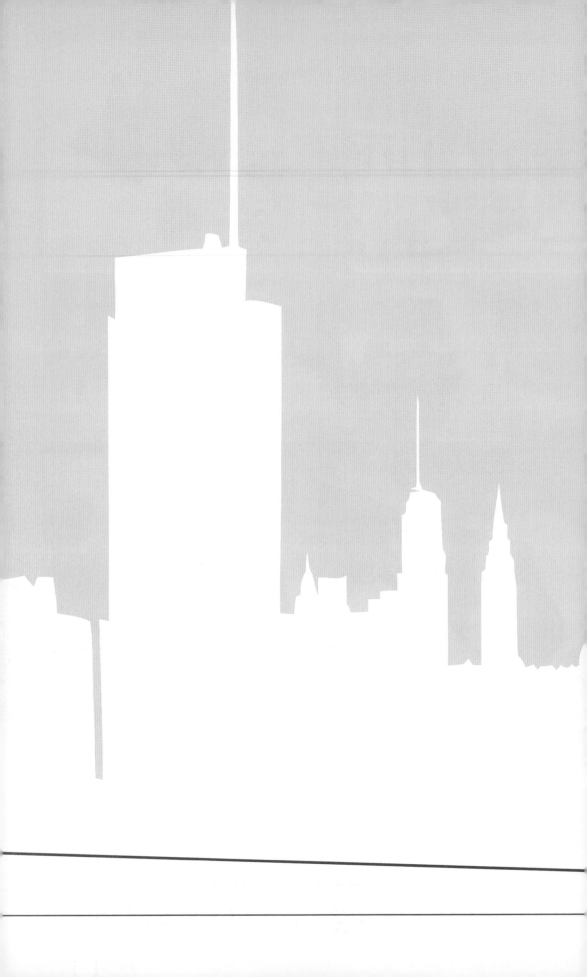

# CHAPTER 5
## Coming to Terms

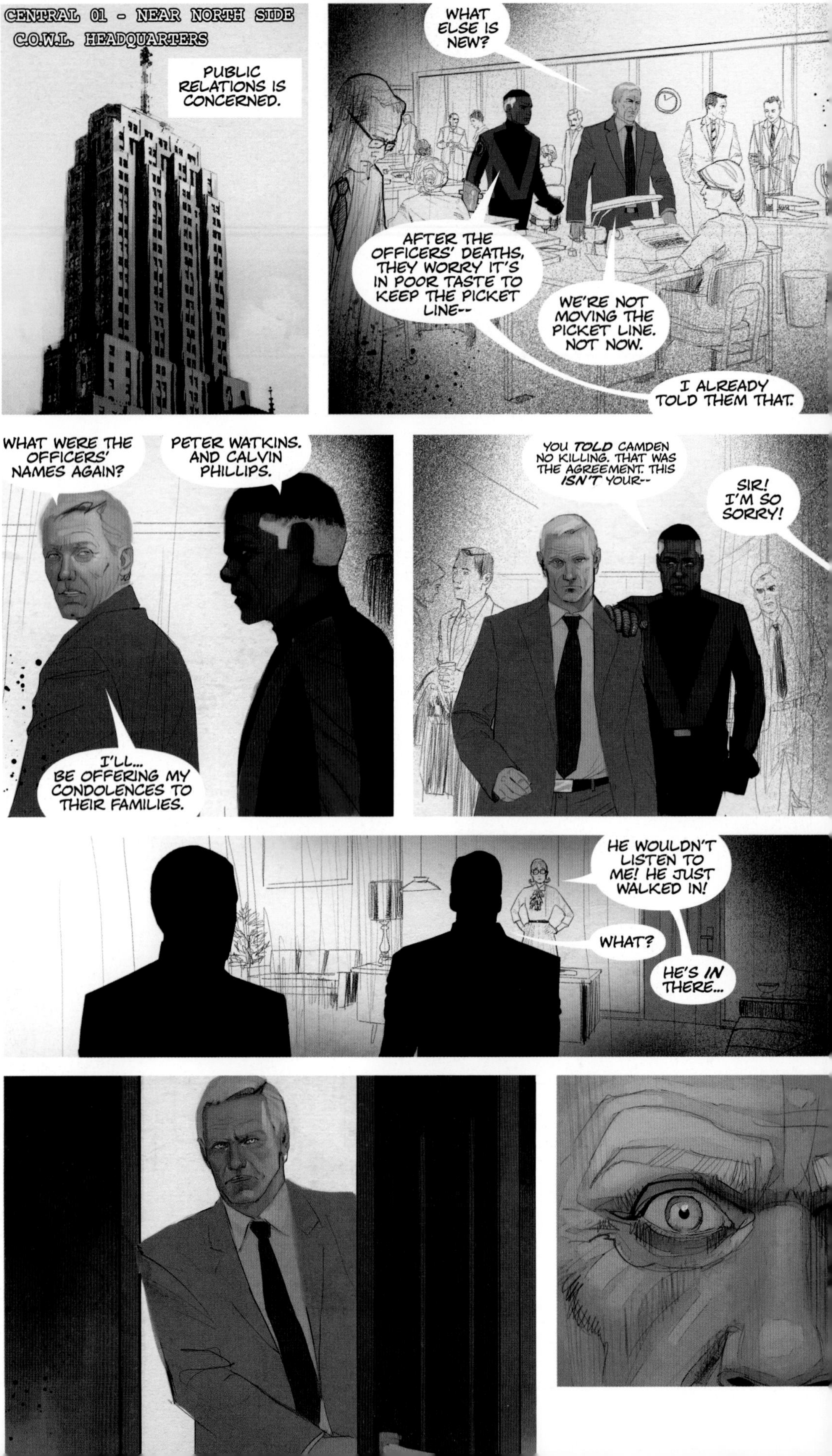
CENTRAL 01 - NEAR NORTH SIDE
C.O.W.L. HEADQUARTERS
PUBLIC RELATIONS IS CONCERNED.
WHAT ELSE IS NEW?
AFTER THE OFFICERS' DEATHS, THEY WORRY IT'S IN POOR TASTE TO KEEP THE PICKET LINE--
WE'RE NOT MOVING THE PICKET LINE. NOT NOW.
I ALREADY TOLD THEM THAT.
WHAT WERE THE OFFICERS' NAMES AGAIN?
PETER WATKINS. AND CALVIN PHILLIPS.
I'LL... BE OFFERING MY CONDOLENCES TO THEIR FAMILIES.
YOU TOLD CAMDEN NO KILLING. THAT WAS THE AGREEMENT. THIS ISN'T YOUR--
SIR! I'M SO SORRY!
HE WOULDN'T LISTEN TO ME! HE JUST WALKED IN!
WHAT?
HE'S IN THERE...

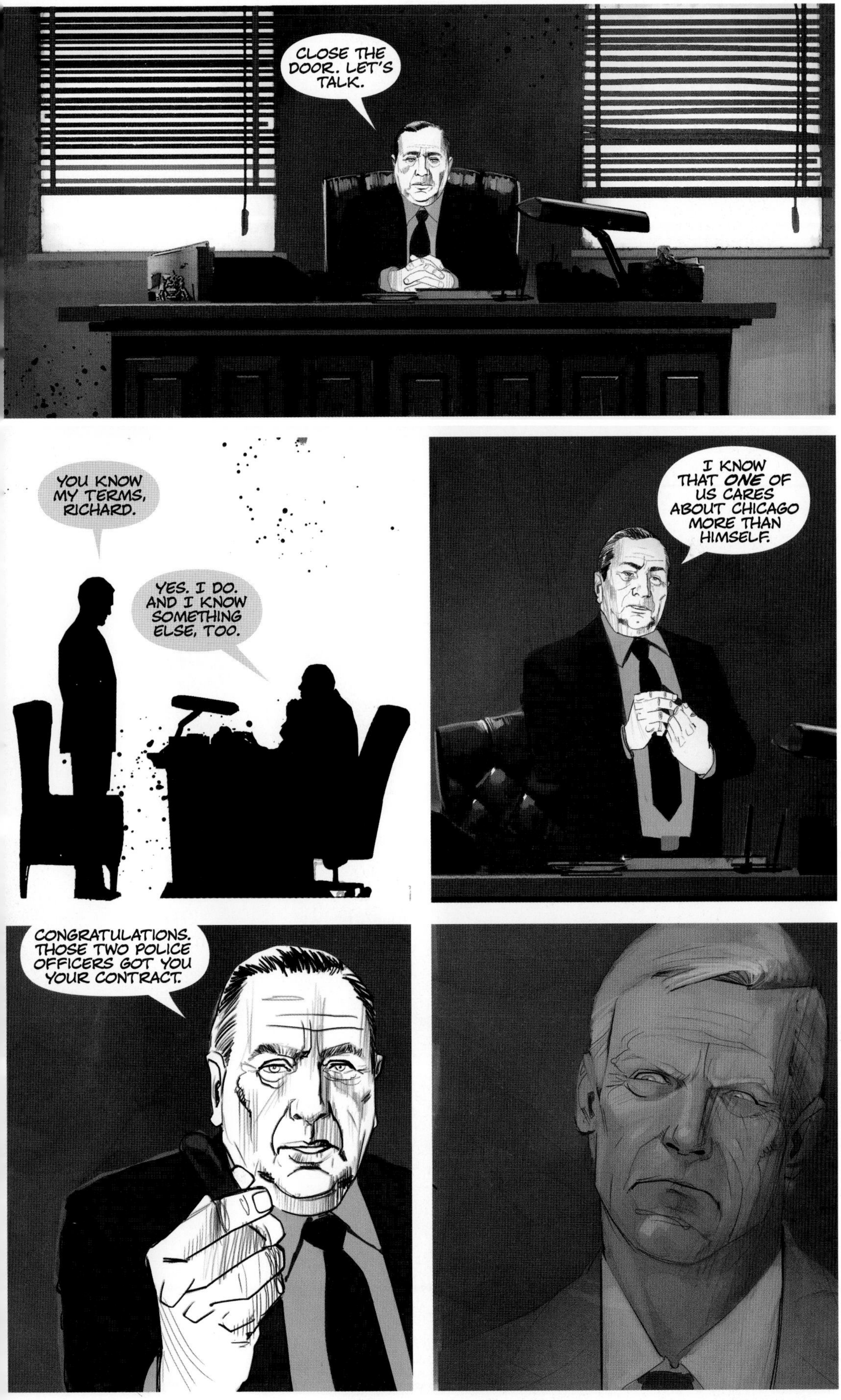
CLOSE THE DOOR. LET'S TALK.
YOU KNOW MY TERMS, RICHARD.
YES. I DO. AND I KNOW SOMETHING ELSE, TOO.
I KNOW THAT ONE OF US CARES ABOUT CHICAGO MORE THAN HIMSELF.
CONGRATULATIONS. THOSE TWO POLICE OFFICERS GOT YOU YOUR CONTRACT.

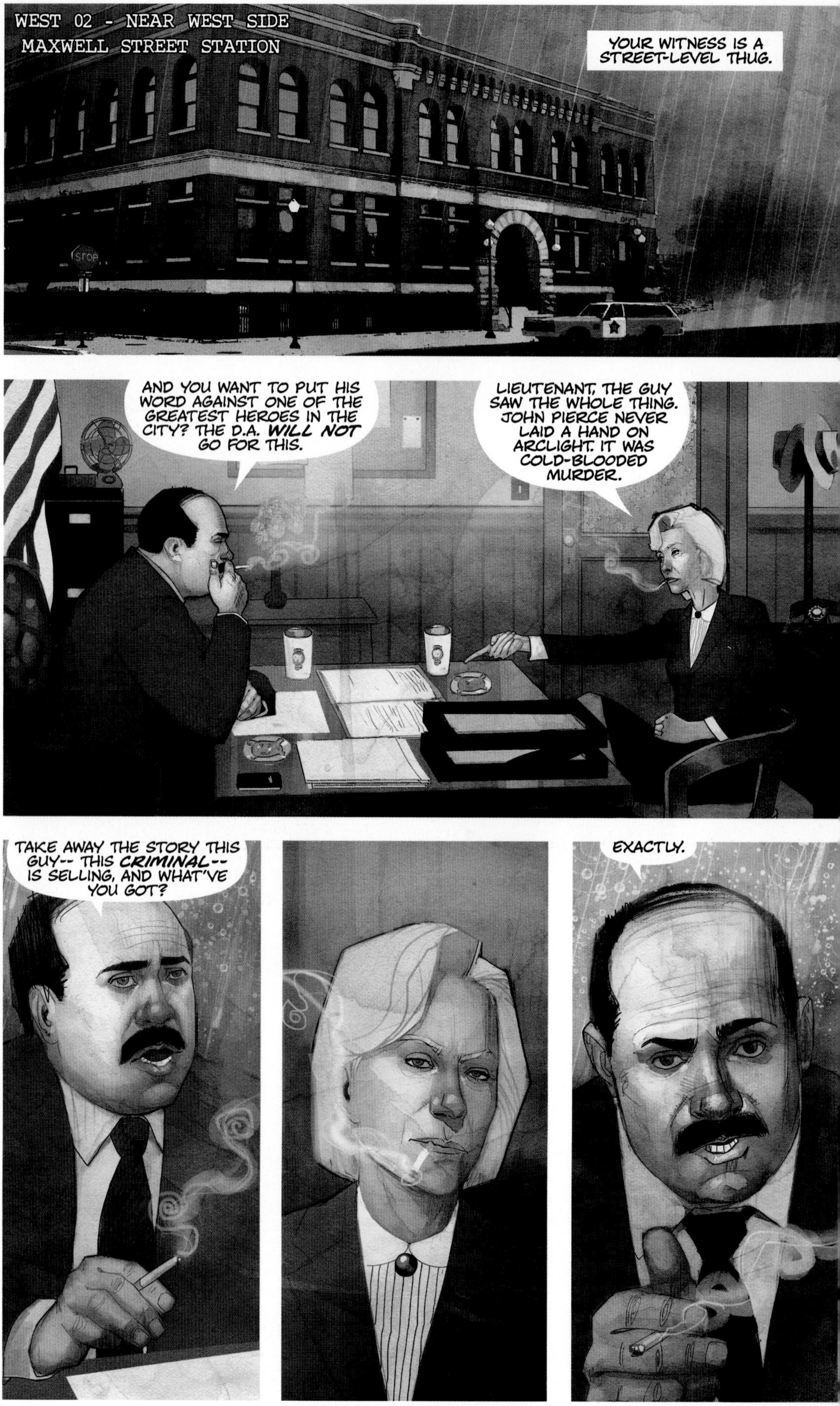
WEST 02 - NEAR WEST SIDE
MAXWELL STREET STATION
YOUR WITNESS IS A STREET-LEVEL THUG.
AND YOU WANT TO PUT HIS WORD AGAINST ONE OF THE GREATEST HEROES IN THE CITY? THE D.A. WILL NOT GO FOR THIS.
LIEUTENANT, THE GUY SAW THE WHOLE THING. JOHN PIERCE NEVER LAID A HAND ON ARCLIGHT. IT WAS COLD-BLOODED MURDER.
TAKE AWAY THE STORY THIS GUY-- THIS CRIMINAL-- IS SELLING, AND WHAT'VE YOU GOT?
EXACTLY.

JOHN TRUSTED ME AND PUT HIMSELF OUT IN THE OPEN. IT GOT HIM KILLED.

THE SUPER'S GUNNING FOR C.O.W.L., SINCE THE CITY HALL INCIDENT. HE'LL SUPPORT--

NOT WITH SOMETHING AS FLIMSY AS THIS. WE DON'T EVEN HAVE *JURISDICTION* HERE, EVELYN.

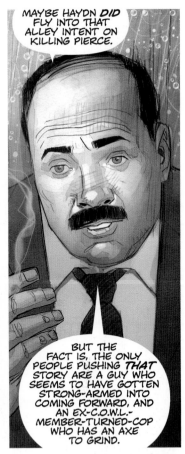

MAYBE HAYDN *DID* FLY INTO THAT ALLEY INTENT ON KILLING PIERCE.

BUT THE FACT IS, THE ONLY PEOPLE PUSHING *THAT* STORY ARE A GUY WHO SEEMS TO HAVE GOTTEN STRONG-ARMED INTO COMING FORWARD, AND AN EX-C.O.W.L.- MEMBER-TURNED-COP WHO HAS AN AXE TO GRIND.

YOU'RE NOT LISTENING TO--

YOU DON'T HAVE *EVIDENCE*, DETECTIVE. I'M TELLING YOU-- THIS DIES RIGHT NOW. RIGHT HERE.

YOU GO BACK IN THE ROTATION, OR YOU TAKE TIME OFF. YOUR CHOICE.

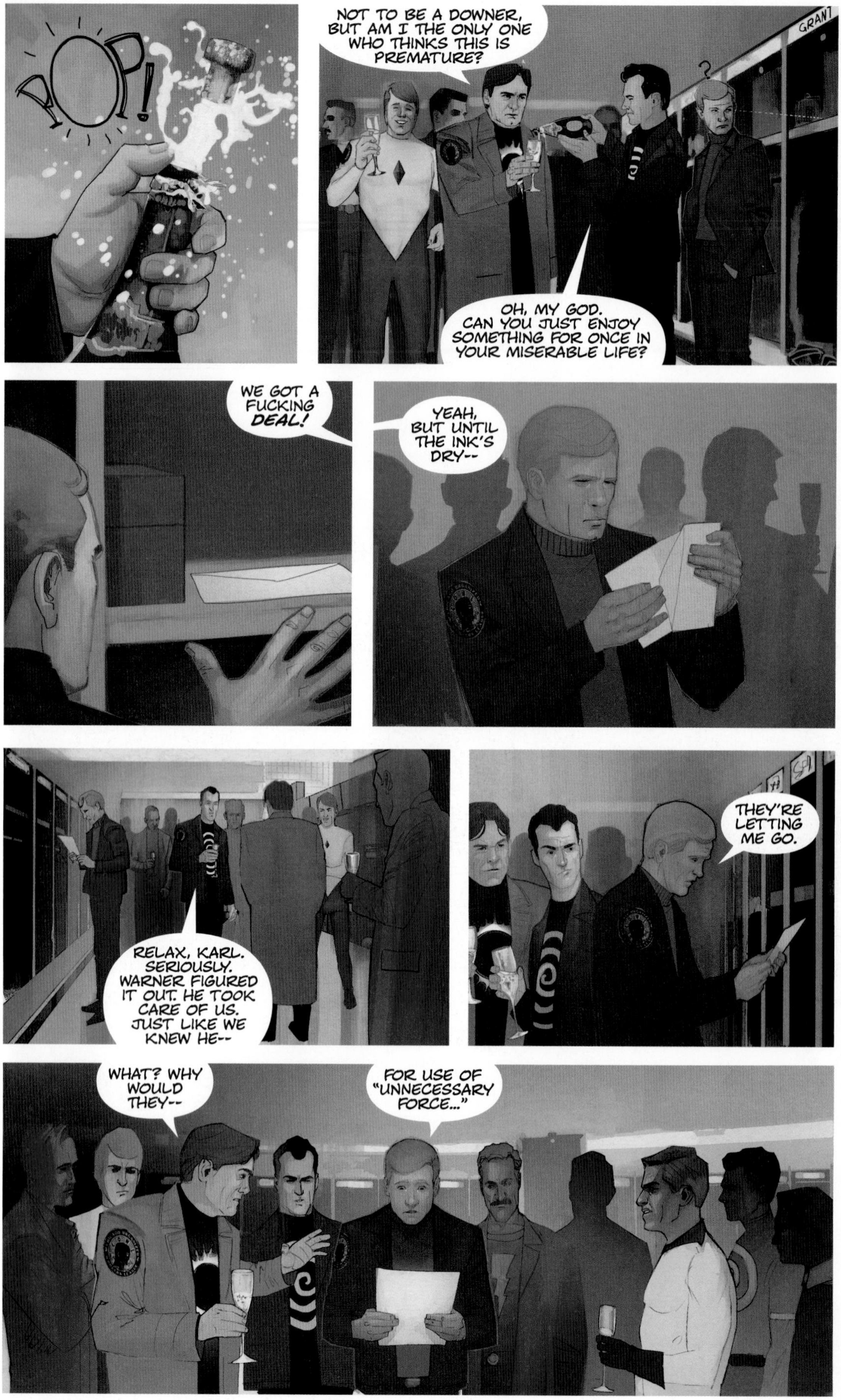

POP!
GRANT
NOT TO BE A DOWNER, BUT AM I THE ONLY ONE WHO THINKS THIS IS PREMATURE?
OH, MY GOD. CAN YOU JUST ENJOY SOMETHING FOR ONCE IN YOUR MISERABLE LIFE?
WE GOT A FUCKING DEAL!
YEAH, BUT UNTIL THE INK'S DRY--
RELAX, KARL. SERIOUSLY. WARNER FIGURED IT OUT. HE TOOK CARE OF US. JUST LIKE WE KNEW HE--
THEY'RE LETTING ME GO.
WHAT? WHY WOULD THEY--
FOR USE OF "UNNECESSARY FORCE..."

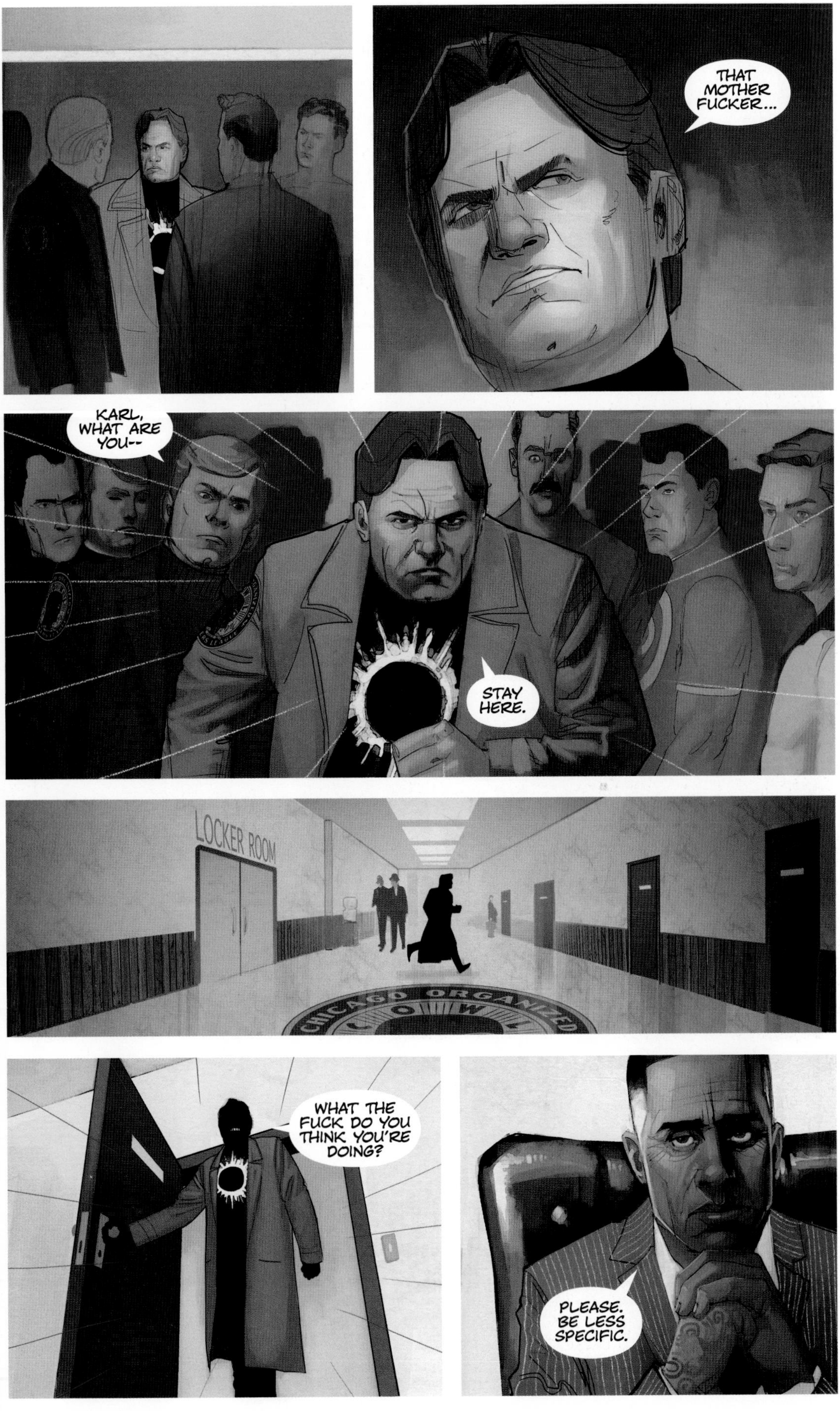
THAT MOTHER FUCKER...
KARL, WHAT ARE YOU--
STAY HERE.
LOCKER ROOM
CHICAGO ORGANIZED
WHAT THE FUCK DO YOU THINK YOU'RE DOING?
PLEASE. BE LESS SPECIFIC.

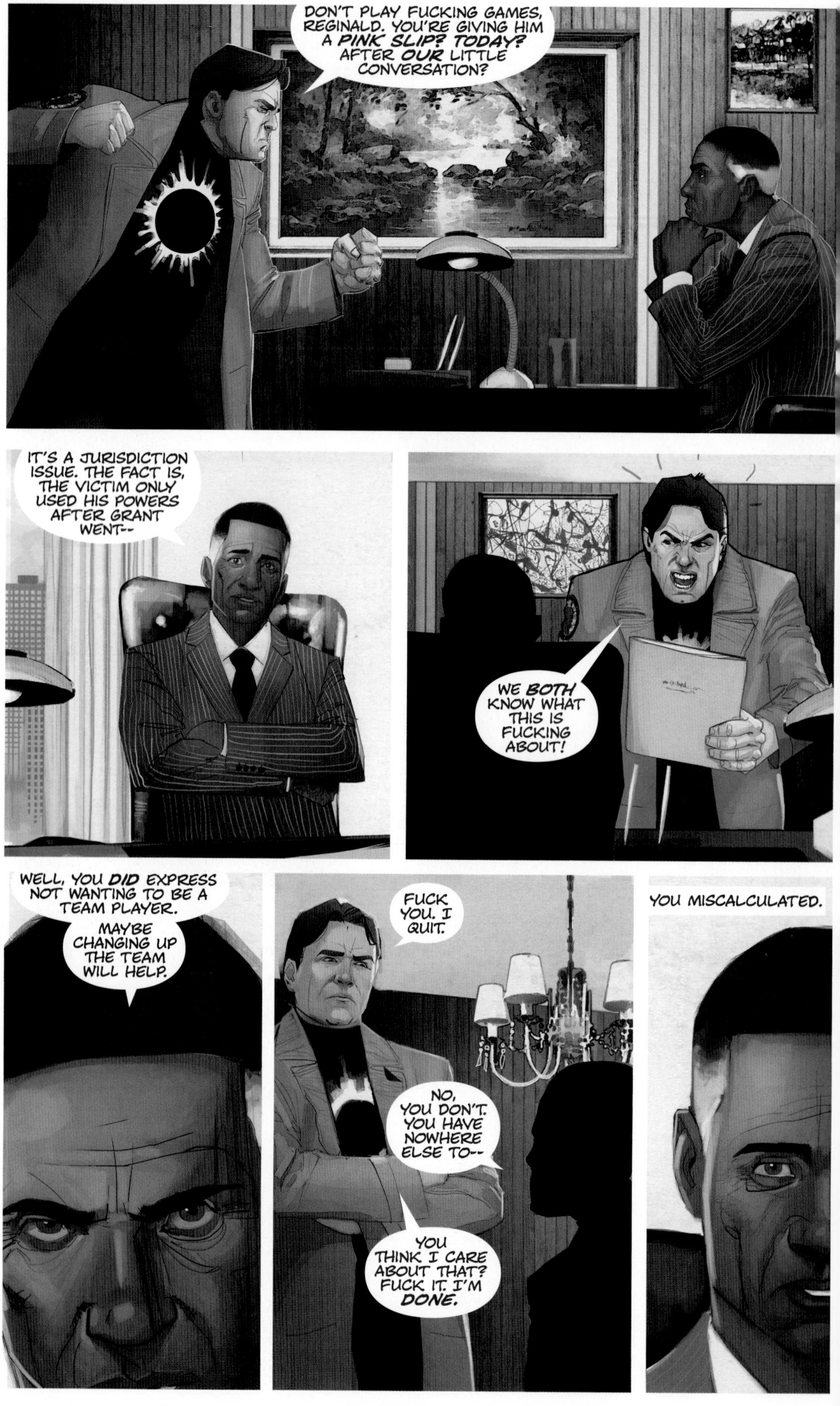
DON'T PLAY FUCKING GAMES, REGINALD. YOU'RE GIVING HIM A PINK SLIP? TODAY? AFTER OUR LITTLE CONVERSATION?
IT'S A JURISDICTION ISSUE. THE FACT IS, THE VICTIM ONLY USED HIS POWERS AFTER GRANT WENT--
WE BOTH KNOW WHAT THIS IS FUCKING ABOUT!
WELL, YOU DID EXPRESS NOT WANTING TO BE A TEAM PLAYER.
MAYBE CHANGING UP THE TEAM WILL HELP.
FUCK YOU. I QUIT.
NO, YOU DON'T. YOU HAVE NOWHERE ELSE TO--
YOU THINK I CARE ABOUT THAT? FUCK IT. I'M DONE.
YOU MISCALCULATED.

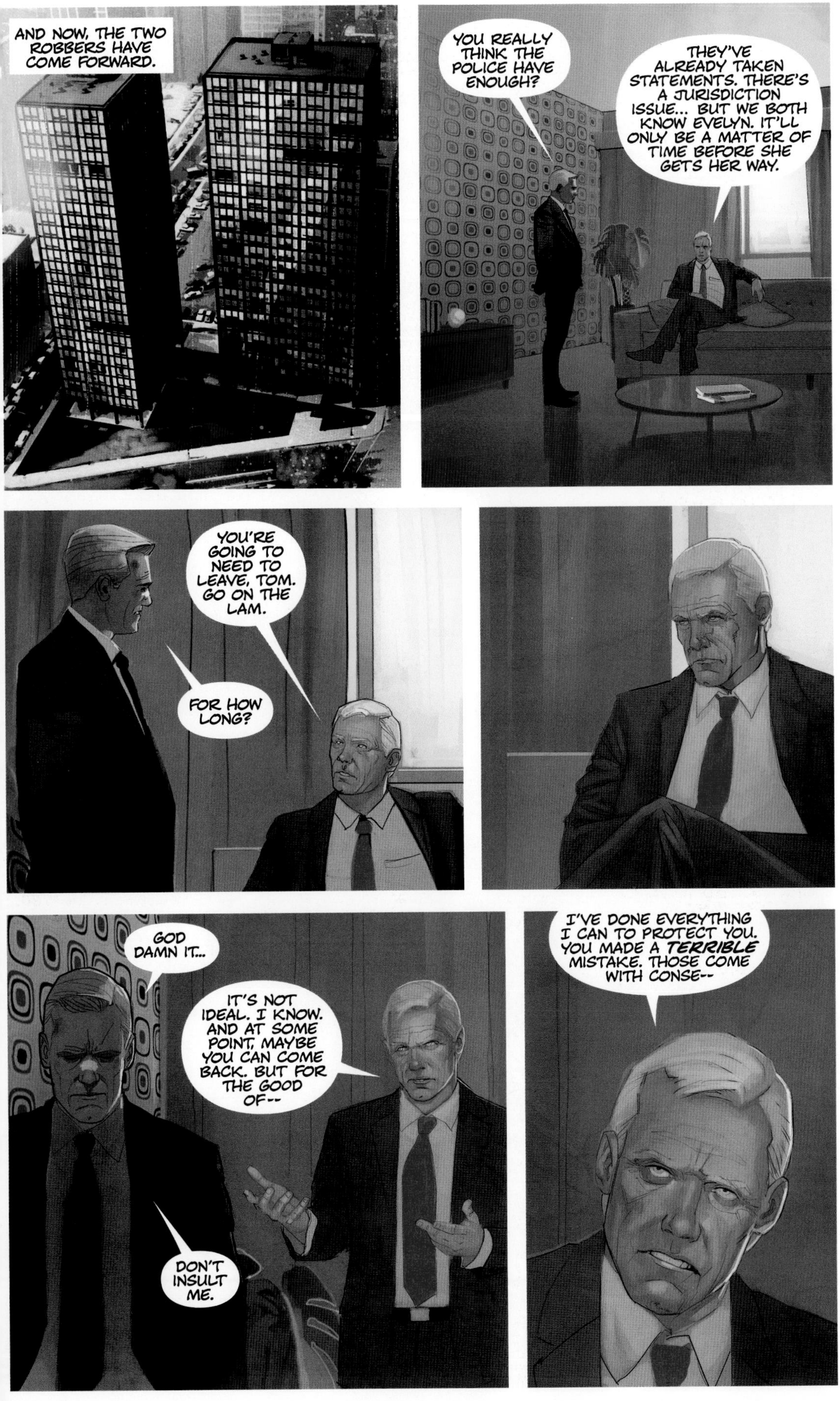
AND NOW, THE TWO ROBBERS HAVE COME FORWARD.
YOU REALLY THINK THE POLICE HAVE ENOUGH?
THEY'VE ALREADY TAKEN STATEMENTS. THERE'S A JURISDICTION ISSUE... BUT WE BOTH KNOW EVELYN. IT'LL ONLY BE A MATTER OF TIME BEFORE SHE GETS HER WAY.
YOU'RE GOING TO NEED TO LEAVE, TOM. GO ON THE LAM.
FOR HOW LONG?
GOD DAMN IT...
IT'S NOT IDEAL. I KNOW. AND AT SOME POINT, MAYBE YOU CAN COME BACK. BUT FOR THE GOOD OF--
DON'T INSULT ME.
I'VE DONE EVERYTHING I CAN TO PROTECT YOU. YOU MADE A *TERRIBLE* MISTAKE. THOSE COME WITH CONSE--

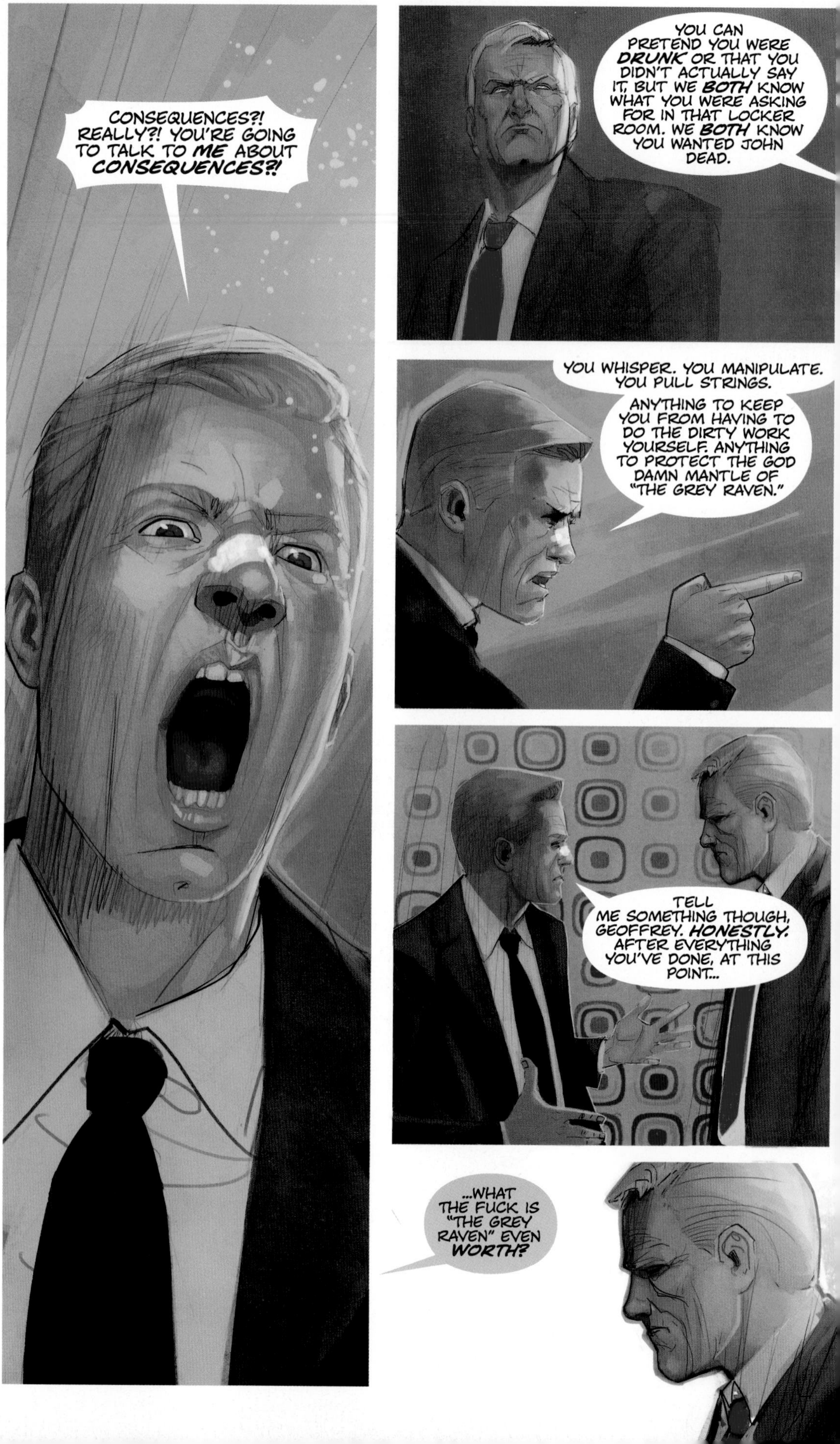
CONSEQUENCES?! REALLY?! YOU'RE GOING TO TALK TO ME ABOUT CONSEQUENCES?!
YOU CAN PRETEND YOU WERE DRUNK OR THAT YOU DIDN'T ACTUALLY SAY IT, BUT WE BOTH KNOW WHAT YOU WERE ASKING FOR IN THAT LOCKER ROOM. WE BOTH KNOW YOU WANTED JOHN DEAD.
YOU WHISPER. YOU MANIPULATE. YOU PULL STRINGS.
ANYTHING TO KEEP YOU FROM HAVING TO DO THE DIRTY WORK YOURSELF. ANYTHING TO PROTECT THE GOD DAMN MANTLE OF "THE GREY RAVEN."
TELL ME SOMETHING THOUGH, GEOFFREY. HONESTLY. AFTER EVERYTHING YOU'VE DONE, AT THIS POINT...
...WHAT THE FUCK IS "THE GREY RAVEN" EVEN WORTH?

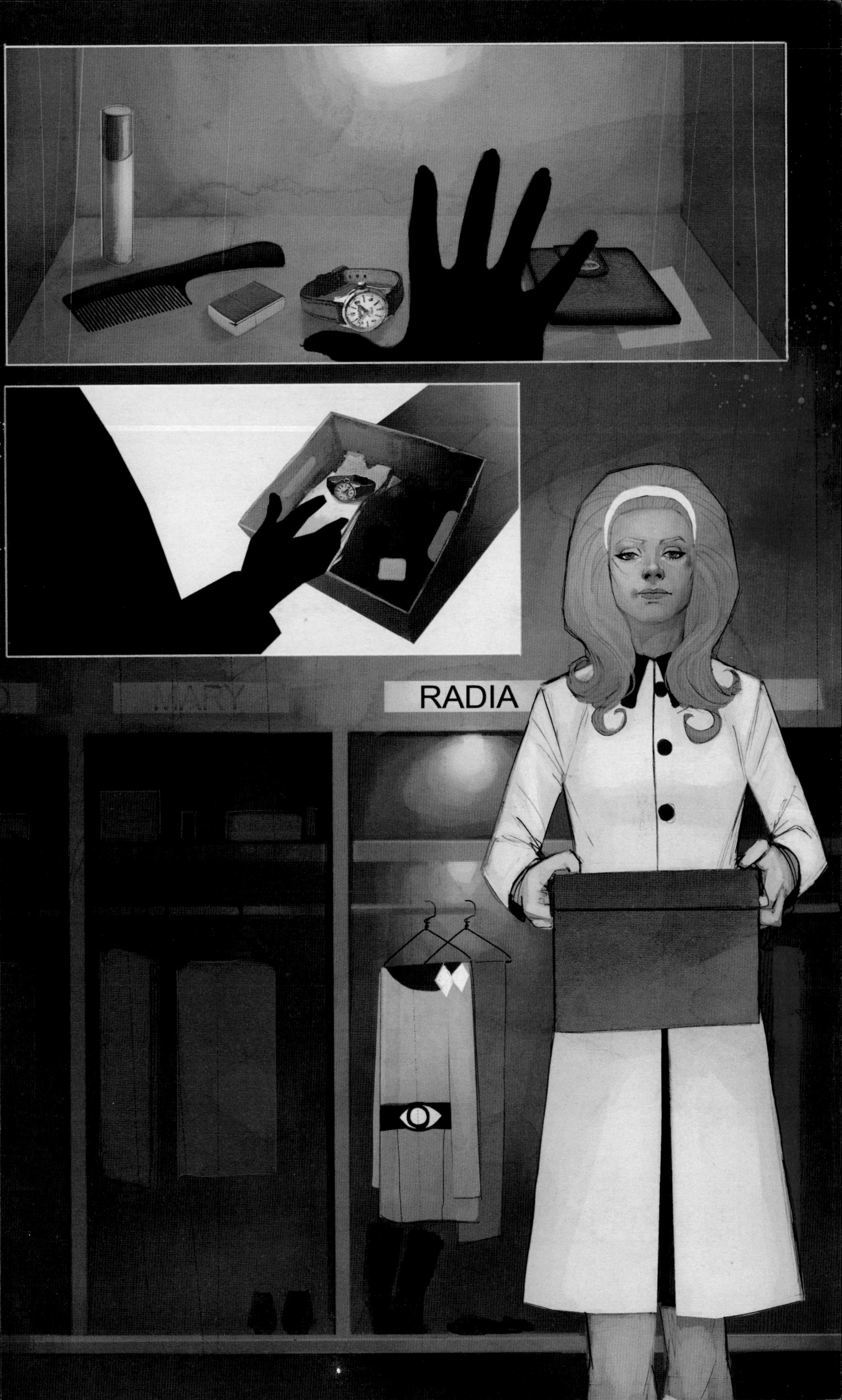

MARY
RADIA

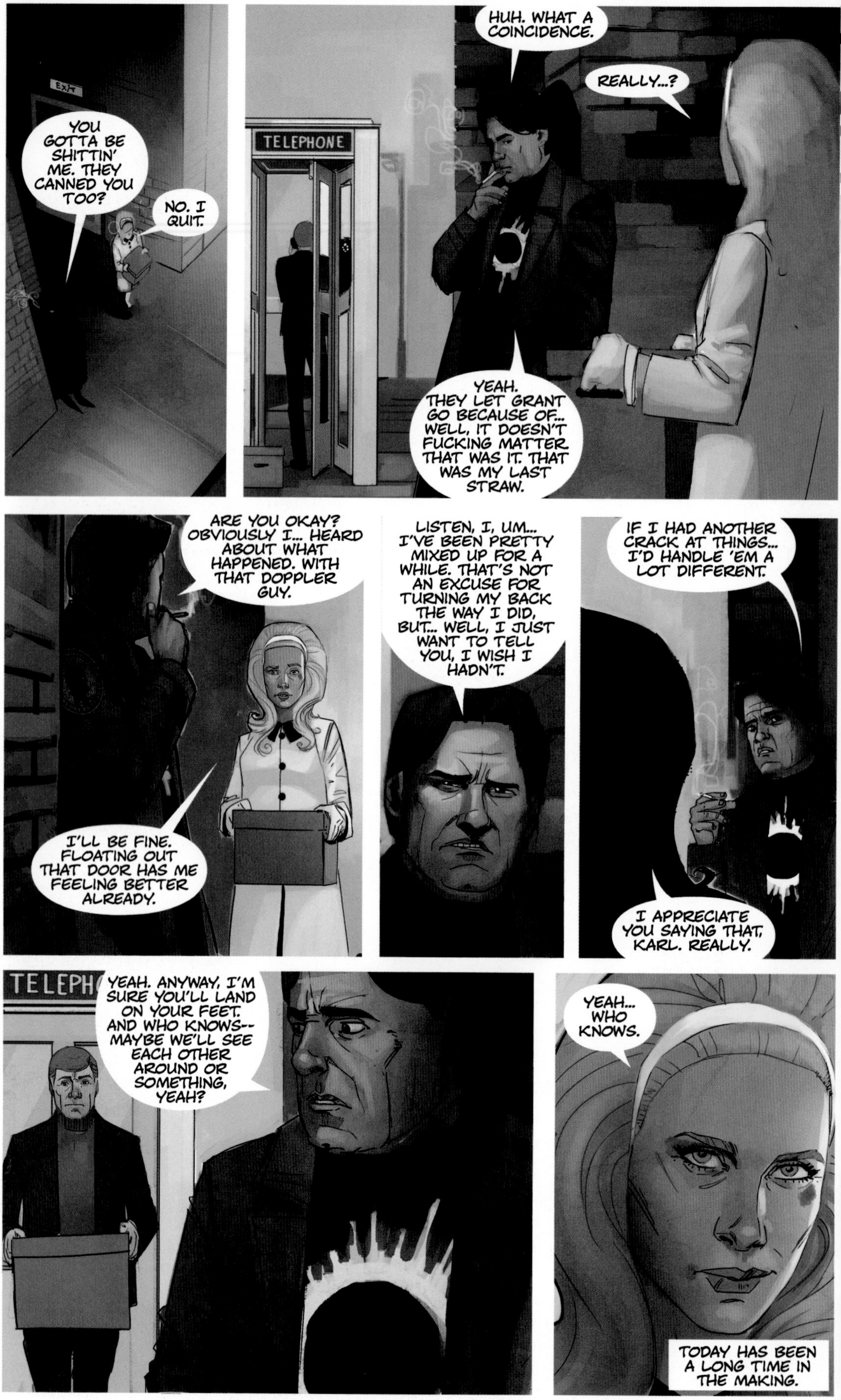
EXIT
YOU GOTTA BE SHITTIN' ME. THEY CANNED YOU TOO?
NO. I QUIT.
TELEPHONE
HUH. WHAT A COINCIDENCE.
REALLY...?
YEAH. THEY LET GRANT GO BECAUSE OF... WELL, IT DOESN'T FUCKING MATTER THAT WAS IT. THAT WAS MY LAST STRAW.
ARE YOU OKAY? OBVIOUSLY I... HEARD ABOUT WHAT HAPPENED. WITH THAT DOPPLER GUY.
I'LL BE FINE. FLOATING OUT THAT DOOR HAS ME FEELING BETTER ALREADY.
LISTEN, I, UM... I'VE BEEN PRETTY MIXED UP FOR A WHILE. THAT'S NOT AN EXCUSE FOR TURNING MY BACK THE WAY I DID, BUT... WELL, I JUST WANT TO TELL YOU, I WISH I HADN'T.
IF I HAD ANOTHER CRACK AT THINGS... I'D HANDLE 'EM A LOT DIFFERENT.
I APPRECIATE YOU SAYING THAT, KARL. REALLY.
TELEPH
YEAH. ANYWAY, I'M SURE YOU'LL LAND ON YOUR FEET. AND WHO KNOWS-- MAYBE WE'LL SEE EACH OTHER AROUND OR SOMETHING, YEAH?
YEAH... WHO KNOWS.
TODAY HAS BEEN A LONG TIME IN THE MAKING.

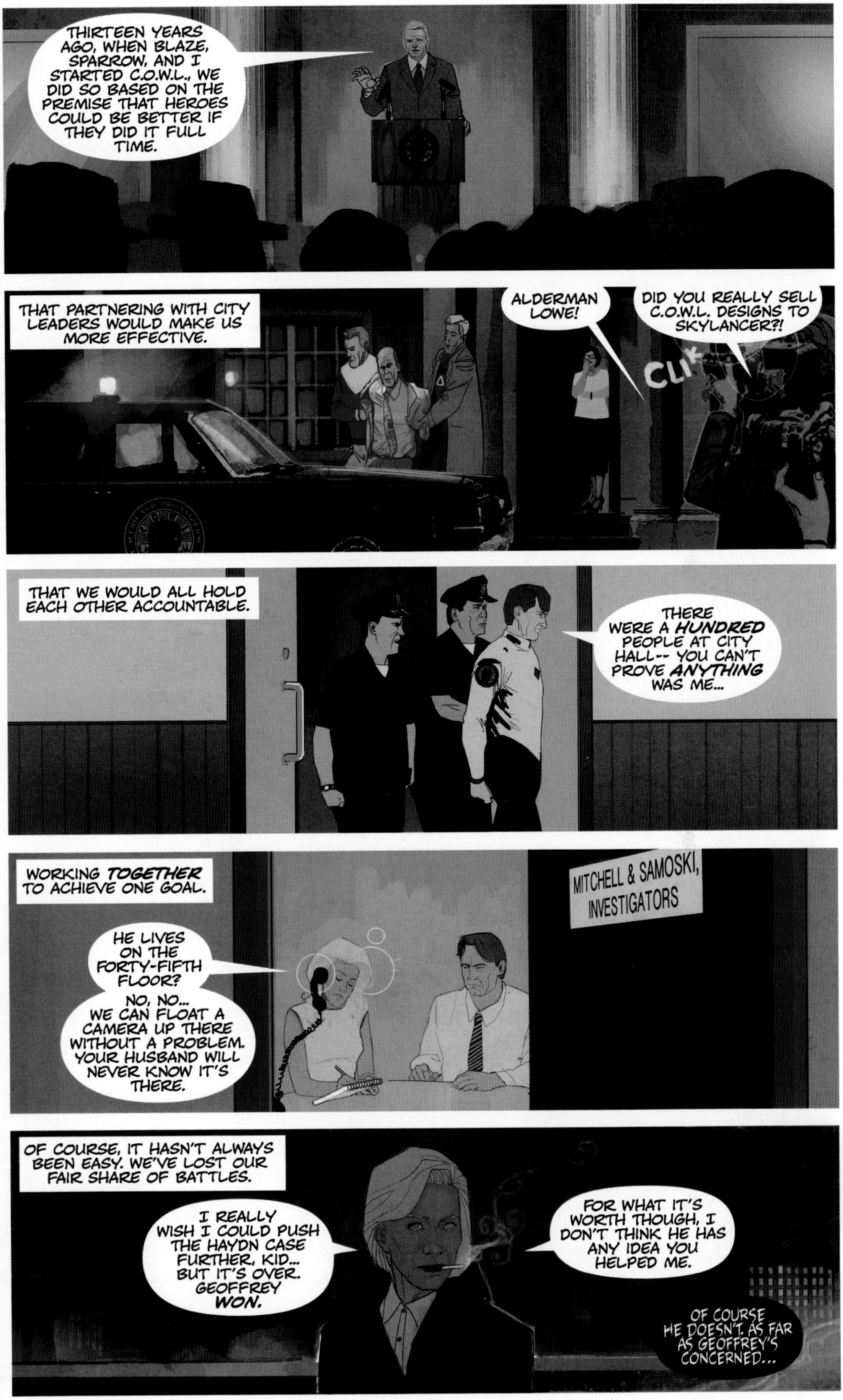
THIRTEEN YEARS AGO, WHEN BLAZE, SPARROW, AND I STARTED C.O.W.L., WE DID SO BASED ON THE PREMISE THAT HEROES COULD BE BETTER IF THEY DID IT FULL TIME.
THAT PARTNERING WITH CITY LEADERS WOULD MAKE US MORE EFFECTIVE.
ALDERMAN LOWE!
DID YOU REALLY SELL C.O.W.L. DESIGNS TO SKYLANCER?!
CLI
THAT WE WOULD ALL HOLD EACH OTHER ACCOUNTABLE.
THERE WERE A ***HUNDRED*** PEOPLE AT CITY HALL-- YOU CAN'T PROVE ***ANYTHING*** WAS ME...
WORKING ***TOGETHER*** TO ACHIEVE ONE GOAL.
MITCHELL & SAMOSKI, INVESTIGATORS
HE LIVES ON THE FORTY-FIFTH FLOOR?
NO, NO... WE CAN FLOAT A CAMERA UP THERE WITHOUT A PROBLEM. YOUR HUSBAND WILL NEVER KNOW IT'S THERE.
OF COURSE, IT HASN'T ALWAYS BEEN EASY. WE'VE LOST OUR FAIR SHARE OF BATTLES.
I REALLY WISH I COULD PUSH THE HAYDN CASE FURTHER, KID... BUT IT'S OVER. GEOFFREY ***WON.***
FOR WHAT IT'S WORTH THOUGH, I DON'T THINK HE HAS ANY IDEA YOU HELPED ME.
OF COURSE HE DOESN'T. AS FAR AS GEOFFREY'S CONCERNED...

...SPARROW'S DEAD.

WE'VE LOST OUR FAIR SHARE OF FRIENDS.

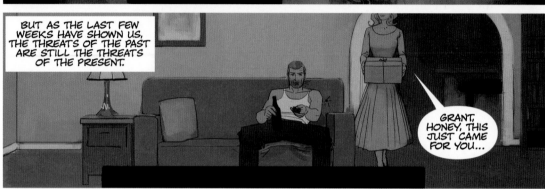

BUT AS THE LAST FEW WEEKS HAVE SHOWN US, THE THREATS OF THE PAST ARE STILL THE THREATS OF THE PRESENT.

GRANT, HONEY, THIS JUST CAME FOR YOU...

AND ARE POISED TO BE THE THREATS OF THE FUTURE.

IF YOU REALLY WANT TO GET THEM BACK...

WHICH IS WHY WE MUST *NEVER* FORGET HOW WE ARRIVED HERE.

HEY, DO I KNOW YOU OR SOMETHING, MISTER? ARE YOU, LIKE, SOMEBODY IMPORTANT?

NOT ANYMORE, LADY.

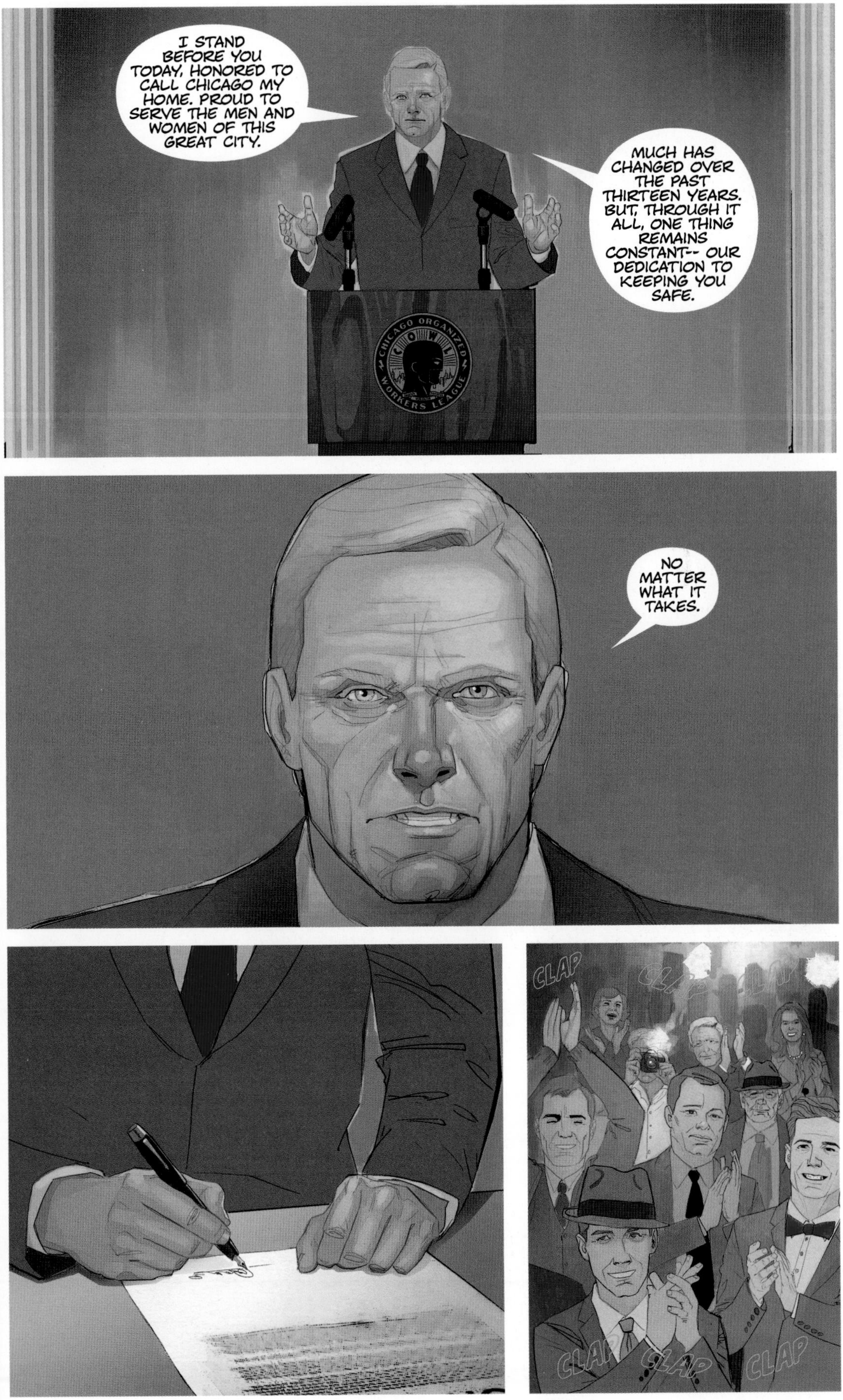
I STAND BEFORE YOU TODAY, HONORED TO CALL CHICAGO MY HOME. PROUD TO SERVE THE MEN AND WOMEN OF THIS GREAT CITY.
MUCH HAS CHANGED OVER THE PAST THIRTEEN YEARS. BUT, THROUGH IT ALL, ONE THING REMAINS CONSTANT-- OUR DEDICATION TO KEEPING YOU SAFE.
CHICAGO ORGANIZED WORKERS LEAGUE
NO MATTER WHAT IT TAKES.
CLAP
CLAP
CLAP
CLAP
CLAP
CLAP

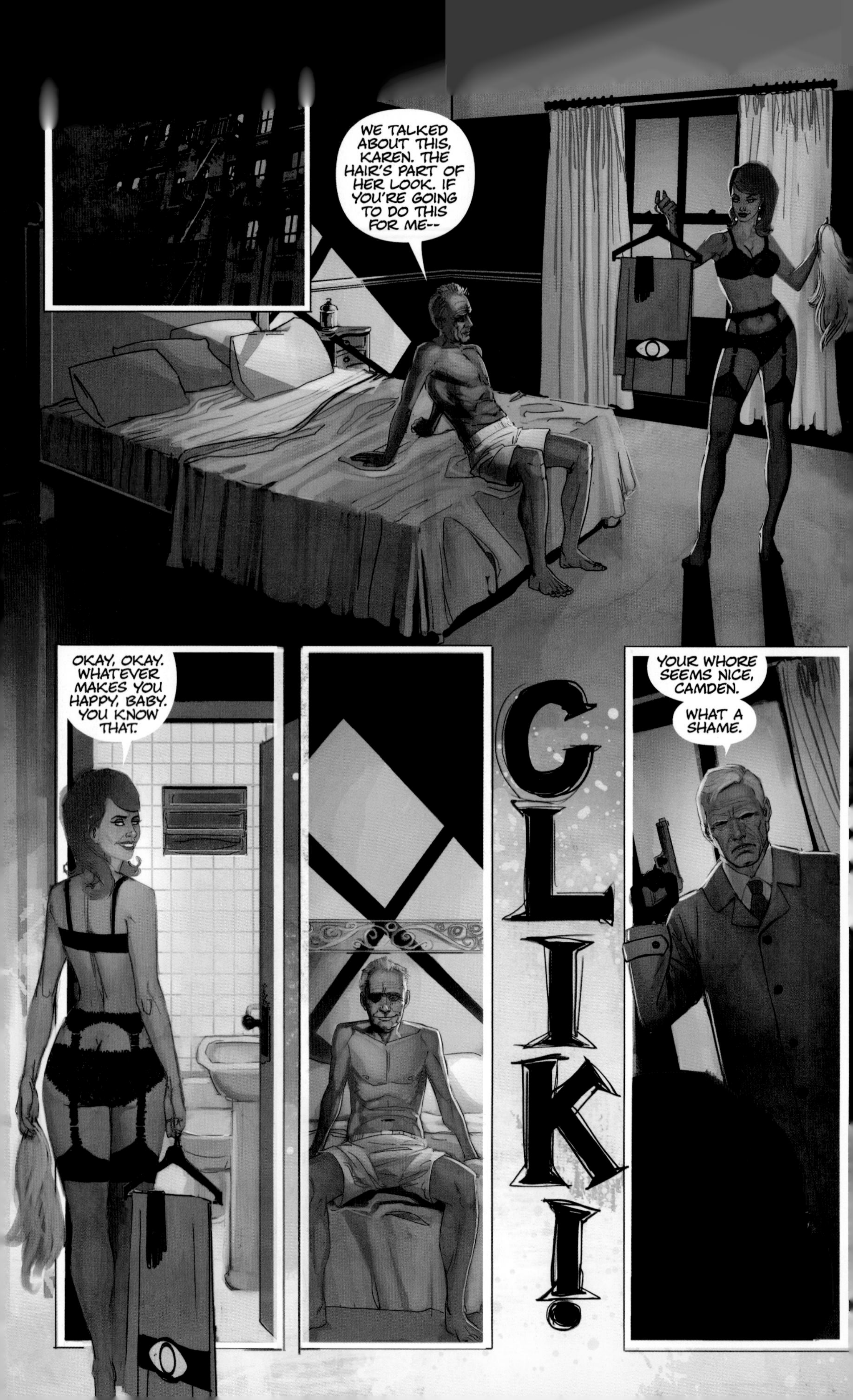
WE TALKED ABOUT THIS, KAREN. THE HAIR'S PART OF HER LOOK. IF YOU'RE GOING TO DO THIS FOR ME--
OKAY, OKAY. WHATEVER MAKES YOU HAPPY, BABY. YOU KNOW THAT.
CLIK!
YOUR WHORE SEEMS NICE, CAMDEN.
WHAT A SHAME.

THINK *CAREFULLY* ABOUT WHAT YOU'RE DOING HERE, WARNER...

I'M CONFUSED. ISN'T THIS WHAT YOU WANTED?

FOR ME TO *KILL* RADIA? AFTER ALL, MURDER COMES SO *EASY* TO YOU.

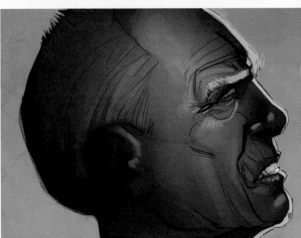

YOU'RE A PIECE O' FUCKIN' WORK, YOU KNOW THAT? NEWS FLASH-- THOSE COP KILLERS *WEREN'T* ONE OF MY CREWS. CONGRATULATIONS-- YOU'VE GOT YOUR FIRST *REAL* VILLAINS AGAIN.

SO, WHY DON'T YOU GET THE FUCK OUTTA HERE WITH YOUR CHEAP INTIMIDATION BULLSHIT.

AT THIS POINT, CAMDEN, DO YOU REALLY THINK I WOULD COME HERE JUST TO *INTIMIDATE* YOU?

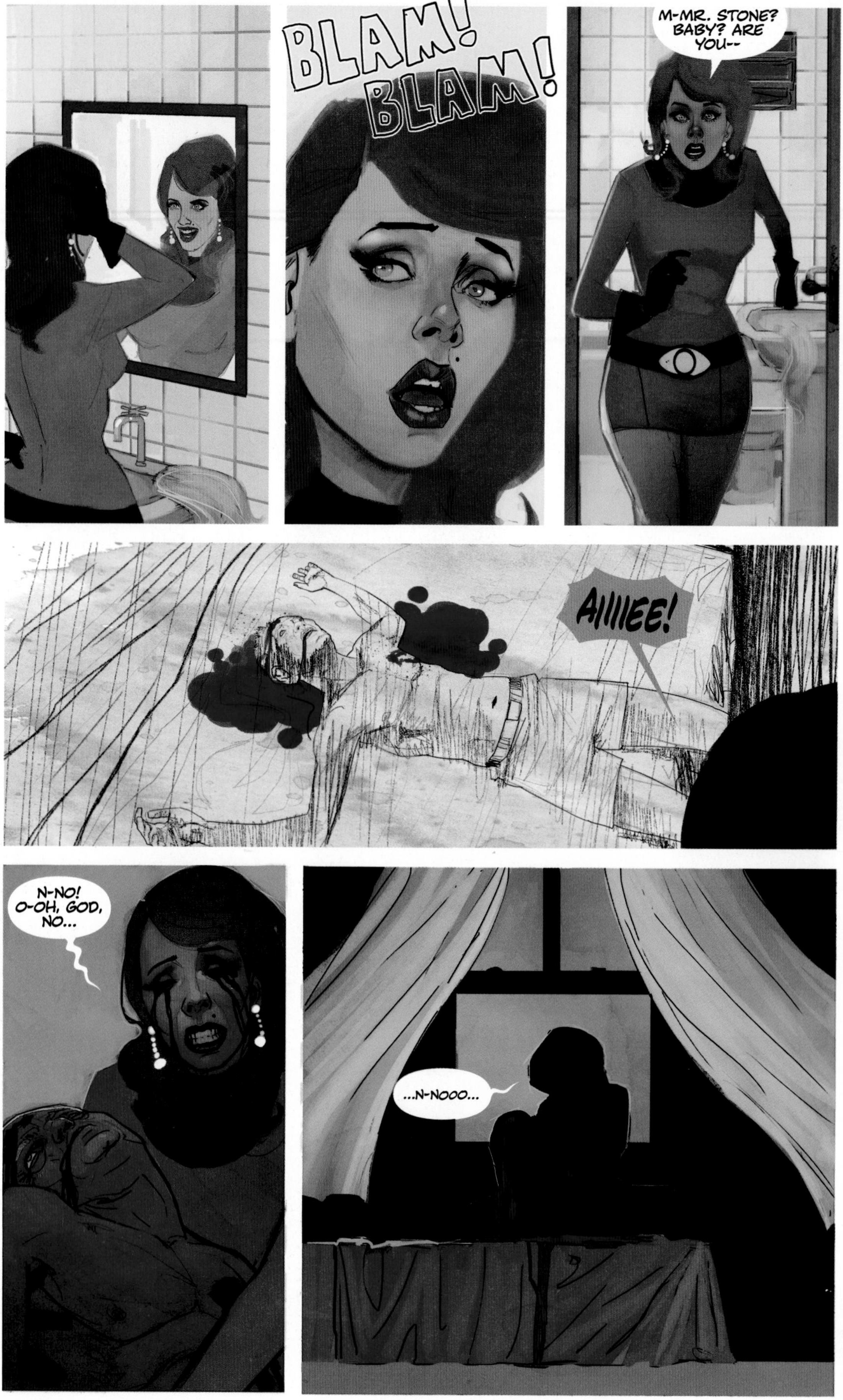
BLAM!
BLAM!
M-MR. STONE? BABY? ARE YOU--
AIIIIEE!
N-NO! O-OH, GOD, NO...
...N-NOOO...

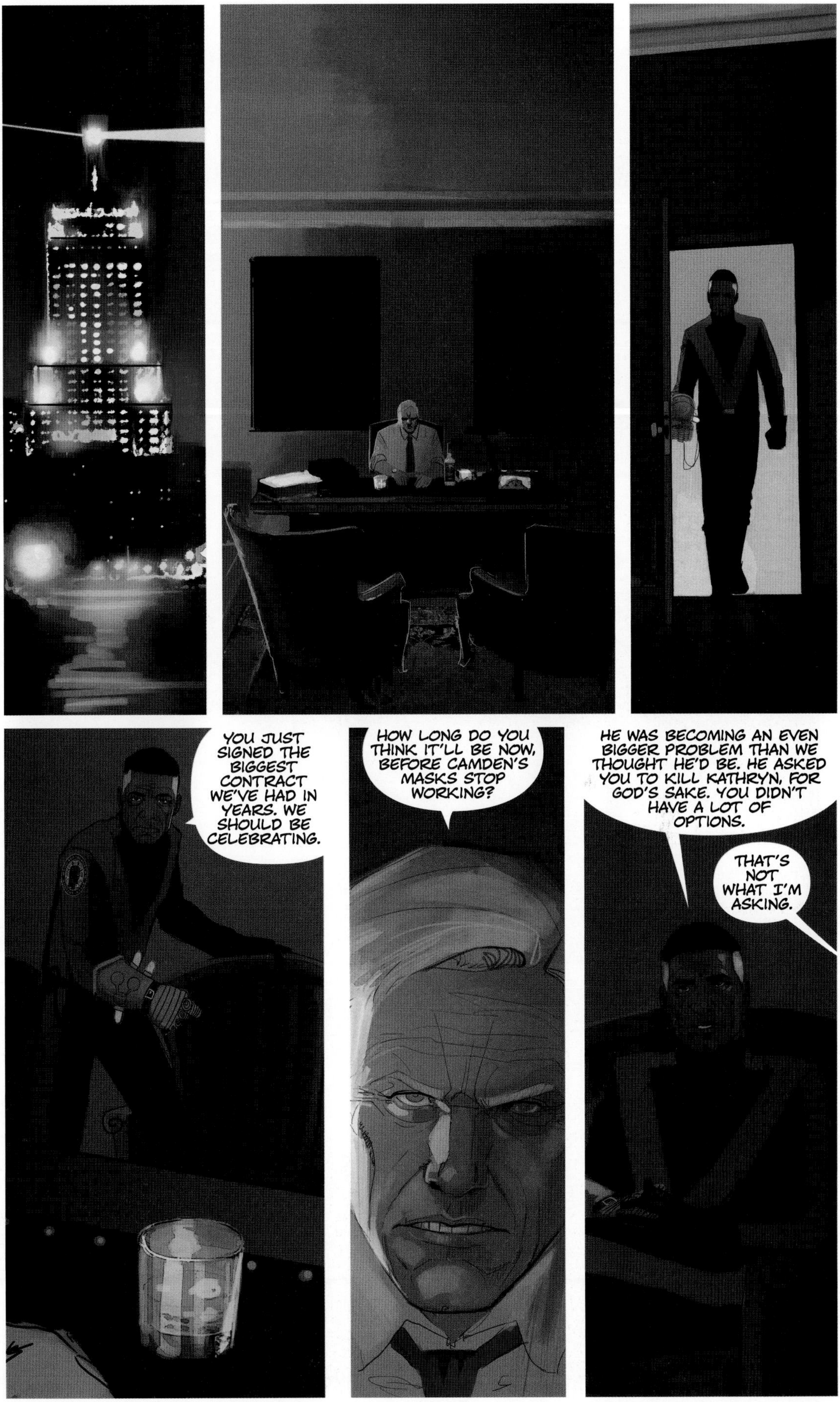
YOU JUST SIGNED THE BIGGEST CONTRACT WE'VE HAD IN YEARS. WE SHOULD BE CELEBRATING.
HOW LONG DO YOU THINK IT'LL BE NOW, BEFORE CAMDEN'S MASKS STOP WORKING?
HE WAS BECOMING AN EVEN BIGGER PROBLEM THAN WE THOUGHT HE'D BE. HE ASKED YOU TO KILL KATHRYN, FOR GOD'S SAKE. YOU DIDN'T HAVE A LOT OF OPTIONS.
THAT'S NOT WHAT I'M ASKING.

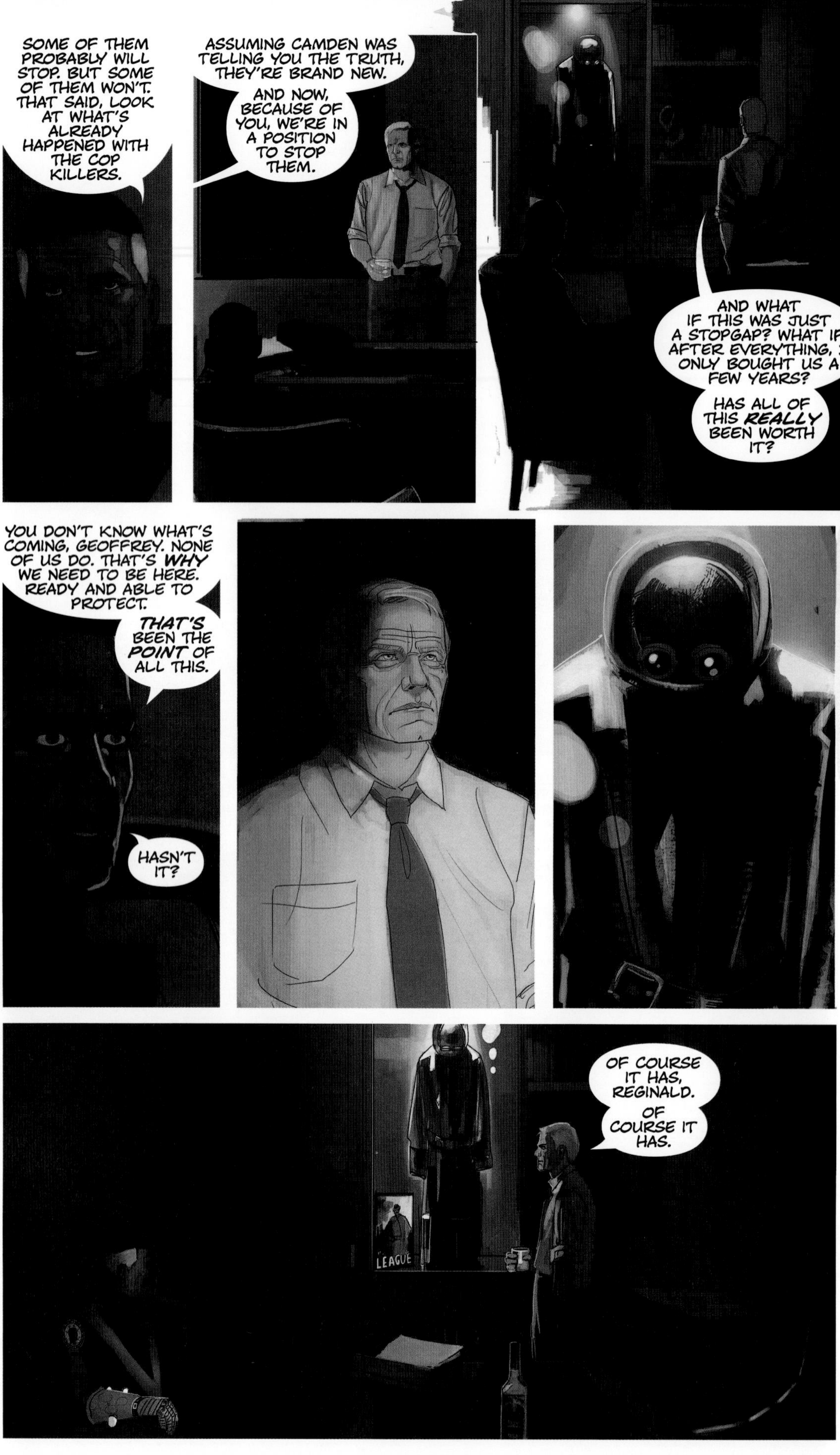
SOME OF THEM PROBABLY WILL STOP. BUT SOME OF THEM WON'T. THAT SAID, LOOK AT WHAT'S ALREADY HAPPENED WITH THE COP KILLERS.
ASSUMING CAMDEN WAS TELLING YOU THE TRUTH, THEY'RE BRAND NEW.
AND NOW, BECAUSE OF YOU, WE'RE IN A POSITION TO STOP THEM.
AND WHAT IF THIS WAS JUST A STOPGAP? WHAT IF, AFTER EVERYTHING, I ONLY BOUGHT US A FEW YEARS?
HAS ALL OF THIS *REALLY* BEEN WORTH IT?
YOU DON'T KNOW WHAT'S COMING, GEOFFREY. NONE OF US DO. THAT'S *WHY* WE NEED TO BE HERE. READY AND ABLE TO PROTECT.
*THAT'S* BEEN THE *POINT* OF ALL THIS.
HASN'T IT?
LEAGUE
OF COURSE IT HAS, REGINALD.
OF COURSE IT HAS.

CHICAGO ORGANIZED WORKERS LEAGUE

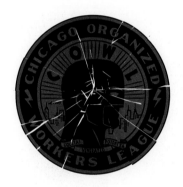

| FILE 006-01 | | | |
|---|---|---|---|
| 1. | SERIAL NO. | 20-1400-0911 | X |
| 2. | REGISTRATION | CLASSIFIED | XF: 03 |
| 3. | CLASSIFICATION | W-706-L21 | |
| 4. | | | |
| COMMENTS: N/A | | | |

| LOG NO. | 5296482368 |
|---|---|
| DEPT. | PATROL |

## C.O.W.L.  DEPARTMENT USE ONLY

Name: Karl Peter Samoski
Date of Birth: 07/22/1926
Place of Birth:
Chicago, IL (West Town)
Height: 5'8
Hair: Brown
Weight: 240lbs
Eyes: Brown

Alias: Eclipse

C.O.W.L. Position: Officer, Patrols

Skills: Anti-kinetics, power disruption

Biography:
Samoski was born in the Chicago neighborhood of West Town where his
father, Henryk, and mother, Daria, ran a bakery. At his mother's
urging, Samoski was active in the Holy Trinity Catholic Church commu-
nity, serving as an altar boy in his middle school years.

Though he was too young to join the armed forces when the U.S. entered
World War II in late 1941, Samoksi and other men in the neighborhood
began working in a Studebaker plant near Municipal Airport (now
Midway) in order to help fill the country's labor needs. There they
helped assemble Wright Cyclone engines for the B-17 Flying Fortress.

It was during the war years that Samoski began to manifest "anti-
kinetic" powers, which gave him the ability to disrupt the flow and
transfer of energy. Before he could use his powers in the fight over-
seas, however, the war came to an end. He moved from job-to-job in
the post-war years, looking for a proper outlet for his abilities.

Samoski found his answer in 1949 with the formation of the Chicago
Organized Worker's League. He joined the organization and became an
Officer in the Patrol Division, a role he's enthusiastically main-
tained ever since.

# CAMDEN HUGH STONE

Photograph taken 1943

Photograph taken 1962

**Alias:** Little Rock

## DESCRIPTION

**Date of Birth:** 3/23/1903
**Place of Birth:** Chicago, IL (Bridgeport)
**Height:** 5'7
**Weight:** 192
**Hair Color:** Gray/White

**CDBC:** 146-A

**Eyes:** Brown
**Sex:** Male
**Nationality:** American (Irish descent)
**Occupation(s):** Businessman, Night Club Owner

## REMARKS

Replaced father (Liam Stone) as head of Stone criminal family in 1939. Prior to this, he was arrested twice, for disorderly conduct, illegal possession of a firearm, assault, and petty larceny. Spent five years in Cook County Jail (1933-1937). Since taking over the family he has been tried for numerous crimes, including racketeering, illegal gambling, murder. No convictions.

He is suspected of using super-powered individuals in criminal activities. Some of these individuals have separately been arrested, tried, and convicted. However, ties to Stone did not hold up in court.

**Note:** As these individuals are no longer known to openly use these powers, the Stone criminal organization is currently outside the jurisdiction of the Chicago Organized Worker's League.

Chief
Chicago Organized Worker's League
Chicago, IL 60611

**Entered CDBC**
January, 1962

| FILE 006-26 | | | |
|---|---|---|---|
| 1. SERIAL NO. | 01-9526-1625 | – |
| 2. REGISTRATION | EXEMPT | AS: 07 |
| 3. CLASSIFICATION | B-723-EB3 | |
| 4. | | |

COMMENTS: NONE

| LOG NO. | 0163849211 |
|---|---|
| DEPT. | N/A |

CLOSED

C.O.W.L.                                    DEPARTMENT USE ONLY

Name: Evelyn Marie Hewitt (Harrigan)
Date of Birth: 12/22/1908
Place of Birth:
Chicago, IL (Bucktown)
Height: 5'5
Hair: White
Weight: 143lbs
Eyes: Blue

Alias: N/A

C.O.W.L. Position: Detective (Retired)

Skills: Expert Strategist

Biography:
Born in the Chicago neighborhood of Bucktown, her mother died in
childbirth and her father was killed shortly after in an accident
along the Chicago River. Harrigan was raised in foster care.

In 1930, she married James Hewitt, a detective in the Chicago Police
Department. Harrigan (now Hewitt) was drawn to her husband's work and
even tried to join the police force herself, but was continually
denied entry to the force due to "physical inferiority."

During World War II, James joined the Marine Corps and Evelyn worked
at Amertorp Torpedo Ordnance Corporation in Forest Lawn. She was wid-
owed in 1944 when James was killed during the Battle of Peleliu.

After the war, Hewitt finally found detective work with the formation
of the Chicago Organized Worker's League. She became one of the organization's prominent investigators and trained many personnel in the
department's current roster.

Hewitt left C.O.W.L. in 1959 and joined the Chicago Police Department,
where she continues to work as a homicide detective.

# DOPPLER

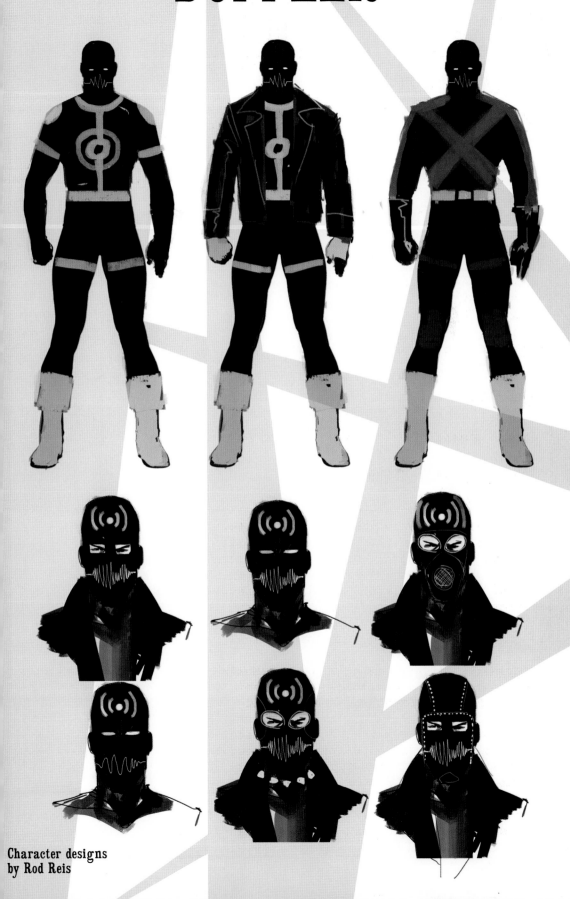

Character designs
by Rod Reis

# THE BRUTE

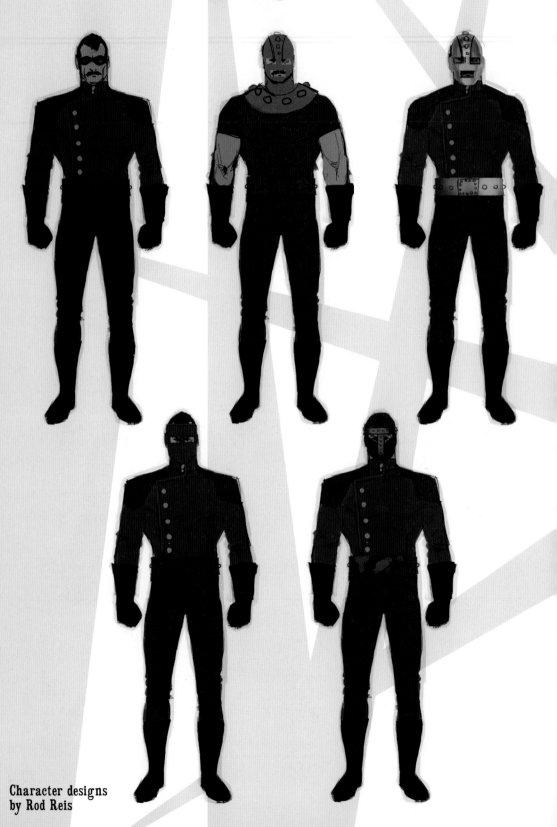

Character designs
by Rod Reis

# PAGE 4

Patrick CRUMPLES the newspapers. The noise is DEAFENING.

SFX: KA-KRUNCH (not sure this is the right sound effect. Any ideas? Maybe just CRUMPLE)

Rod-- I was thinking this would be a fun page to leave to you to design. And... if we do it right, it'll involve a lot of sound effects in the artwork :)

The idea here is that Patrick has audio/sonic powers. He's a bit like Banshee (from the X-MEN). However, instead of screaming sonic blasts... he's able to amplify and redirect sound waves. Meaning, the crumple becomes a weapon. Then, when the man fires the gun... the BLAM sound is a weapon.

So, what's that mean visually? Well, I was thinking it'd be cool if we actually turn the sound effect words INTO weapons. For example-- the CRUMPLE word actually FIRES at the man and woman, like a blast. The man fires his gun... and the BLAM word actually gets redirected at the woman, knocking her off her feet.

The man RUNS... and Patrick uses the KLOP KLOP running sound effects to TRIP the guy.

Bottom line, we want the rest of this page (and the top of page 5) to be vicious... with Patrick laying waste to the store and the man and woman. However... he just roughs them up a bit. He doesn't kill them.

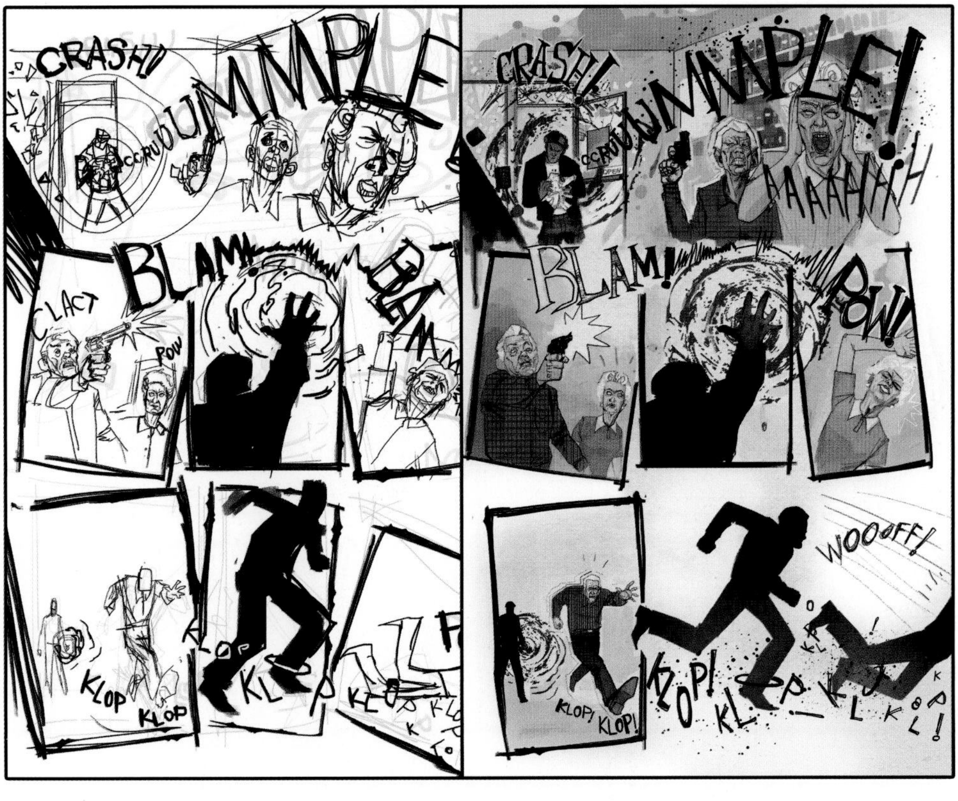
CRASH!
BLAM!
CLACT
POW
KLOP
KLOP
CRASH!
AAAAHHH
BLAM!
POW!
WOOOFF!
KLOP! KLOP!
KLOP!

# PAGE 18

18.1 Radia rushes into the room, using her telekinesis to LIFT Doppler off the floor.

RADIA
Get away from him!

18.2 Alderman Hayes.

ALDERMAN HAYES
Oh thank ***God***!

18.3 Doppler amplifies the "d" in God.

18.4 and uses it to knock Radia off her feet.

RADIA
UNNH!

18.5 Outside, ANOTHER TRAIN goes by.

SFX: KA-CHUNK KA-CHUNK KA-CHUNK

18.6 Doppler takes the sound and it builds over his head... growing in strength...

18.7 ...until all the windows BLOW OUT!

SFX: KACHUNKKK

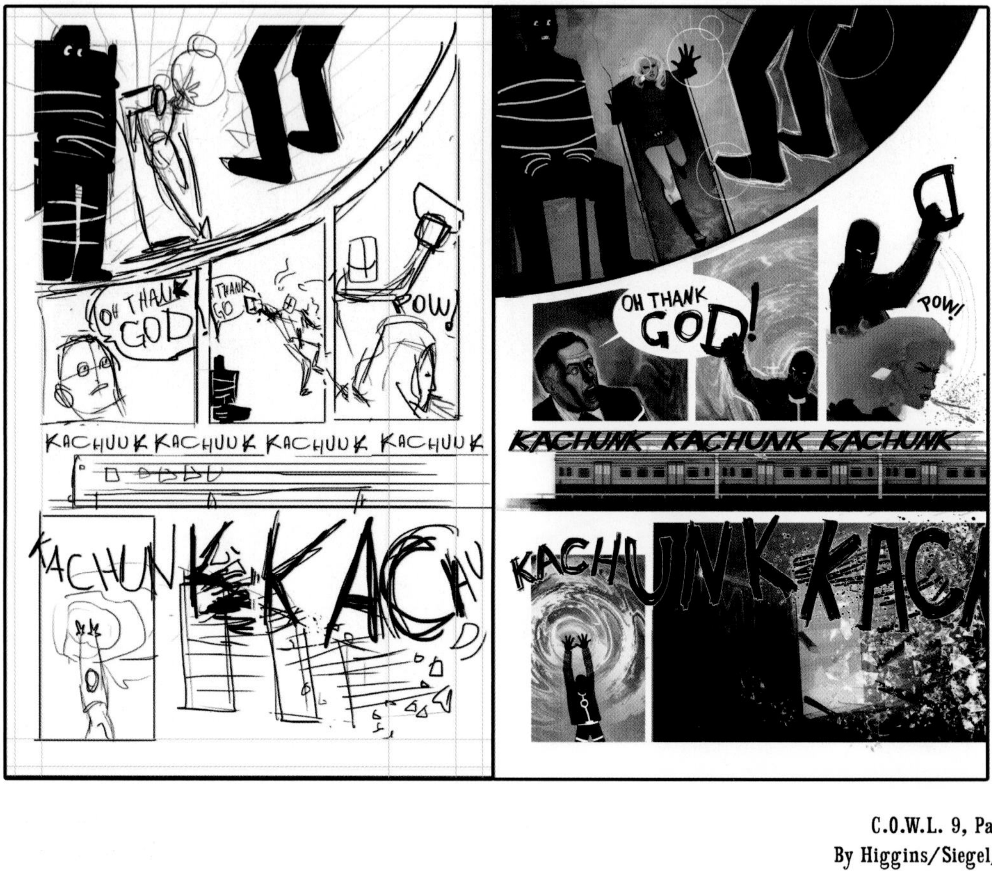

OH THANK GOD!
POW!
KACHUNK KACHUNK KACHUNK
KACHUNK KACH

# PAGE 3

3.1 The two men look around. Confused.

> WRAITH (TAILESS. SCARY)
> I know where you were.

> ROBBER 1 (SMALL)
> The hell...?

3.2 Robber 2 is scared. He's trying to get Robber 1 to keep walking with him. But Robber 1 is defiant.

> ROBBER 2
> Come on. This... Is fucking weird.

> ROBBER 1
> No. Fuck that. Nobody's gonna scare us off.

3.3 Robber 1 and Robber 2. Robber 1 is defiant. Behind them, a BLACK SHAPE drops down. This should be fucking terrifying. Like a horror film.

> ROBBER 1
> You hear me, you fuck?! You don't
> freak me--

3.4-3.5 The robbers TURN as the shape SNAPS a kick. It SLAMS into Robber 1's chest. Right in the solar plexus. Doubles him over.

3.6 Robber 1 falls to the ground. Cringing in pain.

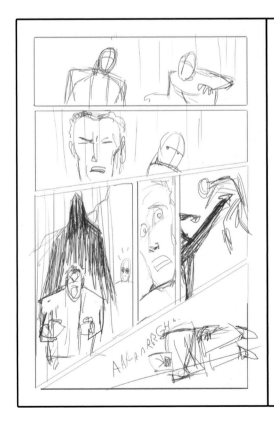

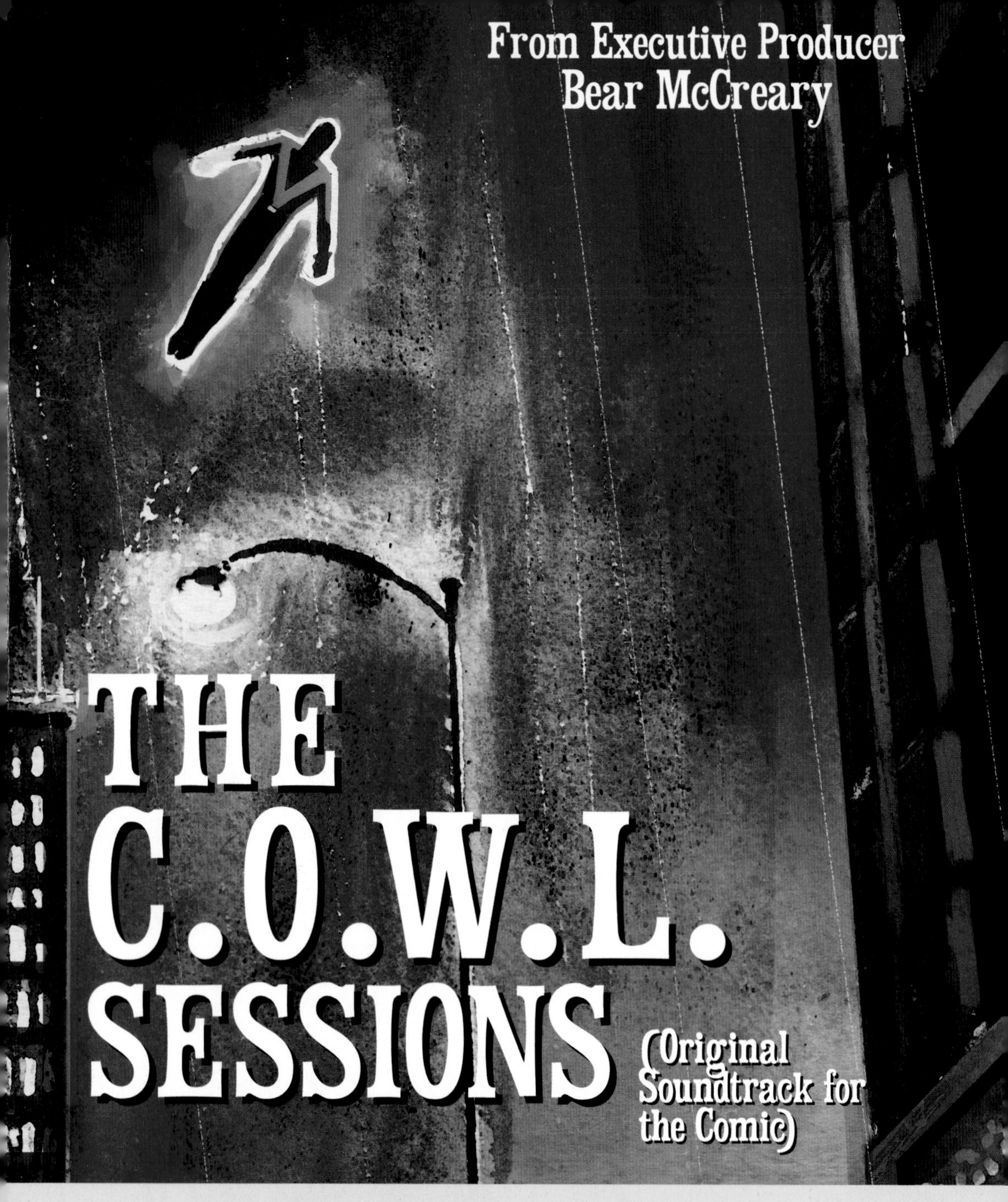
From Executive Producer
Bear McCreary
THE
C.O.W.L.
SESSIONS
(Original
Soundtrack for
the Comic)